All Change:
The Untold Story of
WWI

A Novel

Carol Godsmark

New Generation Publishing

Chapter 1: London

August 2000

Will Digby was about to relive a past life he had all but buried with one sharp ring of his doorbell. Lifting his eyes from the BBC's Grand Prix race between Hill and Schumacher at the Nürburgring Ring, he ignored the bell's intrusion and settled back into his armchair, his arthritic fists tightening during a critical lap.

'Come on, Damon!' he called out irritably as the driver slowed in the drenching, skidding rain, swearing when the buzzer went again. Glancing at his half-eaten crumpet and warm tea on the table, he rose uneasily, steadying himself on the table's edge, the brew slopping over onto the saucer. 'Bloody 'ell, what next!' Turning the TV down he walked to the front door.

Two men greeted him, the younger one carrying a box, the older man a long black case which had seen better days. Will looked them up and down with a scowl, impatient to be rid of them.

'You selling religion? Always two of you – dead giveaway. Before you say anything, no, a devout atheist, me.' Will turned to shut the door.

The older man spoke quickly and with a local East End accent. 'You Will Digby? Not sellin' anything, mate! Was your granddad Ted? Edward Digby? Bus driver in the war? First war, that is! In France?'

Will stopped and turned back. 'Yes. Matter of fact I am. He was.'

The younger man stepped forward with the box. 'Look, my kids found this on an old bus, it's full of family letters. Written to the Digbys. Long story how they found them but we – my dad here – lives not too far away, around the corner in Hackney Wick. Found your address in the phone book, unusual name!'

Will frowned dubiously. 'You sure you're not trying to sell anything?'

The younger man grew impatient. 'No, nothing. We just want to give you some family mementoes.' He reached inside the box. 'Think this could be one of your mother? Sorry 'bout the brown spots, but this is how we found them.'

He handed the old man a black and white photograph, marked by uncertain storage and the passage of time.

Will examined the picture. It was his mum, without a doubt. Ruby wore a white dress, a bow in her piled-up dark hair, and fingered a necklace. She stood between Ted and Norah, Will's grandparents. He turned it over and read, *Ruby's 16th Birthday, June 21, 1914. Bow, London.* It was a copy of one on his grandparents' kitchen dresser which had pride of place.

He smiled broadly, brushed the crumbs off his sweater and opened the door wide.

~

Stop Press…DAILY MIRROR, NEWS HEADLINES, 4 AUGUST 1914

Great Britain Declares War on Germany.
Foreign Office officially stated last night that Great Britain declared war against Germany at 7.00 pm. The British Ambassador in Berlin has been handed his passport. The King and Queen, accompanied by the Prince of Wales and Princess Mary, were hailed with wild, enthusiastic cheers when they appeared at about eight o'clock last night on the balcony of Buckingham Palace, before which a record crowd had assembled. Parliament issued a call for an extra 100,000 soldiers.

Ted Digby edged his way past the crowds and squinted in the sun at the recruitment sign on the railings surrounding the solid brick building. This was the place, all right. He had driven his bus past the central London street housing the army offices a few times that week enroute for Trafalgar Square. The mêlée had caused the bus to crawl along the streets, coming to a halt near the enlistment building. Today the area teemed again with young men, some in excited groups, others alone – like himself – eyeing others up as they joined the throng. Bowler hats jostled with flat caps and broad-brimmed boaters, the mood more carnival-like than war-sombre, would-be recruits spilling onto the cobblestoned road. A mounted policeman, astride a black mare, perspired in the heat while failing to keep the crowd in order.

Not all the men were young, Ted noticed. Older ones like himself also formed a neatish line controlled by soldiers. Posters dotted the walls and fencing, children mimicking Kitchener's pointed finger, aiming fists at their fathers, their brothers and receiving playful cuffs around the ear.

CALL TO ARMS!
BRITONS JOIN YOUR COUNTRY'S ARMY!
GOD SAVE THE KING.

Ted joined the end of the line next to a young man wearing the same bus driver's cap and grinned. 'Seems it's caught on.' The man nodded.

Ted lifted his cap and wiped his brow. 'Your idea or the wife's?' he added mischievously, trying to calm his nerves. 'Getting rid of you, is she?'

'She's not keen, truth be told,' the man replied. 'Thinks we'll all end up – you know.'

He gave an embarrassed laugh and glanced at Ted. 'And you? Same?'

'Norah, my missis, doesn't know I'm keen. Anyway, the talk is it'll be soon over,' Ted replied as they inched forward in the queue, the men silent again with their own thoughts.

'Where do you drive from?' Ted asked as they grew closer to the entrance. 'Take it you're on B-buses - or are you one of them D's?'

'Me? Holloway. B-decker, smart double decker. You?'

Ted nodded, twirling his cap nervously around a finger. 'Dalston-based but before that, horse-drawn carriages. That B's a fine bus but the sprocket shaft can be meddlesome at times, can't control 'em like horses.'

'No, same here, the pinion could do with a twiddle too.'

The man looked Ted up and down, his gaze friendly but questioning. Ted stood a good head higher than him. His dark hair was turning grey, his physique lean, lines on his shaved face indicating maturity beyond most in the queue.

The man cuffed Ted on the shoulder and gave him a sly look. 'Say, you a bit, um, older than the others here? I mean, for joining up? No offence, mind!'

'None taken.' Ted returned the stare. He straightened up and held his stomach in.

'In my prime, I would say, in my prime. Only a few years older than you but I got what they're looking for and...'

'What's that then?' the man interrupted. 'They want youngsters, fit and strong and good mechanics. This is an engineers' war. That's what my mates say - engineers, not them with horse knowledge.'

Ted was silent then gave a faint smile. 'I got both, engineering and horses, two for the price of one. We'll see.'

His stomach grumbled, and he began to feel sick. What was he thinking? Arriving at the army office some hours beforehand, he had joined the queue then slipped away, walking around unfamiliar streets to calm his gut, returning some hours later. He took in deep breaths, trying to conquer his anxiety. He'd betrayed Norah and Ruby, their daughter, by coming to the recruitment office, by even thinking about leaving them.

They stood in awkward silence until the man was beckoned in, Ted next at the top of the queue. Replacing his cap on his sweating head when motioned to enter the building by a bored-looking soldier, he stepped inside. Directed to an office, a clerk motioned him to sit at a chair in front of a desk. Two seated officers looked up from their paperwork at the prospective recruit.

'Name? Occupation?' one said.

'Edward Digby, sir. Ted. Bus driver.'

'Did your bus depot manager suggest you come or are you here of your own accord?'

'Sir, I came to serve. They say it's a flash in the pan, this war and it will soon be over. Funny thing why I'm here, really.' Ted looked up sheepishly. 'I saw a film, stirring it was, at the Empire with Norah, my wife. You seen the one with all that singing? Britons never been slaves?'

The man nodded, looked at his colleague and smiled faintly. 'Very commendable, sir, but the war may last longer than you anticipate. Too many others too, I'm afraid, think the same. We must be more realistic.'

Ted flushed, looked down and toyed with the badge on his cap.

'Age?'

'I turned forty-five in May, sir.'

The officer glanced at him. 'Forty-five, eh? How fit are you, Mr. Digby?'

Ted hesitated then adjusted his position on his chair, his back upright, his shoulders back and looked directly at the officer.

'Sir, fit enough to drive a bus, strip the motor, repair it when it breaks down.' He fiddled again with the badge. 'Me, I joined a cycling club ten years ago, my favourite ride's to the coast, to Chatham. I plays cricket when I can too. Guess my work once with horses also helped me be as fit as I am.'

'Stand up.'

Ted stood up and faced the man.

'Take off your jacket and let's have a look at you.'

Both recruiting officers examined him, put him through minor physical tests, one gesturing him to sit down again. Ted put on his jacket, buttoned it up and sat down quietly, looking at the floor then up expectantly.

Emerging into the suffocating hot evening sunshine with a slip of paper, he walked past the crowds, grinning. Dammit, he was off, and off the marital hook, off the relentless, familiar till-death-do-us-part work and family cycle. Adventure beckoned.

5

The queue on the burning pavements continued to circle around the building. As the men moved forward they advanced to an unknown world, towards the war like moths to a flame. Were their illusions to be shattered into tiny flecks? Or did Britannia really rule those waves?

Folding the paper neatly, Ted put it in his breast pocket then glanced at his watch. Just enough time to have a cup of tea and a meal in the canteen before the night shift. And Norah? When would he tell her of his decision, his acceptance as a driver for the war effort? He knew she would ask the same question as the fellow in the queue. What about your age? And what would she and Ruby would do without him? But Norah would never ask him why, not a curious bone in her slight body.

He flushed when thinking back to the tomfoolery he told the officers about the film he had seen. A load of tosh. Shadows leapt out from long ago taking him to an almost forgotten time when Digby senior had returned from Africa as a soldier, fighting for King and Country.

Alfred Digby had gone from working as a City of London brewery drayman to tending British forces cavalry during the first, short-lived Boer War. Before the sub-Saharan onslaught of mangled humanity and horse flesh, six-year old Ted had savoured being lifted high up on a cart by his father at the brewery before Alf clambered up beside his son.

Alf would command the horses forward along cobble-stones down Brick Lane to Quaker Street on the way to Commercial Tavern and further south to Spitalfields market pubs to unload barrels, the young lad holding on to his leather-apron clad father with filial fierceness. An arm might envelop him when on the straight, Ted's heart bursting. That must have been 1879 or thereabouts, he recalled. A long while ago.

The real reason – truth be told, he argued inwardly – for wanting to join up, came from his father's tales of adventure, his devil-may-care attitude soon turning sour when again amongst family after the war. He terrorised his wife, a woman who lived up to her name of Hope, never giving up on her man despite his temper, but turned a blind eye when their children came under fire.

Ted soon learned to fear the dark scowl, the coarse sneers when opposing his father, a strict hand crashing down on him. Resistance became futile, dull acquiescence taking over, Ted crushed between independence and paternal authority. After years of hankering after adventure, of freedom, and his father dead some years ago, he grasped war's fortuitous timing with a well-hidden exuberance.

However brutal the Boer War had left Alf, he still transferred his love of Shakespeare onto his son. Alf, in a pre-war playful mood, instructed his young son into the world of King Lear, Hamlet and Falstaff. Tucking him up in bed, he would utter, 'The bright day is done. And we are for the dark.' Young Ted's hand would hold on tightly to his father's, Alf gently prising it away when his child slept.

But all that would change when Alf returned from Africa. A cuff around the ear coincided with a Macbethian bellow of 'Looks like an innocent flower but there is the serpent under it!' Ted cowered whenever his father came near.

'O vile, intolerable, not to be endured!' was another of Alf's favoured phrases as he issued another blow to his fleeing son, his mother within earshot but out of sight. No comfort came from her, timidity her middle name.

~

Ted walked down Albion Road, carrying his jacket and cap in the August heat. The bus depot, on the corner of Shrublands Drive, was quiet, only a few B-Buses entering and leaving the garage. Engineers and cleaners sat on the depot's low walls in clusters, some walking to their posts when buses entered the courtyard. A row of double deckers in the yard, blushing red in the brilliant light, always reminded him of playing cars in childhood. He had pushed scruffy metal vehicles – lorries, buses, trains, a horseless carriage – from door stoop to cobblestone and back into a neat line at right angles to their home's brick wall, a brum-brum! brum-brum! accompanying the journey.

'Stop makin' that racket, lily-livered boy!'

It gave him a knot in his stomach to think of these past pleasures mingled with fear. Alfred Digby's drinking had reached fever-pitch when Ted had reached puberty. A juggernaut of gin, replacing ale, had enveloped his life, Alfred throwing himself underneath in self-sacrifice as it rolled along the city, scooping up willing victims.

Ted vowed, as he recovered from his father's alcoholic fumes and blows, that one day a train, a bus, his own limbs, would take him away, far away. Alfred, kicked out of the brewery, took a job as a Bermondsey tanner, the house now reeking of gore and dung, his skin pockmarked by limewash and lye. Raising rough, calloused hands on his young son, he marked Ted who still bore a scar on his neck which had all but sent him to lie deep in the St. James The Less churchyard, Alfred cautioned for minor assault.

Alfred thought he had succeeded in setting his son's character for life. Ted, in maturity, would confound him by gaining inner strength despite Alfred's use of tactics to the contrary, his love of Shakespeare the only legacy Ted kept.

~

Ted walked across the road to the Havelock Arms and joined a group of drivers, the talk solely of war, of anticipation and rumours. Downing a glass of mild before entering the depot, he clocked on and turned into the canteen. It was quiet, the late shift not in evidence, drivers from the earlier one hadn't arrived back for tea, probably caught up in the marches around Trafalgar Square or on the Mall, he reckoned.

He spotted Frank, his usual conductor and nodded, the two exchanging smiles. Ted walked over to him after humming a suggestive song to Rose, an ample young woman who cooked for the depot staff. Her blushing, when Ted came in sight, was legendary. 'Get away!' she laughed when Ted followed up with 'Here's my hand with my heart in it.'

He joined Frank.

'Ted, you're early!' Frank Titcomb sat at an empty table by the serving area. He was reliable, sober, a genial sort some years Ted's senior.

'Join you,' Ted replied, placing his cap and jacket on a chair opposite Frank. He returned from the counter with a cup of tea and a pie, the beef filling oozing from the pastry. Extra gravy, thanks to Rose, spilled over onto the table.

'Looks good,' Frank said enviously, pushing his half-eaten meal away. 'Should have had that, the eel's not much cop.' He rummaged around in a bag, brought out a records book and turned its pages.

Ted grunted and started on his pie. They sat in silence until he had emptied his plate of the last bit of pastry crust coated with dark gravy. 'Won't get that where I'm going, a decent hot pie,' he remarked, moving his plate aside.

'What's that, Ted? Got a mouth full,' Frank muttered, a pencil sticking out of the corner of his mouth. He removed it, put some figures in a column then chewed on the pencil again.

'You'll get lead poisoning, you will!' Ted joked. He moved his tea cup closer to him and reached for the sugar, heaped two spoonfuls into the lukewarm tea and stirred vigorously, the liquid spilling onto the saucer. He sipped noisily. 'You know what I've been thinking of doing?'

'No idea, Ted. Only new thing happening around here is how the war'll change us. Petrol rationing's already talked about.' He shoved the book in his top pocket and put his elbows on the table. 'Fire away. Surprise me.'

'Something related to the war. Yes, definitely.' Ted winked at Frank, put his cup down and wiped away tea stains on the table. He grinned. 'I've joined the ASC. Today. They accepted me.'

Frank stared at him. 'Blimey, Ted! Them lot running the army? Why you gone and done that?'

'Usual reasons, Frank, you know.' Ted hesitated. 'Haven't told anyone yet, not even the guv. Going to tell him when I finish the run tonight.' He paused. 'And pluck up the courage!'

'Guess you're the first here,' Frank replied. 'First I've heard of anyways. Army service must be desperate for drivers!'

Ted shot him a glance then laughed. Frank leant over and patted Ted's shoulder. 'Well done, old man. Well done.' His eyes were wet. 'Wish I had your courage. Too damned old, I guess.'

Ted gave a snort. 'I'm not exactly a youngster, only a good five younger 'an you.' He moved forward and looked at Frank. 'Just something I have to do.'

Frank turned away. 'Don't get caught up in this…well…' He looked at Ted. 'Kitchener and them other posters. Doesn't mean that finger's pointing at you. Why don't you leave it to the youngsters? What about Norah? Still got time to duck out, Ted.'

Ted tilted his chair backwards. 'No one knows, 'cept you, you, and me and the ASC, Frank. Look, it's hard to explain, isn't it? Don't every man want to go to war and fight for his country? Kaiser and his army'll be completely crushed in no time at all. I'll not be chasing Huns with a rifle and bayonet, just driving troops to the Front. These buses are strong, and they're needed. Iron horses, they are. How else is the Army going to get the troops there? They can't all walk, Belgium and France are big places to cover. It'll be a bit of an adventure.' He sipped his tea. 'My dad, well, he went to war, all the way to Africa, right down south with them Boers. He was a …'

Frank interrupted. 'You ain't told Norah, yet, 'ave you?'

Ted looked down at the tea dregs. 'No, not yet. But it's more than about the war, Frank, all them nurses, bound to be there, aren't they now! Or them French ladies.'

Frank leaned forward, grinning. 'I think I get it, Ted, you old dog! Why not, eh?'

'Say, what are you two whispering about?' A voice called out. 'Are you two clocking on this evening or do I have to call the relief out?'

Ted and Frank glanced the canteen clock and stood up swiftly.

'Coming!' Ted laughed, picking up his jacket and cap. Turning, he winked at Frank.

~

Ted parked the bus after the night shift and clocked off. Early sun promised another humid August day. He patted Frank on the back after they signed off in the cavernous depot. Despite the garage's cool air, he felt sick, the smell of a recent oil spill, thick on the concrete outside, hitting his nostrils. His stomach had churned all through his shift with his decision and how he'd tell Norah.

'Not a word to anyone about...' he said. Frank interrupted. 'Course not, Ted, wouldn't dream of it, old son, mum's the word.'

He gave a faint smile. 'What was you going to tell me about your old man? He really went to Africa?'

'Another time, got to talk to Craven now.' His stomach heaved. He walked down the hall to the bus depot's offices. Taking his cap off at the superintendent's door, he mopped London's street grime from his forehead with his kerchief.

He knocked on the door, his hands twisting the smudged cloth into a tight sausage. 'Come!'

Ted hastily shoved the handkerchief into his trouser pocket, pushed open the door and stepped into moist, sticky air, acrid with cigarette smoke.

'Mr. Craven, sir, can I see you for a moment?'

The manager looked up from his desk holding neatly stacked paperwork and an overflowing metal ashtray.

'Of course, Ted. Busy shift? Anything out of the ordinary to report?'

'Liverpool Street was heaving, never seen it so busy early evening.' Ted replied. 'Mostly them marches, a frightful tangle at Whitehall with the queues - maybe over 1,000 in the recruiting line, Frank and I reckoned, clogging up the stops.

11

Frank's a master, did a sterling job of clearing the way so we wasn't too late into Shepherd's Bush.'

'Dependable team, you are.' Mr. Craven sat back in his chair. 'Glad I caught you.' Reaching under a file, he drew out a pack of Woodbines. 'Help yourself.'

'No, sir, thanks. I just wanted to have a word…'

Mr. Craven interrupted. 'Your bus. Tomorrow.'

He picked up a file and opened it. 'You'll have to drive another one, Ted, the advertising's being changed on the upper deck of your usual one. Hackney Gazette's taking up a strip on both sides and the Apollo's adding the new Hawtrey comedy. New Heinz ads too. Life goes on, war or no war,' he chuckled. 'I'll check on the replacement bus for you and Frank.'

'Yes, sir.' Ted paused and moved forward. 'Sir, I have some news.'

Mr. Craven put down the file, lit his cigarette and looked up.

'Not another kid, Ted, after all these years!' He raised hands in the air, the cigarette's red tip glowing in the dimly lit smoke-hazed room.

'No, sir, just the one. Ruby. Now sixteen, few weeks back, in fact, going on twenty- five if you ask me!'

Mr. Craven smiled. 'What's up, Ted? You look troubled, a bit peaky. Anything bothering you? Have a cigarette and sit down.'

Ted nodded and sat. 'Sir, I've come to tell you…to say…to inform you… that, that I've signed up. Volunteered to drive one of the buses taken over by the army, might even leave in a few weeks' time.'

'Well, well.' Mr. Craven pushed the cigarettes and matches across the desk. 'Quite the decision.'

Ted paused then took one and lit it.

'Thanks Sir, I am aware that this'll leave you in the lurch if many of us go but, if you could give me leave for maybe four or five months until we've beaten the Hun back to their borders, I'd appreciate it.'

'Ted, this is, quite frankly, quite the surprise, never put you down for taking on this challenge.'

Ted looked away, his face reddening. Suddenly he felt very foolish.

'Don't look so miserable, Ted! you will always have a job here, don't worry about that,' Mr. Craven said, leaning back on his chair, his cigarette poised in front of his mouth. He brushed ash from his jacket and continued. 'I daresay there will be others clamouring to go to war too, maybe following your excellent example.'

He paused and leaned towards the desk. 'Mostly younger ones with no families, I bet, not like yourself. The job needs doing and you are one of my most reliable, trustworthy drivers. The army lucky to have you. You'll be back and it will be a good day for the depot when you clock on again.'

'Thank you, sir. I am grateful for your generous...' Ted choked back his emotions, stood up, stubbed his cigarette out and placed the remainder in his tobacco pouch.

He put out his hand to shake Mr. Craven's, the depot manager grasping it tightly.

'Now home to tell Norah,' Ted said, moving toward the door.

'Ted! Just a mo'!' Mr. Craven got up and followed Ted to the door after pushing aside stubs to rest his cigarette on the metal ashtray. 'You talked this over with Norah?'

'No, sir. It will take more courage to face her than it was to sign up yesterday.'

'You never know with women, Ted. Norah could be very proud of you or have your guts for garters!'

'More like hanged, drawn and quartered,' Ted chuckled, his laughter forced. 'Norah's got a strong character when it comes to family – and Ruby's just like her mother: got a will.'

He turned to Mr. Craven. 'I will keep you informed of the date, sir. Will I be allowed to keep my badge?' He fingered the blue and white oval metal badge inscribed with 1243 and Stage Driver, Mechanical Power, on the label.

'You've worn it for five years, Ted. The only reason for taking it would be for misconduct. You are proposing quite the opposite by joining up.'

Ted grasped the manager's hand again and closed the door. He leaned against the wall and tried to breathe evenly, his eyes moist. Dragging his sleeve along his eyes to erase his tears, he inhaled deeply then walked down the stairs and out of the building.

~

Walking slowly home, he took the quiet route through Victoria Park. He was tired after his lengthy shift from Liverpool Street to Shepherd's Bush, his mind racing with the probability of a different-yet-same life ahead. He would still be a bus driver but in an altered world, he reasoned. Out of the ordinary, less humdrum, his last chance for adventure, for a small part in shielding Britannia: Rule Britannia. Norah would be dead set against his going, disliking any change, regarding home stability above everything and which he had found attractive twenty years ago, not craving anything else too. Could he, in all conscience, leave her to join the war in France? He admitted to himself only that he was bored, jaded by reliability, by routine. Time to ship out, for a while at least, ditch a principle or two, a chance to cut loose.

He paused by the park's empty bandstand. Of course, he'd understood her concerns, but hadn't he always been a good husband? But she was frail in mind sometimes. He knew that. Norah had never known her parents, her mother dying in childbirth, father unknown, her young life fitting around her grandfather's home and his coal business before being sent to work as a domestic. She had met Ted when he paid weekly visits to her employer's home in Walthamstow to pick up the middle-class omnibus depot manager and his wife, for errands in their pony and trap.

Ted had joined the omnibus company as a horse-drawn carriage driver before moving onto motorised omnibuses. When the Walthamstow depot started manufacturing motorised ones, they were heralded as the end of the horse-drawn ones, red livery the chosen colour for the new breed.

Ted mopped his brow on his sleeve. Back to reality now. Would Norah receive his wages in time to pay the rent, the gas? Food? In his enthusiasm to serve king and country, he hadn't asked the right questions at the recruitment office. 'Sort this out before you talk to her, you dolt. Some hero you'd be in her eyes. Duty to family,' he thought as slowed his pace home.

Passing St. Agnes Gate, the Aviary and the Pagoda before turning right towards Bonner Gate over Regent's Canal, he watched early boaters on the lake then removed his jacket and tie, catching a glimpse of himself in the still water. Was he really fit enough to go to war? His slim body looked longer in the dark water. Bending down, he caught a ripple of an indistinct face with a good head of hair, his face lines appearing less pronounced. Standing up, he was aware that his legs felt sturdy and limber. Life in the old dog yet, his looks suiting more mature women maybe, or even a younger one like Rose if he played his cards right. Frank always teased him about his flirting with canteen staff.

Dropping his belongings on the grass, he lowered himself onto the blades, longer ones tickling his nose. Working on forceful, rhythmic press-ups, his body felt fluid and uncomplaining. Completing more to satisfy himself, he got up and refreshed himself at the fountain, flicking water on his face and neck. Rinsing his kerchief in the spray, he wound it around his neck to cool himself then lay on the grass, his arms cradling his head. His mind raced after the emotional meeting with Craven but soon he slumbered, awaking only when a child's ball hit his head. Getting swiftly to his feet, he threw the ball at the wailing child before picking up his clothing and walking on.

He suddenly felt a fool, a traitor to Norah, to Ruby, to the bus depot. Let others take this on, others who had no ties, those who didn't have grey streaks in their stubble. Only last week, as he turned over in bed to cuddle Norah, she had noticed grey tufts of hair in his ears and had pushed him away, laughing, 'ol' man!' she had whispered. 'But you're my ol' man.'

He would go back to the recruiting officers and admit his haste. He lingered by a set of paths. What if it was too late? What if he didn't act soon? The war was now weeks' old, talk of it being a short scrap, not likely to last long. Accelerating his walk through the park to Regent's Canal bridge and to the recruiting office, he joined the lengthy queue, and put on his cap and jacket when summoned again into the office.

~

He turned into Saxon Road late afternoon, his stomach rumbling. What did Norah have for tea? He'd wash quickly and sit down to table, mumbling an excuse for being late.

The Digby house was a well-ordered, compact, sturdily-built brick workman's terraced home with a yard at the back, the front opening straight onto the cobbled street.

He fitted the key in the door and quietly entered the kitchen after hanging up his coat, jacket and cap on the narrow hallway's pegs. He found Norah in the yard, a small parched gravel and green-turfed patch housing a shed and a vegetable bed where they grew carrots, onions, string beans, tomatoes and fruit. Raspberry canes, planted at the rear of the plot against a worn fence backing onto a church and its graveyard, had struggled in the heat, their laden branches needing attention. Ted looked at them guiltily. The Victorian church's tall spire cast a shadow over Norah's slight frame as she bent over the canes, adjusting them with string. The dilapidated shed door, kept open by a rake, needed attention too, he grimaced.

'Hello, Norah,' he called.

She straightened up. 'There you are! You're late. Thought you was never coming back!'

He gave an abrupt, embarrassed laugh then walked over to kiss her. She shrugged him off, picked up the string, an old knife stuck in the dirt by the raspberries and a bowl of picked fruit and straightened up. 'I'll get tea now.'

Taking the bowl from her, he followed her into the house, his chest pounding. Placing the fruit in the kitchen, he pulled down his braces and washed in the scullery before joining her, towel in hand.

Norah was laying the table, her thick brown hair threatening to come loose from her untidy bun, several strands escaping down her neck onto her cotton blouse.

Ted dried his hands briskly, put the towel on the back of a chair and sat down.

'Had a good day, dear?'

Norah clattered plates on the table followed by tea cups and saucers. 'Not something you'd call a good day, putting laundry into the ringers.'

Ted smiled faintly and was silent.

Norah turned to the kitchener and tasted a spoonful of vegetable soup on the hob. 'More salt,' she murmured before adding 'The smell of them sheets! Just foul. Never get used to it. Then after dinner, Jessie went home sick so I was put on ironing. My arms ache.'

'Then why are you doing the canes then if you're stiff, dear?' Ted asked solicitously. 'The job's too hard on you, Norah.'

'Change is as good as a rest they say,' she said, her back to him. 'Them canes couldn't wait for you, anyways.'

'Sorry, dear, got caught up in some paperwork, Craven wanting to see me after the shift then I had a kip. Long shift last night, all them men still queuing to sign up, bus couldn't get past them. It took longer than usual.'

Norah shrugged her shoulders.

Ted studied her back. Change as good as a rest, she said? But was it the right time for change? For him? Was there ever a good time?

He got up and moved towards her, picked out a hair pin and pinned some of her hair back in her bun before putting his arms around her.

'Don't have to get up too early tomorrow morning, missus,' he murmured. 'You neither, being a Sunday.'

She turned, looked at him sternly then laughed and planted a shy kiss on his cheek. 'Ruby'll be home shortly. Let go! And put that towel away.'

Ted returned to the scullery with the towel. How could he be thinking of leaving? How could he speak to her?

He didn't gain the strength to tell her until they were lying in bed. The night was stifling, neither of them able to sleep. He lay awake waiting for the reprieve, his eyes boring holes into an imaginary Belgian sky, his thoughts twisting around his mind like dark, swirling, murky waters.

He got up and went to the window. The street was quiet below, the silence only broken by the church clock signalling one.

Norah rustled in the bed and sat up. 'Ted, come to bed, dear, you need your rest.'

He grunted a reply but stayed by the open window and looked up at the sky. Was it the same sky, identical stars in warring countries tonight? Were troops and drivers able to find billets? Or were they hunkering down anywhere they could find? Outside in the dark, did the dull thud of gunfire keep them awake? Did anyone ever sleep while fighting an enemy?

Reaching for his cigarettes on the dresser, he moved back to the window, lit a Woodbine and sucked at it, every successive drag giving him resolution. He flicked the final dregs from his fingers onto the cobbles below, a red glow receding as it made its way down to cobblestoned level.

He told her gently, quietly after returning to bed. He wound his body around hers, his arms tightly wound around her breasts. Norah flinched then lay still as she listened to him, her head facing away.

Just one almost inaudible word came from her. 'No.'

Chapter 2: Home Front

December, 1912

*November 1912 report by Times Correspondent Wickham Steed:
The actual beginning of the great Balkan War is a moment of
historical solemnity, sacrifices and victories of Serbian armies
justifying restoration of Albania to Serbia, say Serbs in Sarajevo.
King Nikola of Montenegro informs Austrians he will fight 'to the
last goat and the last cartridge.'*

When the first double decker buses rolled out of the
Walthamstow factory some years before Ted signed up for
war duty, he had volunteered for bus trials taking place from
London to Essex, a War Office initiative directed by Herbert
Asquith's government in December, 1912.

Norah packed some sandwiches with meat from the
Sunday joint for Ted and walked, one cold winter's morning
with him part of the way, to start her early shift at the hospital
laundry. Ted continued on to Upton Garage to the meeting
followed by the trials with the double deckers, the pride of
London streets with their red painted wooden frames and
steel wheels.

Mr. Searle, the chief engineer, stood in front of the crew,
hands on hips, moustache bristling with importance.

'Today is the big army test you've been warned about, to
see how fit our buses are to shift soldiers around in a war
situation.'

A few laughs filled the air, the drivers shaking their heads. 'Not on the cards, sir, but we'll go along with this 'ere trial,' one of the drivers loudly shouted above the voices.

'That's enough, you lot! And mind you don't go over the speed limit. Go beyond twelve and you'll be troubled by me. This is not a country at war! Observe the limits at all times. Them buses' – he pointed to the row of new vehicles behind him – 'might be used for his Majesty's military, even if some of you think this is a jolly, or at worst, a joke, which it isn't. Understood and agreed?'

The drivers nodded their assent.

'Is that a yes?' An officer strode to the front, planting himself next to Mr. Searle. 'Let us be absolutely clear. No speeding,' he said with authority. 'We do not want to alarm those on our way to Chelmsford. We are not at war, as Mr. Searle says! But it may look more like this when we arrive at the barracks and pick up fully kitted soldiers. This is an important trial, worthy of your full cooperation.'

A murmur of surprised voices broke out. Soldiers?

'Lads, enough!' Searle asserted himself. 'Soldiers will board at Warley Barracks, we continue through Essex and back. Each driver will drive one way, the other on the way back. They'll be a breakdown tender with spare parts, grease, oil, petrol and general stores. If your bus develops a problem, considerately – neatly, mind! – drive off the road, a unit helping you. Is that clear? Do remember, safety first. And you city lot, no speeding just because you see an open country road!'

The men laughed and made their way to their allotted buses. Ted, and Bert, his co-driver that day, climbed on board, Bert inside, Ted in the open driver's seat, both dressed in heavy greatcoats, jacket and trousers, cap and goggles.

Ted's thick gloved hands steered the bus out of the garage onto quiet, dark London streets, heading eastwards, headlights picking up thick fog. 'We'll be lucky to do six, let alone twelve miles an hour,' he muttered in low gear, with over thirty miles to Chelmsford.

The single-file convoy made its way northeast and into semi-countryside, boxed in by brittle hedgerows, the sky brightening as they progressed slowly in the white haze. As the buses reached open fields, Ted caught sight the headlights of another one behind, trying to overtake.

'What, the…!' The bus narrowly scraped by on the sloping, thin road, the driver trying to gain control before landing in a ditch. Ted slowed down, struggling with the steering wheel to keep the bus on the road.

'Bloody fool! We was told no speeding!' he shouted. Bringing his bus to a halt, he climbed down to inspect the damage, Bert joining him. The convoy behind them juddered to a halt. An irate officer ran up the road.

'Is this what it's going to be like in a war setting, all of you charging off like racing demons? What if you had a busful of soldiers? Injured before battle, all of them! All that training down the khazi. For nothing!'

The red line limped slowly in single file before turning into the barracks. Fully kitted soldiers waited at intervals to board.

'Blimey, how they going to fit on here?' Ted muttered as he drew the bus to a halt. The bayonets alone looked as if they would scrape the top of the ceiling.

A bellowing order shot through the noise of voices, engines and clanking bayonets as drivers sullenly watched their passengers climb aboard, attentive for any damage they might make to their vehicles.

Bert tried to lighten the mood. 'What you got in them hoojamaflip belts, eh?' he asked one of the laden soldiers. 'You're almost bent double, need a crane to get on the bus!'

'Ammo, 'course! Whadya think I was carryin'? Rum? Encyclopaedias? Watch it, mate! Weighs as much as my girl, over 70 pounder or so.'

A soldier behind gave a nudge. 'You cradle snatchin' again, Tom?' They both grinned.

'Only eighteen inside, eighteen,' Ted called out. 'Here, Bert, get the next lot up on top. Sixteen more up top, mates, that's your lot.'

Bert shouted close instructions over the commotion, soldiers told to move up the staircase. 'What! With all this gear?' they barked. Heaving their blanket and rations inside their haversacks alongside their greatcoats over shoulders, they manoeuvred up on the narrow steps, the attached mess tins clanked angrily, like lanyards flung against masts in a heaving sea.

Ted ran up the winding steps to the top deck. 'You lot, five of you get down below. More space. But standing room only, mind.'

'Make up your fucking mind, will you, mate!' a red-faced soldier shouted, a sideways sashay needed to reach the lower deck.

Ted shook his head. Were these buses really the answer to transporting soldiers?

A wagon drew up to the bus. 'Here's the spare ammo, help me on with it, mate,' the driver bellowed at Ted over the roar of engines.

'There's no space in here for even a rat,' Ted replied, folding his arms.

'What about the driver cabin?' the man said impatiently. 'That's where some have stored it. Don't just stand there!'

Ted scowled before taking one end of a substantial box into the cabin. He motioned to Bert to grasp hold of the other end, the pair adjusting the weight distribution.

'Bugger me!' Ted growled, looking at the square containers of bullets. 'Could easily shift and damage the gearbox.'

Bert dug out a line of rope and they tethered it to the double wooden seat, tightening and pressing with their boots against the seat to give a firm grip.

'Alright, we'll give it a go,' Ted reluctantly agreed. 'All seated inside, up top?'

Bert nodded, then frowned and muttered about explosives to Ted who shrugged his shoulders. 'Must be alright, officers wouldn't allow them on, would they?' Bert's look didn't convince.

The drive to Chelmsford was slow and uneven, four buses slipping off the road into ditches, an axle breaking under the strain, breakdown crews and soldiers setting the buses on the road again.

'Looks like if we don't stray from the crown of the road we'll make it,' Ted said to Bert. He calculated a stately nine miles an hour average mileage through Essex and back to London and into Finsbury barracks. He didn't stop smiling on the return journey, his confidence growing, relishing the change from the usual route he took day in, day out. Finally, excitement! But would war really happen? There was no talk of it. His smile faded as he weighed up the odds of going to war as the bus neared the depot. The vehicle felt girlishly skittish after depositing the soldiers at the barracks with their loads.

Ted arrived home after ten, an orange glow from the street lamp in the December fog capturing streaking dregs of winter soot in the air.

Norah, at the table by the kitchen range with Ruby, was drinking tea, the coals giving off a comforting heat. They were playing dominoes, bent over the wide table with concentration. Norah looked up and gave a half smile.

'Dad!' Ruby got up. She knocked over a few domino tiles and took his bag from him. 'Tea?'

He grinned, reassured by normality. Home. Two shelves opposite the range held jars of flour, oats and other staples. Pots, pans, jugs and cups hung from hooks, some on an old dresser which had been his grandparents'. He'd known it all his life and felt comforted by familiarity.

Next to the dresser was a small recess for boots and shoes covered by a curtain. Taking off his boots, Ted placed them inside, his eyes catching measurements on the door leading to the scullery. The pencil marks measured Ruby's height on her birthday, etched into eternity. An inch or two taller than her mother, she was fourteen when the bus trials had taken place. Ted glanced over at his daughter. Her hair, piled up high, gave her the illusion of height and grace thanks to her slim figure.

He washed in the scullery and walked back to the table, kissing Norah gently on the forehead before sitting down opposite her, heavy with tiredness. She looked up and saw that he was elated, despite exhaustion etched on his face. His eyes were like a music hall performer's, euphoric, in control of the audience. Turning away, she got up and fussed over her sewing on the sideboard.

'Dad can finish the game with you, dear, if you'd both like.'

'Maybe later, or tomorrow,' he murmured.

Ruby shrugged her shoulders, got up and packed the game away. She placed a cup in front of him and put her arms around his shoulders.

'Dad, you hungry?'

'Oh, dear, yes, I am rather. Come to think of it, my sandwiches are still in the bag. Pass them to me, dear.'

He chewed silently on Sunday's leftover beef in stale bread before telling them of his introduction to war on his new bus. Ruby listened intently as he described the bus journey, the soldiers, the ammunition, laughing at the mishaps. Norah forced a smile as she stitched one of Ted's frayed cuffs she pulled from the linen basket.

Ted never mentioned the day again until that critical August two years later when he came home and announced his plans to go to war.

Chapter 3: Home Front

September, 1914

*Daily Mail, September 11: The lake in London's St James's Park
was drained today so that it could not be used as a marker for
German bombing.*

Norah was going to be late for work and Ruby would be too
if they didn't leave the house this minute. 'Hurry up, Ruby!
Past six and we'll miss the bus, young lady!'

They kept a quick pace along the streets to the bus stop,
Ruby's brown hair cascading down past her shoulders under
her white brimmed hat. Norah glanced at her.

'Mind you pin up your hair, Ruby, that machinery will
make mincemeat out of those curls and ribbons.'

'Mum, you know we all have to wear caps on the factory
floor, no two ways about it,' Ruby replied sharply. 'I'll have
the time when I get there to look the part, just like everyone
else. Just like Dad, when he's in the army, like everyone.'

'Ruby, he's a bus driver, not a soldier. And he's not got
any date. Let's remember that.' Norah replied firmly.

'Maybe the war will be called off and he won't go at all,
Mum, did you think of that?'

'Can't say I did. War's never as straightforward as all
that.'

They reached the bus stop, Norah catching one going
north towards Hackney, Ruby to Bermondsey, south across
the Thames.

'Mum, I'll bring a bag of bourbons home, that will cheer us all up, won't it? We always manage to break some. or I'll break some accidental!' she grinned and gave Norah a swift kiss before crossing the street.

'Cheeky! Watch yourself now. Don't get the sack over a biscuit, not even a smashed one!' Norah laughed, but Ruby was out of earshot.

Norah, arriving at her stop, walked briskly to the hospital in Dalston, hurrying past the gates of the imposing brick building with its Dutch gabled design. Passing the stores block, main kitchens, dispensary and boiler house, she walked down the large divided ramp to the laundry, partitioned to keep the processing of infected patients' laundry separate from staff. She knew the drill well, the vastness of the system, its foibles and the staff. As she clocked on, a voice called out from the office.

'Ah, Mrs. Digby! The manager wishes to see you now.'

Nodding, Norah took off her hat, feeling a sudden lurch in her stomach. Was it about the sudden extra load of ironing that had turned up? Was the job not done well enough?

Changing quickly into her long white apron, she smoothed it down over her skirts, put on her cap and went into the laundry office.

A young girl stood waiting with the manager, Mr. Westmann's German accent more acute than ever, Norah thought. The girl looked young, vulnerable, weak. Why was she here? She didn't look strong enough to take on a manual job; there were two vacancies to be filled, due, it was rumoured, to the war. But was it more like prejudice, people frightened off. 'Work with them Germans? Not likely!'

Would this small girl be an asset, able to lift bundles of soiled sheets, clothing and surgeons' infected gowns? Could her back survive the constant bending over rows of sinks and manage the huge, heavy irons or presses? Would she tolerate the incessant clack of machinery, the constant water flowing around her feet? The draining needed attention or all laundry employees talked of strike as their shoes rotted, their feet icy in winter months.

'Mrs. Digby, good morning,' the manager said, rising behind his desk.

'Will you take Miss' – he glanced down at a folder – 'Miss Holton, Annie Holton, on a tour please? And put her to work where you think she will be best suited? I leave it to you, your good judgement.'

Norah had never been asked her opinion or been given any indication that she was to be trusted to instruct new recruits. Giving a faint smile, she hesitated before nodding.

'Certainly, Mr. Westmann. Come, Annie.'

Annie followed her into the washhouse and drying rooms, past the ironing and folding rooms, Norah explaining each procedure as they walked along.

'See here, Annie, if you want to save your shoes and feet, stand on the wooden slats in the washing areas. Like these ones, here, see?' She pointed to boards below vast white tubs.

'What we all do is move the slats around, from basins to wringers so make sure you do too, the other girls helping. But sometimes they gets a bit lazy.'

Annie nodded, looking uncertainly at the work ahead of her.

'And always wash your hands and dry them well to stop them cracking, or even, infected. After each load, mind you; some of them diphtheria and surgery patients leave a right old mess. You don't want to get ill now, do you?'

Annie looked around her, taking in the vast piping, the steam and the heavy, loud machinery. White-aproned capped women pushed large wheeled baskets of soiled laundry towards drums and rows of sinks, Annie shrinking from the raucous banter. Norah sighed then followed the girl's glance up to the high ceiling with its complex series of metal and wood beams and glass panels with winding closing and opening apparatus. 'See that pulley there? That moves the window and…' Norah stopped when Annie lost interest.

'More like a factory, not an 'ospital,' the girl whispered, her voice not carrying above the noise. Norah patiently showed Annie into the last large room to fold sheets 'the way

27

the manager likes them. All uniform, all neat and in the right piles.'

'You got family to keep, to help, Annie? 'she asked as they stood by perfectly folded linen, Norah demonstrating again how to achieve the required neatness.

'We got seven at home – so I got to work, pay for the food, mam says. We're from Stepney,' she added with pride 'Never been as far as Dalston, never.'

She glanced at Norah and made a face. 'Strange here. They speak funny round here; manager's got a, not a normal way of talking.'

'That's because he's German, Annie. It's the German hospital.'

'What do you mean? You mean them Germans are here already and we got to wash their clothes? Mam won't be best pleased, not at all. Eddie – my twin – he's already signed up to fight them.'

'You didn't know this is the German Hospital, Annie? Didn't you pass the sign when you came in the gates, the big one? Can't you read?'

The girl shook her head and twisted her hands.

Norah put an arm lightly around Annie's bony shoulders. 'Never mind, plenty who can't and work here, dear. No need to get upset. All the doctors and nurses are German and we're the English lot, doing the cooking, the cleaning and the laundry. They been here for years, 'round seventy, but, you know, they're just people, like you and me.'

Annie looked unconvinced.

'Alright, just like Prince Albert. He was German.' Norah warmed to her subject, a few other nuggets of Royal information added for effect. 'Queen Victoria? Half German, she was! Bet you got some German blood in you too and all!'

'I got Stepney blood!' Annie said indignantly.

Norah giggled then composed herself.

'Come on, let's get you working now. I've work to do too, on the mangle. I'll show you how too.'

She too had increasing doubts about working in the hospital since war had been declared. Should she be working for Germans, really believing they were 'just like you and me?' She liked her German superiors, however, straight, hard-working people with a care for their own. Maybe she should be wary. She would be judged by her own people.

Annie lasted a day, never to be seen again at the laundry.

~

Norah was laying the table when she heard the front door open. Ted was late home again. He had been on an early shift and had promised to fix the garden shed before supper. A recent thunderstorm had seen to the final days of the door, leaving garden tools, mangle and tin bath open to the elements. Returning from work, she had gone out in the yard expecting Ted to be there, hammering away or at least emptying the shed before repairing the door.

Ted walked in to the kitchen. Giving Norah a peck before taking off his boots, he splashed water on his face in the scullery, the cooling effect united with 'ah, that's better!'

Norah walked over to the scullery, cutlery rattling in a hand. 'Ted, what kept you? You were going to do the shed today. You promised.'

'What, dear?' he asked, rubbing his face with a flannel, leaving a streak of black soot.

'Oh, had to make a detour, Trafalgar Square crowd again.' He grunted. 'Some peace march, women out in force.'

Norah stared at him. 'Women, not with their men?' She laughed and pointed at him. 'You missed where your goggles were, you look like – like a panda!'

'Don't you like the look?' he laughed, peering into the mirror above the basin and rubbing at dark rings around his eyes.

Soon he'd have no time for chores, better mend it now and anything else that needed doing, he thought. Would Norah learn to accept the inevitable, and still believe they were a family, steady as a rock?

'Hard to tell, dear, about their men, but there were loads of them women, shoving and dropping their placards. Had to stop the bus.' He leaned forward to the mirror to slick back his thick hair, grey hairs matching the remaining soot. He turned and winked at her, his voice decisive.

'I'll start on the shed right after we eat, a good crisp evening for it. Or would you prefer to go for a walk? Maybe around the lake, in the park? It's a grand idea, isn't it? Ice cream?'

'There's a storm coming tomorrow, well, Mrs. K. says so, and you know she knows everything,' Norah stated flatly. 'Even the state of our knickers, leans over the fence she does, nosy old…'

'In other words, dear,' Ted interrupted, moving towards her, 'you'd like me to do the shed then go for a walk with my lady wife.' He gave her a squeeze.

Norah grinned shyly. 'What does she know, eh, dear? Let's get out. I had a long day at work, new girl from Stepney not strong enough to push a tub or even do some folding.'

She turned and took out an egg from the cupboard. 'Ruby would like to come too, I'm sure. You can tack the tarpaulin over the door and finish the shed tomorrow if you're on earlies.'

They sat down to tea when Ruby returned from the biscuit factory, their meal of bubble and squeak boosted by an egg on top for Ted. Bread and butter and late tomatoes from the garden were followed by rice pudding.

Norah glanced at her daughter. 'Ruby, can you finish your pudding? Waste not, want not. We want to catch the light in the park. But after the shed's fixed, Ted?'

He nodded and got up. 'Sun'll set just after 7. I'll get a move on.'

Norah and Ruby cleared up to hammering and a few expletives then the sound of the shed door opening and closing with its familiar squeak.

'Can't find the oil,' Ted growled as he walked into the kitchen. 'You seen it, Norah?'

Norah shook her head, wiping down the table. 'No, dear. Probably in that jumble in the shed, surely.'

Ruby stood impatiently by the door leading to the hallway, her hat on and she carried a brown bag. 'Just leave it, Dad, sun's going to set soon. Let's go. Got some biscuits, most broken,' she said, raising the brown bag and grinning.

'Your father has promised us ice cream too, a real treat. It will be quite the autumn picnic!' Norah said, wrapping a shawl around her.

They walked arm in arm to Victoria Park, Ruby clutching the bag. Circling the lake Ted bought ice creams from the kiosk. They passed Speakers Corner, a cluster of young men in loud conversation. The first slight autumn crispness in the air hadn't deterred families from coming out, mostly men in uniform with wives or escorting their girls with a defiant, proprietorial air mixed with pride.

Ruby eyed them and declared 'You'll never get me marrying a soldier!'

'Why ever not, Ruby?' Ted asked, turning towards her. 'They're just like us, wanting to help in our hour of need.'

'Why would I? I could be married already, even at my age! I couldn't bear losing my husband. The end of the world, it would be. Why can't people stop fighting?'

Norah quickened her pace beside Ruby. 'Please, let it go now, let's enjoy the peace and quiet, while we can, dear. What do you say, Ted?'

He nodded.

Ruby turned to Norah. 'We all have the ability to make decisions. We're not meant to fight or kill.'

Ted slowed down and faced them. Norah bit her lip, Ruby looked defiant. 'Ruby, you may be sixteen but you still have a lot to learn. People have to fight to defend themselves. If a bully wants to beat you up, you have the choice of running away or standing your ground. That's...that's why all of these men are going and...'

He paused before continuing. 'To save where you like to live, where your mother likes to live. And all of these people want the same too,' spreading his arms out wide around the park. 'Don't you understand that?'

'Or are they going because they want to look big, Dad, in front of the girls? Do you really think they care that much about everyone?'

'That's a terrible thing to say, Ruby! Really wicked!' Norah cried out. 'Look at their faces! The way them young ones walk so proud! They look honoured, chuffed to bits. We have to trust them. Otherwise, we…'

Ted put his hand up to stop Norah and motioned them to a bench. He sat at the end of the ornate cast iron and wooden seat, his voice breaking when he told them of the date for his departure to the Western Front. It had come through that afternoon, the reason for the detour to the Army Service Corps on his way home, and why he was late back.

He briefly outlined his training, his uniform – an Army one – and the name of his co-bus driver. Billy. Billy Boy Cotgrave, a Hackney boy some twenty-five years his junior. He couldn't tell them how long he would be away, or how he would communicate with them.

Nor did he say that he would be issued with a rifle and ammunition, comment on the route the bus convoy would take to war or his whereabouts. The Western Front.

But he did say he would sort out the paperwork to ensure his salary would be paid directly to Norah. There would be no money or mortgage worries to contend with as long as they both worked, Norah at the hospital, Ruby at the factory.

His goal, his aim, was to be home again with them and resume work at the depot before too long. Christmas – or earlier, he said, as he wiped away Norah's silent tears and faced Ruby's stony eyes. Three months away. Perhaps a few more weeks added on. He wasn't certain. No one was.

Long after they had left the park, the bag of garibaldis Ruby had placed on the bench and had forgotten was snatched up and torn open by scavenging rooks in the darkening sky.

~

Ted left London in late September. As he came down for breakfast in his uniform, Norah brushed his collar down wordlessly, allowing him only a peck on the cheek before he left home.

A tearful Ruby ran after him, and caught up, breathless. Ted rested his hands on her shoulders and looked into her eyes. 'Look after your Ma dear. I promise I'll…' Unable to tell her what she so much wanted to hear, he abruptly turned and walked away.

While gathering his belongings in the bedroom the previous night, Norah had approached him, her red eyes lowered and hit him with her fists. Ted restrained her, pulling her to him and stroking her hair.

'Ted, it's not too late to back out,' she finally murmured.

He was aware of the hope rising in her voice from his touch.

'You won't be any less a…a fine man in my…'

Pushing her away, he whispered forcibly, 'Jesus, Norah! Why do you see me as some kind of Judas?' with a menace new to them both.

~

He drove the double-decker with its distinctive red livery out of London with Billy Boy, Liverpool Street to Shepherd's Bush via Trafalgar Square emblazoned on the vehicle, agreeing to nickname their bus Ol' Bill. They were enroute to a war close to their own borders, the Western Front, the fighting zone in France and Flanders.

Chapter 4: Western Front

September, 1914

Jack and Bill went up a hill to see a Frenchman's daughter;
The Censor's here and so I fear I can't say what they taught her.

Ol' Bill was seventh in line in the bus convoy as it made its way from London to Avonmouth, the Bristol docks their first destination. From there the 75-strong column of double deckers would line up to cross to Rouen, a fleet of steamers taking them up the Seine to join the other one hundred already in France. More than a thousand buses would be put to use straight from the streets of London for the war effort, a third of the capital's transport.

Ted and Billy Boy shared the driving, the bus laden with tins of grey camouflage paint, petrol and stores including provisions as well as their kit and their own few belongings.

They stopped for the night at a Marlborough army base and spread their bedding, rough army issue blankets, over the bus's hard, narrow passenger benches. Ted bagged the left side, Billy Boy the right. After a canteen meal, they joined other drivers for a smoke outside the row of buses, the mood excitable.

'Like the last day of school,' Billy whispered to no one in particular as he drew on his Woodbine. He leaned against the bus, bile rising in his gut. Tossing the cigarette away, he walked back to the bus, Ted joining him. He picked up the unfinished cigarette and handed it to him.

'Don't ever do that again, my son. You'll find them ciggies hard to come by.' Billy flushed.

Later, stretching out in his bed, Ted's arms met windows to one side. Above his head, he could touch the wood and glass panelling separating passenger seating and the drivers' cabin.

'You comfortable enough, Billy?' he asked.

'Me, sir? Used to sleeping anywhere, sir, just about anywhere, not an easy home where I'm from, good to have my own bed,' Billy replied shyly. 'Besides, a small fellow like me can squat down most places.'

'Billy, drop the sir. We're equal, you and me,' Ted grumbled. He paused and moved in his bed, the slats digging into his spine. 'Might use my haversack for a cushion and the greatcoat over me to keep warm in this old tin.'

'You do that, old man,' Billy laughed, adding 'Sir.' They both chuckled.

The morning dawned crisp and clear, Ted cursing his back pain when he woke. Stretching, he sat up and wedged his thick-socked feet into stiff, hob-nailed black boots. After a canteen breakfast he checked his kit. Had he mislaid anything on the way from stores?

He examined his rifle, bayonet, water bottle and tin plate dangling from his haversack, checked his woollen khaki uniform for ammunition in pouches and his pay book. All present and correct. Two smaller pockets on the jacket were for personal items.

'Suit my Woodbines, this one' he muttered to himself. A picture of Ruby and one of Norah were placed in the second one. An internal pocket sewn under the right flap of the lower tunic housed a field dressing. Would a bus driver really need this, he wondered, as he fingered it then put it quickly in the pocket.

He ran his hands over rifle patches, sewn above the breast pockets, preventing wear from the webbing equipment and rifle use and checked the brass buttons fastening his shoulder straps. The buttonholes needed a little stretch. They would in time, he reckoned.

He felt a shiver handling his kit. There was no going back now: *you're no longer a bus driver from the East End, you're in the army now, just like your dad and on your way to war. It's what you wanted, isn't it?*

Puttees! He'd forgotten to wound them around his legs. Forcing a grin when Billy came back on board from washing, he removed his boots and coiled on his puttees from ankle to knee, before stepping into his boots' stiff sides again.

~

Ted drove the bus onto an old tramp steamer bound for Rouen. Earlier in the day, he and Billy Boy had trained in basic musketry cleaning and arms drill while waiting for the dock's chaos to recede, commanding voices clamouring to be heard above the din of machinery and vehicles. Once on board, they listened to the crackling tannoy giving details of the estimated duration of the journey, some three days or more to Rouen. A groan by the new soldiers went up at the length of time taken to reach France, the barrel-chested belly of the old ship soon lurching through the early autumn waves with a soon-to-be familiar rhythm which some would adjust to with ease, others lurching on deck to throw up.

Billy Boy copied Ted and the soldiers in their cramped quarters below deck during the voyage, spreading out his army kit then polishing his rifle, fingering his pay book and imagining the sum mounting up in France. Flipping over his identity disc, a red asbestos circle with his name, number and religion stamped on it, he traced the etched initials, ASC, Army Service Corps, in a horseshoe design with C of E in the centre. Grinning, he thought of playing with his sister along the dirty London canal, fishing out tins to sell to the scrap merchant.

On deck, to avoid the sickly smell below stairs, Ted crossed over to milling servicemen, officers, regular soldiers and drivers, clustered together in excited groups, laughter spilling out only to be carried away by the wind. He paused before joining the drivers.

'Us and them, is it?' he asked one of the drivers who nodded scowling. 'Too good for the likes of us, them officers and regulars.'

They leaned against the lifeboats, tattered paint rubbed off by years of weathering. Other drivers folded their arms on the railings, looking out to sea, some glancing backward to the receding shoreline.

Avonmouth docks disappeared in the sea mist and foam, heads turning towards the distant, unseen French coast. Their faces, eager, reflective, anxious, mirrored their thoughts. Others stared impassively out onto the water and did up their top jacket buttons.

Ted pulled out a pack of Woodbines and attempted to light one before giving up, the strong wind blowing out both match and barely lit tobacco.

Billy caught up with him, took off his jacket and held it out. 'Here, take some shelter, old man, try again.'

Ted took a lungful of smoke as he crouched behind the improvised windbreak and lit one for Billy too. They stood in silence watching the prow of the ship slip into troughs and peaks of waves, trying to focus on the horizon as they smoked. Billy Boy put on his jacket but shivered with cold and excitement, his face turned to the wind, blonde hair whipped by cold gusts.

'Why you keen on joining up anyways, Ted?' he shouted against the breaking waves. 'You got a good job at your age, no need to, sense says.'

'Same reason as you, I reckon, my son, same damned reason,' Ted replied after a pause, looking Billy up and down. 'Country needs you and all that.'

Billy shot him a glance. 'My dad's the same age as you and you wouldn't catch him volunteering, I bet. Category C man, unfit for anything, you ask me. He's got back problems, long bent over his desk. Makes watches, see. Not that he works a lot, lazy bugger! Smokes his pipe all the time too, ash droppin' inside the mechanics. Doesn't even have the puff to blow it out! Don't' get out in the fresh air. Not there's much around us, East End, where we live, truth be told.'

'No, you're right there.' Ted glanced at him. 'You got other family, too, I guess, the bed share and all,' he said, throwing his cigarette stub into the wind. It caught a gust and turned inwards on deck, its glow extinguished in the strong airstream.

'Could say that. Another reason to escape; the pay helpin' the family. Least I don't have to share my bed with no one here.'

'No, you stay on your side of the bus, I'll stay on mine!' Ted laughed. 'Say, how long did you say you'd worked on the buses?'

'I didn't, did I?' Billy turned away and looked out at sea, his face pale.

'You alright, Billy?'

'Sure. Just need a swig of water, feeling a bit, you know…' he leaned over and retched over the side, the sick catching the flank of the ship.

Ted took his elbow and guided him away to a large wooden lifejacket box. Billy sat down awkwardly, holding his stomach. Ted bent over him, unhooked the water bottle from Billy's haversack and handed it to him.

'Here, this'll help. Not the first time you'll be doing that, I reckon.'

'Never been on a boat, let alone seen the sea,' Billy croaked, after taking a few sips.

'Nor I, Billy, 'cept Chatham docks if you count that. Probably quite a few on the ship never seen it neither,' he said, looking around the crowded deck. 'All novices, for sure. Just the sea making you sick, eh? Or somethin' else?'

Billy looked up at him. 'You some kind of priest, full confession time? Think I'm scared, d'you?'

~

They disembarked on a warm late September day after taking the inland waterway to Rouen, the steamer slowly making its way on an unruffled Seine. Ted suddenly felt ready and strangely cheered when he and soldiers lined the decks, pointing out the flat countryside with its neat fields now bristling with stubble after harvest. Housing, a mix of brick and wood, was punctuated by numerous churches. A steady stream of bicycles, mounted mostly by hatted men or labourers in blue overalls, weaved along lines of poplars on the road to Rouen.

When the ship reached the large port, soldiers and drivers leaned over the railings pointing at the vast mismanaged military hub below, laughing. The dock, overwhelmed by equipment, soldiers, horses and shouted orders, spelt confusion. It was their first taste of a foreign language.

Ted and Billy hurried to the bus when the order came over the tannoy. Soldiers, allocated to their transport, clanked up the steps, Billy guiding them. Ted cranked up the engine, dense, choking fumes starting to gather in the ship's fat rusty belly.

The ship disgorged them hastily, adding to the jumble. 'Bloody hell! Too rushed!' Ted swore behind his outsized wheel. He held on tightly, his foot on the brake pedal as the procession of bumper to bumper red buses rolled down the ramp onto French soil.

'There'll be damage done before we've started,' he cursed to Billy. Ol' Bill hadn't suffered paintwork damage unlike others had during the rough three-day crossing, theirs lodged tightly away from less secured ones in one of ship's bays. Ted had instructed Billy to tether all the equipment inside the bus securely. Nothing had shifted, not even the paint pots next to the boxes of ammunition.

Ted glanced at Billy and grinned before driving down the jarring steep gangplank and off onto hard ground, metal wheels clattering over the surface, the buses directed out of town along flat landscape with its avenues of trees. People lined the route waving flags and clapping, Ted staring at their clothing, their clogs and homely farmhouses and well-ordered neatly hoed and ploughed fields. Some thrust loaves at the drivers; Billy shot a look at Ted as he took hold of a warm thick crust, Ted nodding. 'Take it!' Soldiers reached out and grabbed offered wine bottles, others yelling 'none of that tom-tit foreign muck, mercy!'

'Dunno know what I expected,' Ted shouted above the clamour. 'Rousing stuff!'

Billy whistled. 'What a looker, that one!' Ted followed his gaze and whistled too. They shared the bread, Billy eyeing it with suspicion. 'It's all crust!' Soldiers on the top deck sang rowdily.

Singing Glo-ri-ous! Glo-ri-ous!
One keg of beer for the four of us!
Singing glory be to God that there are no more of us;
For one of us could drink it all alone!

The buses stopped in an open field, French soldiers pointing the way to spaces until all seventy vehicles were finally uniformly parked in three rows.

An officer strode into view of the buses. 'Everybody off!' New army recruits were slow in execution, crews taking their time. A strident, harsh voice took up the shout. 'Did you hear the commanding officer, you fresh lot? You listen to your sergeant from now on! The name's Dawkins, Sergeant Dawkins to you! Form your ranks!'

They stumbled off the buses, most of them unshaven, their uniforms rumpled. The journey had taken its toll, their legs unaccustomed to dry land, sea-sickness leaving them weak. They were a boyish lot, the over thirty-fives regarded as elderly. Only Ted and few others fitted that category.

'What a shower you tinkers are!' Dawkins roared. 'Smarten yourselves up, get all your equipment – all of it, mind! – and return at the double!'

Ted and Billy straightened their uniforms, brushed off breadcrumbs and hauled on their rucksacks. Knocking their caps, creased and stained with the ship's soot, against the sides of the bus, they hastily put them on. Heaving rifles on their shoulders, they walked to form a line in front of the sergeant and other brass.

'Rude devil, ain't he?' Billy muttered. 'We're no tinkers!'

Ted gave a short, sharp laugh. 'Billy, not gypsies, he don't mean that. Just a name, who we are. Motor transport.'

Billy shook his head slowly. 'Yes? So? Don't get it, we should have respect!'

'Mostly tinkers. Tinkers. Mechanics! Get used to it. More ribbing to come, boy!'

Billy flinched and leaned forward to steady himself under the weight of his load, his short legs giving him limited ballast.

'Time to stretch your legs! On that boat for too long, a four-hour route march curing you and your sea legs. Stand up straight, Tinkers, shorties all of you! More like miners or sailors than soldiers!'

'Even the drivers? We join them soldiers too?' Billy shouted out.

Dawkins strode over to him.' You in uniform, son?'

Billy looked down at his khaki and mumbled, 'Yessir. But ghost army, sir. That's what they call us, them lot, not real soldiers.' He gestured towards the regular military.

'What's that? Ghost army? You think because you're a driver, you're not a soldier? You drivers are in uniform too, aren't you? Then you're in the army, my son. Got to be as fit as them lads,' he pointed out the soldiers with his swagger stick. 'Do you see the difference, soldier?'

'No, sir, yessir, sorry sir.' Ted, standing head and shoulders above his co-driver, gave Billy a wink as he struggled with his emotions and his kit. He'd show him how to distribute the load more evenly later. Hadn't Billy covered this in training? Lions led by donkeys! Depot managers could teach the army a thing or two, he reckoned.

~

They rounded the corner to the bus park at dusk after their enforced march to the final verses of *Send out the Army* to keep their spirits going.

Send out my mother, my sister and my brother,
but for Gawd's sake, don't send me!

Billy's head leant towards the ground, his legs flung out widely to keep control of his load, his gun straying from his shoulder. He struggled to look up when hearing the drivers' shouts. Blue overalled workers had sawn off parts of the top deck, red, splintered bus parts littering the ground around the row of vehicles.

'For fuck's sake, you Frenchies, what the fuck you doing that for! Get bloody off!'

Dropping their rucksacks and guns, drivers climbed up to the decks and tried to push the workers off. Some landed near boards bearing destinations: *Waterloo, Piccadilly, Fleet Street, Westminster.*

Ted reached their bus before Billy and ran up to the top deck. 'No, no, no! Get off! My bus!' Picking up a Haywards Military Pickle sign, he stepped towards three workers who jumped onto the driver's cabin roof before making the final leap to the ground and ran off, shouting at Ted, gesturing. New ones to him.

Billy ditched his pack and ran towards the bus, adrenaline kicking in. He climbed on board before collapsing and lay on the floorboards breathing sharp, painful lungfuls. Ted climbed down the spiral staircase and rummaged around for some water, sat Billy up, urging him to take small sips. His breathing gradually lost its harsh rasps.

'What they do to Ol' Bill, Ted? Why? They Germans or something? We're here to help them Frenchies and they attack our buses?' Billy gabbled.

Ted sniggered. 'I chased them off. With the pickle sign! They nearly got a battering from me.' Billy joined in. 'Pickle, eh? Ha, ha, ha!'

Ted got up abruptly at a commanding shout. 'Come on, stand up, Billy. Dawkins calling.' Billy groaned.

The drivers clustered around Dawkins, the sergeant barking orders. 'Half the buses will be turned into lorries,

42

more transport needed for supplies to the Front. Others for vital troop transport. Needs must. Dismissed!'

Noisy, angry, indignant voices rang around the vehicles.

Ted spoke up. 'Sir, the workers left before they could finish the job on our bus.' He pointed to 'Ol Bill. 'Guess this means he'll be spared? Sir!'

'Name?' 'Sir, Ted Digby and this here, Billy Cotgrave, William, sir.'

The sergeant sighed before consulting his paperwork. 'Your bus will now be kept as a double decker. For soldier transport.'

Ted and Billy turned back towards their bus, grinning, Billy shot a satisfied look over his shoulder at Dawkins.

'Take that smug look off your mug, chum,' the sergeant called. 'You're on my list now, I'll have you, boy!'

Ted grabbed Billy and pushed him inside. 'Now we have an enemy, you dolt, and we're not even at the Front with the Hun! Well done!'

~

Later, they inspected the bus's interior, Billy's angry mood filling the air. Wooden panels, now nailed onto the window frames, added to the gloom. The benches remained intact as did interior signage – no spitting, be aware of pickpockets – from its public transport days.

'Feels even narrower for 16 of 'em with all their kit,' Ted mumbled to Billy who nodded.

'At least the lighting still works,' Billy said in a small voice.

'Billy, not allowed, is it? Lighting's off in the cabin. If they're on, them Hun will spot us a mile off, 'specially a whole convoy!'

Billy nodded irritably and bent down to inspect the space beneath the benching. He let out a sigh and stood up. 'Let's make some cupboard doors so we can store our own stuff under the seats.'

'Get to work then, Billy, plenty of wood from some of the other buses to work with,' Ted replied with a forgiving grin. 'I'll do the necessary up on deck.'

Ted climbed the narrow, curved staircase to the open top with its boxy groin-high wood sides. The sturdy iron railings would help to steady the men in transit but precious little else would give them comfort, a tight squeeze for all that kit and rifles for eighteen, all open to the elements. But he and Billy needed to store their own kit too. But what about the soldiers, heaving their belongings up the stairs with nowhere to store them? He had mentioned the problem to a sergeant during the trials in Essex but it hadn't been thought through. The wooden benches up top faced the front, their flimsy wet-weather canvas covers not lasting the course, Ted reckoned. Besides which, they took up room. He threw them over the side, climbed down, folded them and stored them under the driver's long seat.

'Hand 'em out in the wet, them covers,' he mentioned to Billy after they toured the bus, examining the changes. Their bedding and belongings were now stored out of sight in the lower deck and in the driver's cabin including Billy's violin. It would have to do. The grey paint would be used soon over the red livery, giving more room for their passengers.

They eyed the lines of soldiers they were to fit on board then motioned them on after Dawkins' order. Shouts and swears and guns clashed as they climbed on.

'Hurry up, move it! No more room, sergeant, in here!' Ted tried to sort out the crush, Billy looking helpless on the side as light rain fell. Ted surveyed the general mayhem before yelling at them again. 'Just you wait til you get to the Front! This ain't nothin'! Ah, c'mon, budge up!'

The convoy finally left for the Front, stopping for the night at Abbeville. Ted took the driver's seat. The soldiers were quiet on the journey, some choosing the top deck for sweeter air than in the sweatbox below, bugger the drizzle. Inside there was little room for manoeuvre, their kit resting on supplies.

'No spitting, no smoking!' Billy had regained his sense of humour after a talking-to by Ted. He admonished his passengers, pointing to a sign and made an explosive sound of ammunition going up in smoke.

'Put a sock in it! Bullshit!' reverberated around the cabin, a few red flecks stubbed out, other cigarettes defiantly lit. Guffaws filled the small space. The globe lighting, allowed for part of the journey, picked up the faces, turning them unnervingly grey-green in the autumn gloom.

Tomorrow, Ted and Billy Boy planned to repair the dented drivers' cabin roof. Ted checked the speedometer. Four miles an hour; barely a crawl. Reaching inside his breast pocket, he drew out three pictures, one of Norah looking solemn yet endearing in a square necked pleated dress, a single clasp holding her fine, dark hair back in her usual loose bun. How he had loved her then, a duty-like feeling now which he was careful not to show. Jesus, married over twenty years, no, longer, twenty-two, or was it twenty-three? He stared at her face for a while before shuffling the next photo into view. Ruby's sweet smile made his heart lurch, her hair piled high on her head, a few strands visible around her high cotton lace neckline. Her inquisitive eyes reminded him of his mother; never at rest but friendly enough. The third picture showed Ruby on her recent 16th birthday, wedged in between Norah and Ted. She fingered a necklace they had given her, her gaze full of confidence, of impending womanhood.

Pulling back the visor, he placed them under a small fold. Their faces were now only visible. He squinted at them in the dim evening light while keeping an eye on the bus ahead then carefully flipped the visor back into place.

Dawkins walked down the line of buses: 'No headlamps, no headlamps! You know the drill! Them lot can see a bloody convoy from a hilltop, miles away! The Hun got binoculars as well as us, you dolts!'

Billy elbowed soldiers to get to the light switch, then jumped down and slid next to Ted. 'Suffocatin' in there!' They drove on in the darkness past blackened villages. Billy dozed off beside Ted, his head lolling down towards his chest then jolting up when the bus went over a rough patch. All was quiet, not even barking dogs heard above the sound of the metal and solid rubber wheels on the coarse country roads.

Chapter 5: Western Front

November, 1914

The race to the Coast: Battles took place from the Somme, Artois, French Flanders, Ypres and Yser to the Belgian Coast as the armies sidestepped one another towards the Channel ports of Calais, Dunkirk, Ostend and Zeebrugge.

'Look lively now!' Ted shook Billy awake inside their cabin. The bus, parked in a field by a makeshift latrine and canteen some yards apart, was partly hidden by high hedging. The war had escalated – Japan had now declared war on Germany – but the German march on Paris had been checked, the mood buoyant.

Ted shook Billy again. 'Dawkins and his henchmen want to see us, all of us, now!'

Billy rolled over on the bench seating and looked up. 'Ted, come on! We been on the go non-stop. Don't we get a rest on one day, just one of them?'

The sound of artillery should have been enough to waken him, the earth's movements spasmodically shaking the bus but Billy had become immune to its snarling rhetoric after three months of war.

He grimaced, pulled off the army blanket revealing the crumpled and stained uniform he had slept in, and put socked feet onto the wooden flooring. Outside on the step, the leafless hedge afforded him a snapshot of passing horses and wagons. Gusting winds caught passing soldiers' uniforms, tipping their caps.

After a quick rinse, Billy slicked back his hair, pulled on braces, boots, jacket and cap and joined other drivers in front of Dawkins, their faces glistening in the light rainfall.

'Those tins of paint, grey, on your buses.'

'Yes, sir.'

'Get to work and paint over the red. Should have been done the first day. Board up all and I mean all those windows too that haven't been done. We're too close to the Front; we don't want that glass shattering over everyone. It's not Piccadilly to Picardy! Got it? Shake a leg then. Jump to it!'

'Have a cup of char first, son, before we slap on the paint,' Ted advised and patted Billy on the back. 'I'll start on the signs and store any we can. Maybe useful for later on, when we get back home.' Billy nodded. Ted got to work when drizzle ceased.

Billy pointed to the signs and laughed. 'Where you going to store them, old man? Thought of that?'

Charlie, working on an adjacent bus, made a face. 'C'mon, Ted! No time for bein' sentimental! Who's going to want Waterloo and Trafalgar Square in this war, eh? Chuck 'em, burn 'em. Not worth a damned thing now, them Germans not hitching a ride to London if I got anything to do with it!'

'Who ever heard of Charlie Hawtrey around here?' chipped in another, nodding at the advert Ted had prised free. 'They won't care to travel to London to see him at the Apollo making a damned fool of hisself!'

Ted was short. 'Mr. Hawtrey to you, mate, the best comedian around!'

The bus, shorn of its signage and advertising, looked naked, unloved, unfamiliar. Ghostly. Ted threw the signs in the fire, flames quickly licking *Horlicks, Nugget Boot Polish, Cooks Shredded Beef Suet* and *Heinz 57 Varieties. His*

Master's Voice, *Haywards Military Pickle* and *Dewars* whisky were the last ones to be fed to the blue flames.

Ted took the Hawtrey ad to the driver's cabin, turned it flat against the rear wall and nailed it to the wood. He sighed. That time with Norah; she had gone and bought music hall tickets for his 44th birthday. She had laughed as he belted out an old Harry Boden song with the rest of the lads in the audience.

On the last bus home at night oft I spy a smart young miss
Who will hail me with her 'mush', then take up her skirts like this
Full inside - on top she climbs, then 'Oh 'er' shout some gay young sparks
Whilst my mate behind keeps warbling, 'Kindly pass no rude remarks.'
Well, to tell the truth I'm going all the way.'
'Late to roam - see me home?'
'Thanks awfully. But what would the missis say?
'Single eh? Oh I say
Well if that's the case
Well then, of course, you might!'

Get a move on, Ted, no time to be soppy, he rebuked himself.

He hurried back to Billy, opened the paint pots and brushed coats over the red livery until sides, back and front were covered.

Ted, head and shoulders above his co-driver, stood on tiptoe on the highest box they could find to reach the top deck. The eight windows, dressed in wooden panels, caught the grey drips, streaking the boards.

'Tommy!'

Billy stepped back clumsily on his heels and spun around.

'You never handled a brush before?' Dawkins roared. 'Don't let the British Army down by sloppiness! Paint it again and do us credit! Before the balloon goes up!'

Billy reddened. 'Yes, sir!'

'While you're at it, slap some on your face, it's as red as that livery! Camouflage it smartish! Bloody Fritz will have it easy seeing you, dead ringer for a sitting duck.'

Laughter spun around the surrounding buses.

Ted quickly walked over to Dawkins, paint brush in hand. 'Go easy on the lad, sergeant, he's trying his best. Why you so hard on him?'

Dawkins drew up close to Ted, his face redder than Billy's. Pulling out a book and pen, he opened it.

'You! – you, old man and that bantam lightweight chum of yours – I'll charge you both with insubordination if you give me any more lip. Never, ever question me or any superior officer! Got that, old man? They let anyone in the army these days,' Dawkins muttered as he turned on his heels, snapping the book shut.

~

Ted and Billy sat down to eat their rations on the steps of the newly camouflaged bus, paint smell lingering over their bully beef. Ted glanced at Billy, reached over and put a hand on his shoulder.

'Look, more of this to come, get used to it or …'

'Or what, Ted?' Billy put his untouched stew down with a clatter.

Ted kept his hand on Billy's shoulder. 'You're sensitive, lad. Army's not like in civvy street. It's going to get a lot tougher, now we're closer to the Front. You're going to see things you and I never seen before, shouted at by people unused to war, like we all are. We have to put up a front – pardon the pun!'

Billy laughed despite himself.

Ted leaned back. 'Look, mate, I'm angry too, Dawkins throwing his weight around, nasty man. But we're all in this together, can't let personal feelings get you down. Not on. And finish that bully, you never know when we'll eat next, nothing certain these days.'

50

Billy looked into the distance. 'Got to confess something to you.' He shifted uneasily.

'Not been driving for long and only signed up, well, my brother Tom dared me to. Said I'd get a white feather if I didn't, the bugger. Right royal goad is Tom. He's in the army and all, first one to sign on in the family.'

Ted nodded with a faint smile. 'Knew you hadn't done much driving, lad. An experienced driver knows better than overheat the engine. You done that least a dozen times getting to the docks, too close to other buses when going downhill, 150 yards needed.'

'I done wrong and you tore me off a strip too.'

'Had to, my bus. Our bus now an' we got to look after it and them soldiers too. Didn't think you had much military before you left either, Billy. You didn't pack your gear well, you know, balance it, not used to handling the load either and you're easy out of puff. Where you do your training once you signed up?'

Billy looked away. 'Didn't, did I?' he muttered. 'Signed up one day, left week after, not even five days apart.' He gave a barking laugh. 'Here's what happened, Ted, a bit different from you, I guess, but maybe not for some of the lads. Got issued my uniform and stuff and told to go to the depot. I can tell you, my mum was shocked. She cried a lot when I told her, even Cissie – she's the youngest one, bit of a sweet girl – hanging on my legs and crying too.'

Ted whistled. 'Quite a baptism, lad. You kept it quiet. No wonder you feel the way you do. You'll learn, and fast. Got to, son.'

'I want to be as good as you, not just some geezer who don't care less about anything, good at my job, not like my dad. Got to get smart, Ted, like you. Got lucky with you.'

'Don't be daft!' Ted gave his leg a punch and got up. 'Come on, let's finish the job, a few more panels to finish off. We want to be home for Christmas! Then we'll be painting Ol' Bill red again!'

Billy laughed more confidently. 'Yes, Dad!'

Ted nodded and smiled. 'You'll do, Billy, you'll do.'

The grey convoy moved on up country closer to the Belgian border, intense army traffic clogging the road in both directions. Ol' Bill, now assigned to the Second Army, had picked up a busload of Royal Dublin troops from St. Venant to Houplines, on the Franco-Belgian border that morning. The traffic mingled with infantrymen, some calling out in jest for a lift with one eye on the sergeants. The cobbled roads twisted ankles, new, heavy unbroken boots adding to already sore feet from endless trudging. Buses, horse-driven carts and other vehicles vied for road space with increasing numbers of refugees, many with dogcarts piled high with wretched possessions. Billy stared at them as the bus passed, a few carts with rugs stretched over the top, others open to the elements. Children, hitching a ride, squealed with misplaced glee, elderly grandparents admonishing them.

Chairs, stacked on solid family tables, each with their own histories, were tied together with rope alongside clashing jangling, metal pots and pans. Children put their hands over their ears with the roar of the army vehicles. No baguettes or wine were offered, a few soldiers instead handing out chocolate and dried fruit to children from their daily rations. Billy waved to a small boy, intent on keeping furniture stable with his thin arms as the cart juddered over ruts made worse by army traffic, one chair cutting loose with the child. They landed on the road, the boy crying.

'Billy, hop to it,' Ted instructed, slowing the bus down to a crawl. Billy jumped down, picked the child up, but was too late to rescue the chair. They stood on the side of the road and watched it being smashed by an army vehicle trying to squeeze between bus and cart. Billy hoisted the youngster back on board and ran back to the bus to the sound of impatient horns and Dawkins' intolerant voice.

The drivers gathered to eat their rations during a break. Dawkins joined the group, berating Ted for slowing up the convoy. Billy edged out of the group and wandered off towards a deserted farm but hurried back when hearing Dawkins' voice calling out 'Let's move, now!' Seeing pails heavy with milk, he bent to smell the creamy liquid. Satisfied it wasn't rancid, he emptied his water bottle and quickly filled it up, spilling it over his boots in his hurry.

'Where were you? Nearly had to go without you,' Ted admonished.

Billy passed him his water bottle. 'Ted, have a sweet swig!'

Ted waved the bottle away. 'What are you doing? Get that out of my face, got my own! Let's get a move on.'

'Different kind of water, Ted, try it,' Billy teased.

Ted looked at him. 'Not now! We're off!' He jerked his head back towards the cabin.

'The men are shoutin' somethin'. Go find out.'

Billy shrugged and climbed back up into the driver's bench after a brief check.

'They don't get it, taking this road, seems wrong to them.'

'Don't make sense to me either,' Ted replied. 'This route nashional is as straight as anything; see for miles ahead. Endless. But aren't we going backwards away from the war?'

'That's what they're gabbing about,' Billy said, peering back into the cabin. The cluster of usually talkative Irish soldiers looked tense, small talk abandoned. Smoke from the top deck swirled around the drivers' cabin.

Ted grimaced. 'What you doin'up there, smoking kippers?' he shouted up.

The roads, Belgian pavé, over the border into Flanders, were rough, uneven, the bus shaking over the coarse stones, their passengers voicing their anger.

Billy turned and shouted, 'Nothing we can do about it!' shrugging his shoulders.

'This'll shake every chassis bolt to kingdom come,' Ted muttered as he steered the bus erratically along the increasingly slippery surface as rain fell. Mud from the fields, dug up by passing traffic, horses and infantrymen, hindered the claggy route. In the distance, through the autumn mist, a cluster of spires emerged. Ypres. They entered the city.

The convoy ground to a halt before urged on by harassed officers. They passed flaming oil tanks licking the air by a pontoon bridge. Refugees flattened themselves against rickety railings to let the vehicles pass, flames lighting their streaked faces. Distant gunfire signalled the Western Front. The Old Cloth Hall lay in ruins, parts of masonry from St. Martin's cathedral falling on broad steps as they passed, stones hitting vehicles.

'That's a close-run thing, could be Westminster Abbey.' Ted shook as he steered, avoiding masonry and twisted metal. The building's imposing entrance mirrored the church he passed daily on his route to Trafalgar Square. He turned away from the burning cathedral and shouted 'Where now?' to passing British officers, their faces and uniform stained by oil. Were they advancing or retreating? They waved them on. But to what? Leaving the carnage behind, the convoy continued to crawl to open countryside before entering a small village and ordered to stop in the square. Ted found a space for the bus by the church and the soldiers disembarked, their heavy hobnailed boots clattering down the staircase, officers indicating the direction to take towards the gunfire. Ted and Billy saw them off with 'wipe 'em out, lads!' They watched them out of sight and sound, until the last muted strains of *'We're here because we're here because…'*

They looked around them, the square now empty apart from buses and clusters of refugees. Straw had been placed around the church. They walked over to settle down in the shelter out of the wind and found themselves next to a woman crouching down with a baby.

'Pardon, Madame,' Ted said haltingly and turned away.

The child, rigid, back arching with anger, protested loudly, his stomach empty.

'Like some milk?' 'Lait?' Billy offered. He'd at least learnt a few words of the lingo already. Swinging his water bottle around from his back, he sniffed the contents then passed the bottle to the woman. 'You better see if it's still fresh.'

She guessed at what he meant, snatched the bottle from Billy's hand and lifted the bottle to her lips, tested the milk and nodded her thanks. The baby, fed, slept.

'You turned into Jesus or something?' Ted asked Billy back on the bus. 'Next time, turn water into some ale, OK?'

Billy gave a short laugh. 'Whatever you want, dad.'

~

That night, at a makeshift bus depot in the village, the drivers sat around a small coal fire with their rum tot and dwindling rations.

'Could do with some sardines now,' Ted said as he rummaged in his haversack in case he had missed a tin.

'Sorry mate, can't help you out there, but one of them biscuits, yes!' offered a driver.

Ted turned to him. 'Did you know that Billy here can turn water into milk?' Billy turned red, ashamed of his pilfering.

'Mate, you have to do what you have to do,' the driver replied. 'Make mine cream next time, to pour over some thick porridge, maybe a rasher of bacon to follow on toast, none of them foreign thin sticks of bread, mind.'

Dawkins walked over with post, bending toward the fire to read the envelopes. The drivers looked up expectantly.

'Lane!' 'Here!' 'Jameson!' 'Flippin' 'ell. Here!' 'Digby!' Ted stood up and grabbed at the letter. The post had finally caught up with them. He had written home but hadn't heard back. Was Norah still angry with him for leaving? Or had she turned a new corner, one of acceptance? Shoving the letter in his pocket, he walked around the quiet streets before returning to the fire and opened the envelope. Billy sat empty-handed in silence.

Her writing, small and concise, was perfectly readable if he moved closer to the fire. Squinting at the pages, he read.

My dearest Ted

I am sitting in that little wood in the park and it's a cold day. It's where we sat together all those years ago – 20 years now – and when you asked me to marry you. I couldn't write in the house, too many memories so came here to be by myself but with you. Thoughts come in to my head here, my best boy in the world. Ruby is upset with you for leaving and I am too. The house, so empty, so nothing without you in our lives. I don't mean to make you feel bad. You're doing what you feel you have to but at your age shouldn't be left to the youngsters, them with no family to care for? You have a big heart, guess that's why you're doing this, a patriot one. Maybe for just Ruby and me next time, not the others. Is it wrong to feel this way? Never apart you and me, the same face every breakfast, every evening. The girls at the laundry talk about their men and sons like they think they'll never come back and they never to see them again. I listen to them and think that too then I think, no, Ted's strong and sensible, he'll not put himself in danger because he wants to come home to Ruby, to me. It's strange at the hospital, English staff leaving. Just like rats from a sinking ship more like. Them that know we work with Germans jeer us. I don't know if I can trust them Germans anymore, the rumours too much sometimes but they have always been perfect good to me and I like them. To give up work would feel like betraying you, our family, like a divorce. Failing the war effort. I feel I am on the wrong side. I should look for other work. We have to live, pay the house costs. But them feelings for anyone German is moving fast. We was all shocked when the German sausage name had to change to luncheon sausage! And your pub's now called the King of Belgium, not your King of Prussia! The papers full of German butchers and bakers' shops smashed, everyone on the lookout for spies. But the silliest thing is that them injured Belgian solders being treated by our German doctors. From the frying pan into the fire, if you ask me! I am sorry, dearest Ted, these thoughts not a help to you when you are far away, looking after these brave soldiers. Too long a letter. And I'm cold. I'll finish with the news that the shed door is still keeping the elements out. Ruby is a support around the house, her

mending skills improving too. Wonders never cease! Life the
same outwards but very different inside us. Maybe you too.

May God bless you, your devoted wife Norah. Write.
Please. Are you eating enough?

Ted folded the letter neatly, put it in his breast pocket and
stared into the fire. He had cause many times to think of his
decision to go to war while he idled the engine in convoy,
cleaned his bus and his boots from the muddy Flanders fields.
Pride? To prove himself at his age? Patriotism? The Empire
and its position in the world? It certainly wasn't the money at
a shilling and tuppence a day. Nor the cold, the stinking mud,
the latrines, the food rations, the monotony, the uncertainty.
The comradeship, yes, adventure in his life, not the mundane
day-to-day Euston to Shepherd's Bush he knew like the back
of his hand. Oh, yes, that was the reason, well, one of them.
French women were lookers, no doubt about it, and not
plump like Hackney and Dalston women in the main,
matrons before their time.

Lighting a Woodbine, he smoked part of it before
stubbing it out. Placing the half-smoked tobacco in the
packet, he reached in a pocket for his mouth organ. *Three*
Blind Mice from the harp filled the air around the fire, men's
voices taking up the tune, at first with the accustomed words,
followed by ones new to Ted.

> *My Nelly's a Whore!*
> *My Nelly's a Whore!*
> *She's got such wonderful eyes of blue*
> *She uses such wonderful language too,*
> *Her fav'rite expression is 'Bollocks to you!*
> *My Nelly's a whore!*

Ted abruptly put his harp away and headed into the darkness.

Chapter 6: Home Front:

November, 1914

National League of Defenders' propaganda on British streets, November 1914: "ENGLISHMEN! Your Homes Are Desecrated! Your Children Are Starving! Your Loved Ones Are Dead! ... WILL YOU BECOME GERMANS? NO! ... You have England's Millions beside you. ... Let us exterminate every single man who has desecrated English soil." "ENGLAND'S MILLIONS ARE READY TO RISE!". Let 'England for Englishmen' be your battle-cry and avenge the blood of your wives and your children."

Norah, bundled up against the late November cold, closed the front door and hurried down the road to see if a bus came by. Or she'd have to walk the three miles to the hospital, over an hour away. Transport was increasingly patchy, no timetables adhered to. Maintenance crews had signed up for soldiering as well as bus drivers, a third of the buses now taken over by the army for ferrying soldiers in France and Belgium.

There was talk of training women to learn basic mechanics but diehards dismissed the discussion as pure hoopla. To save pennies and time waiting for a bus, workers, like Norah, had taken to walking.

Norah squeezed onto a crowded bus which would take her halfway to her destination. Before arriving at the hospital, she swiftly covered her face to pass a small group of gesturing people at the gates and walked down the ramp to the laundry rooms past Mr. Westmann's glassed office to clock on. The manager rose to his feet. Waylaying her he smiled faintly and gave a slight bow.

'Mrs. Digby, good morning to you. Will you please come to take a seat in the office for a moment?'

Norah frowned and hesitated. His gracious manner seemed at odds with the talk of war, of German barbarity circulating around pubs, homes, on the streets, in shops.

'Please, nothing to be alarmed about!' he frowned. 'I have some good news to tell you.'

Norah threw him a puzzled look, took off her coat, folded it over her arm and entered the orderly office, a model of planning and efficiency mirrored by the smooth running of the laundry. Wash smells and noises of pumping, pulsating wringers lessened when Mr. Westmann closed the door.

'Please, sit down,' he gestured. She moved to the chair opposite the desk. He motioned to tea and biscuits. 'Here, take. You can see we Germans have an addiction too to biscuits and learn how to dunk them, as you do, English fashion.' He gave a small laugh.

Norah stirred a spoonful of sugar into the hot brew and thanked him with a nod. Did Ruby pack this box, she wondered, and then stopped herself, such trivia going through her head. She declined a garibaldi.

'Ah, you do not have the habit of dunking?' he asked.

'Please, Mr. Westmann, say what you have to say,' Norah said quickly before she lost the courage to do so. 'I have work to do.'

'Forgive me, Mrs. Digby. There have been changes to management recently. You are aware of them, I feel sure.'

Norah stopped stirring and nodded.

'We have unfortunately lost two supervisors. I have not to explain why to you. The hospital now needs new ones.'

Norah looked at him expectantly.

He continued: 'We will pay an extra one third of salary and I offer you one of these jobs. Is this of interest to you, to be an even more valued member of the workforce? To help those at this terrible time in our lives?'

She was silent for a moment then tried to pick up her cup but felt unable to, her hands shaking. Placing them on her lap she was aware that they turned and twisted with startling ferocity. She gripped them and steadied them on the chair's armrests.

What would Ted say to this sudden help in their finances? Or would he suggest she'd taken leave of her senses working for any Hun, fighters or the non-fighters? Propaganda against the Germans was a daily mischief. She had recoiled in horror when given a New League of Defenders pamphlet, the heading startling and frightening.

Your Homes are desecrated! Your Children are Starving!
Your Loved Ones are Dead! Will you become German?

Norah looked at Mr. Westmann. 'Sir, I can't say yes or no for now. Give you an answer this week when I have time to talk it over with my family?'

'Ah, of course, with Mr. Digby.' He stood up.

'No, not with Ted, no. He's not around.' Norah's voice wavered. 'He's, well, fighting you lot.'

'Oh, I see.' Mr. Westmann gave a shake of his head and sighed loudly.

'We ordinary people do not wish you the slightest harm. As you know! I hope. You have been part of our German-English community for quite a time and I pray you understand us as people wishing not to hurt you. Or anyone! Our mission here is to protect and cure. And to shelter from illness, not make things more difficult than already exists, in this time of our shared lives.' He stopped and pushed his tea away.

'And here is a funny fact for you, Mrs. Digby,' he added, and smiled. 'Your Florence Nightingale, she trained here. With us. We were Germans then. And now.'

Norah, caught by the absurdity of it all, gave a high-pitched short laugh. Leaving the office, she hung up her coat by the entrance and tied on her baggy white apron. Moving slowly through the different departments – washing, bleaching, ironing, pressing, folding – she looked at the workplaces as if the first time. She set off home after her ten-hour shift, retracing her steps along the fog-bound streets to Bow.

Turning the key, she wished she could hear Ted's voice calling out. Instead, all was in darkness. And in the gloom, she wept.

~

That evening, she and Ruby finished their meal of rissoles and preserved runner beans from the garden, rounded off with a box of biscuit remnants. A pot of tea, swaddled in a knitted cosy, remained on the table after supper. Norah stood by the kitchener after clearing the dishes, leaning against the cooker's warm surface.

'Join me?' She gave Ruby a slight smile, her voice faltering. Silence, peppered with forced good humour, had been the order of the evening. She patted the space. 'It's ever so lovely and warm. Comforting.'

Ruby got up and huddled in Norah's arms. 'Ooh, you smell nice, like – like, carbolic soap!'

'And you, so yeasty and lovely, what biscuits you been working on today?'

'Bourbons, mum. Can you get a whiff of chocolate?' Ruby leaned over to the table and picked up her cup. 'We had a visitor today, high-class lady in the canteen over lunch. Better spread than usual, for some anyway. We got a dollop of pickle on our plates, first time ever.' She made a face. 'You could teach them a thing or two about a proper mustard pickle, ma, those cooks are a lazy lot.'

Norah poured her some more tea and put an arm around Ruby's shoulders. 'Do you know, maybe there's not enough allspice or maybe vinegar, that's what I reckon. Piccalilli's only good made at home, never in a factory. Oh, no. Small batches. Got to be homemade.'

'You're right, Mum. Nothing like yours,' Ruby paused. 'That woman today…'

61

Norah interrupted. 'Can it wait, dear? Something I have to tell you. Talk to you about.'

Norah told her about the sudden offer of promotion, the financial gain to the family coffers, her own disquiet, the deeply hurtful commentary from those at the hospital gates throwing words – *Traitor, conspirator, whore, German spy!* – at her and others.

'Mum, I don't want to hurt you, really, you know I don't. But how can you work for Germans here, when dad's working to take soldiers to kill them in France?' Ruby reasoned.

'Not right! Even if the war'll end soon, so Dad says, anyways. Why do you stay on there?   It's all too hateful, Mum!' She looked down at the patch of chipped flooring around the kitchener.

Norah removed her arm. 'I tell you why! They don't know these are kind people, people with heart! And they care for us, not only the Germans living here. They look after all the poor sick and us – and us! Everyone! Just everyone who needs help. We have to pay for care if we go to the doctor's. They do it for nothing. If we all leave, many won't have doctors looking after them. Them poor people, they got nowhere else to go. Nowhere. Not as if I agree to the war and all. Far far from it. The hospital's just looking after sick people, not killing them.'

They remained silent at the kitchener, Ruby watchful, Norah's look passive, almost resigned after her shrill outburst.

Ruby hugged Norah. 'Mum, you stand up to those bullies who never been in the place and don't know what they're talking about. That is, if you want to stay. If you can stand it.'

'The money's tempting,' Norah murmured quietly and hugged her. 'Sweet girl. It don't grow on trees.'

~

A week later, Norah accepted the job as supervisor. That same week she received a letter from Ted and sat down at the kitchen table to read it.

Dearest Woman,

Finished reading your letter last evening. I lie. Finished re-reading your letter for the tenth, or was it the eleventh time? My dear, what fine memories you brought back of those days when I scarce had the courage to ask you to marry me. You then had my love and you and Ruby will always have my devotion. You will consider them fancy words, I know, not like me! But it's true what I write to you, a new strong kind of love in my heart for the dear precious woman who stood by me when I meanly decided to leave to serve - my hasty decision. My girl, my girls, how I miss you. At night I lay awake and think of you, the roar of the big guns giving way to pictures of you both before my eyes. I too go back and-travel the road we have known together. You and me, girl. My girls.

Billy Boy – I mentioned him to you in previous letters – is coming on just fine after some trouble getting used to army life, a fine young man keen to do the best he can, poor upbringing or not. He's toughening up. He has a lovely, light voice and can sing 'Oh for the wings of a dove' most beautiful. I play my harp and he sings it, and other stuff. But words are different at war. Not for you and Ruby's ears! Then sometimes he gets out his violin and has a go at harmony or the tune.

We took some poor injured soldiers to the makeshift hospital this morning and drove into a town to find something called, well, a bit like a canteen but nicer, estaminet, they call it, homely place. I had an omelette and a rum for about a halfpenny. So, we're eating, don't fret. Tea's funny out here, must be the water. Not like home.

I worry about you and working at the hospital, all those people by the gate making a damn nuisance. You decide for yourself. I am not there, can't judge. Ruby's your support now. Glad to know the shed door is holding up. Get Ronnie, that old geezer who's always on the lookout for a farthing or two to see to it if it's causing you problems. He's a proper carpenter, not like your loving husband, Ted.

Norah gave a short laugh then replaced the letter in the envelope and flung it across the floor. She thumped the table with a strength that surprised her then folded her arms on the worn wood and stared into nothingness, resisting the urge to howl.

Chapter 7: Western Front:

December, 1914

By the end of 1914 the battles of movements, of gains in the first weeks of the war had been brought to a halt. Carefully selecting the most favourable high ground, the Imperial German Army began the construction of a strong defensive line consisting of trenches, wire defences, mined dugouts, deep bunkers and reinforced concrete emplacements. Gradually, building and digging was carried on both sides of the wire along a distance of 450 miles, creating a more or less continuous line of trenches separating the warring belligerents along The Western Front.

Soldiers lined up on claggy, winter-darkening roads waiting to be assigned to their buses. Their clothing and equipment was covered in marl, yellow, watery clay found in these parts. It clung to their boots, puttees and any other part of their uniform. Faces, streaked with mud and fatigue, were proof enough to Ted and Billy that their passengers had endured a battle day of consequences on the Franco-Belgian border. Their destination now was to Armentières in French Flanders, away from Ypres on the Belgian side of the disputed land.

'Go and help them on,' Ted said firmly but quietly to Billy, who stood jiggling on the soles of his boots to keep warm.

Ted walked to the front of the bus and cranked up the engine, swearing as the motor failed to engage, more vigorous winding finally rewarding him with a splutter then a whiff of petrol, followed by a robust engine noise and a shaking chassis.

Jumping inside, he turned on the lights for a short while to guide the soldiers on board before switching them off. Flares lit up the sky, the shape of the churned, mottled flat lands distorting in the flashes, the sudden jarring of light focusing on stretcher bearers.

Billy tried a joke at the bus steps. Sometimes it worked. 'Wipe your feet before getting on this bus bound for Piccadilly, lads!' Some cuffed him playfully on the shoulder as they made their slow way up to the top deck or inside the airless, shuttered bus, their hobnailed boots forced sideways up the narrow steps. Others scowled at the feeble joke before their faces resumed a passive look. Only one with still enough spirit exaggerated his boot wiping skills in theatrical style, earning him pats on the back and a lively kick. Billy pushed those, unable to muster strength, from behind on their mud-marked rucksacks, his grip catching their mess tins.

Royal Army Medical Corps vehicles passed the bus slowly, drivers nodding to Ted.

'Full up to the gunnels,' shouted an orderly at the back of one of the vehicles to another attendant while fastening the door. Ted could hear piercing cries of young voices and wondered if he'd ever become immune to their pain.

In the canteen, an orderly sat with Ted and Billy drinking tea while they waiting for the order to drive to the trenches. Fiddling with his mug, the medic talked in a quiet voice. 'Too dog-tired, some of these men. No wonder they get slow, can't keep up the pace them generals want. They're just fodder for the Huns, don't get enough rest.'

'We can only do what we can,' Ted replied, draining his drink. 'Help them keep up morale; being cheerful's the best thing, I reckon.' His weak voice belied his true feelings.

'Least we're not in the line of fire,' Billy offered. 'We got the rifles too but we're just drivers, the lucky ones, I guess. Like Ted says, keep cheerful.'

'You may see yourself as lucky, boy – but we're not! Some of them injuries I've never seen the likes of; just getting them to the clearing stations is sometimes the end of them on these god-forsaken roads. Don't even make it to hospital for treatment.'

~

The bus made its way along increasingly slippery roads in the torrent of rain sweeping across Flanders fields until they reached the next French town where they would stop for the night. Ted and Billy drove onto the curb several times to remove mud from the wheels and the front of the engine as it became overheated, climbing back on board after knocking clumps of mud from their boots. Ted, in the driver's seat, wrapped the tarpaulin he'd saved around his legs to keep out the rain while Billy moved inside with the troops for warmth and listened to the banter inside the bus.

'Took us an hour to climb out of our trench,' boasted a burly soldier.

'Step over the bodies next time, useful even when dead, our Tommies,' another muttered under his breath.

'Jesus Christ, Not the Huns that killed them, the trench water more like,' added another.

'Drowned and never said goodbye to Mother.' They laughed but without humour.

'I'll have his rum rations!' called out one.

'And me too, and all,' shouted another.

The convoy stopped in a nondescript village, its houses facing a small square with a church at its centre, its steeple pockmarked by battle scars. The parish looked like a poor place with no visible lights or people. Ted checked the time, angling his watch towards the scudding cloud-lit moonlight to check the hour. It was past midnight.

Soldiers disembarked and were shown the way to their billets, Ted and Billy told to knock on a cottage door where they would kip for the night. An old man welcomed them then pointed to their muddy boots.

'Ah, OK, we take them off,' Ted said, bending down. It occurred to him that he hadn't been in a house since leaving his own, boots rarely off now. The bus, mess tents and latrines were their natural habitat since leaving England over three months ago.

'Do the same, Billy.' Ted directed.

Placing them near the front door on a frayed mat, they followed their host, the heat catching them unawares in the semi-darkness.

The man turned up a gas light, revealing a simple sitting room cum kitchen.

'It's like Buckingham Palace!' Billy muttered to Ted. 'Feel that heat! Not felt anything like this for months!'

Ted stepped forward to the man and clasped his hands. '*Merci, merci!*'

They looked at the bare floorboards and basic furniture, the warmth and their host creating a homely feel. The man gestured to seats around the table by a long black stove where a coffee pot, bowls and bread were laid out.

An elderly woman turned around from the stove. '*Asseyez-vous, messieurs, vous êtes les bienvenus!*' She turned back to the pot she had been stirring, tasted a spoonful then filled a tureen with hot potato and leek soup, placing it in front of the drivers.

'What a… a feeling to be in a real home again!' Ted exclaimed, dipping his bread into his soup bowl. He tried some hesitant, staccato sentences, the couple nodding encouragingly. Billy, eyes closed, pushed his bowl to the side and struggled to his feet. He stretched then threw in a phrase, *dormir, me*, two hands by his head feigning a pillow.

Their beds that night in the warm room were hard, but not as hard as the bus's slats. Peeling off thick woollen long johns, vests and socks by the stove, they hung them up to dry over kitchen chairs before slipping under sheeting and a rough blanket. Billy looked at the stiff *oreiller* bolster before deciding it was a pillow, not a foot rest.

'Beats sweeping out the mud and sleeping on the benches,' he murmured contently in the dark. All he heard was Ted's rhythmic snore.

~

They rose early in the dark. Ted opened the shutters to rain and groaned. Searching in his rucksack for something to leave the couple after pulling on his clothing, he drew a blank.

'Billy, you got a little prezzie for the couple, a little thank you? I'm fresh out of anything like that, only half pack of ciggies left.'

Billy looked inside his bag and found a jar of strawberry jam sent to him by his sister. He had been keeping it as a keepsake, a good luck charm. Lifting up the jar, he looked at it for the longest time then put it on the table.

'Well done, Billy,' Ted said, touching his arm. 'Well done.'

~

Later that month, Ted and Billy picked up the first batch of Indian soldiers to join the forces and drove them to the trenches. Most wore turbans, a silver clasp holding the cloth in place, others adopting the British military cap. Full beards and curled moustaches contrasted with shaven British soldiers, moustaches, however, their only acceptable facial hair. Since their arrival in Flanders the Indians had suffered heavy losses. Ted and Billy had witnessed a self-imposed segregation, British soldiers ignoring the newcomers. But as weeks wore on, they had seen the two sides meshing, respect growing for the Indian Corps' courage and uncomplaining character.

German counter-attacking was now further up the line, defences needed swiftly. 'Get a move on!' Dawkins barked as Ted helped the newcomers on with their heavy equipment; despite their smaller stature, they were surprisingly strong, showing great limb strength and silent resolve.

'Fine, fine, that's what we're doing,' Ted answered brusquely. Sleep-deprived, he dropped his subservient tone.

Dawkins tapped him on a shoulder and shouted in his ear. 'Then do it faster. Faster!'

'Sir!' The hint of sarcasm wasn't missed. Dawkins strode off after a swipe at the driver, Ted ducking in time.

Billy nervously pressed the gas pedal, the engine's revving adding further tension. He didn't want it to die away after he and Ted had got it going; he knew from bitter experience how easily cold could affect the mechanism and what a blasting Dawkins would belt out.

Flares in the distance lit up rows of bare, desolate vineyards and stone houses as the convoy headed towards the offensive. After four hours of skirting around the Front's winding farm roads, the buses came to an abrupt halt, the soldiers ordered off.

Ted's tenuous grasp of home life began to feel like a figment of his imagination. Driving a bus around Piccadilly was too fantastical, a fairy tale of blinking, riotous colour, not of monochrome landscape. Khaki landscape, khaki-green-brown-grey. Only an occasional piercingly cold blue winter sky heightened the drabness of the French countryside at war.

He stepped aside to let the soldiers off, giving a hand where he could to the shorter Indians, the reach from step to mud difficult with their large loads. The clash of rifles and boots dimmed in the distance as they made their way to the front. They had already endured hours of stop-start, stop-start in cramped quarters, no sleep possible. Now the real work started.

Ted and Billy stretched and yawned and got out their tea kit after brushing out the mud from the two decks. The horizon offered light in the freezing cold. Billy went for a piss as the water heated.

Dawkins appeared. 'Ted, head back to the night's stopping point and pick up another load!' he growled.

70

'But Sarge, we already done a fair day and night. Jim and Tony over there,' he nodded in the direction of the bus alongside them, drivers snoozing on the drivers' bench. 'They had the whole night to rest here.'

'Digby, are you countering my orders?' Dawkins asked in an uncharacteristically quiet tone. 'And use my full title. It's sergeant, not sarge. Got it?'

'Yes, sir, but just pointing out that it would be fairer to…'

'So, you want some fairness in life, is that it, soldier? You are a soldier, are you not? Not a civilian? Have I got that right? Have I?'

Ted didn't answer. Infuriated, Dawkins got out his book, his voice rising, his words exaggeratingly slow.

'Do – you – know – what – I – am – writing – down?' Ted shook his head, beads of sweat forming. He took off his cap and wiped his face.

'And you dare to take your cap off in my presence too! I'll cashier you before too long!'

Billy ran up at speed at the loud exchange, Ted gesturing him away. Dawkins turned around, saw Billy and called him over.

'I suppose little man would like special services too, a nice lie-in suit you? Both of you lazy buggers, I'm timing you. Back here with a full complement within the next four hours.' He strode away.

Ted motioned to Billy to zip up his mouth as they gathered up their tea kit, climbed onto the drivers' bench and drove back in the cold dawn.

Horses sped past them to the Front, their hoofs flinging up mud on the riders' uniforms and on their firearms. Their air of urgency, coupled with the horses' snorts and dispatch bags, almost airborne against their flanks, suggested a mission unlike that of others passing by more slowly in the melée. Ted watched the animals' buttocks disappear in the fog and felt unexpectedly, strangely cut off from the action. Keeping one hand on the large wheel and his eyes on the road, he bent to touch the rifle at his side. He too should be fighting, ending this war by all means possible. Or aim the rifle at Dawkins; now, it seemed, he had enemies on both sides. Acute homesickness attacked him. He shouldn't be turning away from the enemy but driving towards them, all hands to the pump. Finish the job off! Kill the buggers messing up all their lives!

Only a week to go to Christmas. Jesus! He promised he'd be home for Christmas. Promised. Why did he think it would be over in a flash? What would Norah be thinking as the date loomed closer? If he couldn't be trusted, who could she trust? She worked with Germans. And what was he doing? Not even fighting them but driving. Just a driver. He could be doing this at home, in London. At home.

Stop it, you bloody fool! He glanced at Billy's tightly coiled fists then lit two cigarettes, smoke wavering in the wind of the cold light of dawn. Where was his galaxy of good intentions now?

~

It was early Christmas Day morning, the date ignored by many. Told to line up after their rations, soldiers were reminded of the festive season when handed a present by officers, a tin from Princess Mary alongside an extra tot of rum and a slap on the back or shoulder, their false bonhomie not reciprocated, apart from the Indians who looked gratefully at the unexpected royal gift.

Billy examined the tin's contents and pulled out tobacco and cigarettes as well as a pipe, lighter, and pencil and paper for writing home. Lifting up the paper, he searched for a sweet snack and closed the lid after taking out the pipe.

'Ted, Ted. I'm now my pa!' he clowned, clenching the pipe in his mouth. 'Get away with you!' Ted replied, grinning at him. He'd keep the tin when emptied of its useful contents, maybe for extra baccy from home.

Their bus was at full stretch at the Front after breakfast.

'Here, Billy, help that lot on,' Ted instructed, a hard edge to his voice.

Billy nodded but without energy. Dawkins remained undiscussed since their last altercation with the sergeant, the passing weeks seeing a hail of sneering orders not visited on other drivers. The Indian soldiers became Dawkins' new targets.

Billy half carried, shouldered injured soldiers onto the bus, the vehicle increasingly used as a makeshift ambulance, his small stature staggering under their now-useless bodies. Their boots, welded to their feet after standing for long periods in cold, dank, stinking grey-brown trench winter water, had to be prised or cut off at nursing stations, their feet treated for rot or amputated.

Billy's stomach turned when helping his first group with trench foot, unable to keep his rations down. He could now smell putrefied flesh yards away.

'Gangrene, lad, get used to it!' was Ted's sharp remark when Billy retched.

Their bus returned for more injured soldiers on Christmas morning. As they neared the Front, a band of snow and sleet moved to the east. Teasels, piercing the snow, lay defeated on their sides, their brown, prickly stems and conical seed heads appearing to have given up the ghost.

Excited shouts simmered before ricocheting into the slate-grey sky. Ted, his thoughts elsewhere, jerked back to the present. 'What's going on? What's up?' he shouted at a passing driver while adjusting his coat collar in the bitter cold.

'Ceasefire, old man, ceasefire!' shouted the driver.

'No, doubt it, doubt it very much!' Ted replied, confused.

The urgent voice continued. 'Brass briefing us now, well, that's the rumour. Maybe we all get to go home, fucking good news, eh?'

'I'll believe it when I see it with my own eyes,' Ted growled. Ordered to park his bus by a zigzag of trenches, he jumped down from the cabin, Billy joining him.

Dawkins approached quickly. Sighing, Ted put a protective arm around Billy.

'Not so fast, lads,' Dawkins shouted. He came to a halt alongside a captain and addressed the drivers and soldiers.

'Only a temporary one is the word.' He smirked and studied the assembled group, his gaze resting on Ted and Billy.

'You. And you. Get your shovels and help bury the bodies!'

'Oh, god, no!' Billy muttered, 'not in no man's land again, my boots can't stand much more of those water craters!'

Ted pushed Billy. 'Don't goad him, just do it!' he hissed into his ear.

'You know the drill by now. Remove the ID tags first, lads,' Dawkins called out after them. 'Return them to me. Quick as you can!'

'As if we didn't know the drill,' Billy sneered as he and Ted put on masks. They worked methodically after climbing down into the waterlogged pits, turning bodies to find their identity numbers, some caught up in bullet-torn uniforms and flesh, others more challenging to locate.

'Poor buggers, what a way to die,' Billy muttered through his mask. He gagged often and cursed the war. Ted worked silently beside him, his coat's wet, muddy hem dragging him down.

Picking up a photo and a diary, Ted smeared the mud off and stuffed them in his coat pocket alongside a clutch of identity numbers and a penknife with a pearl handle he had found on an officer. His family would be reunited with the number and the penknife. He left the bibles, some chewed on by rats. He chased the animals away with their shovels or showered them with blows.

One of Dawkins' trench recruits, an Indian, shouted at them. 'Dirty vermin, don't send them our way, please, sir! Kill 'em, sir!'

Ted swatted at the animals, catching one on the back. The squealing rat managed to get away, scrambling up the bank towards enemy line.

Ted groaned in pain as he stretched his spine. They had shovelled and stacked bodies neatly in the opaque light for hours. Placing his shovel against a trench bank, he cupped his ears. Silence. Stillness. Sounds of warfare, of blasting shells, hand grenades, machine gun fire, sniping, horses neighing with terror – all were conspicuous by their absence. Maybe it really was the end. If it had only been a ceasefire, it would only have lasted a short time before guns blazed, men were mown over as they went over the top.

He motioned to Billy and raised his head above the trench. They gazed at the wintery pale colours of the land, the clay, mud, broken drainage bricks and coils of barbed wire which stretched into infinity. Everything was still, just a pall of smoke rising in the far distance. Other diggers joined them.

'Get down, you fucking idiots!' Dawkins bellowed from the ground above, never far away. 'I'll have you court-martialled, you lot! Get back to your duties!'

Ted held a restraining hand on Billy who was poised to climb up out of the quagmire.

He slid across to Ted. 'Why not? Into no man's land for once. What a story to tell your grandkids, Ted! I'll tell mine, for sure!'

Ted shook his head, he and Billy watched soldiers, defying Dawkins' orders, climb out and advance toward the barbed wire. The enemy was nowhere to be seen, the quiet unnerving. Some turned tail and scrambled clumsily back down into the trenches when shouts went up, others braving the unaccustomed freedom, waving their arms at the non-existent enemy. Dawkins took notes on the sidelines after a heated discussion with the shrugging duty captain.

~

Billy settled down in the bus on his bunk bed after brushing off the mud from his uniform and boots as best he could before supper, the bus now a distance away from the Front, but he couldn't sleep. He sat up in the dark and thought about the day, Christmas Day like no other he had experienced. Or likely to do so again, he reflected. They'd be going home, back to civvy life. Surely.

Ted stirred in his makeshift bed opposite, cold breath visible. 'What's up, Billy?'

Billy moved on the wooden slats. 'Do you think that's really the end? Maybe we don't have to shovel no more bodies in the ground, Ted? End of the war, d'ya think? All go home soon?'

'Can hardly believe it, all seems so strange, Billy. Suddenly we're fighting, then it's ceasefire. Your prediction's as good as mine. God only knows. We'll find out soon enough. Get some sleep now.'

Billy wouldn't let the subject go. 'D'ya suppose everyone's really the same everywhere, Ted? Everywhere in the world? No one wants to fight but we're all caught up in this, this…?'

'You mean, not really knowing why we're fighting, Billy? You're right, sometimes even the smallest thing can seem big to us when it doesn't really matter. Just say sorry and get on with our lives.'

'I volunteer!' Billy laughed. 'I'll say sorry! To anyone. The first German I meet!' He added, 'After he says sorry to me first!'

'Makes sense to me, lad,' Ted replied quietly, turning over in his narrow, hard bed. He tugged on the blanket. 'Wouldn't mind a few creature comforts right now!' he chuckled. 'Pull the covers over and get warm, Billy.'

Soon the bus was quiet inside.

~

The truce lasted only twenty-four hours. French army chiefs and civilians, hearing of the fraternisation along the trenches some distance away from where Ted and Billy had been burying the dead, concluded that the British were now against them. Rumours and facts flew: The Royal Family were really Germans, not English. The Kaiser, a cousin to George V, their reigning monarch, was all the proof they needed. It all added up.

Chapter 8: Western Front

December, 1914

The alarm went out after midnight, the ceasefire declared over. The ground where both sides had been so congenial and where Germans had wished the opposition a Merry Christmas, was now covered with the dead. But the truce, although widespread, was not total. In some parts of the Front, however, shelling and firing continued with deaths on Christmas Eve to Boxing Day.

Ted found a warm corner spot in a Red Cross makeshift canteen away from milling soldiers and drifted off to sleep. In front of him lay pen and paper from Princess Mary's tin and a tea mug. He stirred as he dreamt he was underground, beneath enemy trenches, a terrible vision emerging of Ruby, trapped by Germans who waved frantically at him to help her then laughed at him. He started to crawl over corpses, over rat-bitten bibles, Ruby dragged further down a tunnel.

'Ted! Ted, wake up!' Billy shook him awake. Ted wiped dribble from his mouth and sat up.

'You was talking to yourself! Asleep!'

Ted stared at Billy vacantly, recalling the nightmare, then shook himself. 'Just going to write to Norah, must have dozed off.'

'Say that again, you did! Here, I'll get you a fresh cuppa.' Billy walked purposefully through the canteen to the counter.

Reaching across the table, Ted picked up his pen. He had angrily screwed up his first attempt to write to Norah, the paper now a taut ball under the table. He tried again, tempering his feelings.

My dearest Woman and Ruby

December 26, 1914

How are you both? Ruby, are you keeping well, dear? I think of you every day and wonder how you got on over Christmas. You'll be surprised to hear that we spent our Christmas in the trenches and that Christmas Day was a very happy one thanks to a tin of baccy we got from Princess Mary. Can you believe it? Bloomin' odd, I know, something I never thought possible, something from the royals. Still shaking my head. We shared the plum pudding you made for Billy and me. Highlight of the day. Apart from the truce, of course. Never tasted anything so moist and fruity, Billy said. Today it is all over. Back to war. No sign of coming home yet but Billy will be, his dad very ill. Give him a warm welcome when he comes by, dear. He don't have close family like us. A good lad, brave and true.

His letter crossed with one from Norah, dated December 25.

My dearest Ted

I got your letter dated December 15 and hope you are in the best of health despite the privations. Ruby and I are as well as expected at present. Christmas was hardly the same without you but somehow we managed to keep a strong faith, our celebrations small, no like other years, I guess not surprising, dear. We dug out the old ornaments but didn't have a Christmas tree – too German! But Ruby and I didn't have the heart to do anything with them and put the box away. Didn't seem right, you not having a Christmas either. The hospital invited us all to a Christmas tree party with singing on Christmas Eve, Ruby too, but we didn't go. Just couldn't. I saw it lit up in the entrance hall with candles when I left work. It looked very beautiful. They are all so nice to us. Why, when we are at war? I don't understand anything anymore. Thank God for our daughter who keeps my spirits up. You should be proud of her – at such a tender age too. Is anyone getting home leave? Why ask eh, my heart in my mouth. When will you, my dearest one? I long for your arms, your eyes shining on me once again. You are not to worry about us. Just keep yourself safe, for all our sakes. I pray for you always. Your loving Norah.

Ted folded the letter carefully and put it away with the others in a bundle.

Chapter 9: Home Front

Daily Express, Wednesday 13 January, 1915:
*BATTLE FOR A FORT. GERMAN TRENCH INSIDE FRENCH
WORKS. DESPERATE FIGHT.*
*French Official, Paris - The following communiques were issued to-
day: - On the Aisne, to the north of Soissons, there was some very
lively fighting around some trenches captured by us on January 8
and 10. The enemy, in the course of yesterday, several times took
the offensive, but were repulsed, and we captured fresh sections of
trenches.*

Billy stepped off the train and looked around the station.
Charing Cross seemed untouched by war, people going about
their business just as they had the day he left so swiftly
without warning for the Front. Belgium was just as hastily
left four months later when the captain informed him of his
father's stroke.

His mother's successful, pleading letter to the Army gave
him little time to assemble belongings, let alone bathe before
he was on his way back to London. It was four days after
Christmas, the oddest Christmas he had known. Before
leaving, he carefully wrapped his violin in its case and shoved
it with other belongings on the bus, Ted entrusted to keep an
eye on it.

The Army had checked up on his father's health before
granting him compassionate leave. Alfred Cotgrave lay in
Hackney Hospital with little chance of survival. Bending over
his watchmaker's bench smoking for long hours had seen

him alter from a young, fit man thirty years ago to someone aged before his time.

Billy would nip home first to surprise his mum and Cissy, he'd then go to see his old man. He had promised to pay a visit to Ted's family too, after the older man had insisted.

His kit bounced uncomfortably on his back as he hopped on a bus going towards Hackney. Home, a short walk from the bus stop, looked more neglected than he remembered, his new life erasing his old one in more ways than he cared to admit.

Doors were never locked on these streets. He stepped into the hall and peered in the kitchen. His mother bent over a pan on the kitchener, intent on supper.

'Hello, Mother,' he said quietly as he put his bag down on the kitchen floor.

'Oh, my God. Billy!' She dropped a wooden spoon in the pot and rushed over to him, one small, dry kiss brushing a cheek.

Being away from home has changed her, Billy thought, returning her embrace, a first time for everything.

She tripped back. 'What's all this crawling over you?' She looked closer. 'Lice! Disgustin'! You bring them all over with you?'

Billy looked down and brushed his uniform jacket. 'Oh, these. I'm so used to them now, we call them chats over there.'

'You're not spreading them around this house, my boy! Get outside with you!' She pulled him by the arm out onto the street. 'Strip, Billy!'

'What, here, right here, Mother?'

'Right here!' She had always been a determined woman. He did as he was told.

He stepped in the tin bath with a modest foot of hot water which his mother had heated in a pot on the kitchener and squirmed as she applied force with carbolic soap and a stiff brush, his skin turning blotchy red. Reaching for the Lysol, she didn't listen to his cries of 'Go easy, Mum!' as she scrubbed him with renewed vigour. He was a child again. The smell was overwhelming yet oddly comforting.

In France, chats lined his trouser seams and in deep furrows of long thick woolly pants. One trick the army had taught him was a lighted candle, chats popping like Chinese crackers.

His mother had bundled up his clothes on the street, leaving them outside the house in an untidy khaki tangle. Ice and snow blanketed them overnight, the frozen lice shaken off before he brought in the uniform the next day.

Billy sat with her over a cup of tea. Dressed in civvies, his skin still sulked from his mother's fierce grip and scrub, the nearby fire making him itch. He looked into the flames. 'They're usually worse but they don't like the winter cold too much. Still, some like my warm blood! But standing on the street stark naked, Mother!'

'Well, I couldn't take you through to the yard, could I? Droppin' them lice everywhere!'

They exchanged a look. Billy ended the awkward silence.

'Now, what's Dad been up to, eh, the old bugger?'

~

His father died the day after Billy visited him. He barely recognised the gaunt, twisted figure in the hospital iron bedstead. He had seen that look a hundred times or more on the battlefield, the mouth agape, the staring, uncomprehending eyes, the chalk-grey skin. Another unfulfilled life extinguished. But he wasn't sorry; the old man had always given him a hard, brutal time. He and his brother had been singled out for beatings, their sisters left alone.

The next day towards dusk, Billy hurried along darkening streets in the bitter wind, heading towards the address Ted had given him. Norah opened the door and frowned at the slight figure.

Billy gave her a smile. 'Mrs. Digby?'

'Who wants to know?'

'Billy Boy Cotgrave, Mrs. Digby. I've just come…'

Norah stepped down to the street and squeezed him tightly then let go swiftly, with a joint look of shame and eagerness.

'You seen my Ted! Oh, please, how rude of me, what possessed me to do that to you, I…'

He put up his hand and laughed. 'Well, quite a welcome, quite a…'

'Come in, come in! Ruby! See who's here,' she called as she entered with Billy in tow.

Following Norah, he caught a glimpse of the layout and décor of the formal, tiny front room and tried to visualise Ted living here and failed. Ted was a practical outdoor man, used to privations, dealing with them without complaint. But Billy had seen Ted's pictures on the driver's visor, noting too the carefully concealed letters tucked under floorboards. A family man without a doubt.

He struggled to recall when the two of them had entered a house in France. No, in Belgium, that time in Flanders, Armenty or something like that, the first in the four months. The bus was their natural habitat, where they slept and ate but sometimes they had a meal in some canteen or other. Soulless places. But warmer.

Family portrait photographs hung on walls over a small worn sofa and two stuffed chairs were stoutly positioned by the decorative iron fireplace which was only big enough to take two logs or a small shovelful of coal at a time. The room was not only at odds with his and Ted's lives but also his own meagre home.

Norah beckoned him through into the kitchen and took his coat, hanging it on a peg by the kitchener.

Ruby, seated at the table, glanced up from her needlework. She was the spitting image of Ted. He'd recognise her anywhere, on any street, any bus. Ted's girl. The girl in the picture, under the visor. He had memorised her features, the bold uplift of her mouth, her brown, direct eyes, her dark hair piled up, pillow-fashion.

He blushed then plucked up the courage. 'Ruby.' He held out his hand. She nodded and gave a shy smile.

'Sit down, sit down, dear!' Norah commanded, a tremor in her voice. 'Some tea? And when did you eat last? We just had suet pudding if you'd like some. Now, tell us.' She paused. 'How's our Ted?'

'Mum, let him be. Catch his breath.'

Billy sat awkwardly, not knowing if he should face Norah or Ruby. Norah unhooked a cup from the dresser, leant over the table and poured him a cup of tea, then placed a plate of suet pudding and a fork before him. He looked at her gratefully and picked up his fork.

'Forgetting my manners, I'm sure,' Norah said hastily. 'You're here, for your father. I trust he is recovering. Back at home, is he?'

'No, Mrs. Digby, no.' Billy replied, hastily chewing a mouthful before answering. 'Died yesterday. Hackney, in hospital. No great loss, not like your Ted, not at all. Still, he had his chances. Just didn't know how to take them, poor sod.'

His directness startled Norah who had always been brought up to believe only to speak of the dead in a virtuous tone.

Billy stirred some sugar into his tea. 'What me and Ted seen these past months can stop you in your tracks or...'

'Billy, can you stay for the funeral, stay a while, or are you back prompt?' Norah interrupted. Ruby glanced at her mother then turned to Billy.

'I want to hear, Billy. Carry on.' She filled up Billy's cup.

He told them about his and Ted's lives on the bus, what the French and Belgians were like, the food and presents given to them for helping them fight the Germans.

'Les Boches, they call them, slang. Fritz too.' But he didn't use the word 'fight,' Ted's instructions ringing in his head.

'Don't tell 'em too much, Billy, don't tell them the dangerous stuff, some of the sights you and me have seen. The shrapnel,

*the trenches, terrible wounds, killing, digging graves. Keep it
light, keep it simple, not too much detail. Women, see?
Gentle, delicate. They worry.'*

He told them about their first day in France after a long
march to find their buses being sawn in half, Ruby laughing
at his story.

Encouraged by Ruby, he continued how he and Ted
painted the buses a camouflage grey. Where they slept ('you
get used to never turning over, else you're on cold deck!'),
the landscape, the Sikh soldiers' exotic turbans, the rum
rations, stories about barking sergeants. Dawkins' name came
up often. Billy told them too about the German uniforms he
had seen on prisoners, the Christmas football match played at
the Front, down the line from where they had been, his tone
regretful that he had missed out.

'You allowed to tell us all this, Billy? Don't seem right
somehow,' Ruby chastised him. 'What would the War Office
say?'

Blushing, he put down his fork. He had to keep to Ted's
wishes but had said too much as he warmed to his subject,
wanting to impress Ruby.

Norah rebuked her daughter. 'Why did you stop him,
Ruby? I want to know all about your dad's life. Don't seem
too bad to me, in all honesty.'

Ruby left the room, muttering something about her
uniform needing mending.

Billy raised his head after she had left the room. 'Guess
I'd better be moving along, Mrs. Digby, sorry for the…' He
got up.

'Stay a while longer, Billy,' Norah urged quietly. 'Just
need to hear more. Please, sit down.'

They sat for a long time, Norah asking innumerable
questions. Was Ted eating properly? Getting a bath? And
receiving her letters regularly? Did she need to send him
some underwear? Winter clothing? Biscuits? When was he
was likely to get home leave? She omitted any questions
about the war, preferring to know about Ted's life and not the

lives of others, their suffering, their privations, their cruel deaths. But what were the French women like? She heard they were pretty.

He answered Norah as best he could, some questions easily dealt with, others ducked after remembering his promise to Ted.

'He's like a father to me, he is,' he said proudly. 'A real gent. Helped me toughen up in them early days when I didn't know what hit me, this signing up business.'

He looked at Norah. 'Sorry, Missus, shouldn't really be talking like this, the day my dad died and all. Ted shows me how a real dad cares. Never had nothing like that. Tops, he is.'

He buried his head in his hands and let out a stifled howl. Norah got up and put her arms around his shaking shoulders then topped up the teapot with more hot water.

They barely noticed Ruby returning and taking a chair in the corner by the light to sew. The clock ticked by the dresser, the hour late, Norah not tiring of questioning him. He was unsure of Ruby, her manner now brittle, her unfriendly eyes occasionally flickering in his direction. His dinner plate remained on the table, greasy from the pudding gravy and marked with vigorous scraping as he had tried to get the most out of the homemade meal.

~

Norah met May, Billy's mother at the funeral, a reserved, determined-looking woman who showed no emotion when her husband's coffin was lowered into the grave after the chapel service. Norah insisted that Ruby come along to support Billy, his arm shaken off by May as they walked away from the graveyard. Only Cicely, her youngest child, managed a kiss from her remaining parent, the cold embrace followed by a smack for dropping her black arm band.

In the small East London cemetery chapel, Ruby gazed at the stone carvings after the sparsely attended service. The cluster of Worshipping Angels, of Passion, of the Earth and

Sea, all soaring sculptures, were pitted with age and industrial detritus of the city. Was this a fitting end to a life, any life, even an unfulfilled one they had gathered together to put to earth? During the service she had turned to look at Billy in the front pew with his mother and small sisters. Only his brother, on the Front, was missing.

Billy put his hand in his pocket for a wake at his father's favoured pub, the Rose & Crown on Mare Street. Ruby tasted sherry for the first time, declaring it a fine, warming drink. She had shaken off her initial feeling of distrust towards Billy after watching him with his family. He'd soon be gone anyway, back to the bus. But Dad would ask him about her. Better be friendlier towards him. But did Dad remember – or care – how she felt about soldiers?

Chapter 10: Western Front

London Gazette, April 14, 1915. British Break the German Line in Artois

The Battle of Neuve Chapelle (10th - 13th March 1915) was launched with the aim of capturing the high ground of the Aubers Ridge and in so doing, to create a threat to the German Army in occupation of the city of Lille. German losses in four days' fighting were estimated at 18,000.

Ted walked into the *estaminet* with other soldiers and signalled to a waiter. The bar, overlooking the square, was busy despite the surrounding devastation, the town hardly recognisable from when he had last passed through five months ago. Only the bare shell of the church remained, the interior lost to view beneath the debris. In the churchyard the dead had been plucked from their graves, coffins and ancient bones scattered. A scattering of monuments remained, two large stone crucifixes reared up at grotesque angles. Both were pitted with bullet marks, Christ looking down in mute agony. Workmen, in blue overalls, bent over collecting bones and making neat piles of fallen stone.

Monsieur Laurent, the owner, came out from the kitchen clapping his hands. '*Monsieur* Ted, you back here!'

Nodding towards the rubble surrounding the café, he clasped Ted close to him. 'The café goes on, life must go on, ' he whispered. 'But,' stepping back he added loudly, 'we still have some food for you.' He wiped his eyes. 'Come, a table!'

Pointing to one in the centre of the café, he collected a bottle of wine on the way with a few stubby glasses. Ted and the others followed him and sat down.

'Et messieurs, à manger.' Des omelettes, un potage de pommes de terre aux poireaux...' Setting down the glasses and wine. He poured it and continued. *'Mais, la viande? Pas grand chose aujourd'hui. Rien que des lardons. Je suis desolé.'*

Ted smiled and introduced him to his companions. *'Mon ami monsieur Laurent,'* before rattling off the egg and vegetable options, no meat today, 'just those little bacon strips them French like.'

'You do the parlee voo, Ted?' one asked, admiration in his voice.

'You would too, after months here, near eight months in fact, no leave at all, Pete!' Ted declared and helped himself to wine. He now preferred red wine to the rum portion, after more than one soldier had drunk his ration and fell down dead, the rum having been decanted into a bottle used for Condy's disinfectant.

He looked around, took off his cap and threw it on to an empty chair.

'Billy'll be here in a minute. Save a chair for the young 'un. He and I was here before Christmas, the front wall blown out, a right old mess. The bagatelle table was still standing though, still with the balls and cues!' Emptying his stubby glass, he continued. 'Laurent was clearing away the damage so we helped him a bit, time to spare before we moved on.'

He glanced at the church ruins opposite and recalled an abandoned, crushed hearse and a howling, starving dog somewhere in the town's ruins.

'First hot meal I'll have since being here,' a soldier said.

The assembled group were all new recruits to the army and to Ted's bus. Billy joined them and sat down next to Ted before ordering a beer from monsieur Laurent. Ted winked at him and pulled off his cap.

'Pay your respects to the *monsieur*, Billy!' Billy removed it with a sheepish nod.

Ted turned to Pete next to him. 'What did you do in civvy street?'

'Was a butcher, in Smithfield, wasn't I,' Pete laughed. 'From one slaughter to another!'

The party let out a snort of laughter. Ted looked at another soldier. 'An' you?'

'Me? Clerk, for steel works in Lancashire. A lifetime ago already.'

'Well, I'm from Salisbury.' said a third. 'Student, a theological one. Kind of funny story, how I got recruited.' He started on the bread. 'Well, I said theological to the sergeant and he said to another recruiting officer, 'ask him what he is.' So I repeated theological. And what did they do 'cept scratch their heads?'

'No idea, tell us, go on, waiting for the punchline,' Ted grinned.

'Put me in the medical corps, 'cos they thought it was biological!' He guffawed and slapped his thigh. 'Can't tell the difference between a vein and an artery, me!'

Laughter ricocheted off the damaged walls.

'Soon put them right so here I am, a soldier in this godforsaken country.'

They were silent as they attacked their omelettes with lardons of bacon interlaced in the delicate folds.

'Got to watch how they make this,' Billy sighed, pushing his scraped plate away. 'See if they give me a lesson. My ma's cooking's more like leather, a good waste of eggs she can't afford.'

'You all done, lads?' Ted asked. He pointed at a swelling of soldiers converging on the square. 'Looks we got reinforcements.'

Dawkins came into view. 'Dawdling again, Ted! Bloody typical! Come on, lads, get those buses revving. On the move!'

Ted and Billy Boy downed their drinks, Ted hastily sandwiching the remainder of his omelette into bread. Feeling

91

Dawkins' watchful eyes burning into his back, he pushed his chair back, pressed *sous* into Laurent's hand and sprinted back to the bus parked in the nearby rue des Anges.

~

Some months before they had arrived back at Neuve Chapelle, they had ferried soldiers close to the labyrinthine trenches near Cuinchy. Their passengers were a number attached to 251 Tunnelling Company, Royal Engineers, billeted in nearby Béthune. Their role was to act as 'beasts of burden,' working underground, removing spoil excavated from the face by more experienced miners.

Valuable German equipment had been captured alongside many German soldiers, Dawkins sending Ted's bus back to pick up prisoners and take them to an internment camp. There they would be fed thin soup and a hunk of bread.

Ted noted their sense of relief, their sly smiles of surrender as they boarded the bus. He drove, Billy keeping a cocked rifle inside on his human cargo.

The bus had returned to the area with more new recruits in April, the action now eastwards. They knew this route well, the Front constantly altering in favour of the Allies before falling once again to German forces, Neuve Chapelle the most hard-fought area in the Pas de Calais.

They criss-crossed a triangle of roads with damaged churches, housing, walls, crushed gardens and orchards strewn with discarded warfare.

'Never seen so many troops,' Billy muttered to Ted as they sat side by side on the driver's bench, the vehicle swaying under the load, every chassis bolt loosening as it shook under the strain of the rutted roads. After an enforced stop, they continued at night. The single pavé road, thick with grease, was lit by moonlight, dark shadows forming on the convoy of clanking battalions and snorting horses.

Ted caught the occasional snatch of song before the tunes filtered away in the night and hummed them quietly. Billy, by his side, shivered in the open cab, their muddy, wet clothing catching an unseasonal cold wind.

Ted glanced at him. 'Least the cold keeps the lice down, eh, boy?'

Billy muttered something inaudible as he fingered the latest letter he had received from Ruby. In the months since his return from Hackney to the Front, his rucksack now bulged with her letters, tucked in a leather wallet he had taken from his father's belongings.

He closed his eyes, trying to recall details his and Ruby's final moments together. Wrapping his arms around his chest, he bent forward and recollected his departure morning at the station. She had come with him, an arm entwined in his, her head nestling against his shoulder. A band played with brassy, bold, patriotic gusto.

'Don't tell my father just yet about us, dear,' Ruby said loudly above the music and engines as they reached the barrier.

'Why ever not, my angel?' Billy had picked up the expression from a song, using it to his advantage.

'He'll say I'm too young to know what's for the best. Besides,' she looked mischievously up, 'on one of his last nights with us, Mum and me in Victoria Park, I said I'd never marry a soldier. Never! Not for me! Want to do things with my life, not just be in the family way, but…'

He pulled her towards a less noisy corner away from the barrier. 'But what, Ruby? What else is there? For a woman?' Before he allowed her to answer, he added quickly, 'but I'm not a soldier, me, I'm a bus driver, just a driver. Don't want no part in killing.'

'Billy, you may be but you're wearing a uniform, you're a soldier!'

Letting go of him, she moved back a pace. 'Anyways, what are you saying? Nothing for a woman to do 'cept have babies, have a man? Don't you know nothing about them suffragettes?'

Billy shook his head. The word had passed him by.

'Plenty of work now for women we never had before,' she said impatiently. 'Thanks to men leaving for war, that's why, one reason. And we want to work, not just have baby after baby, year after year. Like your mother, like…'

Shaking his head, he pulled her to him but she had resisted.

Ruby's face relaxed when she took his resigned look as defeat and put her arms around him.

'Sorry, Billy, just gets me cross when men don't see other values women have. If they're allowed to do what they'd really like to do, that is.'

He returned her hug and gazed at her shyly. 'Guess I don't know women well, Ruby, but this is not the time to talk about it.'

~

He also recalled a conversation with her on their last night together, their talk about the future. Should he desert, invent an injury or sickness, report a family hardship to stay at home to look after his mother and Cissy? Ruby had dissuaded him from taking a drastic step.

'Don't be a fool! Go like Joy's brother and be court-marshalled?'

He reluctantly agreed that she was right. Billy had never talked to anyone so openly – not even Cissy.

The train coughed into life and shrill whistles blew. 'All aboard!'

Billy held Ruby tightly before being engulfed by billowing smoke. Ruby choking, held a handkerchief to her face and disappeared into the tangle of parting couples, her head bent.

Pushed onto the train by army personnel, Billy lost sight of her as the engine gathered speed, the music swelling then receding into a void.

~

Billy's head lolled awkwardly as the bus rumbled along the pavé, the suddenly braked, a 'damn and blast!' from Ted waking him. The bus stopped briefly then continued slowly over debris. Hardening his body against the cold, he closed his eyes again and began composing a letter in his head as the rumbling of the guns grew louder in the distance.

My Angel, dearest darling Ruby,

Somewhere in France. But a letter from you! Amazing they get to us! And you think about us. Good, my sweet. Do you remember those beautiful kisses? Do you remember the last one we gave each other between tears? You was braver than me. And maybe always be... You want to do other things with your life but I hope they will mean with your ghost army boy. I cried on the train and still do when there's time to think about you, about home. Ted thinks I met someone. Too right I did! He says I moon around, not drivin' well or just staring into space with a silly look on my face. I ache to tell him how much his daughter cares for me and how I love her and will always do. I...'

The bus jolted to a stop. Billy opened his eyes, the rattle of hobnail boots on the stairs bouncing him back into reality. Ted nudged him sharply. They jumped down, helping the new recruits – the clerk, theology student and butcher – balance their load as they climbed down the step, rucksacks and rifles juggling on their backs as they disappeared from view.

Flares shot into the dark, mottled sky, the roar of the guns, the pounding of howitzers rattling the bus. It was just past seven, a cold, grey dawn emerging on the flat landscape. The shelling of enemy lines and reconnaissance flying corps aircraft, a new addition to the war, added to the confusion near the Front.

Billy, pissing in his pants, ducked down beside the bus away from the artillery fire then flattened himself alongside Ted as shells bounced in the foreground. Billy held his hands over his ears and buried his face in the muddy earth, ignoring the body fluids.

'Ruby, never meant to be like this!' he muttered angrily.

Over a briefing in the Red Cross tea tent after the battle, an officer blustered that powerful artillery support enabled the allies to secure the whole of the village of Neuve Chapelle yet again and the roads leading in all directions.

'Make no bones about it, it's a good outcome,' he added. Telephonic devices cut by the enemy's fire, let us down, but a decisive victory!' Some cheered and chinked their metal mugs of tea, their expressions not matching the wished-for positive effect by brass.

'We need them damned clever pigeons,' Ted said to Billy as they drank. 'They'd sort out the parley, get them messages out. Don't see none around here but what about the truth about the bodies we seen, eh? We passed enough of them, not quite the so-called victory yet.'

Billy nodded unconvincingly. He hoped that Ted and the others couldn't see the stains on his trousers.

Chapter 11 – Western Front

April, 1915

"Saint Vaast Palace's cellars in Arras," reports officers from the
Service de Protection des Oeuvres d'Art, *"protected from the daily
shelling by a thick wall of earth and stone which made them look
like a fortress, received a steady flow of works of art. Statues,
paintings, pieces in precious metals, rare ornaments and delicate
pottery, humble pieces of stone and fragments of sculpted wood,
were stored there and the depot soon developed into a veritable
treasure trove."*

Ted and Billy joined the other drivers one late April morning,
their buses ordered to line up in rows close to ruined Arras
but away from the Front. The sun shone and they got out their
cans to cook breakfast some distance from the latrines.

Ted eyed his rations, groaned and picked out his
remaining bacon rasher. Lifting it to his nose he smelled it.
Cook it now or chuck it for sure, he grimaced. The bacon
spattered in the can, the smell of sweet, salty meat filling the
air. Ignoring envious glances, he carefully lifted the crispy
slice onto a slice of rough bread. Chopping up a cube of
cheese, he dropped it into the hot fat adding a few drops of
tea from his Dixie to stop the cheese from sticking. Scooping
up the molten mass, he piled it onto the bacon and groaned

with satisfaction as he bit into his meal. Fat dribbled down his chin.

'Just like hot cream,' he called over to Billy when he'd chewed the first bite. Billy, stretched out on the grass some feet away, grunted, stared up in the sky and thought about his letter to Ruby. How to start it? Better make it a good one or else.

My Angel, dearest darling Ruby, he whispered, rolling over on his stomach away from Ted. Recalling some of the words he had composed last night, he added to them, re-writing them in his mind then sat up. He reached into his rucksack for paper and pen and started to write. A willow warbler sang nearby, the whistling suddenly jolting into an urgency, from hopeful major key to an insistent disturbing minor key.

Ted joined him, tin mug in hand. 'Writing to your sweetheart?' he said, playfully punching him on the shoulder.

Billy reddened and looked away.

'Ah! Got it in one, did I? Someone you met when you was back home?' Ted grinned mischievously.

Billy put away the pen and paper. What did Ted know? Had Ruby spilled the beans to her father?

'Don't let me get between a good love story and you, Billy,' Ted said, walking away. 'You go right ahead and write. Want to stretch my legs anyways.'

Billy stared at Ted's back as he disappeared into the woods. His pen began to flow.

My Angel, dearest darling Ruby,
    Somewhere in France. Last night I received a letter from you and curse our separation...'

He wrote a few more endearments then stopped, swiftly aware of a commotion, the earth shifting and pounding. Jumping up, he jammed his writing materials into his rucksack, crumpling Ruby's letter. Where was Ted? The other drivers? French soldiers in red coats, red trousers and caps came into confused view, a rush of rats before them. All fled toward the woods. What the fuck? Ted was nowhere in sight.

'*Allez vous en, allez vous en*!' The soldiers shouted before disappearing. '*Les Boches*!'

A green cloud unexpectedly emerged in the blue sky and drifted in the wind towards the stationed buses. Where could a fog had rolled in from so suddenly? Billy asked himself. They were nowhere near the sea. He caught a robust whiff, almost pepper-like but more cloying. Chlorine? Just like the smell of the sewers at home. But it was stronger, more potent than he remembered. Maybe enemy shells damaged a factory, he thought. His eyes soon smarted. Half-covering his mouth and eyes, he coughed as he ran towards the bus for shelter. Maybe Ted was there after all.

'Must be lyddite from them shells bursting on Jerry's bank,' a driver gasped, choking.

'Gas! Gas!' The commanding officer barked as he ran up towards the group.

'What we s'posed to do? Hide down a rabbit hole?' the driver shouted.

'Piss on your nose rag!' someone shouted. 'Hold it to your nose, save your lungs!'

Billy looked at drivers turning their backs and pissing on a piece of cloth but he had heard of better method.

'Stick something metal over your head, like a helmet, a bucket,' was one rumour floating around the canteens. Buckets, used in nearby latrines, might do.

He ran to the toilets, emptied one and stuck it over his head. Holding his breath, he gasped for air, his lungs picking up the poison, his body shuddering from the impact. He flung the bucket aside, laughing drivers surrounding him. Billy touched his hair, his hand matted with faeces. Ruby, he'd never deserve her.

Ted pointed to the woods. 'Here, lad, take yourself off and find the stream, just to the right. Go and wash yourself down.'

Billy ran to the stream he had walked by a while ago. Tearing off his rucksack, he ducked his head in the fast-running water, his arms flailing as he rid himself of the shit. Gasping for air, he plunged his head again in the cold water. Moving upstream he drank the water, gulping it down, his lungs still unable to function deeply.

A whistle blew vigorously. Getting slowly to his feet, he felt dizzy then walked to the edge of the woods. Buses were on the move, Ted revving the engine.

'You look a darn sight better. Get in.' Billy threw his rucksack on the seat and climbed on board. Water dripped down his back. It felt good, calming him.

They came across a group of soldiers who had been blinded by the fumes. 'Get in, get in!' Ted shouted, slowing down.

In the distance, they could hear 18 pounder field guns, the sound diminishing as they drove away. Ted inched the bus through the next town. Many structures were on fire, columns of soldiers running the gauntlet between scorching rows of buildings. Heat blistered the bus's paintwork.

Driving the gassed soldiers to a Red Cross hospital, Ted turned to Billy. 'You need to get seen to, son, that's awful coughing.'

'Don't make such a fuss,' Billy said, gasping for air. At the hospital they walked the injured to the wards, a nurse stopping them.

'You'll have to wait your turn! See this one here?' She pointed to a young man on one of the rows of cots, fighting for breath, his lips the colour of an over-ripe plum. 'Canadian. They all are. They were the first to get it full blast.'

Ted instructed Billy. 'Move our lot back to the bus and wait there with them. 'I'll stay here and see when they've got room for them. You feel up to it?'

Billy nodded unconvincingly. Ted patted him on the shoulder, a hug almost. 'Have a lie-down in the bus,' he added. 'I'm going to stretch my legs.'

He rolled up his sleeves in the bright sun and wandered down a path beside the hospital before lighting a cigarette, a dog barking in the distance, the air cool and soothing. Rounding a bend, he stopped.

A courier driver waved to him in the distance then eased off a sputtering motor cycle before bending down to examine the bike, the sound dying. It looked as if the driver was checking the cylinders.

Waving again – or was it a gesture for help? – the rider got out a kit. Ted walked over. He was very tiny, about the same height as his Norah and with equally good ankles. God, now he fancied a courier, he thought, must try to get some leave, just to hold a woman. Marion, a nurse, had seen to his needs some months back, meeting now and then when chance would have it, a nice looker. Marion didn't make any demands on him, nor he on her. After all, she was engaged.

'My, you look relaxed,' said the courier, removing a khaki woollen cap. Platted hair emerged, any loose ends tucked back behind her ears.

'Well, I never!' Ted exclaimed. He suddenly felt shy, unsure of himself. 'I never!' he muttered again.

'You never what?' the woman laughed.

'Seen the likes of you. A woman in breeches, an' all. Never!' He scratched his head then hastily rolled down his sleeves and did up the cuffs.

'You can roll them back up again, if you like and see what the matter is with this bike of mine,' the woman said. 'Name's Kitty. I take it you know a thing or two about mechanics? This time the problem has me flummoxed. I've fixed it many times before, maybe the part's just worn out. Have a look, will you?'

'Yes, miss. Ah, name's Ted, Ted Digby.' He rolled up his sleeves again. 'Bus driver. In the army but you'd never know it. I calls it the ghost army, in the army but not really, not seen by regulars as one of them.' He stopped, embarrassed, and bent down to have a look at the bike. Kitty knelt beside him, her tangled hair obscuring his view. Ted brushed it gently away. Kitty smiled broadly.

Chapter 12: Home Front

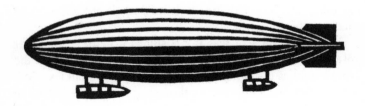

Reported by The Times, July, 1915. "AFTER THE AIR RAID. THE "MYSTERY" CAR."

Since the visit of the Zeppelin early on Friday morning the district has been full of rumours of mysterious motor-cars with flaming headlights which, passing along the highways, guided the airship to the area where the majority of bombs were dropped. Of all the stories of motorist spies which have been retailed during the last day or two the only one which has a plausible appearance is that of a car with exceptionally brilliant headlights which is alleged to have passed along the road through town near the Zeppelin. At about midnight Mr. and Mrs. Woods both saw the flaring headlamps, which lit up their bedroom. It was travelling quite slowly. A few minutes later the car was heard by the old couple two or three miles away. Nearly half an hour later it was heard making its return journey, but, as with headlights of much diminished brilliance.

Ruby walked slowly on her way home one July evening. She struggled for breath as she walked uphill from the Peak Frean factory, the smell of sweet biscuits turning her stomach. But it was not the sickly stench of the garibaldis lingering in the air that troubled her, more a nausea of uncertainty, of war, of family, and of Billy. Oh, yes, certainly him, top of her list. She hadn't been kind to him at first, quite the opposite. But that was months ago, last winter when he was home on compassionate leave.

While Norah sat with his mother and other family members after Billy's father's funeral in the pub's parlour engaging in life's difficulties and challenges, she had gone over to him. He was sitting alone, a pint in front of him.

'Billy, join you?' Before he could answer, she sat down. 'Now, tell me more about my dad. What's he up to? Any chance of him coming home? Does he miss us? At all?'

Billy laughed. 'Steady on, one at a time!'

He had called at the house the day after the funeral, offering to take Norah and Ruby shopping for a present to take back to Ted. Norah, exhausted by work, suggested they go together, and handed Ruby some money which she slipped into her coat pocket at the front door then waved them goodbye.

Ruby recalled that afternoon in detail, the search for an appropriate present proving elusive until she spied a wrist watch in an ornate West End shop window. She leant her head again the glass to examine the card balancing on the timepiece.

Mappin's Famed Luminous Campaign Watch.
First used in great numbers in the Omdurman, a desert experience, the severest test a Watch can have.
It is fitted with a luminous dial which shows the Time on the blackest of nights.
This fine movement wristlet watch has wire lugs attached to the case.

'Wouldn't that be perfect for dad!' she exclaimed. 'Think he could get a lot of use out of this timepiece, Billy?'

He had nodded, impressed by the gadget. 'A fine gift, very useful, very smart, quite the officer style. He's got a cheap one but it don't work no more.' He didn't tell her that Dawkins' metal-tipped swagger stick had come down hard on her father's arm, his uniform cuff not saving the glass. He looked at the watch more closely. 'Must cost a lot. Let's move on.'

Ruby looked crestfallen. 'We've been to every shop, it feels like, Billy, my feet ache. Let's just call it a day.'

'Wait a mo, Ruby. Let's go in and see.'

They examined the watch's large, easily read numbers, its separate circular second-hand embedded in the face by the figure 6 'and the glass is unbreakable too,' assured the salesman, tapping it with a small mallet with showmanship flair. He covered the watch with a black velvet cloth, inviting Ruby to duck under the counter to test its luminosity. She emerged, grinning.

'The perfect present! How much?'

'For a serving soldier, you say?' The salesman beamed. I'll knock off five shillings, now just over £2 for you.'

Billy watched Ruby's face fall. Outside, he suggested a visit to a friend of his father's.

'Why, Billy? You're leaving in a few days and I want to make sure you take a present with you. Don't be silly, wasting time like this.'

Billy tapped his nose and smiled. 'Got an idea, I have.'

He guided her back to Hackney backstreets in the late afternoon, the dark January sky threatening snow. She shivered and he put his arm around her shoulders. She didn't shrug him off.

Billy looked up at the house numbers along a shabby narrow street. 'This is getting us nowhere!' Ruby said crossly, wriggling away from him. 'Let's go home now.'

Billy stopped. 'Here we are. Number 12.'

An old man came to the door, his bright grey eyes taking in the pair.

'Well, if it ain't Billy! Come in, son! This your fancy woman? She's a girl, more like, you naughty man, just like your dad! Mustn't speak ill of the dead!'

Billy shot him a look.

'Mr. Slater, sir, this is Ruby. Her dad's my boss on the buses, you know, in France. We was wondering if you had any second-hand watches, them ones like the Campaign type, luminous, for him, a present, but, well, not too dear.'

Slater looked the girl up and down and murmured a faint whistle before opening and beckoning them in. Billy pushed her in. 'Used to work with my dad years ago, took over his business when dad got ill, better at it too!' She nodded with disinterest.

Slater interrupted. 'Let's have a look. Come with me, son, and you, Ruby Red.'

In a backroom workshop, Slater took down a box, dusted it off and opened the lid. 'Got two here, both commissioned and engraved but the poor buggers – pardon my French, dear! – never made it through, widows cancelled 'em.'

Ruby snatched both and examined them. They were new, replicas of the one in the smart shop. She put them down. Maybe it was bad luck to chance buying one for dad. He might be next in line.

Glancing at them again, she hesitated before snapping, 'They've got to be the same price as the one in the Strand, Billy, why did you bring me here, wasting time?'

Turning them over, she pointed out the engraved initials on the back. 'Another reason why they're no good for my dad.'

Slater looked at her. 'You went up to West End to buy a watch?' He gave Billy a mocking look before turning to Ruby. 'Look, Ruby Red, how much you got to spend?' She told him.

The watchmaker frowned then grinned. 'As a favour to Billy, done.'

Ruby laughed with relief. 'Really? Really?' before her pessimism returned. 'But they've got the initials of them dead soldiers, can't give him one of these!'

'Course you can,' Slater replied emphatically. 'What's your father's initials, dear?'

'ED. Ted Digby, Edward.'

Slater picked one of them up and turned it over. 'See here? I can engrave it easy enough, alter the lettering.'

They settled on ED, Driver, France 1915, Slater engraving the watch as she stood admiring his work.

Ruby hugged Billy on the street before pirouetting under the gas lights.

Billy laughed then stopped outside a pub. 'Slater's son, now, he runs this place. Good fireplace and all. Let's celebrate your good fortune!'

'And dad's! I could do with some warming up too.' Billy kissed her then and again later on, and after unaccustomed drink, she had kissed him back. He kissed her again in the pub's dark hallway before taking the small back stairs to a room used for storage. It was cold, the sloping window covered with hoar frost, a thin veneer of snow lit up by a yellow street lamplight.

Wrapping his arms around her, he touched her face and lips. His kisses and her eagerness overtook them, sacks forming their impromptu bed. She recalled how he had spoken to her beforehand and during their love-making, her only desire was to be near him, his soft, low voice the sweetest recollection of all.

She recalled too his hands, his active, searching tongue, his increasingly urgent kisses on her throat, her breasts, her stomach as he pulled off her many layers and then his. She gave in gratefully, willingly, enthusiastically, ignoring the pain.

Afterwards, Billy found sheets of paper for Ruby to clean herself with. She dressed hurriedly, her back to him, then patted her coat pocket for the boxed watch.

Walking to their homes with barely a glance as they parted, Ruby shifted uncomfortably in her clothing next to Norah in the kitchen. She felt stifled.

'Windy out there? Your hair's a mess, Ruby! You're quiet. Get anything for your father, dear?'

Ruby said nothing, handing her a letter she found on the doorstep. Norah grabbed it and examined the envelope. Ted's cursive handwriting, the ornate M of Mrs, the h in Norah that looked like a hook on which to hang a hat, was all she hoped to see.

'Come on, Mum, what's dad got to say?' There was just one small sheet of paper which Norah swiftly read and

106

replaced in the envelope. She didn't answer. Ruby patted down her hair, a tangled, dishevelled mass.

~

Since that day, six months on, she had concealed her increasing girth with an extra layer and a shrug of the shoulders when her weight gain became apparent to all.

Her Peak Freans factory colleagues teased her. 'Taking your work home with you?' 'Taking the biscuit, you are!'

Norah was distracted, her mood taken up by war news, her thoughts constantly elsewhere. Examining herself for the first time in a long time in the chipped mirror with its faded silver backing, she shied away when seeing her taut features, the skin on her cheekbones more thin and wan than ever. What would Ted say?

When the *Lusitania* had gone down with a loss of over 1,000 lives in May in the Irish Sea, she couldn't eat a thing. She and Ruby had pored over newspapers in the kitchen, their tea getting cold. They took turns too, re-reading stories of widespread looting from London's German shops, their discussion not only of the escalating war but of Norah's safety at the hospital.

They had witnessed a rising anti-German orgy, anything with Made in Germany an excuse for possession or destruction. Why, even their favourite bakery, Engels, down Clapton Road, had been stormed. People of previous good character – Meg, their dressmaker friend, Liza who made soap, Jack, the tobacconist – all found themselves up before the courts for assault. All got off lightly.

Ruby had shuddered when hearing about the mob attacking the bakery, two men holding back the angry crowd to safeguard the baker's heavily pregnant wife.

'I ask you, went to school with Meg! Nice quiet family!' Norah had admonished, taking Ruby's wincing as testament to her revulsion at Meg's arrest.

They read too of internment camps springing up in London, one not too far away in Alexandra Palace's

107

cavernous Great Hall, another one nearby in Stratford. Ruby nodded with satisfaction on reading of their privations.

'Giving them a straw pallet and horse blanket, a mite too good for some of them,' she declared.

She heard too of another internment camp in Islington. 'More of a holiday camp if you ask me!' she sniffed. 'Look, ma, private rooms! Barber shop, laundry!'

She tried to regain a sense of perspective but failed. The Germans were the enemy, as simple as black and white. When Zeppelin raids bombed London near their home, her hatred towards German turned even more intense.

'Ma, you'll be seen as a German or, worse, a traitor if you continue at the hospital. You've got to leave, change your job, to please me, to help Dad know you're safe.'

But Norah wasn't of the same fighting stuff as her daughter. She wasn't able to make decisions as quickly as either Ruby or Ted. Never one to rock the boat, she had always been a more a safe, careful, trusting pair of hands. What other work could she do anyway? London was in a state of turmoil, Home Front changes were forcing everyone to adjust their lives, but without clear guidance. She listened to Ruby informing her of suffragettes' actions and had quickly decided that mutiny wasn't for her.

'Ma, there is a way out, you know. Quite simple, really. Don't know why we didn't think of it before. Guess things, being what they are, we need new thoughts.' Ruby paused and looked at her. 'But it would mean a distance to work. It's safe, away from all the dangers.'

'And what would that be, Ruby? Nothing much going on except at munitions, and even garage work. Don't think I'm cut out for these jobs, do you?'

Norah listened as Ruby outlined her work at the biscuit factory. An early start, as early as the laundry and no more rotting shoes, soaked feet in cold, dank water swirling around each departmental slatted floor. A safe job, and free biscuits and lunches too.

Norah, folded her arms. The pay wasn't as good as at the hospital, and she had been promoted. Nor had she considered working in a factory, it never appealed. But there was merit in the move despite her misgivings, she admitted, while lying in bed in the early hours. Write to Ted, he'd know. After all, she had been given new responsibilities at the laundry, extra pay since last October. Didn't that count for something, for the family coffers?

Chapter 13: Western Front

July, 1915

Bent double, like old beggars under sacks,
Knock-kneed, coughing like hags, we cursed through sludge,
Till on the haunting flares we turned our backs,
And towards our distant rest began to trudge.
Men marched asleep. Many had lost their boots,
But limped on, blood-shod. All went lame; all blind;
Drunk with fatigue; deaf even to the hoots
Of disappointed shells that dropped behind.
Wilfred Owen *Dulce Et Decorum Est*

Sunday July 4th, 1915

Dearest Ted,
My thoughts cross over to you every hour of the day, your last letter, more a paragraph really, not giving Ruby and I much information what you're up to, where you are, but we both are relieved to hear at all. And about Billy too, someone who Ruby mentions. They only met a few times but he's a looker, catching our daughter's eye, maybe? And a good man who cares for his mother, his sister. You can't say fairer than that. One of the strangest things about life is how we get used to situations. Over here, there are few buses on the road,

everything horribly crowded, all the young passengers, most in khaki, talk about the Front, no idea if they will return to the old country again or rest, for all time, where you are. I am getting maudlin. You don't need this, my dearest love, working so hard, away from us. But, like you, I see so many with bandaged heads, so many missing limbs, no one even taking a second look at them no more. London's fearful of them zeppelin raids, no music halls lights to gladden the spirits. It's a danger crossing roads after dusk, all blinds pulled down, no street lights. Papers say we need three million pounds a day to spend on this horrific war. Imagine! But there's talk of war going on for another six months. But I think, as long as there is an Englishman alive to fight, he will. Pity they don't take Ruby in the army. She'd knock their heads together and sort it out smartish! She is persuading me to leave the hospital – Germans aren't liked, lots of looting, bad business going on – and join her at Peak's. More travel, less pay, but there are free biscuits! And lunch. Oh, dear, I don't know what's best. I'd love to sit down with you over a cup and talk about it, no chance of that. Ruby went on a march yesterday, begged me to go. Women's March with flags, banners. She says women want to play a bigger part in the war effort, like making munitions! I ask you. She came home with a tummy ache and went straight to bed, no supper. Right as rain this morning. You know that shop on Old Street, the one selling pots and pans we bought the new roasting tin from last year? Closed after a crowd thought they was Germans. Owners chalked up 'We're Russians, not Germans.' Can't see different, myself.

Ted put her letter away with the others, tapped his pipe against the bus's railing and filled it with tobacco. He lit it and looked over at Billy, bent over double, coughing. The bus, stained with burns and shrapnel, was in better shape than his co-driver, he thought. He had written briefly to Norah and Ruby about the gas and its effect on Billy but told them he was on the mend so they wouldn't worry. But he was troubled.

He put his arm around him then reaching down for Billy's water bottle. He glanced at the unappetising Maconochie stew lying in a grey-brown mass in the tin.

'Here, have some water,' he ordered. Billy took the bottle and tried to force some down his burning throat but retched.

His sallow skin was traced with green, blisters forming, crusting. They both could still smell burning horse flesh despite being a distance from the rotting mass.

'Billy, time to get you to see the doc again, you're not right at all,' Ted said when the rasping started up.

Billy looked at him through rheumy eyes. 'Can't even pee right,' he managed, as he stood up and leaned against the bus. Strong sun hit his blistered skin. Quickly turning his face away from the heat, he closed his eyes.

Ted drove him to the field hospital, parked the bus near the quartermasters' stores and helped Billy down from the back of the bus where he had stretched out, the coughing intensifying during the uneven drive. In the flat countryside, rows of canvas tents housing nursing and army field operations shimmered in the evening haze.

'Gently does it, son.' Putting Billy's arm over his shoulder, he guided him to the nursing station.

Billy tripped over guy ropes as they passed the cook and mess tents, canvas flapping in the wind, Ted gripping him.

The nurse helped Billy to a cot in the crowded tent, took off his boots and helped him to lie down on the narrow bed. After patting his face with a damp towel, she turned to Ted. 'I'll be back with the doctor.'

Ted sat on the bed and made a feeble joke. 'Green's so fetching, the latest Paree colour, don't you know!'

Billy laughed and sat up quickly, phlegm forming around his mouth. He wiped it away with the cloth. 'Ah, that's foul, just foul! Ted,' he grasped the driver's hands. 'Ted, do me a favour. When you write home, don't tell anyone I'm sick as hell. Don't want anyone to worry on my account. I'll be up in no time, just need some medic to give me some more of that ointment for me face, even if it stings like billy-o.'

Ted looked at him. 'Can't do without you, son, your family neither. Sure, you'll be up and at 'em. You got youth on your side too, a winner. We need you. I'll be back in a day or two. Don't fret. You're made of strong stuff, you Cotgraves.'

Ted moved through the makeshift field hospital, passing patients queuing for the mess tent or smoking by the post room. He spied a friend. 'George, my old mate, how you doing?'

The man gestured angrily at his loose-fitting boot and his balloon-like ankle.

'Did me foot in, didn't I? Stepped on a mine, something like that anyways, can't put any pressure on it, turning black so here I am. Infected, like.'

'More like a Blighty one, if you ask me,' a nearby soldier muttered. 'Stick a Frenchy pitchfork in your toes and, hey, presto, on the boat,' he continued. 'No more fightin,' rollin' round in Frenchy clay for the duration.'

'Nah, not like that, 'course not! Fighter like you I am,' George replied, eyes to the ground.

The soldier gave him a hard stare. 'Bet you're on that boat sharpish, home to Mummy or that bint of yours!'

Ted uttered an expletive, patted George on the back, made his way to the post room and picked up a letter from Norah. Stuff this for a game of soldiers, he thought as he pressed the envelope in a pocket. Maybe doing a Blighty's not such a bad plan.

Ted drove away with a full bus of turbaned Sikh soldiers. Dawkins came over to him, a demanding, accusing look of an order etched on his heavy face. Ted felt very alone despite the company of men.

Chapter 14: Home Front

August, 1915

DUNLOP CONTRIBUTIONS TO THE WAR. THE RIGHT SPIRIT.
One thousand, five hundred Dunlop men have enlisted.
The rest, in shifts, are loyally working day and night and week
ends in order to meet the demands created by the war.
Are you buying Dunlop Tyres?

August arrived with a weight in the air, of sweltering humidity coupled with people's heavy hearts. One year on and the war showed no signs of ending, the prospect of another winter's battles and privations creating a crescendo of pessimism and silencing optimists. Norah, in the former camp, speculated if any men would be left to fight, daily reports of their rate of extermination in France and Belgium too grim to accept. She didn't take into account slaughter in other parts of the world at war, her focus on Ted and his survival. She didn't dare think what kind of a world it would be if only women survived. Life without her Ted was unthinkable. He hadn't been given any indication of home leave, recruitment slowing to a limp pace now that realities about the war had sunk in. White feathers fluttered from the hands of women like confetti, on buses, in the streets, in parks targeting young, fit men who shied away, dodging the feathers in the crowds.

Ted's letters were mostly about the long hours they worked but omitted Billy's health, Norah guessing he had recovered. Billy's letters to Ruby, she noticed, had dropped off. Maybe their sudden attraction had flattened, withered and died as quickly as it had arrived that winter's evening so many months ago, no case of absence making the heart grow fonder. After all, they hadn't really known one another well in short time he had returned for his father's funeral. Ruby barely mentioned him and when Norah did, Ruby would just turn away wordlessly.

The gossip on the streets and at the vast hospital tub wash lines was of the Kaiser, that slayer of millions as English hospital workers called him. Said to look haggard and weary, he had aged twenty years. Norah became aware of a slowing of pace of her German colleagues, their manner hesitant, nervous. Voices were muted, as if afraid their accents would betray them. Norah's superior, the kindly Herr Westmann, had shrunk in size, wasting away in his black frock coat and now too-large trousers. Even his head looked smaller, as if he wanted to disappear. At least he was over the fighting age and not interned yet due to his essential work, the hospital looking after the local poor as well as their own.

German staff came to work in groups. Safety in numbers, Norah thought, and watched as they regrouped into pairs when leaving the hospital. They had given up long ago using the front entrance to avoid the name callers and the homemade placards with hatred written on them. Protestors hadn't located the tricky-to-find back entrance, an old tunnel taking them to an adjacent building which led to a park. But they would.

Most of the English staff had left, preferring lower wages over taunts and spitting. Norah felt a chill, a constant discomfort at work. This couldn't continue. She wanted to rejoice in the bulletins of 'Great British Victories' from news vendors keen to sell more papers, cynics dismissing the triumphs as false news. She didn't know what to believe, what to expect.

~

Ruby left her work after only completing the morning shift and reported in sick. Hurrying home in the heat, her chest heaved, her layered clothing hiding her pregnancy. She turned the corner of her street, put the key in the door and went to the scullery for water, drinking a large glass after splashing some on her face and neck. Removing layer after layer of clothing, she scooped them up over her arms and walked up the stairs to her room, gripping onto the handrail. She closed the door and lay down.

She had only been asleep a short while, her hands resting on a turbulent belly, before being woken by banging on the front door. Hastily putting on a layer, she held onto the railing down the narrow stairs to the parlour's heavily curtained window and raised a corner. The caller was hidden from view.

Moving to the door, she cried out. 'Who is it?'

A young boy's voice shouted 'Letter for Miss Ruby, miss, ma sent me.'

She opened the door a crack to take the letter, snatched it and closed it swiftly. Tearing at the envelope, she took out a piece of paper with uneven, jerky handwriting.

'*Dear Miss Digby,*

Ruby, Billy's mother here with bad news. He asked me to let you know if anything happened to him so I am sending you this telegram. It's in the same envelope. I don't want it in my house, enough bad things going on in my life. It only upsets Billy's young sister, Cissy, you saw her at her father's funeral, to have it here too. You only met him a few times but I am respecting his wishes.

She searched inside the envelope and took out the telegram.

'I am very sorry to tell you of the death of Army Service Corps Driver William Boyden Cotgrave who died in hospital due to chlorine gas injuries...'

Ruby didn't read any further. Her loose clothing crumpled onto the street as she ran from the house, clutching the papers. Hammering on her neighbour's door, she shouted 'Mrs. Flynn, Mrs. Flynn!'

The door opened and a child peered out. 'Me ma's in the back, Rube.'

Mrs. Flynn hurried out from the scullery. 'Whatever's the matter, Ruby? Child, calm down.' She put her arms around Ruby's shoulders and sat her down in the front parlour, the drab mustiness making Ruby retch.

'Quick, Molly dear, there's a good girl, fetch Ruby some water.'

The child disappeared.

'Read this… this…,' Ruby whispered.

She ignored the water offered to her, sat down abruptly on a stuffed armchair and passed her the note and telegram. Mrs. Flynn looked at Ruby and took the papers.

'Dear Mrs. Cotgrave,

I am very sorry to tell you of the death of Army Service Corps Driver William Boyden Cotgrave who died in hospital on August 5, 1915 due to mustard gas injuries. He put you as his next of kin, hence this sad news delivered to you. He asked for the enclosed letter to be given to you with this official letter. You will be given further information as to his burial and…'

'This your boy, then, Ruby, somethin' special to you?'

Ruby stood up and held onto the armchair. 'Yes. Yes he is.'

Before Mrs. Flynn could catch her, Ruby had fainted, her clothing showing her advanced pregnancy. Mrs. Flynn clucked vigorously before helping her home and up the stairs to Ruby's bedroom, Molly ordered to stay put.

~

Norah put the key in the latch earlier than usual. Laundry staff had been sent home, the heat unbearable in the pressing rooms, several passing out.

Taking off her frayed straw hat and scuffed sandals, she paused by the door into the garden and caught a glimpse of an over-ripe dark hued tomato to add to tonight's supper. She carried her sandals up the stairs to her bedroom to avoid the clack, clack, clack on wood, the sound irritating her, scolding Ruby if she didn't do the same. She would tend to the vegetables first then get supper for her and Ruby, the vegetable patch wilting under the unrelenting heat despite her attempts to keep the rows of runner beans and carrots refreshed. Food for the pot, keep the costs down.

She tried to recall the last time she and Ruby had meat, bread now a dear commodity, a light supper for them both using the broad beans and marrow picked yesterday.

Ruby hadn't seemed too hungry recently so she'd keep it light, neither of them with much of an appetite these days. Reaching the top of the stairs, she frowned when seeing Ruby's closed door. Why had she not taken her advice and left it open to let a through breeze in? Opening the door, she let out a cry.

Ruby was on the edge of her bed, rocking back and forth in pain, with small steady moans. Mrs. Flynn looked up as she applied wet cloths to Ruby's forehead, clothing exposing her large belly and spread legs. Norah dropped her hat and shoes on the hard floorboard with a clatter and rushed towards her. 'Ruby? Ethel? No, it can't be!'

Mrs. Flynn shot her a warning look.

Norah put an arm around Ruby and bent down to lift her daughter's heavy dark hair from her forehead, touching her perspiring, tear-stained face.

'No! No, mother! Go away!'

Ruby threw out an angry arm towards her, the pain causing her to double over. Norah let go of Ruby's hair. 'Tell me, how bad's the pain, dear? Let me help you!'

Mrs. Flynn bent down towards Ruby's thighs. 'The head's already showing, Norah, won't be long now.' She steadied her arms around Ruby's and looked firmly at Norah, rattling off a list of items to fetch.

The child cried out loudly, a troubling cry enduring long after emerging. It was as if the child knew it would never know a father, now buried in France. Ruby named the child William Edward Cotgrave Digby. She couldn't bear to look at him.

Chapter 15 – Western Front

August, 1915

Amsterdam – Reuters report.
A despatch from Berlin reports that during a recent visit of the Kaiser to the Western Front where many Germans had been killed, the Emperor alighted from his horse and kneeled on the ground where he offered a prayer. Rising, he said: "Oh God, I did not want this war."

Ted gathered up Billy Boy's meagre belongings from the hospital and walked towards the bus with his co-driver's knapsack, violin case and small satchel of personal items. Placing them in the bus with a shove of anger, he wiped his eyes with a jerk on his sleeve and lit a Woodbine.

Stubbing out his cigarette with a grimace, he pulled out the violin from its battered case and examined it. The strings still looked taut, the bow somewhat frayed, loose hairs needing attention. Billy was always meticulous about his violin but, recently, he played with little vitality despite willing himself and hadn't trimmed the drifting hairs. Ted's fingers caught rough grooves on the violin's maple wood back. He frowned. Billy always wrapped it up carefully in a frayed silk scarf before storing it in the case. How was it damaged? He turned it over and exclaimed at the crudely engraved words Billy had etched on the back since leaving home.

A descending line of destinations they had reached were engraved on the veined, stained wood. Billy must have filched an engraving tool from his father's works toolbox, Ted thought. His eye caught several places on the long list where they had carried soldiers to the trenches, recalling Billy's duties, his boisterous, somewhat misplaced sense of humour. Ted snorted with laughter then wiped his eyes.

William Boyden Cotgrave. Billy Boy! was the first engraving.

Left Hackney! – 15.9.14
Seine – France! – 23.9.14
Bassee Canal – 10.10.14
Messine battle – 12.10.14
Festubert – 23.11.14
Wytschaete – Belgium! 14.12.14
Xmas Day – St.Yvon – 3:2 Fritz won footie
Home – dad died 29.12.14
Neuve Chapelle – 10.3.15
Gas! – St. Julien – Apr.15

The dates had tailed off after his lungs had ingested the chlorine. Half-hearted attempts to add a reminder of his war from April to August were barely documented, Billy's strength deteriorating. But he had soldiered on, refusing to let go of his work as a driver, pleading with Ted to keep quiet about his illness. Ted covered for him for a few months, Dawkins using it as a further lever to work them hard.

'Protecting your little man?' he had mocked as Billy coughed with sudden bursts and glittering, too-bright eyes.

A mania seemed to grip Dawkins before ordering them to further duties, his face contorting as he spewed them out.

Billy had sat by Ted's side in the warm air after a foray, his marked, blistered face turned to the summer sun. Surely this was better for him, Ted reckoned, than lying down in a hospital cot, coughing his rib cage to breaking point. He might catch other germs and infections from the seriously injured and ill. But he could put it off no longer and took him to hospital with a gnawing fear in his stomach and throat.

Ted continued to trace the violin's uneven engraving, pressing fingers against its rises and falls but stopped when he came to one name and one date. *Ruby – 2.1.15.* A poorly-scratched heart with an arrow through it was etched next to her name. Ruby? His Ruby? Or their Ruby?

~

He had stood over Billy's freshly dug grave that morning and mourned his friend, his ersatz son, alongside a few colleagues. Dawkins was nowhere to be seen. Army Service Corps members, caps over hearts, stood with the army chaplain, local grievers and army personnel, all well versed in mourning. They saluted his coffin as it was lowered into French soil. Ted had written to Billy's mother after the ceremony with a description of the burial and service and his condolences. Words flowed from his pen.

'*You would have been proud to see changes from a timid youngster to a right fine young man in the eleven months and eight days since we sailed from Avonmouth, a father and son close-like feeling growing all the while when we worked and lived tightly on this bus of ours.*' He paid tribute to the son she had borne, commenting on '*his confidence as a grand soldier and how he had taken on challenges men twice his age would have run from, no coward your Billy.*'

He composed a verbatim description of the funeral:

'*We walked alongside the coffin to the church from the hospital. I was one of the pallbearers. Men was deep behind us, even some French officers and nurses who had looked after him. As we walked, we came to the little Protestant Church and some German prisoners with a Dragoon escort were marching. They halted and presented arms and even them prisoners stood to attention. Even the enemy! For Billy Boy. A short service in the church followed then we went on*

122

*to the cemetery where head of motor transport spoke very
nicely about Billy Boy and the work he had done. You would
have been proud. There were several wreaths too, beautiful
they was.'*

He lied about Billy's wretched death, his gasping and
wrenching for air, his whispered cries in fear and in pain. He
did not put on paper descriptions of her son's weeping
blisters, his blind sticky eyes, his lungs constantly fighting for
breath, his voice a mere whisper, his throat closing, choking.
But he told her that he had held her son's hand to the last
breath and had covered his body with a sheet. Ted muttered a
prayer he did not believe in but considered it was the right
thing to do. Enclosing Billy's bus badge in the envelope, he
closed it with the sigh a parent would utter.

He also wrote to Norah describing the day and what Billy
had meant to him. *'Billy came out of his shell the more we
worked together, didn't shirk any task or take advantage of
any situation, for the most part, that is! After all, he is was
only human. When we was in Ypres this last time – when he
caught the gas – we was all tired out afterwards, out of the
threat area. Billy went scouting about and found an old tin
bath in a shed full of junk. Huge, it was. He just emptied it
and we both fell into it and went to sleep. Thought we'd be
safer there. When we woke in the light, we found tobacco
hanging from the loft. It was drying, see. Billy rolled as many
smokes as he could and stuffed our rucksacks with them. Just
like him to think of pulling out the middle bits of tobacco
leaves, stripping them veins. Then he rolled them up and tied
a piece of string around each one. Only trouble was, they was
terrible. Awful!*

*When he got back from his pa's funeral, somethin'
changed. Kind of a daydreamer after that. Maybe his ma
tried to get him to come back home. Man of the family and all
that. But he'll never do that now. He felt like a son. Came
back glowin' 'bout you and Ruby, the best family ever, he
reckons. Reckoned. He was right, you are.*

Ted finished the letter, sealed it and walked over to the canteen which doubled as a post office. Soldiers and nurses sat at long trestle tables with cups of tea, the atmosphere muted. Joining the long queue for post, he glanced at the envelopes, thinking of their contents. Damn! Why didn't he mention the violin to Mrs. Cotgrave and to Norah about Ruby's name etched on the back? When it was his turn, he gave the envelopes to the lad on duty who looked at the name.

'Digby, eh? Just a minute, think there's another letter just come in for you, your lucky day.'

'You sure? Just had one from Norah, my wife, yesterday.'

'I'll check for you. Digby.' Adjusting his shirt which stuck to him in the August heat, he walked over to the alphabetically labelled cubicles.

'Hurry up, mate, got to get on the road,' a soldier barked behind Ted.

The post lad turned and gave him a look. 'Wait your turn, you'll not be wanting your news if the missus run off with the milkman!'

A guffaw went up in the queue, the soldier given one or two whipping cuffs.

'Go dig a trench, sapper! Where you belong, down a hole, not with us civilised lot!'

The lad pulled out a slim envelope. 'Thought I was right! Here you are.' He handed it to Ted.

'The wife. Again,' he grinned to the lad. He started to walk away. Was she quitting the hospital?

'Still want to post these ones?' The lad shouted over the din of clatter of tin cups and boots, holding up Ted's letters.

'Oh, yes! They're important.'

'My turn now?' the soldier behind him said sarcastically.

'Sorry, mate, all yours,' Ted said. 'What's your hurry?'

'Blimey, don't you know there's a war on?'

'Digby!' Ted turned when hearing his name. Dawkins stood by the canteen entrance.

'Get a move on, Digby, on the double! Looking for you everywhere. Your bus is needed. For officers. Now!'

Ted stuffed the letter in his top pocket and made his way to the bus. He hadn't the heart to get on the bus, not without Billy. His temporary driver, a weasel-faced small man, complained bitterly all the time and didn't keep the bus clean. Not like Billy. No one quite like Billy.

Only later on he remembered the letter in his breast pocket as he lay down to sleep on the hard bus seating. He was dog-tired. It could wait until the morning.

~

Dawkins gave him a new order the following morning to take officers further down the line, their cars out of action. Shrapnel had seen to that. After a long, monotonous convoy crawl towards the Front, the commanding officer ordered Ted to stop the bus while the officers' batmen prepared a meal on the hard ground overlooking a wood.

Ted, handed a plate, sat a little distance from them, listening to their talk of war in the Dardanelles and their mistrust of Westminster politicians as he picked at the grass surrounding his tin plate, imagining each blade representing deaths, soldiers and civilians on both sides, large clumps of grass pulled up with jerking, virulent haste. What had been achieved? How many others in the world would be dragged into the war? He longed to be at home, for his past life.

'What do you think, driver?' Ted startled, looked at the speaker.

'Was you speaking to me, sir?'

'Yes, I certainly was. You must have some views, man. Been out here a while, have you?'

Ted stood up, plate in hand 'Yes, sir, almost a year. Lost my co-driver, buried him only yesterday, matter of fact. Gassed, he was. Only a young 'un. Never had no chance to live a proper life, no family ever now. Don't make sense.'

'Sorry to hear of this, ah… Digby, that right?'

'Yes, sir, Billy was one of the best.'

'More to come to take his place, Digby,' the officer said. 'More to come.'

Ted threw him a look of anger, followed by one of resignation. He nodded and made his way to the bus. He'd wait for them there.

The convoy twisted around ravaged corn and potato fields towards the Front, farming now a futile way of life. A plough lay rutted in a dip by the side of the ridged road, other farmyard implements twisted like odd sculptures, not vital tools of the trade, of livelihood. He parked the bus after dark on one of the cracked-earth fields, his mind on the officers' global warfare talk, not just along this stretch of the Front.

~

The sun bore down on the bus, Ted waking in a sweat. Pulling on his trousers and boots he went in search of a latrine. Arriving late last night he hadn't familiarised himself with the lie of the land, the weasel-faced temporary driver nowhere to be seen. Peeing in a bush he returned to the bus, made some tea and sat down on the step to drink it in the early dawn, his thoughts turning to Billy's mother. Would his letter help her at all? Would knowing how her son was buried with such respect comfort her? Remembering Norah's letter, he got up and stepped onto the bus to retrieve it from his jacket, returning to his seat in the warm sun.

Ted,
August 30, 1915
I don't quite know how to tell you but tell you I must. Your daughter had a son yesterday. No, I had no inkling of her in the family way. No one did, always covered in layers. We just thought Ruby was eating too many free biscuits, not getting fat at home, not from vegetables from our patch and soups. Meat's too dear, bread too. Anyways, it's happened now. Ruby named her son William Cotgrave Digby, he's a big boy. Billy's son. Did you know about this, that he was sweet on her? You keeping something from me, Ted? I hope not, truly I do. Ethel helped in the delivery, a real dear. Ruby had a telegram about Billy from his mother. It sent her into a shock,

126

poor love. Ruby's not well in the head, doesn't know if she's
coming or going. Please, please, try to come home. We've all
gone through enough in one year.
   Your wife, Norah.

He stared at the letter, re-reading it over and over, his
thoughts ranged from bastard to despair. Billy! Traitor! His
daughter! How could she? Why would she? Only seventeen
and with a bastard son, a misborn, a mutt. The sun no longer
warmed his back.

Chapter 16 – Western Front

September – November, 1915

Daily Mail: *Youngest soldier, 13, fought in the trenches at the Somme for six weeks before his mother showed the War Office his birth certificate.*

'Sir, permission to go on compassionate leave. Sir.'

Ted faced his new commanding officer, mangling his cap, the brim twisted until it resembled a rag in his damp palms. He had tried to get home leave since Ruby had given birth. This was his third attempt after identifying new commanding officers who might show more consideration than previous ones.

'Blurt it out, Ted, why don't you? And put down that damned cap. You'll ruin it. Army's not made of money to replace it.'

The officer sat stony-faced in the improvised office surrounded by paperwork. A harassed junior officer hurried out with an order ringing in his ears. Ted put the cap under his left arm, squeezing it tightly and clenching his jaw.

The officer continued. 'No leave, not these days. You're indispensable, you drivers. Can't get replacements. You knew that, I daresay, before even asking, your new driver gone absent. Didn't leave a forwarding address. Just you driving your bus now, Ted. Just you. No frills in this war.'

'Sir, it's essential. Family problems, my daughter...'

'Still alive, is she?' the officer interrupted. 'If this is the case, then, sir, you have no leg to stand on. We need you more than home does. Do you understand?'

'Sir, please listen. She's just had a child, unexpected –like, my wife…'

'Congratulations are in order then, Ted. You can't expect to go home to kiss the baby, toast the happy couple in times of war. Good news, I reckon.'

The officer gestured to the paperwork. 'That will be all, Ted. No doubt, we'll drink a toast to your grandchild, your first?'

The officer didn't wait for a reply and called out for a staff member. Ted didn't move.

'Sir, please, listen.'

'Driver Ted Digby!' the officer roared. 'Leave now!' He stood up and pointed stiffly to the tent flap. 'Return to duty!'

Ted paced up and down outside before lighting a Woodbine. Maybe telling him that the child was Billy's, who lay in his grave not a few kilometres from the area, might swing it. Deciding against it almost as soon as the thought came into his head, he headed slowly for the canteen after glancing at the watch that Ruby had sent him via Billy.

'Sod Dawkins! Sod the lot of 'em!' he thought, his chest tightening.

Finding a table in the recesses of the tent, he sat down with his tea. Feeling short of breath, he covered his face to stop an urge to howl.

'Penny for them,' a voice said quietly. He parted his fingers. Kitty slid onto the bench, a slim buttock cheek resting on the hard surface next to him. She took his hands in hers. Ted straightened up, a watery smile emerging, his eyes unyielding in their helplessness.

Kitty looked at him. 'What's up, love?'

Ted shook his head at first, unable to speak.

~

When they first met five months ago at the hospital after Billy had been gassed, he had repaired her damaged bike, Kitty brisk but friendly.

'Must move on soon, if this damned cycle can make it,' she said, pointing to her bike leaning against fencing. 'Will you have a look after a cuppa? That your bus there, heat up a brew on it?'

Ted had never heard a woman swear, let alone invite herself to tea. An involuntary laugh escaped from his lips and he hurried back to the bus, Kitty following.

'Water's from a stream nearby, miss' – he said, pointing to a hollow before farmland – 'not the jerry can stuff.'

'Good, upsets my stomach a bit, that whiff of petrol in the water.' She picked up a tin, one of the tea items hastily assembled by Ted. 'I'll have a drop of this milk if you can spare it.'

They sat on a nearby log, Ted scraping moss from it in a gallant move, Kitty thanking him extravagantly with an 'oh, kind sir!' and they drank their brew in the watery mid-afternoon sun.

Ted listened as Kitty explained why she was in the area close to the Front; a recent battle at Givenchy was no place for a woman, he reckoned.

'Part of the Women's Emergency Corps, we are,' Kitty said, swilling her tea round the tin cup. 'Only two of us in these parts, Dora and me, both nurses. We run a unit as close as we can get to the front line.'

Ted glanced at the bike, thinking of the stir they'd cause.

'Trusty Triumph!' Kitty declared as she followed his gaze. 'And why the bike for nurses, you're asking?' She formed a fist, knuckling his arm lightly, almost playfully.

'Well, it is a mite odd!' he eyed her, nodding brightly at the touch. She smiled back.

'Not really, just different! Dora or I go to the Front to see what's needed. We get the wounded back quick as we can to our first aid unit and if we can't look after them on the spot, it's a case of moving 'em on to a hospital or patching 'em up.'

Ted gave her a quizzical look.

'No, silly! Not on the back of the bike, patients holding on for dear life!'

Kitty outlined the practice she and Dora used, assessing patients, helping ones that they could before resorting to more advanced medical aid. 'They can do without a long journey over rough roads to a Red Cross infirmary.' As well as the two motorbikes ('one for Dora too, she'd hate to miss out!'), they also drove a small ambulance which took badly injured patients to hospitals.

Ted glanced admiringly at her, his thoughts turning to apprehension that women could play this vital role at the Front. Whatever next? He tried to visualise Norah here, the image failing him. But Ruby? Could she cut the mustard? Probably, but over his dead body, even if he allowed it.

'We've been given this rickety old farmhouse for the duration and have a small first aid unit in what was the dining room,' Kitty continued, pouring another mug of tea and adding a small dash of condensed milk.

'We cover quite an area of the Front and whizz them back to it. Poor buggers, with their trench foot, terrible swollen feet, all colours of the rainbow, smelly gangrene setting in.'

She looked at him. 'But you've seen all this, 'course you have! And the VD cases! We're always running out of mercury, Dora and I. The lot, really, truth be told.'

Putting her mug on the ground, she gazed across at a nearby wood, a breeze gently stirring the young poplar buds, the tree's grey bark enhanced by circles of lime algae and diamond shaped fissures. Her hair, caught by the wind, blew around her face. Smoothing it back, and tucking longer wisps behind her ears, she continued softly, telling Ted about her patients.

Ted longed to reach over and stroke her hair. He looked away but listened to her soothing voice. 'It's soil infections mostly though, bodies not removed from trench water, the living ones contaminated by it.'

Ted turned back towards her, struggling to keep his tone neutral.

'Me…me and Billy, we took injured ones to hospital – and them Germans too, prisoners with the same injuries.'

They were quiet for a while before Kitty broke the silence. 'Never get quite used to the lice though!' she laughed.

'Who would? You're the brave ones, a wonder I've not seen you before.'

Or the foolish ones. He had yet to decide. Looking up at the sky, he noticed the sun dipping further west and got up reluctantly. 'It's getting on, Kitty, better have a look at your bike.'

He went over to the bike and whistled when examining the 550cc side-valve four-stroke engine, running his hands over the three-speed gearbox and belt transmission. He gave an excited whoop. Kitty, laughing, quickly got to her feet and followed him.

~

They had initially kept in touch by letter, Ted reading Kitty's before opening Norah's, his guilt lessening over the months, Ted visiting her field unit farmhouse after their first chance meeting. He found the cellar rank with water, the walls cracked and panes of glass blown out by mortar shells. Despite the privations, the two nurses, with funding, had fashioned three warm, clean nursing stations within the farm's walls. Beyond dense growth at the back of the house lay a vegetable patch.

'Ours,' Kitty introduced briefly. 'For soup, mainly, we grow hardy vegetables. See those tufts? Onions. Soup's the only thing some of the sick can keep down.'

Ted viewed the poorly tended garden next to their parked vehicles. Norah would have a field day here, her green fingers working miracles, but he quickly dismissed his wife from his mind as they stood by her bike.

'Dora and I need to fund our work; the only way we do it is by donations back home. We've got quite good at it, raising enough for my bike last time. Yes, that bike!' She laughed, adding, 'We need money for first aid supplies,

132

swabs, bandages, medicines, that kind of thing. Socks, too, never seem to have enough of them. Even commodes, specially commodes!' she giggled. 'I'm leaving in a few days to drum up money, that shelling knocking our stock to smithereens. And our windows.'

Ted felt a sudden, inexplicable sadness. Would he never see her again?

~

Over the weeks, he guessed that her sudden inability to repair her motorbike was a ploy which he was only too happy to exploit. A missing fuse here, a tightening of a bolt there was usually all that was needed, a bent wheel taking a little more time to repair as their hands and eyes met, as if by accident.

Their lovemaking, mostly on a narrow bed in Kitty's and Dora's flat in town, was spontaneous and quick at first, Kitty whispering how to slow Ted down by undressing her unhurriedly. His mind, over the decades, would return to the first time he unfastened her stockings, rolling each one off. She taught him other ways before too long. A quick, eager learner, he initiated moves too, Kitty urging him on before burying her face in the *oreiller* to smother her cries, both falling about laughing. She often checked beforehand if Dora was in her room down the short passageway. 'Asleep, snoring for England,' Then steered him to her bed.

His intentions were only to hold Kitty that first night together – that not to be forgotten night – maybe talk about Norah, his shy aim giving way to swift ardour. Norah's name was never mentioned, not even when Kitty told him months later about her aggressive husband, the war giving her the opportunity to leave him. But she had also left her young son behind with her parents.

'He's eight now, Lesley. He understands, a good boy and I'll see him when I go home.'

Ted buried his head in the bedclothes when hearing she might leave again. He turned to her, leaning on one elbow. 'Won't let you go again!'

She wound her arms around him and kissed him. 'Let's not talk about it right now,' she murmured. Reaching for her breasts, he gave a sigh and rolled on top of her. They lay comfortably in each other's arms in the dark, Ted learning over the months not to feel shame, nor recalling his and Norah's monotonous, lacklustre sex.

Ted sat up. 'You were saying, my love?' he whispered, brushing back her hair from her small face.

'Don't spoil it now, dear, let's just…darn, now you've got me back to reality, you mean man!' She fumbled under the blanket and tickled him, Ted laughing, his eyes intent on hers.

She pulled the blanket up to her breasts. Ted felt for her thighs. 'You naughty man!' Her voice softened. 'Oh, Ted, you have to laugh to get through it. That last shelling hit a room where we patch up men, where they read their letters from home. A boy got it, mangled he was, his legs smashed to pieces, even his hands were mutilated. So, we start all over again, back to London. In a few days' time.'

Ted was silent. He removed his hand from her body and lay back, his eyes wide open.

~

'Digby, there you are! On the double!' Dawkins would bark every time he caught sight of Ted, his sergeant's greatcoat handing from his shoulders. Dawkins had not –would not – let up. Even though Billy had recently died a painful death, he had shown no compassion or understanding. The evening of Billy's funeral, Ted sat a bar with a few drivers drinking rough wine, got up to leave as a very drunk Dawkins joined them, Ted's arm grabbed. 'Sit, man, that's an order!' A maudlin diatribe about his early days in the army in Egypt as a cadet followed, Dawkins filling Ted's glass and drinking from it. In charge of other cadets and map reading, the goal was to reach a hilltop fort. 'But you know what? Bloody lost the magnetic compass as we crossed that god-awful terrain, three of them soldiers dead. Got lost, simple as that, didn't we?' he cackled. 'But they never charged me, never, never, couldn't prove it, could they? I told them the compass was nicked, never lost it, me!' He laughed, pulled it out his pocket and passed it around, blaming others for the lack of promotion over the years. 'Me? Part of the awkward squad!' Ted stared at it uneasily, refusing to touch it. Dawkins grabbed it, threw the remaining wine at him and stumbled out.

The next day, Ted, with a clearer head, recalled Dawkins' boasting as he cleaned his uniform. The red stain faded over time but not cheat's lying, always putting the blame on others. 'War does somethin' terrible to people, make no mistake. Maybe we're all victims,' he tried to convince himself. But Dawkins? A victim? He dismissed the charitable thought with a snort.

~

Dawkins adjusted his greatcoat one November morning at dawn. 'St. Eloi. You must know where that is by now!' He jerked his head towards a line of soldiers. 'Some passengers waiting for you, Ted! Move!'

'Sir!'

Kitty was in London and not sure when she'd be back, Ted in a daze. He wanted to tell her about Ruby and her baby, maybe Dawkins' confession. Barely glancing at the sergeant, he nodded curtly and climbed on board after helping soldiers onto the two decks, his human cargo barely acknowledging him, eyes down. They'd had enough and so had he.

A thin mist and drizzle circled the area. Grabbing his coat on the seat while inching forward in the convoy, he quickly put it on and jammed on his cap against the rain, pulling over when a lieutenant, in command of the platoon he had transported to the Front, vigorously mouthed and motioned 'Stop here, now.'

Driving as far as he could towards the ditch, he put on the brakes before helping soldiers disembark, guns and shovels rattling as they stepped down from the bus.

'Stop for the night, driver,' came the order. He nodded, shook the rain from his coat and reached in his top pocket for his cigarettes then started a letter to Norah in his head but the shellfire in the distance put him off.

What would he say to her? 'No, dear, the army won't give me leave. Already told you. Tried three times, makin' a bloomin' nuisance of myself. I want to put my arms around you, around Ruby in this hour of ...' Of what? Our first grandchild? No, why should he celebrate something so hurtful, so out of kilter after Billy's death? But did he really want to envelop her, hold her or would the vision of Kitty get in the way?

Or would he write, 'Ruby, how could she? Our girl do this? Our girl wasn't brought up like this.' He didn't know what to feel anymore, life never as senseless as now. Only Kitty's presence stopped him from disappearing into the blackest of thoughts. But even she was far away. Would she return or be persuaded to stay by her family to look after Lesley? To desert or to stay and serve king and country, as his father had done? But he had returned home an embittered, callous man. Like Dawkins. Would this also be his fate?

He wandered into the night, the blackness briefly lifted with sudden flares of light then sounds of death, of destruction. He glanced at sides of the bus, illuminated in the light, recalling its red livery on Piccadilly, the pride of the bus fleet. Now it was a mechanical grey war horse, sowing destruction.

Suddenly, on hearing the clatter of guns close by, he swung in the direction of fire, his eyes adjusting to the shadows. Soldiers stood in a line in the distance, away from the raging battles in the far flat French expanse of land. What were they doing, pointing their guns at such a distance from the Front?

Darkness fell then the sky lit up again. Ted caught sight of men in front of the line of infantrymen, their heads held high. He watched as guns were raised and the row of men falling. No. No! Their own, killing their own? Or were they the enemy? But they were not on the battlefield. What enemy would line up to be shot? No, it had to be their own. He put his hands over his face, stifling a shout.

Later that night, back at camp, the talk was of deserters being shot. Englishmen shooting other Englishmen. Desertion? These were the lowest of the low, no sympathy shown from colleagues as they drank their tea and smoked their pipes.

Ted didn't believe deserters were cowardly: they didn't dare stand up for themselves or their beliefs. He'd like to tell the sergeants how he felt about ferrying men to war, in trenches for months on end, enough to turn your thoughts to escape, to regain sanity, to take to the road for home. Or disappear forever. No one mentioned loss of nerve, no moral fibre was the general consensus. Shoot them dead, better off dead, that type of Englishman. Shameful, not setting a good example.

He turned away from the fire into the night and thought of Norah and her last letter. *We've all gone through enough in one year. Your wife, Norah.* He left the group, walked into the shadows and wept silently, not for Norah but for Kitty's departure.

~

A few months after the shootings, Ted was stationed near Rouen. The grey bus, pockmarked by shrapnel, would be unrecognisable by hailing Piccadilly passengers, their seating equally unidentifiable. Ted called it the Shed, sometimes the Cavern or the Shack. But, more often, nothing. He felt nothing unless he was with Kitty, now back after her fundraising mission. When she wasn't there, he had turned into a mechanical being, mirroring his bus's grinding gears, not feeling, not caring.

Letters to Norah and to Ruby were equally unemotional. He missed Billy but equally felt his betrayal. Kitty was his only salvation, her spirit and love keeping him from throwing in the towel, feigning a Blighty wound.

Outwardly, he was the reliable Ted, up early to clean his bus as best he could. Despite his feeling of emptiness, he lavished attention on the vehicle, a touch of grey paint here, a nailing of a floorboard there. Soldiers, in hob-nailed boots, punched him manfully on the arm as they embarked and disembarked. Quite a following, never a grumble from Ted. No sir. Not Ted, and he was on his own, no second driver, recruitment at a standstill. He was grateful not to have to talk to anyone in close proximity, day in, day out. Facelessness, obscurity, driving mechanically, that suited him best.

He drove to a Rouen railway siding shed to pick up passengers. Arriving earlier than expected, he parked the bus and made his way through the crowds of soldiers resting in the town's square and found the canteen he remembered from previous visits. A cup of tea and a Woodbine would suit. Taking off his cap, he entered the makeshift building, trying to ignore the dispossessed around a fire near the town's squalid bombed shelled buildings in the early winter mist.

The large tearoom was packed but oddly quiet, just one voice heard. *Not another pep talk from on high,* he thought. He hadn't heard any rumours about top brass arrivals. But the crowd was unusually respectful. It must be someone important, on a flying visit.

The man's generous, thoughtful tone held him but he couldn't make out the words clearly. Inching his way around the side, he finally got a glimpse. A short, squat man stood on a box, hands gesturing to the crowd. Some would describe him as ugly, his jaw jutting out from an uneven face, hair like dense burnt straw. But his eyes, darting around soldiers, held them. Most stood, others seated at tables or crossed-legged on the floor, Ted moved closer. An elbow jammed into his side.

'Sorry, mate,' he muttered and backed off. He leaned against the wall and stretched up to get a fuller view. Words came more clearly now.

'Britain will win the war because Tommy is morally superior to the Hun. And why? The British sporting tradition. British soldiers know how to win, German soldiers do not.

But Tommy is surrounded by temptations, the temptations to vice appealing, yet' he paused for effect, 'appalling. Better the guns of the Germans than the Devil's pull. Men, you lead heroic lives but many fall and lose what they can never gain again, save the grace of God and the absolution of the church.' No one moved, unlit cigarettes dangling in mouths.

'Like you here, I too have been in the trenches. Some captain whispered to me today as I stood by one, 'You'd better get in' as something whistled near us but before he could finish I was in it. Never moved so quickly in my life, my friends!' A laugh went around the canteen and they fell silent again when the speaker's hand went up.

'There was a silence, a strange silence for what seemed an age once in that trench…'

'Bet it was just a minute, guv,' came a voice.

'You'd be right, sir. But the men had ceased to dig in the crowded ditch side by side. And for good reason. A hail of machine gun bullets burst over us with a noise like bitter hatred and foul words, a cry or grunt telling me some were hit. Then it stopped. I said the Lord's Prayer and bent over to offer comfort. One of the brave wounded soldiers looked up at me and said 'Gawd, blimey if it ain't the padre! What you doin' 'ere?'

He looked around at the assembled crowd. 'I go where you go. I am with you wherever you are, in body or in spirit. Remember me, as Christ said. I say, remember us all. Let us pray. Dear Lord. Thank you for days when life's easy and straightforward. When it's not, when it's turned upside down, help me to discover what's real and lasting.'

Ted cleared his throat, his eyes smarting. 'Who's that?' he whispered to a nearby soldier who turned to look at Ted and said loudly. 'Dunno, gov. But his voice don't 'alf talk to you. Could be reciting the dictionary for all I care.' Heads turned. 'Shhhh! Shut up, you lot. Shut the fuck up for Cane!'

Ted looked at the square man with his unruly straw thatch and then noticed his collar. Cane? Geoffrey Cane? Didn't think he'd ever come across him, the Army chaplain with quite a reputation for holding initially unwilling listeners spellbound. Even working-class men like him. No shuffling of feet in the crowd, just a few lungs coughing in the damp air.

Cane advanced towards the men. 'My dear comrades, let us finish with the words which may comfort and give you courage. My door is always open wherever you find me.'

He leaned forward and looked at them. Ted felt his eyes on him, even far away, the honeyed voice speaking to him and only him. He watched the chaplain walk into the throng and distribute cigarettes to the men, pausing to light their Woodbines before lighting one for himself. Some walked away after taking the free smoke, others bending forward to ask for advice, for comfort, the chaplain's eyes steadfast, listening intently to each speaker. Ted moved towards him to catch the words.

'...kneeling up to me waist in water, padre, couldn't take any....'

'.... I says God! God! God! Machine gun burstin' all over us, I'll not see another...'

'...wanted to get out to the Front to have the experience...bloody mad.'

'Son, would you like me to pray for you, for your family...?'

'No, son, it's not because you're a sinner, you're here. You're a brave, good lad, fighting for what's right and just.'

Ted stumbled out of the canteen with his free Woodbine and walked back to the bus. Billy, oh Billy. He was just a bus driver, not a soldier, but he felt strangely comforted. Cane got to the hearts of people in the midst of horror and waste. Most of the talk on the bus, in the canteen, in billets, was brittle, unfeeling. No one spoke from the heart, not wishing to stand out as a coward, not up to the task.

~

Later that month he sat immobile in his driver's seat, hunched up with cold despite his thick uniform coat and cap. The ration of rum hadn't helped to whittle down the fierce chill an eastern wind had brought to the flatlands around Ypres and St Eloi.

He had learnt of new tactics by German defenders during the autumn battles, his passengers debating them as they took their rum and tea. huddled inside the bus.

Casualties were high, minds aching as well as bodies. Ted was well aware of the emotional damage being done, many suffering from sleepless nights, afraid of shutting their eyes, of the dark, of ghosts of comrades returning to torment them. He observed bravado slipping away.

After driving battle-wearied soldiers to their billets near St. Eloi after an attack, he watched some heading off towards the sign *'Washing done for soldiers here.'* They were not in search of clean clothing but what awaited them in the upstairs farmhouse, hang the consequences. They deserved it, they ribbed one another, hang it! And if the outcome was an uncomfortable remedy for the clap, hang it too! He had Kitty, enough for him. Driving a busload one day, his passengers jeered as they passed lines of soldiers undergoing the penalties of pleasure. Queuing to place tubes into their penises, an orderly turned on a tap to fill up their bladders, men moving swiftly to spill the infected water out in a ditch behind water tanks Not for him.

Sitting in his cab after the day's troop-carrying, he dozed off. He was shaken awake by the commanding officer.

'Looks like your prayers are answered, Ted. Good news.' Ted stirred and stared at him. He sat upright. 'You mean, I am given leave to go...'

'Home?' The man gave a curt, embarrassed laugh. 'No, 'course not. You know the shortage of drivers. But you will be joined by another driver. Couldn't wait to enlist, I'm told.' He shook his head. 'He'll be here tomorrow. Name of Dickie Lovelock.'

He walked away and called over his shoulder. 'Shake a leg now. Leave the bus in the square and get some shut-eye. Long day coming up.'

Ted stepped down from the cab, his legs stiff and cold. What day wasn't long? He headed for his billet after shutting

141

the cab door and securely storing the starting handle away. Dickie, eh? A young 'un like Billy? Wonder if he plays the mouth organ. Or maybe the violin. Like Billy. Prayers? Partly answered, he reasoned. Take some of pressure off him. With Dickie here, he might have all his wishes seen to – to go home. But with Kitty, his love.

Chapter 17 – Home Front

January, 1916

I work at Woolwich Arsenal now,
"Give my message to your chums,
"Girls are working 'midst the shells and guns
"Altho' 'tis tiring, as you're requiring ammunition for the fighting
line,
"We'll do our share for you out there."
She Works at the Arsenal Now by Robert Donnelly

Ruby called to her mother from the hallway. She had her coat on, the cord of her bag cutting into her shoulder.

'Time to go, Mother. Will's next door already.'

Norah came out from the kitchen, nodded to her daughter and picked up her coat from a hallway hook. She reached for her winter hat and thrust it on over her greying hair.

'Has Ethel got the extra flannels?' she asked.

'Yes, the pile I folded up last night in the scullery's gone to Ethel too. Along with Baby.'

Norah hesitated then took off her coat and folded it over her arm. She stood by the coat hooks, her brimmed hat clamped to her head.

Ruby stared at her. 'Mother, what are you doing? We decided. Let's go. Please!'

Ruby had started to call her Mother, Mum and Ma now consigned to childhood. There was no discussion about it, ever since Will's birth five months ago. She had shrugged her shoulders when first being addressed as Mother but frowned, irritating Ruby. Everything seemed to annoy her daughter now. The house had turned into a home of duty, of mechanical doings. Looking after Will gave little pleasure to Ruby, Norah quietly enjoying her unexpected grandson but not allowing herself to show any outward emotion towards Will. It would have displeased Ruby.

'Ruby, I don't know. Seems like a nasty job, making stuff to kill others.' Norah hesitated. 'Laundry was so – well – helping others, a worthwhile clean job and a decent wage with the hospital, I...'

'Mother! You were working for Germans. In a German hospital! How did that help anyone? Tell me that!' She tightened her grip on the strings of her bag and moved to the front door.

'Well, you coming? More money and better war effort and all. We've got to get there for the interview and you know I registered our names, Mother. They're expecting us and we're going.'

Norah had weighed up the benefits and less appealing sides to the job she knew little about, making ammunitions for the Front. There was a strong argument for the War Effort, of course. With Will's sudden arrival, it made sense. At least to Ruby.

She bit her lip often dealing with home life with Ruby. When she climbed into her cold bed at night, she didn't allow her thoughts to dwell on their lives, uncertain of any return, sooner or even later, by Ted. Now in his 15th month of acute absence, she felt numb, disconnected with the new world evolving around her.

She looked at Ruby and put on her coat, hurrying behind her to catch the bus to the Arsenal, a journey south of the river.

The Royal Arsenal. Massive Grand Stores had grown up along new wharves by the Thames, their new place of work, should they pass the interview and medical. It had been a man's world until now, women needed to take up the slack as men where – and might be – conscripted for the war effort. Besides which, women's hands were smaller and more able to work on fiddly armaments requiring precision. Or so the recruits were told. Flattery never went amiss in recruiting staff for the war effort. Norah looked uncertainly at Ruby on arrival. She did not return her nervous glance, her face impassive. Walking swiftly in front of Norah, Ruby pushed open the double doors into a large hall. They joined a queue of mostly young women who looked curiously at the newcomers then turned back to others in the line, chattering, the excitement tangible. Three long tables had been set up, would-be employees motioned towards interview staff when chairs became vacant.

Ruby pressed Norah ahead of her when a chair was freed then took the next unoccupied one. They met in the hall after the interview.

'Well, Mother?' Norah didn't return her gaze right away. Finally, she looked up.

'Well, Ruby, not what I... they want to check our hearts, nerves and eyes. They blue or green-blue, they kept asking? Like I wasn't there!'

Ruby sighed. 'They got to know if your nerves are good, blue eyes, like mine they told me, are just the job for inspecting and all.'

'Well, I don't know. Anyways, I got a job on the production line. Something about cartridge caps. They think my small hands are useful,' Norah said. 'Usually men do the work, they said. But they're not around, are they?' She paused, looking over Ruby's shoulder to the other women. 'Don't know nothing else about the job. Pay's good though, they say. Guess I'll stick it, the war and all.'

Ruby forced a smile. 'I knew you was like that, Mother. Really.'

'Difficult to see what it's like to work there,' Norah commented on the return bus home. 'They didn't even take us around the factory to see for ourselves. And what will we wear? Didn't mention that either.'

'Why didn't you ask, Mother?' The cold tone returned too quickly. The bus passed a shop with *'We are Russians,'* signs written on the boarded-up windows, an anti-foreigner crowd gathering threateningly. Norah felt sick.

Ruby broke the awkward silence. 'We get a kind of uniform, long jacket and cap. And we take them home to wash too. Even with explosive stuff on them, not a good idea with Baby.'

'Disgusting!' Norah agreed. 'Shouldn't be allowed!' Anything to keep the peace, to be in tune with Ruby.

They returned the following day to the Arsenal before sunrise to start the 12-hour shift at 6 am. Will had been taken next door to Ethel who had agreed to look after him 'but only if you both work on the same day.'

Norah, assigned to the copper cap work shop, stored her clothes in a large changing room, the uniform too baggy for her slight frame. She wore a pair of stout shoes of her own and bent down to roll up the cuffs on the trouser legs before entering the workshop.

Her guide, a young woman, stared silently at Norah's attempts to dress. 'Put all of your hair in the cap, some's sticking out,' she said curtly. Norah rolled up her cuff to smooth her hair into the cap, the rough, worn cotton scratching her scalp.

She turned and faced her guide. 'There, good enough now?'

'It'll do.' The woman pushed open a bulky door and motioned her inside. Norah covered her ears at the incessant, crashing sounds coming from the bulky hanger with its large, glaring pendant lighting. High windows and waist-high tables lined the room.

She stared at the lathes and fat vats, taking in the rows of bomb cylinders standing erect on the tables. Women bent over them, filling them with explosive at one end then fitting them with caps. The intense heat had an industrial smell, like rotten eggs. It permeated the building.

Her guide took her to the far corner of the hangar holding big pressing machines. Norah watched as copper sheets, fashioned into caps by a stout woman of her age, tumbled to the floor, a glittering mass lying around the machinery.

'Pull and pull hard,' shouted a cheerful voice over the din. 'You'll soon get the hang of it, dear. Here, you try.' She motioned Norah over.

Her guide said. 'I'll leave you with Mrs. Forster here, she'll show you the ropes. Dinner break at noon.'

'She's a right smiler,' Mrs. Forster grinned. 'I'm Geraldine and don't look so, so…'

It was all so strange, so manly. 'Used to a laundry, me,' Norah said.

Geraldine touched her on the shoulder. 'You'll have to speak up around here, a bit of a racket! Don't worry too much. You'll soon fit in. Now, just watch what I do and copy me on this presser.'

Copper sheets, a waist-high pile, were stacked by a machine. Geraldine picked up a sheet, placed it accurately at right angles and brought the lever down with a thud. Norah did the same on hers. The copper bent a little, the sheet clattering to the ground and narrowly missing Norah's feet.

'You're going to have try harder than that, dear!' Geraldine laughed. 'Look!' Her hambone arms flashed the lever with force onto the copper, a neat cap tumbling to the floor.

After several tries, Norah rubbed her right shoulder, the copper unyielding to her touch.

'Tell you what,' Geraldine said. 'You pick up the caps and put them in the bins here and try again later.'

~

Ruby found Norah in the canteen at lunch, as they queued up for tea and a pie. 'Mother, there you are! Find seats for us and I'll bring dinner over to you.'

Norah nodded and walked to one of the trestle tables. In silence, she ate the pie and drank the strong tea Ruby put before her then wiped her mouth.

'What did they give you to do?' Ruby licked her suet pudding spoon and put it in her bowl. 'I quite like it where I

147

am. In the filling station. We have to stem the powder into shells with broom handles and mallets.'

'Brooms? Don't they give you proper tools to do the job?'

'Odd, but it works! You see, you have your shell and the broom handle, your tin of powder. And you put a bit in, tamp it down, put a bit more in, tamp it down again. It takes all your time to get it all in, very hard work but I'll learn fast. Or I won't get much pay.'

'What do you mean, Ruby? You're paid to do it, by the hour. Aren't you?'

'Well, mother, you see, it's piecemeal. The more you fill up, the more you'll find in your pay packet end of the week.'

'We didn't have to count the number of sheets and flannelettes we washed and ironed in a day in the hospital! Doesn't sound right!'

'Well, here they do, Mother. There are supervisors everywhere, counting and marking.'

'I won't make a bean then,' Norah gave a giggle. 'I just picked up caps, copper ones, and put them in the bin. Couldn't get the press to press.'

'Don't worry, Mother,' Ruby said sharply. 'They'll give you another job when they see you're not strong enough.' Her tone changed. 'But give it more of a try after dinner. You'll see.'

Norah was moved the following day to inspect fuses, sixteen separate small hand actions needed to achieve each fuse. On Sunday, she wrote to Ted.

Dear Ted,

Home, January 26, 1916

Hoping you are in the best of health as it leaves us all at present. Dear little Will is thriving, his care by Ethel, when not at home with Ruby and me, comfortable and loving. In fact, Ethel shows more motherly instincts than our daughter, unhappy as she is at her loss, Billy forever in her heart it would seem. Not that she tells me anything. But we soldier on, both of us taking a job at munitions, The Arsenal at

148

Woolwich, you know, a fair distance from home but it pays well. Gave us quite an interview before we was taken on, blue eyes good to have for some of the work. Did you know that! You think it's not womanly to do, this kind of labouring work, but Ruby and I are both thinking of our little boy and his needs. Ruby, even though she's so sad, is thinking of the future, a brave, good girl, our daughter and takes after you, my dear husband. She's working in the shell department, filling them shells with just something we use at home – a broom handle! Mashes the powder down nicely. She's getting on famous. My small hands are doing assembly work, in fuses, which suits me well, the women working with me helpful. We're all in the same boat. My job is putting holes in fuses of shells. And you work to a gauge. You do so many, then you put your gauge to the particular hole you were drilling and if it was oversize, you call your foreman and he checks it and makes it suitable. Can you imagine? A new world. And the food is good in the canteen. Saves on home bills. Herr Westmann was sad to see the back of me, the hospital not finding laundry staff, Dorothy, my jokey friend in pressing, you remember her? tells me. She's still there but finding it harder and harder, German feelings run high, they do.Ruby is cross with the council for closing Victoria Park on Sundays this winter and is getting up a group of people fighting it. Goodness knows when she will find time. Our only park closed! Saving money, their excuse but she's having none of it. Turning into a right little Suffragette!

No word from you this month, just a field card saying you got the parcel with the soap and the powder to control the bites. Any sight of a second driver? Very unfair to burden you with all the driving and maintaining the bus too but, knowing you, well, what I can say. You will do what it takes, to the end. As will we. Goodnight and hoping for a letter from you tomorrow. Ruby sends love. Your wife, Norah.

Norah did not tell him of the skies lighting up at night with searchlights, guns thundering away at Woolwich, uncanny sounds ricocheting around London disturbing Will's sleep, hers and Ruby's needed rest after the 12-hour shifts with only Sundays off. She didn't write of the rumours of Zeppelins flying more frequently over London. Nor did she mention her heartache or of Christmas, another Christmas without Ted.

Chapter 18: Western Front

March 1916

'Every night we would work,' said George, who remained on the front for four-and-a-half years, only returning home on leave twice. 'I slept at the roadside on those buses, with no cover. Each night in the winter we had to get out of our beds and start the engine every two hours. We had to be ready at any time to rush out and pick troops up from their billets. London buses were engaged in every battle that happened, from Antwerp to the Somme.'
George, London B-Bus Driver on the Western Front.

Dickie Lovelock walked over to the makeshift canteen at St. Julien. Missing the bus he was due to catch with the other soldiers, he had cadged a lift to the small town outside Ypres with a delivery van. The late March ground frost and ice crunched beneath his feet. The uniform suited his tall frame. He ducked into a small canvas service entrance, avoiding the congested one for soldiers and looked around. Spotting a sergeant at the far end, he crossed the chilly space, weaving between soldiers.

'Sir, Lovelock's the name. Come to meet my co-driver, sir.'

The sergeant looked up. 'Ah, you finally made it, took your time, driver. What kept you?'

'Sir, transport from Calais not too reliable. But I 'spect you know that. Time for a cuppa? Parky out there.' He rubbed his hands and moved to sit down.

He didn't mention he'd stopped off to visit an old antiques acquaintance he knew in St. Lô, weighing up business to be had with the French dealer who agreed to take on Dickie's wares. He had found the warehouse after a search and, over a meal of local beef stew laced with red wine and onions followed by several types of cheeses, they talked over possible profiteering tactics during days of war. Thanks to a particularly good Cognac he missed the army transport.

'Don't sit, man! The name's Dawkins, Sergeant Dawkins. And you want tea?' he spat sarcastically. 'You must be new to the army. Follow me. And take your cap off next time inside. Show some respect!'

'Sir.'

Dickie's long legs covered ground quickly as he followed the burly man's back, shifting his army gear on his shoulder, his rifle clanking against the metal water bottle. It held a mix of water and brandy picked up in St. Lô.

As they crossed the square and down a side road past milling soldiers, Dawkins spat out some information to Dickie. 'Ted, your co-driver, is doing a spot of maintenance in the depot. Your bus got hit by shrapnel last night and I suggest you get to work with him right away. On the double!'

'Sir.'

Ted, jacketless, crouched down by the side of the bus, painting over blistering, uneven metal. Hearing footsteps on the cobblestoned courtyard, he unfurled himself and stood up.

'You must be Ted, Ted Digby,' Dickie said, holding out his gloved hand. He stood several inches above him.

'And you got to be Dickie Lovelock, a welcome face!'

Ted put the paint brush down and grasped Dickie's hand, pumping it enthusiastically. Mid-thirties, he guessed. His just-too-long hair, a dark brown, must have caught Dawkins' eye. How had he passed inspection? It framed his handsome face nicely, women, picking him out in a crowd, taking him for an officer with his batman-polished buttons and upright posture.

Dawkins hovered. 'Put him to work, Ted. Expect a callout this afternoon. The bus will be ready. And get your hair cut, Locklock! By tomorrow!'

Dickie just nodded.

'Put your kit in space under the seats.' Ted instructed. 'I've left room on the right for you. That's your bed too,' he added.

Dickie surveyed the narrow wooden bench. Not quite what he was used to but needs must. He stowed his belongings, removed his greatcoat and placed it on top.

They finished off the damage to the side of the bus before stopping for a break.

'You done this type of work before, looking after your bus?' Ted queried, looking at Dickie's unmarked, smooth hands.

'Course!' Dickie flashed him a quickly fading smile. He didn't elaborate.

'Time for a break, hungry?' Ted took out stores and placed them on the bus steps. 'Anything to add to the pot?'

Dickie shook his head. 'What's this?' he asked, pointing to a tin which Ted had placed in boiling water on a camp stove.

'Dinner, Maconochie stew. You not got any in your pack, mate?'

Dickie smiled and shook his head. Ted nodded. 'I add potatoes, sultanas, and onions, other stuff handed out too. You should too. I find anything really to give it a bit of flavour,' he paused, 'sometimes dried biscuits. Bulk it up a little. You get used to it.'

Dickie hid his distaste. 'No field kitchens? That's not what I heard.'

Ted shook his head.

The mess of grey-brown food, bubbling away, turned Dickie's stomach. Two square hot meals a day was the signing-up deal not this foul-looking lumpish dinner.

'Few months ago, we could find some decent food – local – but it's not easy now,' Ted said. 'Just get used to it. Don't breathe in when eating, my advice for nothing!' he chuckled. 'Oh, and avoid turnips, they'll do something else to you!'

Dickie reached for his water bottle, took a swig of the mixed brandy and water, and watched as Ted wolfed down his dinner.

'Guess if you're that hungry, you'll eat anything,' Dickie scoffed.

'Just don't think about it.' Ted advised. 'Battalion food's the same. Industrial-size vats, everything tastes the same. Just wait to you get a whiff of the pea-and-horse flavoured tea. Count on comforts to jolly you along.'

'What's that? You mean, local girls? They jolly?'

'Dickie, if you want to get the clap then seek 'em, find 'em. They're everywhere. Stick to nurses, my bet.' Ted got up and wiped his dinner can with a rag.

Turning to Dickie he added, 'Stuff sent to us by folk back home, maybe chocolate, sometimes malted milk tablets, helps. They're the best, biscuits always go stale or soggy. You got family?' He slapped his body for warmth. No answer. 'Come on, let's go,' when he heard Dawkins' raised voice.

Ted quizzed his new co-driver as they drove slowly along the mud-covered, rutted roads. Dickie's immaculately polished boots were soon heavy with clay, the soles set to rot away in time.

A Londoner like Ted, Peckham-born Dickie had been a milkman and brewery drayman, like Ted's father, before becoming a chauffeur to Lord Harmsworth, the Mail newspaper proprietor. Dickie had never driven a bus before joining up a few weeks ago, this fact kept from both army, to whom he blagged about his skills, and from Ted.

Ted pumped him for news of home, also checking facts he'd read in the Mail, thousands of copies sent to the Front every day which soldiers read avidly. Ted commented on Harmsworth's blistering attack on the Secretary of State for War too which hadn't gone down well with high command: 'Lord Kitchener has starved the army in France of high-explosive shells.' Kitchener was seen as hero by many, Ted

154

no exception, and disputed the article, Dickie sticking up for his past boss.

But one thing puzzled Ted. Why did Dickie give up such a safe, cushy job? Dickie airily explained away his motives for joining the war effort as an essential British must-do. Ted remained baffled but, whatever his motives, Dickie had a winning way about him.

~

Demoralisation had set in with the troops that winter. Harmsworth had been right. They were pitifully short of ammunition, infantry having to endure German shells without any retaliation from their own guns. Dickie, inside the bus with the troops, did his best to keep their spirits up with songs he'd learnt as a lad, the words changing to suit his audience. The eased mood helped them to get through the winter night convoys to the Front. Soon their bus was the most sought-after transport, soldiers jostling for a space.

Oh, what a life, living in a trench
Under Johnny French in the old Frenchie Trench.
We haven't got a wife or nice little wench,
But we're still alive in the old French trench.

Different versions filled the air:

Sergeants stealing rum,
the heroes of the night,
we'd sooner fuck than fight.

In a lull, a voice shouted out to Dickie. 'So, tell George here' – the soldier pointed to a thin youth by his side – 'not heard the story from the horse's mouth! About when you was a milkman, Dickie.' Dickie didn't need prompting.

'Well, when I was a milkman, in Plumstead. Since you ask. And you ask too, where's Plumstead, you northern lot? Middle of nowhere in London, that's where. Well, the notes

155

them women used to leave me on the doorstep, right confusing but I followed them best I could. Do love the ladies but their thinking's not too clever. Like this one. Milk needed for the baby. Father unable to supply it.' Guffaws went up around the cabin.

'And what about this one? Milkman, please close the gate behind you because the birds keep pecking the tops off the milk. Compree?' Shouts of compree went up.

Ted played his harp and joined in the singing when Dickie took the wheel. Cheered by Dickie's presence, laughter came more frequently.

~

Ted's second French Christmas had come and gone without celebration. A warning notice was distributed along the Front by sergeants, Ted and other drivers given leaflets to distribute. Ted had not taken down the notice in the bus since it was put up in before Christmas which Dickie read out in the freezing bus late one afternoon months later as they drank their tea.

'The G.O.C. directs me to remind you of the unauth, inauthor… unauthorised truce which occurred on Christmas Day last year. Nothing of this kind is to be allowed on the Divisional front this year. Every opportunity will as usual be taken to inflict casualties upon any of the enemy exposing themselves.'

He laughed. 'Exposing themselves, eh! Too parky to do that! Want to go home fully functioning, me. Guess the Hun would too!'

Ted chortled. 'Me and all too, mate.' He paused. 'A good time last year.'

'You there?' Dickie asked in a distrustful tone.

'Well, that truce stretched over 70 mile along the Front, didn't you see it in the Mail? It's not just in one place, lots of men over the top on both sides! Billy and me, we got caught in a trench, couldn't turn the bus around. We was ordered to dive into a sap, one of 'em godawful trenches, our first time, but we'd seen them up close, too close, before. Didn't have no choice that day. We dug up bodies, Dawkins choosing us, the bastard, to do the dirty work.' He lit a Woodbine. 'Seems ages ago now.'

Blowing fumes in the cold air he leaned back in the bus seat, his cigarette glowing in the dark. 'Billy was there, a lovely....' He became silent.

'Who's Billy?' Dickie said. 'You keep mentioning him like I should know him.'

'Told you before! You listening to me or not?'

'Oh, you mean that sick geezer I took over from?'

Ted swore at him and didn't utter another word until they reached their destination for the night.

Later that evening Dickie disappeared down the road, returning later with a bottle of champagne and a sturdy beige ceramic pot with something grey under the lid which he offered to Ted. It looked even more unappetising that that stew they had warmed up.

'Here, try this. Something them Frenchies eat. Leftover from Christmas but should be OK. Covered in fat, keeps it fine. Fuwogra, or something like that. Goose anyways. Tuck in.'

Ted stared at the grey, smooth mound and sniffed it. Maybe Dickie knew his stuff, more classy than the average driver. Breaking off a hunk of dark bread Dickie handed out, he smeared some on with the tip of his knife and tried a mouthful. It was as light as a feather and oozed with flavour, a definite step up from Maconochie stew.

Ted grinned at Dickie. 'Never had goose. Like it but it looks very, um, well, off.' He took a long drink of the wine Dickie poured into his tin mug.

'More of this where this came from but mum's the word, eh?' Dickie murmured as he thickly spread the paste on the bread.

Ted didn't ask where Dickie had found the delicious food and drink, fine with him. Best not inquire.

Later that night, Ted thought of what he'd write to Norah. He might not mention champagne though. She might wonder about the company he was keeping. But Kitty, well, she'd love it all, be around in a flash for a glass.

~

Dawkins climbed on board their bus a month later with a drably dressed, down at heel local man, notebook in his hand. Lifting sad eyes to the pair, the Frenchman solemnly introduced himself.

'*Bonjour, messieurs, M. Robert à vôtre service.*'

Dawkins ordered the drivers off the bus. 'You're no longer ferrying troops, you're off the road for conversion.'

'Conversion! Into what, sergeant?' Ted demanded.

Dickie added with a laugh. 'The Ritz, Ted, with good food, steak and ale pie served from the steps with a little grouse from the Moors, the champagne kept in them cupboard seats.'

'More like pigeon pie, you two,' Dawkins replied, looking sharply at Dickie. 'Ted, you've run this bus to the ground, in a terrible state, so bad it'll be made into a pigeon wagon.'

Ted flinched then looked sullenly at Dawkins who avoided his hard stare. The sergeant pointed to the man with miserable eyes and a pencil.

'Carpenter, see? He'll make wooden structures for a loft to be fitted on the top deck. You will be cooperating with him, scraping off mud, making good where you can and helping him. Do you understand? It must be ready to go by next week. No question.'

'And then what? What do we do after, like?' Ted muttered, his feet shifting stony ground by the bus.

'You'll drive the bus as usual, of course, Ted. What did you think? Both of you. Just a different set of passengers, four birds at first up top and you'll help Ralph, your bird handler. He'll be sharing the lower deck quarters with you, so budge up.'

It was Dickie's turn to flinch. He'd have to shift his goods smartish.

Dawkins studied their faces. 'Oh, now, men, did you think you were going home?' He gave a short laugh and walked away.

~

Ralph Gant moved in with his pigeons the following week, rain lashing down on the new loft on the top deck. It jutted out on both sides, creating difficulties for Ted and Dickie over narrow roads. Robert Marchand, the carpenter, showed Ralph and the drivers how to fold the top deck cages flat when travelling but it still looked unwieldy.

'Dunno what it'll be like on these potholed roads,' Dickie said, his driving skills not up to Ted's. He was more used to a Daimler or a Rolls for Lord Harmsworth.

'You're forgetting the cages fold in like this.' Ted demonstrated a flat motion with his arms. Dickie looked dubious.

They helped Ralph up the steps with his cages, baskets, message carriers and boxed message books, the staircase encased in wire mesh after the move. The drivers inspected the loft once all the equipment had been placed to Ralph's satisfaction. The pigeons would have a perfect vantage point and living quarters, the bottom deck now overcrowded and dark. The pigeon handler, a slight 20-something man of few words, would have to share the space with the drivers to sleep, eat and store belongings in the tight squeeze.

'Oh, to be a bird,' Dickie joked mirthlessly, his big frame appearing gargantuan in the converted space.

'You're a right big old Dickie Bird! 'Ted laughed. 'Lucky for us Ralph's small.'

'You'll have to store your gear up top, old son,' Dickie, said, ignoring Ted, challenging Ralph then brought up the subject of where he might sleep, trying charm first before adopting a strident tone. 'Look, old man, there's just no space for you below. Get it? Understood?' Ted rocked uncomfortably on his heels before Ralph blurted out, 'I'll sleep with my pigeons, 'course I will.'

'Fine, son, fine, if that's what you want to do,' Dickie readily agreed with a knowing smile at Ted. 'Here, I'll help you move your gear upstairs.'

Ted stopped rocking. 'Get some grub now and you can tell us about your birds. Can't for the life of me understand how they find their way to the right place and back again.'

'Are you sure they're the same birds you let out or just any old bird come back for free grub?' Dickie mocked. Ralph turned his back on them, ran upstairs and put a finger into the cage of one of his birds, stroking its feathers. Reassuring coos ricocheted around the makeshift loft.

~

Over the next weeks, Ralph, who didn't speak unless forced to, reluctantly showed them how he worked his pigeons, first attaching a tiny balloon to a small basket. They craned forward as he pointed out the mechanics. 'See this metal band? Makes the whole thing work like a clock. Clockwork, see?'

Picking up a pigeon and stroking it, he placed the basket holding a message and attached it to one of its legs. Ted and Dickie jostled for space when he moved to the window then watched as Ralph threw the bird with an upward thrust into the bright air. The drivers laughed childishly as they watched the pigeon fly away to the northeast, his return anticipated before nightfall. They whistled when Ralph blurted out, 'they do 50 kilometres an hour, can fly over 100 kilometres, more than this ol' bus, for sure!' he boasted.

The stench of bird droppings didn't seem to bother Ralph, nor the small space in which he worked and slept, the air a ripe mix of sweat and fowl. When they all had been trained, Ted got a terse grunt from Ralph that he could drive the loft to the aerodrome at Maubeuge, the Royal Flying Corps close to the Belgian border.

Part of the flock on-board would be for use over occupied Flemish and French territory and let loose from Avro 504 biplanes. The remainder would stay in Ralph's care and used for sending and receiving intelligence from the Front.

But first they had to check the pigeon carrier's roadworthiness. Ted, then Dickie drove the bus a few short kilometres to familiarise themselves with the new load, the bus shifting, tilting with its top-heavy loft. A vehicle sounded its impatient klaxon behind them on the narrow road, Dickie leaning over the side with a gesture.

'Need some ballast for sure down below,' he grimaced. 'What you reckon, Ted?'

'You'll get used to it in no time, mate. Look at the load ahead, them Frenchy trucks dead slow.'

'They got men and horses in them, we only got bleedin' birds!' Dickie laughed.

Reaching the aerodrome along slippery cobblestones behind horse-drawn ambulances and a confusion of weary soldiers retreating from a plumed-smoked horizon, an officer waved the vehicle in. Ralph eyed the landscape with suspicion before releasing two birds in the direction of frontline headquarters. Egged on by Dickie, Ralph grudgingly showed them how he logged proof of pigeon missions in a black notebook he kept tucked away behind the cages.

'What's this column for?' Dickie pointed to a tiny handwriting, heading Rewards.

'Gives 'em pressies just for coming back and keeps a record!' Dickie snorted to Ted over a brew later, the loft moved to the edge of the aerodrome. 'More than we get!' He swilled tea in his mug. 'But, hang on! Couldn't they be shot down, them Huns knowing about our troop movements and all?'

'Guess that's the chance they take, but it works both ways, don't it?' Ted mumbled.

~

Dickie was bored after a week at the same position near the Front. He took off one morning, his greatcoat collar hunched up to reach his ears. Rain dripped down onto his face from

161

his cap. He returned late that afternoon, April skies giving up its incessant rain for a brief period. Climbing on the bus, he emptied his coat pockets of some items examining each one before hiding them away.

Ted climbed on board. 'There you are! You could have told me you were going somewhere, Dickie! You've been gone most of the day! What if we had sudden orders to move, eh?'

'Then you'd have gone without me,' Dickie said calmly, his palms sweating. Ted glared at him and stepped off the bus.

The following evening, the low weather front had moved to the east, rain ceasing, clouds lifting. Ralph declared it good enough for a pigeon flight. Ted was in the loft with Ralph, Dickie below on his bed with a smoke, his long torso squirming uncomfortably on wood.

Ralph reached for one of the prepared pigeons, choosing the bird's strongest tail feathers to position the strong wire and basket. His deft hands folded the message inside the tube attached to its leg, the bird now ready for action.

He gently held the docile, fat bird, throwing it up in the air. It vanished in the pale blue sky, another one following. Ted became aware of Ralph's sweetness, his concern and care with his flock. They were his family, not people like him and Dickie.

~

The pigeon loft moved along the Front Line for the rest of the spring. Ralph remained mostly mute, a small, reticent figure on the top deck who ducked at the sound of shells, at any sudden movements in the undergrowth when the bus was stationed, a deer or wild boar usually emerging. He rarely ate with them, preferring to prepare his food up top.

Ted and Dickie, on the open drivers' bench, made up lines of poetry to amuse themselves while driving during the dark nights. Dickie started in a low, seductive voice.

'The handler's hands gently wrapped themselves around
  my body.'
'Do your duty like us soldiers, for us, he whispered.'
Ted joined in. 'Oh, saucy, saucy!'
'I feebly lifted off and reached the level of the bare trees.'
He nudged Dickie, lost for the next line, Dickie obliging.
'Flying in a tight circle, I could not get my instinct to
  guide me in the right direction for my reward.'
'Not sure that's poetry, Dickie, but they're lovely, them
words!'

Dickie nodded before adding, *'Hot fragments of steel*
sizzled past me.'

'Oh, nice one!' Ted interrupted, envy in his voice. His
voice rose as he fought to match him but words failed him.
Dickie butted in.
'My strength was low so I returned to my master,'
Who cooed forgiveness.'
I lifted off again, my wings heavy.'
'Nice try,' Ted granted, cross with himself for faltering.
Dickie continued before Ted could draw breath.
'I could see the river and a wilderness of brown earth,
Hot air and mud. I could see the town and the cathedral
  spire,'
And then hot fire, burning fire.'

Ted interrupted. 'Bugger! You're not going to kill the
pigeon off are you, Dickie?'

'Not sure. It would be a pity. Ralph would be upset so
let's not.'

Dickie whispered more lines under his breath later when
lying on his slatted bed, his head propped up on his knapsack,
his greatcoat spread out over him. Big guns had kept the pair
awake. The top deck was quiet, no floorboards creaking. In
the lull he murmured, giving up on rhyme. No rhyme, no
reason.
'How or where I alighted, I know not.'
'Plumes of gas and flame throwers were my unwanted
  companions.'

'I had not breathed properly for some time,'
my tiny lungs filled with nausea.'
'But what was the strange message I carried?'
I shall never know.
'It was all strangely quiet. I saw nothing. Ever again.'

He sighed and turned his head to the boarded wall, his thoughts turning to his stash of goods hidden in the bus and how to get them to the dealer. He started when Ted spoke.

'Bugger, that was sad, Dickie. Even the pigeons get it.'

~

When the birds fall, they land in the soil dug up to bury the men on both sides. Not all of the soldiers' bodies are identified. Shellfire, from mighty blasting howitzers and bombs, and made by the likes of Norah and Ruby and others in other lands, would close these lives with annihilating vengeance.

Chapter 19: Western Front

April, 1916

The Ypres shops were crammed full of German soldiers. By way of payment, some offered German coins, some had paper notes. Others gave pre-printed coupons to the shopkeepers for food and clothes. There were stories of damage to the railway station, stealing from local peoples' homes and drinking. Every day the bakers were ordered to have 8,000 bread rolls baked and ready for 8.30am the next morning to distribute to the troops. Pilfering or breaking into a house in search of plunder would result in a court martial and the death penalty.

'End of April already! Can't be!' Ted exclaimed as he examined Norah's letter, checking its date. April 27. *'Husband.'* He read the short letter, noting her care and concern for him, stories of the now-crawling grandson *'The image of his father,'* but little about Ruby and herself except for *'Ruby's interested in fighting causes. Don't know much about this yet. But she tells me we're the saviours, we really are. She says. More like the likes of you, don't you think? Don't know what's going on in her head but she says if they not got rid of limits taking on women labour, we'd be in trouble during this terrible war.'*

He sighed and stacked the letter away in the box under the cabin floorboards next to Kitty's prized letters, now outnumbering Norah's. Stretching outside in the faint spring sun to ease his muscles, his thoughts turned to their last meeting some weeks ago, Kitty locating another house for them before revving up her bike and disappearing towards the Front. Emerging from their temporary home, Ted, uniform unbuttoned, had flung his arms around Kitty as they parted. Her hair tumbled down onto her shoulders. As they kissed, the nursing equipment bag slipped from her shoulder, their embrace interrupted by a shout.

Dawkins advanced on the pair. 'The last straw, Private Digby! Positive vulgar display in the ranks! Loutish! You will be severely dealt with!'

Turning to Kitty he sneered. 'How much do you charge, you Frenchy tart? Old duffers like Ted get special rates, sweetheart?'

Ted took a swipe at the sergeant, knocking him to the ground. 'Leave, Kitty, now!' he commanded.

Ignoring him, she knelt down beside Dawkins, examining his cut forehead.

'You'll live, old man.'

Reaching into her bag, she fished out a cloth and tossed it to him. 'Ted, let's go.'

He shook his head at Kitty before hauling Dawkins to his feet. The sergeant looked at him with loathing. 'Reported! You'll be done for! Book'll be thrown at you.'

Ted spent two nights in detention, his pay docked for a month, the sentence justified, according to Dawkins' captain, for gross contempt of a superior officer, a further penalty of no leave for six months thrown at him for lack of remorse. He returned to duty, the bus continuing its zigzagging along the Front. Ted's sense of resentment was steadily growing out of control.

~

Ted, reading an old copy of the Wipers Times outside the bus, grinned at the spoof entries in the paper.

For Sale. The Salient Estate. Complete In Every Detail.
Intending Purchasers Will Be Shown Round Anytime Day Or
Night. Underground Residences Ready For Habitation.

Another one caught his eye.

Are you a victim of optimism? You don't know? Then ask yourself the following questions. Do you suffer from cheerfulness?
Do you sometimes think that the war will end within the next twelve months?

He read down the list.

We can cure you. Two days spent at our establishment with effectually eradicate all traces of it from your system.

He laughed and slapped his thigh with the paper. Kitty would find this funny. But not Norah, her sense of humour never a strong point. He folded it up when Dickie approached from the direction of a château near where they had parked last night. His uniform was rumpled, straw clinging to his jacket.

'Fall down a trench? Go on a bint hunt? Find a good kip shop?' Ted joked as Dickie neared. 'Good-looking lad like you needs some comfort after five months in this hell hole, I reckon. Bet you didn't sleep, you old rogue.'

'No, mate, I did sleep. Had to sleep off my dinner - *and* the wine. Slept on the stable floors last night with my new *amie*.' The stink of barnyard filled the air.

'What you on about, you rascal?' Ted said, fanning his face with the paper to blow away the bad stench. 'You'd better not let the sergeant see you looking so rough. You don't 'alf pong, mate.'

Dickie ignored his comments, brushed down his jacket and removed his clanking knapsack. Ted raised an eyebrow.

'Had quite a time,' Dickie said later over tea, the air sweeter, his outer clothing flapping in the breeze on a nearby tree.

'Couldn't sleep, too quiet around here. So, got up, had a smoke then heard some music from over there.' He pointed in the direction of the château.

'Turns out the old man, you know, that field marshal who came on board yesterday to see the pigeons, well, he and field ranks was having dinner with the owner. Lovely violin playing. Should have brought Billy's violin along for someone else to play.'

'Yes, and…? The grub, other stuff? Women?' Ted impatiently asked.

'So, I creeps over when I hear glasses clinking and find myself in the kitchen. Big woman, cook, you know, invites me in and sits me down. So, I eat. The food! Heavenly grub!'

'You're a bold one, aren't you!' With Dickie's thick dark brown hair and strong features and bearing, he could have warmed her heart in less than a time it took for a pudding to rise, Ted reckoned.

Dickie smirked. 'Didn't come back empty-handed!' He pulled out bottles of red wine, a round cheese and different meats from his knapsack, two loaves of bread following.

Ted stared at it, grinning. 'Share, Dickie?'

Dickie nodded. 'Course, my mate's got to have a treat after what he's been through with Dawkins. That man's going to get his come-uppance, for sure!'

Ted threw him a grateful look before Dickie continued. 'The lucky buggers had some of this grub. Now it's our turn. Pigeon man about?' he glanced up at the loft.

'No, having a session about his pigeons with top brass and probably hating it. Back tomorrow. We're on pigeon guard.'

They closed the extended cages in Ralph's absence and settled down to a meal outside in the cool air. Ted lit a lamp while Dickie laid out the food before tucking into game birds' legs and cold venison pie. They drank the estate's wine straight from the bottle while sprawled on makeshift seating, a pair of logs dragged together out of sight behind the bus.

Ted eyed an odd-looking cylindrical packet wrapped in leaves after wiping his mouth on his sleeve and sighed contentedly. Poking it with his finger, he pushed it closer to Dickie.

'What's this?'

'Ah, don't turn your nose up at this find! Look! 'Dickie untied the raffia holding the cheese together and showed it to him.

Ted leaned forward and caught a strong pungent whiff then peered at it from a distance.

'Smells a bit, Dickie! Here, look, gone rotten too, 'he said pointing to mottled black mould when the leafy wrapping was removed. 'Don't they have paper where you got this from? Leaves, I ask you!'

'You just leave the whole cheese to me then, mate!' He tucked into the Montrachet. 'Oh, I do love a goat!' he mumbled through a smearing on bread. 'And it's not gone bad, just how it is, matured, like.'

'Goat? You'll never catch me eating anything like that, give me a Brie any time.'

Ted, initially put off by the local soft cow's cheese with its white mould and ammonia-ripe smell, when he had arrived in France, looked at it again. Anything to take the taste of Maconochie stew away, he reckoned.

Dickie shifted from the log to nearby grass and lifted the bottle. 'To us, mate!'

Ted sank down on the patchy grass. The lack of jarring war noises, the view of a peaceful horizon not bursting into flames added to a sudden sense of peace. They watched as darkness fell gently over the tilled soil in the distance.

'Finest meal I've had since crossing the Channel,' Dickie said, wiping his knife on the ground. 'Apart from last night, that is!'

'Me too, by far,' Ted laughed, helping himself to more bread and cheese.

'Just like at the Harmsworths,' Dickie added. 'You'da liked their grub, their wine. The cellars stretched for miles under the house, the London one. And the country pile had one too, them dinners quite the affairs. Lloyd George, he came,' he paused for effect. 'I was given his carriage to look after, special one. Churchill was a guest too. Do you know something, Ted, me old mate?'

He pointed the bottle at Ted. 'Harmsworth told him about them Germans on our doorstep, but no one listened. And Churchill the Lord of the Admiralty! Can you credit it? Now we're here and we don't have to be. They'll all bloomin' idiots but not Harmsworth. No sir. Trigger-happy, the men at the top, more like, just can't wait for a good scrap, can they?'

'Your Harmsworth chap,' Ted said, after a pause for wine, 'hang on, saw it in the papers. Didn't he write once *them in government's no master of policy but...'*

Kitty, better educated than he was, had read it out to him last week as they lay in bed.

Dickie interrupted: '... *the slave of unforeseeable and uncontrollable events.*' 'Memorable, eh? In the Mail this week. God bless the paper, the only way we know what's going on.'

'Why'dya give up chauffeuring for the likes of him then?' Ted asked, his voice slurred. 'Right cushy job, if you ask me. You didn't have to sign up, so...' He looked expectantly at Dickie.

'Fancied a change, that's all. Now, about this here Ralph, a right secret fellow, don't talk to no-one if he can help it. But them birds, they get a look-in.'

Ted nodded and pointed upwards to the loft, his voice attempting a lower pitch, forgetting Ralph wasn't there.

'I heard tell he did some soldiering and got a thin end of the wedge near Wipers. Couldn't stand it no more, jabbering wreck. Not exactly a deserter, a traitor, I'll say that for him, more just, well, a crushed man.'

They sat in silence for a while, listening to the birds' soothing sounds above them.

'Just listen to them! All that cooing!' Ted whispered. 'You'd think they didn't have a problem in the world! D'you know, the bus would still be a bus if them telephone lines weren't blown to bits by artillery! No need for all this pigeon malarkey.'

He laughed. 'From Piccadilly, a red double decker stunner, to grey boxy carbuncle in France, more mud on it than you can shake a stick at, and shrapnel holes to boot! You'd find a pretty white caged parakeet on the top deck in London sometimes, travelling from Selfridges to Mayfair and taken to a smart home by a servant, not a shedload of these here birds!' He giggled helplessly, Dickie joining in.

'Here, Dickie, slather of some of that cheese on this bread,' he ordered, throwing over the rest of his hunk. 'Not bad at all! Might even get a taste for it.'

Dickie ignored the bread by his side, leaned over and poked Ted's leg. 'Nearly forgot to tell you!' he guffawed.

'Dawkins, he's got a fancy woman, husband's put out, to say the least! But best bit is,' he guffawed again, and took another swig. Spilling some wine, he swore as he wiped it off a trouser leg, a red stain emerging. '...best bit, mate, is he ditched her for her sister, now he's got two husbands on his tail!'

'And he has the nerve to throw me in the clink for...bloody hypocrite!' Ted stood up, unsteady on his feet. 'I'll blow his brains out!'

'I'll join you an' all,' Dickie said. 'Doesn't deserve to live!'

~

The bus was on the move one hot May morning. More pigeons now lived in the loft, Ralph training sixty male and female birds in the overcrowded space.

Ted, in the drivers' cabin, drummed his fingers on the large black steering wheel. Dickie appeared from the shadow of nearby poplars wearing his greatcoat. Ted called out impatiently.

'Dickie, come on! Time to go. Where you been?'

'Back in a mo.'

Dickie walked purposefully, hauling himself on board. Glancing up the eight steps to the top deck, he listened for movement. Ralph was cooing to his birds. He removed several objects from his pockets and admired them briefly before storing them carefully away. That clock will fetch a pretty penny, those watches and the silver drinks tray and cigarette box too, he reckoned. The initials on a handsome, ornate box bothered him but his contact at St. Lô had intimated he could 'adjust' any tell-tale ownership clues.

Finally, he removed a cheese, several bottles and an impressive hambone and stored them in his improvised food locker, formed from bits of wood left over from the bus conversion. Folding his coat up and stowing it away, he walked around the bus to Ted in the driver's seat.

'Don't hurry, for Gossake, will you? Crank up!' Ted tossed him the crank.

They drove slowly away from their latest vantage point. Dickie turned to look at the large house on the edge of the village near their overnight stay and sighed with pleasure.

'Where you been?' Ted said. 'You missed Dawkins' orders, not very pleased with that, I can tell you for sure.'

Dickie laughed. 'Man cannot live by Maconochie alone!' he said. 'Well, this man can't anyways. Had to say a fond *au revoir* to *mon amie*. Couldn't resist givin' me, well, us, some good grub to see us on our way.'

'Say, where we headed now with them birds?' he added, wiping sweat from his face. The coat was perfect for hiding a multitude of items, Ted turning a blind eye.

'North northeast,' Ted said. 'Closer to the Front further up for messaging, maybe too close for comfort. We'll see.'

Traffic had come to a standstill, artillery lorries clogging the route with their heavy loads, foot soldiers haphazardly moving out of the way, sergeants bellowing 'Step in line, step in line!'

'Worse than a Piccadilly traffic jam,' Ted said, watching the mayhem.

'Must be near the Front,' Dickie muttered, surveying rifle and machine gun ammunition carried by soldiers, ungainly trench mortar fire loaded onto their backs. Others heaved by with heavy sandbags, timber, duckboards and bundles of unruly barbed wire, coiled into weights of half a hundredweight, two men carrying them on a pole resting on their shoulders. Ted grimaced when the wire came into view, recalling panicked horses, caught up within its spiked mesh. He had turned away when the sleek beasts were shot as they flailed in vain to escape.

The bus was motioned down a track by a marshal and followed a tiny ridged trail going east. The carbuncles on either side clumsily brushed against newly budded, sticky chestnut trees. Ralph shouted abuse from the loft, he and the pigeons hurtling from side to side along the rough track.

Ted slowed down and stopped at an abandoned farmhouse. 'This is far enough,' he decided, putting the gearbox into neutral. 'I'll ask Ralph what he thinks, a better view up there for him.'

Taking the stairs to the pigeon loft, the smell of pigeon droppings caused him to gag. Feathers, dust and feed covered the floor, the pigeon cages visible in the haze. Ralph was talking in a low, calm voice to his charges, his red face mirroring the stuffiness of the loft.

He looked up. 'Bit jumpy for them, Ted! Slow down, eh?' They gazed out at the flat countryside, seasons-old unharvested corn crops now bleached and bowed by the sun. Further away, hills creased the once productive fertile land.

'Must be Aubers Ridge ahead.' Ted pointed to the right, rubbing his eyes, now red with dust. 'And the Bassée Canal over there.' There was no movement, no sign of life, the profound silence unnerving Ralph.

'Too quiet! None of my birds'll will fly, don't want to lose any of 'em!'

Ted nodded. 'Whatever you think, Ralph. You're the boss. Dickie and I – well, Dickie wasn't there when Dawkins briefed me – we've been instructed to help you. To help you train them.'

Ralph whined. 'I don't think so. Sergeant doesn't know what he's talking about.' His face reddened. 'You do your job and I'll do mine!'

'Sarge said we should know how to handle them too, in case anything happens to you, I guess, you know, like a sniper injures you. Never know, Ralph, eh?'

'All my birds are trained, they know what to do.' Ralph moved back a step and reached inside one of the cages, picking up one. 'Look at Noah here. You saw how he flew for over five miles at first then thirty a day, trained every early morning, just as they should. Ready to go. You couldn't do it!'

'Did they go out with messages or just flying?' Ted asked, scratching his head after removing his cap in the scorching loft.

'Look, Ted. You're a driver. You know nothing about trainin' 'em.' Ralph's voice became even more heated.

Dickie appeared at the top step leading to the loft. 'What's going on?'

Ted turned to him. 'Sarge – Mr. Dawkins, sir! Our lord and master! – said we should help Ralph in case he gets injured but I guess you and I better stick to driving,' he mocked.

Dickie gazed at Ralph. 'You know best, squire, you're the skilled one but Dawkins won't like it!'

'They like one person, one person who shows affection. That's me, they're mine.' Ralph whispered. 'Not yours. And they have a message carrier on their leg when I lets them out so they're used to 'em,' he added.

He turned his back on the drivers. Ted motioned to Dickie to leave. They walked silently down, Dickie stifling a laugh. They heard the door bang shut, then the shutters closing.

'Well, that's telling me to mind my own business,' Ted growled as he and Dickie prepared supper. Dickie shrugged.

'He's missin' out on some fine ham,' Dickie said loudly, carving slithers of pink meat from the bone and scooping it onto Ted's tin plate after putting a large chunk in his mouth from the tip of his knife. 'Stubborn cuss, he is,' his mouth full. 'Not my sort.'

'Ah, don't be hard on him, Dickie. We don't know the half of what goes on in his mind. He don't want our help, nothin' we can do. We'll just tell Dawkins a lie and have done with it.'

Dickie picked up the knife again to carve. 'Good plan, mate. The only way, lying.'

'What's this, lying about, not helping Ralph?' Dawkins' voice came from nowhere. Dickie covered the food quickly with his jacket then jumped to his feet. Ted moved swiftly to bar Dawkins' view of the meal.

'Ah, sergeant Dawkins, sir, Ralph says he doesn't want us to…'

Dawkins interrupted. 'Now there's where you're wrong, driver. Very wrong.' Coming closer, he reached down and pulled the jacket off the remains of their meal.

'Ham, a whole leg, I see. Not the usual ration. And wine!'

He picked up a bottle and read the label. 'Château-bottled, no less! Not your customary plonk! Are you both aware of what this means?' he questioned, every word slowly enunciated. 'Stealing from locals?'

'Ah, Sarge, stealing a moment of little pleasures that life offers, far from the thunder of guns, of oppression! Never did anyone any harm! But who says we stole it?' Dickie drawled, removing the half-full bottle from Dawkins' hands.

Ted looked at the scene with alarm, his bowels loosening with fear, reminding him of his father's dark glare when faced with the slightest opposition. He moved back and into the bus's shadow.

'Private, stay right here, alongside him!' Dawkins shouted, pointing to Ted then at Dickie.

'I'll get the redcaps. You'll be lagged for sure, and court martialled.'

Lagging, leg irons, was for serious misdemeanours, not for being given food, Dickie's excuse to date, not stealing as such.

'Mr. Dawkins, sir, we seem to be in the presence of a hypocrite, your fun and games with two sisters rather out in the open, I fear! Fraternising with the locals is also frowned upon, I believe,' Dickie ventured, his posture upright, imposing. Dawkins, by contrast, seemed to shrink in his presence.

Dawkins coughed and stepped back, thwacking his swagger stick against his boots.

He spat at them. 'You're both to be court-martialled! Ted, yet again for severe insubordination, Dickie for the vilest of offences too numerous to list, not least the crime of

175

plundering – and gross slander! You know the consequences to the plunder charge alone!'

Ted nodded and looked at his boots, trying to keep his legs from shaking, Dickie laughed uncomfortably. 'Oh, now, Sarge! A little over the top! Here!'

He bent down and picked up the ham bone, still fleshy with copious pink meat, and an unopened bottle of wine. He looked at the untouched blue cheese, sighed and added it to the items.

'Here, have these! Mum's the word!' He passed them over to Dawkins who scowled but took them after a pause. Dickie handed him a spare army bag he had carried them in. Dawkins placed them swiftly inside then directed his swagger stick at them, waving it intimidatingly.

'I'll be back with redcaps shortly. Do not move from here, do you understand?'

He turned to go.

Dickie called after him. 'Why don't you take the shortcut through the fields, Sarge? Save you a bit of time, that sack a little on the heavy side too.'

Dawkins looked at the field then headed out across it, the lights of his regiment on the field's rim seen in the distance in the fading light.

Ted sat down on the bus steps and put his head in his hands. Thoughts of Kitty emerged at first more strongly than images of Norah, followed by Ruby's and Billy's son he'd never likely see or cuddle, share his carpentry skills with, give him his father's violin or show him the watch his parents had bought for him, pressing it against the child's ear to watch his face dissolve into wonder, into laughter lines.

His last days. A jumbling of life, past and present, mingled with the bleakest, most finite of futures couldn't be ducked. A sense of shame followed, then denial and anger towards Dickie. There must be a way out of this.

Dickie stood by the edge of the field, watching Dawkins as he stumbled across the cratered land, the sergeant taking even more of a shortcut to reach his company unit before nightfall. He disappeared from sight followed by an anguished cry. Observing the area where Dawkins had been lost from view, he shaded his eyes to see any movement. Dawkins, if he had fallen, had not got up. Or had he disappeared into the encroaching gloom, reaching the regiment and he had missed him? He called out to Ted.

'Seems our friend's got himself into a spot of bother, mate. Let's have a dekko.'

'What do you mean?' Ted roused himself.

'I mean, he's fallen, maybe into a trench, poor rascal. Or the scallywag's teasing, having a kip. Maybe settling down for the night to have the ham and wine to hisself.'

Ted got up, his desire to beat the living daylights out of Dickie not lessening. 'Where?'

'Can't see him now, the dunderhead! He's fallen, see, gone! Just like that! Let's go see, shall we?' Dickie offered casually. 'Or make a run for it? Take the bus and go missing ourselves?'

Ted studied the undulant folds of landscape, its gentle slopes ebbing into wood copses in the distance. The battle had moved on some weeks previously, debris only remaining.

He muttered to Dickie. 'We have to see if he's alright, don't we? Only right. Light's fading.'

Dickie shrugged. 'You're the boss.'

They set out, Ted striding through tiny tufts of corn which hadn't caught direct shell hits, his breathing shallow. Dickie followed on languidly. The field, increasingly pockmarked by missiles, gave way to the first of the traverse, angled trenches and a series of support ones closest to the enemy. The silence unnerved Ted. He listened for noises before searching, peering over trench banks, the heavy clay slippery from the morning's early showers. Sheets of corrugated iron, used to bolster the sides, hung loosely over damaged, waterlogged duckboards and sandbags.

'You go that way and I'll go right,' Ted said in a whisper which Dickie barely caught, Ted's clenched fist directing him left.

Dickie heard the moaning first. He gazed into the trench and saw Dawkins, his legs sprawled beneath his torso, his head gashed and bleeding. The army bag had split open revealing the ham, cheese and the bottle. A rat gnawed on the meat, others scampering closer for a feed. He watched as a hand went up to ward them off. Dawkins' head swivelled upwards, Dickie staring at the sergeant's terrified eyes.

He saw Dickie. 'Get down here, pull me out!'

Dickie gave a short, sharp laugh. Ted heard him and walked warily back in the receding light. Catching sight of Dawkins down the bottom of the trench, he gave a small grunt.

'Nine feet, at least, down. Where's the steps? Need to get him out now!'

'Dunno, mate. Too dark to see much. You know how it is.'

Ted looked at Dickie with incredulity. 'What are you saying? Leave him there?'

'Did I say that? Don't think so!' Dickie replied with a tap on the side of his nose and a grin. Ted turned abruptly away and walked down the line, the zigzagging trench in the gloom making it increasingly difficult to locate the steps. Reaching a wire tangle defence, he turned back.

'You or me going down there, Dickie? Only way's to jump.' He took in Dawkins next to a mass of shells and cartridges, discarded Maconochie tins and a tangle of useless telephone wires lining the trench.

Dickie laughed. 'No point now, bugger's dead. Look, his eyes are closed. No swatting at them rats no more, is he?'

Ted squinted in the dying light. Dawkins wasn't moving, only the rats. His body lay as if in on the cross, his head now bowed in acceptance of his fate. Taking one more look into the trench, Dawkins' right arm appeared to have shifted, Dickie dismissing this with a retort. 'Your imagination, mate!'

Ted faced him. 'OK, nothing to be done, but we have to report this, Dickie!'

'You must be joking, mate,' Dickie panicked. 'This will get us into such trouble, just as Dawkins said we would if he had made it back to camp.'

Ted stared into the trench, turned and walked quickly back to the bus, stumbling into clay troughs of Picardy land. What were the consequences of not reporting Dawkins' death? What if he wasn't dead? He didn't care about Dawkins, about anything or anyone anymore. Couldn't. Only Kitty survived in his new reality.

Back at the bus, Ted heard the squeak of one of the shutters was being quietly closed. Looking up, he saw the outline of Ralph's arm in the dark before the shutters were latched tight.

Later, he was aware of Dickie stumbling about in the black as he lay in his bunk. In the morning, a bottle of clay-splattered wine clanked near Dickie's bed as Ted stepped onto the boards, looking for his boots. He ran outside and retched.

~

Martin Roberts, their new sergeant, was a beaten man, his long war unending, punishing on mind and body. In his 20th month of battle, he now chose a route of least resistance with his charges which Ted and Dickie encouraged. They had barely exchanged words since that night. Dawkins' body was discovered days later, his identity badge helping retrievers.

Ralph came down the next morning to find the drivers still in their cabin. They did not emerge until later but Ralph was too engrossed to notice, only interested in his charges, all flying back home after he had liberated them with their messages. German marksmen, deployed to shoot the birds down, had missed, none of Ralph's touched by hot metal.

Ted, to distract his thoughts of Dawkins, read the printed placards lining all routes as he drove slowly along in convoy. He understood the gist of the message written by Germans' command in French and in Flemish.

*Any persons who find one of these homing pigeon baskets
must, without tampering with it, report to the nearest military
authority. Inhabitants disobeying these orders are liable to
the severest punishment. If they attempt to escape they will be
shot instantly. Any town in which these pigeons are hidden
are to be fined 10,000 to 100,000 francs.*

Now a veteran of one year and nine months on French and
Belgian soil, Ted could read the message with a good degree
of fluency. Hell, he now had dreams in French with a few
Flemish words thrown in. His mind often took him to dark
places, mostly rats gnawing a ham bone and a face. His.

Ignoring Dickie as best he could, he ducked mealtimes
and looked sideways at Ralph, fearful of what he knew of the
events surrounding Dawkins. He longed for Kitty, to tell her
the truth. But would he have the courage? Or would he bury
his guilt, trying to forget what had happened?

As the bus rumbled rhythmically along the cobblestones,
the mantra, the constant refrain beat out *Daw-kins, Daw-kins,
Daw-kins!*

Chapter 20: Home Front

Late April, 1916

"We 1,200 women in the International Congress assembled in The Hague, protest against the madness and the horror of war, involving as it does a reckless sacrifice of human life and the destruction of so much that humanity has laboured through centuries to build up."
The British government, for its part, prevented most of its planned 180-member delegation from traveling to Holland by suspending regular commercial ferry service between the British port of Folkestone and the Dutch port of Flushing.

Ruby joined the crowds pushing into Central Hall, Westminster. Women only were present except for helmeted policemen outside the entrance with their truncheons. Ruby noticed one smirking as she entered the narrow doors into the building and threw him a look of contempt.

Egged on by Frances Spash, a co-munitions worker on the conveyor belt alongside her filling shells with explosive, Ruby had agreed to attend the meeting. She followed her to a row of remaining seats in the back of the vast space.

A leaflet was thrust into their hands with order of proceedings, a song first. Ruby listened at first before catching up with the words on the sheet.

Lead, kindly light, amid the encircling gloom,
lead thou me on.
The night is dark, and I am far from home;

lead thou me on.
Keep thou my feet; I do not ask to see
the distant scene, one step enough for me.

The organ droned to a halt. Ruby stood up to see the platform and who was on stage, trying to see past the wide-brimmed hats.

'Sit down, girl, we didn't come to see your backside!' someone called out with a cackle.

Frances pulled her down onto the seat. 'See, this is who's going to speak now,' pointing to the leaflet.

Ruby nodded but the name meant nothing to her. Shifting on the hard Methodist pew, she found a gap to view the speaker whose voice was loud and clear.

'My dear co-workers!' A roar went up from the audience.

'My dear co-workers, let me continue! Those of you at the last meeting will recall our call for the war to end, for senseless destruction of family, home, hearth and menfolk to cease. On that we are all agreed, no dissenters here! We shall not tolerate the ruin of our lives, of centuries of work to create our society, to wreck our homeland! This week we shall address the lives of women who work. Yes, you!'

Another cheer rang through the hall, the speaker raising then lowering her arms for quiet.

'As we are aware, the press are not inclined to print true stories of our lives, the lives of working women – you! – in 1916. You represent industries working hard for the war effort, however menial it is! But it is vital work. Important work! You may be in the nursing profession, in armaments, in factories, probably in unhealthy conditions with arguments about wages. The work you do is equal to men's work but you are not paid equally, merely shunned when asking for better pay and conditions.'

More cheers went up, Ruby was now on her feet. She couldn't care less if those behind her couldn't see, they could do the same.

'Instead, the press project the image of all men as fit patriots. Not women, despite' her voice rose and fell 'doing the same work which many of you do.'

The speaker paused and looked around the hall at the keenly nodding hats.

'The government has chosen the route of censorship, denying any rumblings of discontent from women workers, ignoring strike action, denying us demonstrations, or, at least, putting obstacles in our way to show our disapproval, our anger, our fight for equality.'

She moved forward on the platform. 'Are we not just as worthy as men? You know the answer to this! Instead, the press gives the impression that production continues the same way it has always done, ignoring the sex of these workers. Women! We now number millions up and down the land, filling those jobs which our menfolk have left, to join the forces. They are seen as the only heroes, not women.'

Shouts rose in the hall.

The speaker shushed them before continuing. 'Too many people judge women by what they *can't, shouldn't, mustn't* do. We're here to celebrate what women *can* do. There's no stopping us!'

Ruby flung her hat in the air, landing several rows ahead. She scrambled to retrieve it.

The confident voice calmed the hall again.

'Women, if we are to be seen in our own right, we must appear more alert, more able to criticise our working conditions, ready to take a stand against those who oppress us. We are different women now in this age of war, women of even from the lower classes now strengthened with the knowledge that their voice will and must be heard. But, fellow workers. Listen! We have another obstacle to overcome. From our own.'

Nervous laughter rippled around the hall. 'If management only employs women of a certain class, a higher social status, with no more knowledge than those who come from the lower classes, those without the status will obey them without question. The saying, 'I know my place' is not acceptable in today's society! Join the union and let us move forward! Sign up, join now. Step forward!'

Cheers grew deafening, the crowd surging forward to the stage to pledge support, Ruby and Frances amongst them. The organ swelled and voices joined in the final verse of *Lead Kindly Light*.

So long thy power hath blest me, sure it still
will lead me on,
o'er moor and fen, o'er crag and torrent, till
the night is gone;
and with the morn those angel faces smile,
which I have loved long since, and lost awhile.

Ruby slept fitfully that night. She lied to Norah, unable to tell her she'd been up west where Zeppelins were rumoured to be headed after raids on Southend and along the Thames Estuary. They wouldn't bomb the poor East End, Ruby reckoned. No sense in that, she reckoned.

But that night a single Zeppelin, approaching from the east in a full moon, dropped their incendiary bombs. The first fire was quickly put out in Stoke Newington, on Pond Road, near the Digby home. A neighbouring Jewish family, sheltering in a doorway on their way home from the cinema, didn't survive the attack.

Will woke in his cot and whimpered, Ruby quietening him. 'Shh, little man. Don't wake your granny, she's had a hard day.'

But Norah lay awake.

They were up before dawn the next day, Will was taken next door to Ethel who filled her ear with details of the bombing raid.

'No park today with Will, dear,' Ethel said, hands on ample hips as Ruby stood in her neighbour's kitchen holding her son. 'Too close for comfort last night. We was out of the house to see the damage quick as anything, a row of houses just matchsticks, burnt ones at that. Stumps left. They got the kiddies out in time but they say the father perished in one. What them bombs do!'

Ruby voiced her agreement, no park today. Where were her bombs landing? The ones she had packed so tightly with explosive, then shipped to France, to Belgium and other countries? When she tamped down the powder with her broom handle, she only thought of the Huns as the target, German soldiers, fat German soldiers with their menacing helmets. It did not occur to her that the bombs might kill kiddies, old women and men, mothers, fathers, shopkeepers, firemen, workers – workers like her.

Ruby hastily left Ethel and her son and silently made her way with Norah to the Woolwich ferry to start their twelve-hour shift. Smoke, acrid black plumes, not of burning coal but of smouldering, burnt houses, rose from neighbouring streets, sounds of wailing klaxons and sirens circling the area. Newspaper vendors shouted out lurid details. Norah faltered and sat down on steps leading to the ferry.

'Look,' she said in a whisper, and pointed to a vendor, his newspaper's headlines condemning German murderers. Under a picture of an 11-year-old girl, a caption asked:

'*What had she ever done to Germany?*'

Ruby sat down beside her. 'Mother, get up. We must get to work.'

Norah reached into her pocket and found a sweet. She sucked on it before trying to get up but fell back, Ruby helping her up. She hadn't put her arms around her for months, not since Will's birth. Norah's frame always slender, was now bone, just bone. Why hadn't she noticed before? Had she been so blind to her own misery and shock – losing Billy, gaining Will – that she had become careless, thoughtless? She hugged her mother with more intensity. 'Mum, yes, we must. For Dad, for the others. Billy. No question. Billy.'

They crossed onto the ferry, the wind catching Norah's hat, whirling it up in the air into the blue sky tinged with scudding clouds. It blew away down the Thames before either could catch it. Ruby jumped up on a ferry's wooden slatted seat to grab it before it disappeared but failed, nearly losing her balance. Norah laughed in a way Ruby hadn't seen her laugh in many months but it was more like hysteria than mirth, she concluded later as she plugged the powder into the next bomb.

After last night's Zeppelin attack, deaths were surely now only streets away. If Norah couldn't be strong, she must be, or she'd be just another number, another life without meaning.

Chapter 21: Home Front

June, 1916

From Reuters: *The Zeppelin LZ.38, commanded by 35-year-old Hauptman Erich Linnarz, had already flown four other raids on Britain before striking against London. It had a crew of 13, was 536 feet in length, could fly at about 50mph – wind permitting – and carried 120 bombs. Forty-one fires were reported in Hoxton, where two cabinetmakers' premises were gutted. Most damage occurred to private dwellings, but bombs also struck the Shoreditch Empire Music Hall during a performance and smashed through the glass roof of the Great Eastern Railway's Bishopsgate Goods Yard. In Whitechapel, bombs struck damaged a church, a synagogue and a bonded warehouse full of Johnnie Walker's whisky. They killed seven people and injured another 35.*

Ruby did not hand over her wages to her mother now. Roles were reversed, Norah wordlessly giving up the household finances to her. Working sixty-five hours, longer by five hours than at the German Hospital, she did not feel capable of doing the books, the allocation of monies to the tradesmen, the doctor, insurance man. Ruby assumed control of the family budget and gave her mother pocket money. She calculated the dues coming in from Ted as well as their own wages and put a small sum aside each week for Will's current and future needs. She also kept a stash for going out with Frances, for union funds and for drinks at the pub afterwards. Norah didn't have to know everything. Ruby didn't want to add to her worries, unions not seen in good light for a woman to become involved in. That was men's territory.

Norah pored over discarded newspapers at dinner time after her morning shift, too tired to enter into much talking with excitable women next to her in the canteen. She left this to Ruby who seemed to have many new friends. She watched Ruby in animated conversation with a rather knowing, older-looking girl with soft brown hair and a direct gaze and noticed that their plates of food going cold as they talked. Such a waste, she thought. Ruby can't – mustn't! – throw away food.

She returned to her reading. The papers told the same story over the months about out of control females '*blowing wages on luxuries, squandering money now that they worked,*' munitions workers singled out as infiltrating men's world and therefore suspect. Articles trumpeted about '*assertiveness, highly undesirable, smoking and swearing, having fun on their day off rather than going to church in a demure fashion.*' They warned of '*promiscuity, illegitimate children, venereal disease, the notion of misbehaviour not for ladies with conventional, respectable minds.*' Norah shook her head. The world order was not what it had been or should be.

She stole another glance at Ruby and her companion. Well, they certainly didn't fit these warning descriptions, just bouncy, lively young women, proud of their new, important jobs. Granted, Ruby was somewhat sharp-tongued, but not like the papers described women workers. Ruby dressed modestly and hadn't splashed out on unneeded fripperies.

Norah didn't dwell too long on her grandson's parentage and Ruby's lack of a wedding ring. Somehow, it didn't matter. Norah could see why Ruby would be attracted to be with other people, not cooped up at home with a baby and housework. There was bound to be changes as fathers were often absent. But some things didn't change. In her own family, fathers hadn't played a role, nor in Ethel's. Ted's family was of the marrying kind, fearing the church '*for better or for worse.*' She hadn't known who her father was, her birth certificate reading 'begotten in fornication.' At least Will's was filled in with his father's name.

Nora could sense that Ruby was getting over Billy, her manner less brittle, her laughter returning. Norah finished her dinner in silence, cleared her plate at the hatch with a nod and faint smile to Mrs. Slattery, the friendly cook, and walked back to work, shifting in her uncomfortable uniform.

Ruby and Frances ate their now-cold food quickly when they noticed the canteen emptying and made their way arm-in-arm to the filling station.

'You know what we need,' Frances said conspiratorially as they pushed open the door to their area.

Ruby looked at her. 'No, can't say I do, chum.' They hurried to their places when a supervisor approached them. 'Tell you later. Meet me afterwards.'

The woman, in her 40's, scowled at them and pointed to the large clock on the wall.

'Young ladies, you will have your pay docked if even a second late on your next shift.'

Ruby flashed a winning smile at the supervisor and quickly started on the bombs as they inched forward on the long tables, shovelling the TNT gradually in the metal cylinder, tamping down each addition with precision. With every thump, thump came further thoughts. Could she go out evenings, once every so often, to another union meeting to hear about new attitudes? Go to the pub with Frances? Did she dare? Would she tell Norah the truth?

Frances walked with Ruby and Norah to the ferry after their shift, Ruby, next to her friend, whispered conspiratorially to her. 'You started to say something to me. '*We need,* you said.'

Frances wound an arm around Ruby. 'You keen to go the next meeting? Tomorrow night? You going to tell your ma what you're up to?'

'Don't know, Frances, it's difficult as Ma hasn't been quite herself since Pa went overseas. She don't seem to live without him, always quiet before, now like the grave 'round our house. 'Xcept for Will that is. He makes her smile.'

Norah stopped, waiting for them to catch up with her. 'Say, what are you two whispering about, thick as thieves?'

~

Ruby met Frances the following evening, wearing her old tailored ankle-length skirt and long, matching jacket and shoes with a heightened heel to make her look older. A blouse, with neat tucks and a masculine-style collar and tie suited her on in cool June weather. Returning home from the Arsenal in a sudden downpour, her piled-up hair was still damp.

'Look, there's a bus coming!' A double decker with *Piccadilly* on the front drew up at the stop. 'Run for it!'

Frances held her back, laughing. 'No need, our meeting's right around the corner.'

Ruby stared at her. 'What, in Bow? Unions around here?'

Frances took her by the arm and they walked along the main road, a crowd of women outside a large building. 'Bow Palace' Frances explained. The cavernous building, at the rear of the Three Cups public house, jutted its its square brick footprint on both sides of the dull solid pub.

Ruby looked at the structure. 'Well, I never!'

She had passed the pub many times but had avoided looking at it, men often drinking outside.

'Suffragettes used to come here,' Frances offered as they joined the queue. 'You must have gone down the Roman Road market and seen them there! They ran a stall selling posters next to the fish curing one. You know the one!'

She poked Ruby in the ribs. 'My big sister used to buy their newspaper, *The Women's Dread,* or something like that. For working women and their interests – our interests,' she corrected herself.

'Couldn't be called the dread, surely, Frances! Sounds more like women's troubles!' Ruby giggled. 'I'm surprised the men in the pub allowed them in!'

'You don't argue with Mrs. Pankhurst! She had to fight for us lot. Told you about her when we was at the meeting last week!' when Ruby looked blank at the name.

Ruby nodded. 'Course, Frances, 'course!'

They took a seat in the large, plain interior close to the podium with a row of chairs. Five women walked on from the wings to loud applause and sat down, one remaining standing. She looked at the crowd.

'How many of you work in the laundries?' Hundreds of hands went up. 'And in textiles?' 'In tailoring?'

Many hands were held in the air.

'And in munitions? Where are the munitionettes?' Frances stood up. Ruby followed, many more joining them.

'I see you are a proud lot of women! Women of all ages. Of all backgrounds!'

Ruby stood up even straighter, forgetting her pinching heels.

'We are here today, this evening, at this union meeting...' the woman paused. 'How many members are here? For the National Federation of Women Workers?'

Ruby and Frances put their hands up proudly.

The speaker looked around the hall. 'More than half, good! Now, turn to those who haven't put their hands up and tell them why you joined. And why they should. Or might consider, I should say.'

Ruby turned to Frances and shrugged, not knowing enough to voice her feelings. She listened as Frances launched into concrete reasons to women behind them.

'Women together...give us more power as a group...put safety into work...show men we can do the work, 'specially where we work, in munitions...learn new skills...need same wages as them men...fight for it.'

'Alright, girls, now settle down,' came the command from the stage. 'Those who are not yet members may have learnt from others who are. They have shown we can fight for equal pay, better working conditions. Is this too much to ask for?'

'No!' came a chorus.

'Last year, when war began, women demanded the right to work in jobs men were leaving. But unions feared us. So, what did Lloyd George do? Dropped restrictions to women workers but only, dear friends, for the duration of the war.'

She repeated *duration of the war* with emphasis. 'It was abundantly clear that our work was to be temporary – temporary, I ask you! Legislation made sure that this was so.'

Ruby snorted. Surely not. She had learnt new skills, earning more than in the biscuit factory and felt a worthwhile member of the war effort. Progressing to even more skilled jobs when the war ended was a goal, with better wages and workplace conditions to give her and Will a better chance in life.

'So, you see what we are up against, not only the wage question, safety issues and other benefits in the workplace of all types but we have a different obstacle to overcome, keeping our jobs after the war.'

They filed out after further debate and speeches and made their way down the street.

Frances stood still at the corner. 'Let's have a drink, go to a pub. I know a quiet one down here we won't get any jip.'

Ruby nodded. She wanted to talk, to learn. 'I want to fight alongside you, Frances. What should we do next?'

Frances squeezed her arm and kissed her. 'You're rather wonderful, you are.'

Chapter 22: Western Front

June, 1916

Daily Mail report, June, 1916: *The combined Franco-British offensive attacked eastwards against the German Sixth Army during the past few weeks. Led by General Foch, the alliance formed a 20-mile front between Arras and La Bassée. Medical facilities on the First Army front at Loos included dressing stations, ambulance trains also in place, as were barges and road transport to evacuate wounded men towards the coast, Our brave nursing staff looked after our valiant forces.*

Norah dear,

June 10th, 1916

Scribbling a letter last evening, I had to cut it short as we was moved to a new area. I have a moment now to spare to get on with our chat. I don't think I've told you how much I admire our pigeon man, Ralph. Did I write to you about how he trains these little clever creatures? He's as calm as anything and speaks to them so quiet, whispering-like. He don't speak much to me, only when needed, and never, ever to Dickie. Something between 'em. I think he'd really like to coo than speak! Ralph, not Dickie, of coose! Ha Ha! Do you know how far they can fly, these little grey birds? Up to 100 miles without batting an eyelid (but a lot of wings. Ha! Ha!). And they go faster than this bus. 50 miles an hour! – and with a message attached to them in these funny little baskets. Do you like my drawing of one? For Will, he might like it. They don't

fight them off, scratching 'em wires off, just resigned, accepting. Like us in a way, my dear. We're lucky if we get up to a few miles an hour on these rough roads. We move around so our Ralph can train his new birds. Dickie is getting on my nerves rather but he's good at ferreting out some good grub too, don't know how he does it. Good looks do it, always did turn a girl's head. Missing the soldiers in some ways, the bus a bit cleaner in the cabin though, those muddy boots making a real mess. But it's pigeon droppings now, imagine the smell, the mess up on deck. But you get used to anything, anything in this war, you too my brave wife. Must close now. I see the courier arriving with something, God knows what, out of the way here too. Don't know how he tracked us down. Good talking to you, dear. Mind how you go and thanks for sardines – 3 tins! –and my favourite baccy. Must cost you a fortune. Mind you ease up when you can at work. No sense in killing yourself. Ammo still tight, mind you.
Ted.

Hearing the pop-pop of a motor cycle, he hopped down from the driver's seat after quickly stowing the letter away. Kitty! He ran to her and put his arms around her. She took off her hat, let her hair spill down to her shoulders and learned forward to kiss him.

'Got you something,' he whispered.

'Naughty man,' she laughed.

'No, really!'

Climbing back into the bus, he emerged with a finely wrapped cardboard box with a red ribbon and opened it.

'Have one. No, two, three!'

Kitty stared at the beautiful, handmade pastry. 'Haven't seen these for a while!' She eagerly drew out a Madeleine and scrutinised it before eating it. 'So elegant, so…so…well, French!'

He laughed and held out the box again. 'What are you doing here, anyway?'

Kitty wiped her mouth and chose a second pastry. 'Glad I came! Usual, on a flying mission. But I haven't been here for a while, we've been further down the line. I guess that's why I missed you. Oh, how I missed you!' She blew him a sugary kiss. 'Think I'm running out of petrol, the usual pitstop not around. Can you spare any, dear?' Kitty asked, wiping her mouth.

'We're short too, same reason.' Ted looked at her with a grin. 'Just have to stay here the night, darling one.'

'Hmm, nice thought! Now you'll think I ran out on purpose!'

A voice interrupted them.

'Allo, allo, what do we have here?'

Ted turned around. Dickie's shirtsleeves were rolled up and he carried a knapsack. When he saw Kitty, he took it off, rubbed his shoulders where the straps had dug in and advanced towards the pair.

Kitty stood up and held out a hand. 'Kitty Howard.'

'*Enchanté,* Madame!' Dickie took her hand and bent over to kiss it.

'Mademoiselle to you, or Nurse Howard if you prefer. Just plain Kitty will do.'

Dickie looked her up and down. A bit small, he thought, but very attractive, in a dishevelled way. Her hair must look a treat when it was brushed shiny. Or lying on a pillow. 'Nurse, eh? 'He pointed to the motor bike. 'Not on this?'

'Oh, dear, here we go again, you old bigot! Even out here, near the Front!' Kitty mocked.

'Well, you must admit, it's unusual,' Dickie said. 'But very, very welcome, you little coquette!'

'Never been described like that for my work!' She forced a smile. 'We go at the same lick as a general's outrider to save a life or two. On the Front, no less,' and pointed to her medical armband. 'We're the only women allowed too, the authorities banning women in a three-mile radius. Ridiculous!' She looked at Ted, 'Well, any gas to spare or do I stay here with you?'

Dickie bowed, mocking her, and smoothed his hair back.

'Guess we can show the young lady a good time on the bus, eh, Ted?'

Ted ignored him.

Kitty threw Dickie a direct look. 'I am quite capable of looking after myself, might go by foot, back how I came. Shouldn't take long.'

'Wouldn't advise that, dear,' Dickie swaggered up to Kitty. 'Listen.'

Kitty looked at him then out into the distance across the fields. 'An 18 pounder, I reckon,' she said.

Plumes of smoke rose above far hills, acrid smoke following.

'That's settled then. We'll get you to your destination tomorrow. Without fail,' Ted said quietly. 'It's getting late anyway.'

Kitty nodded. 'Fine with me.'

Dickie carried his knapsack inside the bus and Ted showed Kitty the pigeon loft, Ralph more tongue-tied than ever.

Dickie unlocked his makeshift box and placed several more items in it before locking and closing it hastily when he heard footsteps and laughter on the winding staircase.

He came to the lower deck entrance, barring the way with his tall frame.

'Why don't you set up a space for eating over there, move a log or two in a square and I'll serve up some grub in a jiffy?' he suggested. 'Ralph joining us?'

'No, he's feeding his flock now and says he'll turn in for an early night. Guess he'll do a stock check too,' Ted replied. 'Muttered something under his breath about it.'

Kitty helped Ted fashion some logs into some semblance of an eating area.

'Shall we help him? Seems very independent-minded, your Dickie.'

'No, he'll surprise us with a feast, I reckon. Leave him to it.'

Kitty's eyebrows went up. 'Really?'

She stretched out on the grass and looked up at the sky between the trees, the evening air now clear of black smoke.

The only noise was the vague clatter of metal and glass from inside the bus.

'Dinna is served,' Dickie announced in a lugubrious butler tone. Kitty laughed and sat up as he approached the makeshift dining area with a clean white napkin over his arm, his face expressionless.

Ted joined in the spirit, pointing to a log. 'Would modom like this seat over hea' or care for that one over there?'

'Kind sirs!' Kitty smoothed the grass from her hair, brushed the log and sat down.

She expected the usual, or even less than the normal fare as the bus was far from supplies, and exclaimed in delight as Dickie offered her hams, cheeses, a tartine and cured river fish served with bottled peas. Granted, the *petits pois* with baby onions and herbs were cold but oddly delicate and delicious.

Dickie retraced his steps to the bus and returned with a bottle of champagne and rustic bread. 'Saving it for a special occasion, this wine here,' he said and poured it into glasses.

'A glass!' Ted exclaimed. He held a stemmed one up to the fading light and examined it.

Kitty picked up hers. 'Dickie, where did you get these from? You walked here. But from where? Nothing around here!'

Dickie shook his head and put a finger to the side of his nose.

Kitty tucked in, the different types of meats and cheeses, groaning with pleasure. Declaring the fish to be her favourite, she leaned against Ted and gave a deep sigh.

In the dark, later on, Dickie rummaged around in his food and drinks cabinet and pulled out a bottle of port. Jokes flowed from him, Kitty laughing loudly. Not to be outdone, Ted tried a joke.

'What time is the Frenchman's watch set to? Five minutes to one.'

Dickie and Kitty exchanged glances. Exasperated, Ted shouted, 'Dinner Time! They like to get their legs under the table!'

'Ah, got it, Ted, nice try!' Dickie said condescendingly, adding another joke, Kitty doubling up.

Ted retreated from the conversation. Finding a quiet moment to talk about Dawkins to Kitty fluttered in and out of his mind, like a moth on a window.

When Ralph cried out 'Quiet, you lot! My birds!' Kitty and Dickie fell finally silent. That night Ted and Kitty slept outside, Ted attempted to tell her about Dawkins.

'Oh, go to sleep, it can wait to the morning,' Kitty said drowsily, the port having an effect. Shame ate through him like a hot knife in butter.

~

Next day the hot spell continued. Placing Kitty's bike on the bus, they drove to her field unit. Dora was nowhere to be seen, her motorbike missing. Kitty and Ted disappeared into the house. Dickie looked around the property, and finding nothing of interest, yawned and returned to the bus. Ralph came down from the top deck, agitated. He searched for Ted and found him repairing a window frame, Kitty laughing at him as she handed him some stout nails. 'My birds need to fly, Ted, let's go now!'

~

Ted caught a glimpse of Kitty some weeks later, her motorbike speeding past the parked bus near Loos. The town, dominated by ironworks, was in grimy pit mining flatlands northeast of Paris, southeast of Ypres. He squinted after the disappearing motorcyclist but failed to make out if it was really her. Or was it Dora? A nurse's white and red armband was visible on the diminutive figure driving with determined energy.

An offensive attack, eastwards against the German Sixth Army during the past few weeks had left the allies in disarray with many losses. Ralph cried silently in his loft for Desirée, a little blue chequer pigeon which he had trained and nurtured from being hatched. She was shot down after being despatched with a message to the Front Line that the Tenth Army would make no further attack in the area due to dwindling ammunition supplies. She lay in the rain for hours but had sufficiently recovered to struggle back to the loft with a return message. Ralph untied a vital message from a division in difficulties from her lacerated leg. When she died the following day, Ralph buried her, Ted carving a wooden cross for the gallant bird's resting place.

Chapter 23: Home Front

November, 1916

Daily Mail report: *Britain is facing a huge shortage of munitions on the front lines of the war. The Government recently appointed David Lloyd George as munitions minister, prompting the construction of new shell factories across Britain. Women, some 950,000 working in munitions, are surprising men with their ability to undertake heavy work, and efficiently. They are already regarded as a force to be proud of, part of the glory of Britain. However, their entrance into the workforce is greeted with hostility for sexist reasons, male workers worried that women's willingness to work for lower wages will put them out of work. But instead, women are doing the same job that a male skilled worker would do. They are even driving trucks around the factory, operating lifts, man's work.*

Frances caught up with Ruby in the long canteen line.

'The Welfare Supervisor, Ruby, she wants to see us. Don't know what for, do you?'

Ruby stamped her feet to keep warm. A cold November draught whistled through the canteen. The Arsenal, with its own railway lines criss-crossing the site, didn't suit those with chilblains.

'The super? No, no idea.'

'One and the same person,' Frances replied, wrapping her arms around her body for warmth. 'And no clues at all why. Right after we get food down ourselves.'

Ruby barely touched her rissoles or the skin on her rice pudding, a delicacy, she always reckoned. But she couldn't eat knowing that she and Frances were to be hauled before Mrs. Stockwin.

She tried to trace back any lapses in the production line over the past few days. Certainly, she used the TNT as delivered, no mixing of the compounds to get the balance right. It couldn't be that. Not enough explosive in the shells perhaps? No, no supervisor had pulled her up on this work. Or how fast she now moved those filled shells on?

Her piecework was shown as a model of how to work well when new recruits were taught the ropes. They looked admiringly on, watching the speed at which she managed to achieve so many fillings.

Was it the time when she and Frances were minutes late after the dinner hour or the time when she had to leave early as Will had a bad case of the croup? She missed two days' work because of his illness, Ethel unwilling to look after a sick child as well as her own brood.

'Shall I save this for you for later?' asked the motherly woman in the canteen's washing up area as Ruby returned the plate to the kitchen. She always made a fuss of Ruby and the younger women.

'Please, Mrs. Ford. I'll come by later and take it home.' Waste not, want not.

Mrs. Stockwin got up from her desk to greet Ruby and Frances. A tall, imposing woman with thick steel grey braids wound loosely around her large head, her demeanour pointed to an assertive, no-nonsense approach.

She moved from behind her desk to the girls.

'Now, ladies, I need to find out from you…'

'Was it because we were late one day, Mrs. Superintendent?' Ruby interrupted.

'I will take the blame, miss, ah, madam.'

Frances shot Ruby a look.

'Why do you think I asked to see you both?' Mrs. Stockwin asked, 'That is not the reason why at all.'

She picked up a report from the desk behind her. 'You both have an excellent record of time-keeping and work, no question of pulling you up on any of these fine attributes. They all help to run this factory smoothly.'

Ruby gave a small sigh of relief.

Mrs. Stockwin looked at her and smiled. 'No, what I would like to talk to you about is something to benefit all women who work here.' She paused and noted their demeanour.

Ruby looked less alarmed now, less under threat. Frances showed no emotion at all.

'I would like to move you both from the filling station. You have both demonstrated that you are more capable of less repetitive work.'

Ruby twisted her hands, Frances ribbing her with an elbow.

'But before we come to that,' Mrs. Stockwin broke off, 'we should sit down together. Take a seat over here.' She gestured to a table by a window overlooking part of the factory floor.

'Now, girls, I hear that you have both joined a union. National Federation of Women Workers. Correct?'

'Yes, ma'am, we have, we did, I did, Frances…'Ruby said.

'My suggestion, Mrs. Stockwin,' Frances interrupted. 'I got Ruby to go. We think change is needed for women workers.'

'Specially in this line of work,' Ruby added. 'Not fair on many counts, I reckon. We reckon.'

'Fine, fine, girls. Fine.' Mrs. Stockwin said. 'It's admirable you wish for change. As I do. Women workers need support and I want to see advances around here since my appointment in charge of you this year.'

'That's, that's good, ma'am,' Ruby said. 'Well, what I hear is from women with children. What they say. They pay, well, we do, to have them looked after, the money we get just disappearing. My Will, well, I pays my neighbour a fair sum to look after him six days a week. He's only a baby, nearly

202

year and a half, barely knows me now, thinks I'm a stranger! If we could have our kiddies here and pay less – or nothing! – well, it would really help us girls with no men. No other wages, see? My mum, we share the cost. She works here too, you know, and…' she tailed off, embarrassed.

Frances stared at her in admiration and patted her on the shoulder.

'That is one thing we can discuss, certainly, but difficult and dear to put into practice,' Mrs. Stockwin said. 'The subject can be put on a list.'

'But what about benefits for all women workers, not just ones with kids?' Frances, childless, suggested.

'Such as?' Mrs. Stockwin asked.

'Our long skirts. They trail all over the place. They're dangerous, caught up in machinery, get filthy, our shoes too. We need something more practical.' Frances looked Mrs. Stockwin in the eye.

'Granted, it's not ideal, far from it. What do you suggest, Frances?'

Ruby joined in before Frances could give an opinion. 'Overalls, like the men, ma'am, and sturdy boots.'

'And clean washrooms, enough of them too!' Frances added.

'And we need to be warmer too, and not so noisy, the workplace, not us! Can't have a decent conversation and nowhere to sit, on our feet for twelve hours…'

Mrs. Stockwin put up a hand. 'Don't forget you sit at dinner break, Ruby. Now, I can see you are both keen for change, some of your suggestions good ones. But today, what I wanted to talk to you about are your jobs. Would you like to learn new skills? You both have the capacity to learn, bright young women like you.'

'Like what? Jobs men have? They won't thank us for barging in to their territory,' Frances reasoned. 'They think we're inferior for a start.'

'They say we're frightened of machines, not womanly to do this work,' Ruby said, reddening. She stood up. 'They say we're not strong enough, fit like fleas, not like they are.

They're frightened we're taking their jobs over but we don't even get the same wages in what we do now. So, what are you going to do about it?'

Mrs. Stockwin motioned her to sit down. Ruby eyes filled.

'My, quite a firebrand, aren't you, Ruby? Believe me, I am here to make work better for you. And the others too at the Arsenal. As you both know, more men are needed at the Front. This means more will be leaving here. We need people, strong women like you, to train and work in their place. Slowly does it, slowly but surely. Just remember! Think back to this time next year and you will see how we have changed things. You are a vital cog in the war effort, be proud.'

'Wages too, Mrs. Stockwin?' Frances countered. 'Will we have equal pay? This year? Next year?'

~

The following week Ruby and Frances moved from the filling stations to new jobs. Ruby was taught how to drive after a test to judge her vision and to gauge space, Frances not passing. She was moved to small arm cartridge cases and taught all the machinery steps from indenting, forming rims, tapering, necking the end, to washing the finished articles in acid baths and finally, stamping each case with numerals.

'I'll get one of those supervisors' jobs when the men go to the Front, more likely, wish they'd get a move on,' Frances declared, shocking Ruby one night as they walked through the throng to local transport.

'Better not let anyone hear you say that!' Ruby cautioned. She didn't let on her excitement of her new job until she got home and let out a whoop after picking up Will and throwing him up in the air.

'Crane driver, my little man. Your mother's going to be a crane driver!'

Norah was appalled but kept it to herself. This was a man's job, not for a girl.

Ruby went out more often after she had put Will to bed. Norah didn't ask where she went but it seemed always in Frances' company. Norah assumed they went to the cinema although Ruby never came home laughing about the latest Chaplin.

On those evenings when Ruby was absent, Norah invited Ethel around for tea, a gossip and a game of tarot cards. Norah got out the frayed red box and they spread the cards and fools out on the kitchen table and took turns in divining the future.

She turned over the Jaunty Fool, murmuring 'Ted!'

Ethel looked up with a perplexed look. 'Why Ted, Norah? What you on about?'

'Stands to reason, doesn't it? He has that kind of victorious look and...' Norah pointed out a travelling bag, 'he's off to war!'

Ethel shrugged, turned over the Two Lovers and examined it. They stood naked below a vengeful winged god dressed in deepest red velvet, storm clouds gathering over the lovers' heads. 'Next you'll be telling me these are Ruby and Billy!'

Norah nodded. 'Could be, depends on your reading. Or your Sarah and her beau.'

Did the carefree naked child on a white horse below a hot sun on another card represent Will's future? She saw Ted in all of them but mostly as The Fool. He might as well be drawn at the wheel of a bus waving goodbye to her.

Ruby would come home and find Norah elated or silent after these sessions. Or she would be upset when an Opened by Censor stamp was marked on a letter from Ted.

'Strange prying eyes reading letters for my eyes alone is too much!' Norah complained.

Ruby grew exasperated. 'But mum, they have to know if anyone is sending out information that would help the Hun!'

'Your father, dear! Your father! As if he would! It's a personal right, a private personal right to have our letters without someone else reading them.'

205

'But, Mum. Isn't he just writing of his day to day life, nothing about troops and where they are, or where the pigeons are flying to? But what if he wrote something he shouldn't, but isn't careful, like how the pigeons are used, or…'

'You don't understand, dear. It's personal. Between your father and me. If someone else reads it first, it's not the same, between three people now.'

Ruby took Norah to the cinema on their next day off to take her mind off the censored letters, Ethel glad of the extra pennies to mind Will.

'You need to get out more, Mum,' Ruby said when she suggested the outing. 'Just the two of us, like old times.'

Norah agreed. She hadn't set foot in a cinema since Ted had left, over two years ago. Twenty seven months ago and five days, to be precise. Or was it more time since an outing with Ted, even just before the war? Maybe it was a music hall, their last evening together at an amusement. No, it was definitely to see a Chaplin film, Norah remembered with a sigh as she and Ruby set off under cold blue skies, arm-in-arm, to the Broadway Theatre.

Seating over 3,000, the main auditorium's grand architecture boasted a painting of Peter the Great, the proscenium stage sporting a projecting ship's prow. Ruby pointed at the two posters by the box office, one of *Birth of a Nation,* the other featuring Fatty Arbuckle.

'*Tin Type Tangle* sounds lighter, dear, whatever it means,' Norah remarked, staring at both posters, pictures of a civil war brewing in America, President Lincoln receiving a bullet and Fatty, sitting on a park bench, looking uncomfortable with a woman seated next to him.

'As Ted would say, what a tangled web we weave!' she laughed as they stepped out onto the crowded pavement after the film. 'Just watch out who you sit next too. Married woman and all asking for trouble!' She took Ruby's arm in hers and squeezed it. 'Thank you, dear, a treat.'

Ruby hugged her, a relief to see her mother less tense. She almost identified with Fatty and his search for love, no one catching her eye at the Arsenal. Anyway, she thought, as they walked down the street towards home, many men would be gone, gone to war, better not get attached, stay clear. She had work to do, a son to look after.

~

Ruby and Norah returned to work after the Christmas one-day break. Ruby had been working for less than a month as a crane driver, Norah transferred to shell-filling, the War Department demanding more for the Front. They walked to the Arsenal's works entrance on Beresford Square from the bus stop, the internal train taking the workers to various departments. Norah got off first, Ruby waving goodbye to her and blew her a kiss. The train jolted and continued its slow run to other departments.

Ruby craned through the steamed-up windows to catch a glimpse of the tailors' shop making gloves, felt buttons and cartridge bags of various sizes. Canvas and cork items hung up including saddlery and cartridge-carrying cases. Passing the coopers' shop she saw wheels and barrels being repaired from wood brought into the sawmill and cut into sheets then planks. Very young or disabled men, some of the remaining male force, had been chosen to work inside the Iron Foundry, sparks and heat flying as steel was shaped with drop hammers and giant shears.

Ruby's workplace was at the end of the line past the brass foundry castings, taking in large guns' ends being shaped and bored by automatic rifling tools, mountings being tested in the fitters' shop. She and other crane drivers drove the finished shells and guns taken out of the factory to the train and barge, the end of the line the pier or station. Prejudice poured out from the male drivers.

'Here she comes, make way for a woman!'

'Take the strain off your feet, dear? Seat's not big enough for your bottom.'

'She won't last! Money won't suit her needs!'

Sometimes, mock play-acting took place, drivers pretending to take the king's shilling. Others were more forthright, *bugger off our territory!* was the unspoken message. Some mock-pleaded: 'Oh, miss, please leave and leave me my job!'

But she had lasted over three months, since before Christmas. Keeping her head down, she had learnt the ropes, avoiding insults which continued despite ignoring them and showing her worth.

Only Jack, drawing the short straw as her teacher, gradually showed some support.

'Leave off, why don't you?' he had said to the other drivers after Ruby's first month. 'Just leave off. Doing her job, ain't she? No special treatment, no bother. Just gets on with it.'

Ruby brought him scones or biscuits she made on her day off. A short slim man of a similar age to her, Jack was a shy, patient teacher, Ruby a quick learner.

Ruby met Frances at dinner times, Norah occasionally, but her dinner hour often didn't coincide with hers.

Jack took a ribbing from other drivers when he was seen next to Ruby.

'Can I sit here?' He held a plate of stew and dumplings. She nodded, slowly eating her dinner. She looked at him over the rim of her tea cup. 'You look chirpy today, Jack.'

'Matter of fact, I am, rather, Ruby. Just moved into one of those new homes nearby, want to have a dekko?' He fished out a photograph from his overall pocket and handed it to her.

She held the picture in one hand and gazed at open spaces, trees and the neat terraced housing, different styles lining the road, all so different from the uniformity of her Victorian terraced street.

'You live here?' Close by? Ever so smart!'

'Thanks, Ruby. Me and my parents, just got lucky, I guess, all of us working here meaning we qualified. We put our name down smartish, I can tell you!'

She walked slowly back to work. A home of her own. Her parent's home by contrast looked tired, exhausted by living.

Done in. So did the street and too many parts of the East End. She didn't want to end up there. Nice little home in the country in Kent where the air was clean, with fewer people and better for Will. Away from the crush and industry. But those Garden City homes nearby, they looked a treat. She would find out about them.

Chapter 24: Western Front

March, 1917

Daily Mail: *Few can imagine, when the Germans stormed the town of Verdun, near the border with Belgium, what the repercussions would be. On the first day alone, the Germans - who sent 140,000 soldiers to attack the French town at the start - had 1,000 guns pummelling the earth, the town and cathedral in ruins. The aim, said Erich von Falkenhayn, the Army German chief, is to 'bleed the French army white'. The war looks set to continue as the British and French armies carve gaps in the German ranks with our shells, our heavy artillery bursting forth in fury, the whole valley turning into a volcano.*

Dickie sat on the drivers' bench, the bus parked in murky countryside near the Front just outside a village. A stiff-limbed battalion marched by, their uniforms muddied, each painful swollen step, etched on the soldiers' faces, pointed to ordeal. Some, with cocksure bravado, had their boots laced together and worn over their shoulders, giving the air of successful hunters with prey. Their mess tins, dangling from large backpacks, clanked against their guns, resembling the sound of a discordant army of reluctant, grudging musicians. It was a now-familiar echo on the French dirt tracks and Belgian pavé stones.

Dickie glanced at the first line of men, muttered an uncharacteristic 'poor devils' and went back to reading a pile of letters, holding them up to the faint spring light. The occasional belly laugh caused several soldiers to turn their heads and glare at him, but he was unaware of them and unaware too of an approaching officer.

When his brown boots came into view, Dickie hastily removed his large black ones from the wheel and jumped down from the cab.

'Sir! Just catching up on my reading,' he said, picking up a Drivers' Orders manual Ted had been studying. He had uncovered a fault, a piston needing replacing. The nearest repair bus depot was housed in an old jute factory alongside a canal some 15 km to the west.

'You're looking too relaxed, Lovelock!'

The officer, Lieutenant Whitehead, now stood at arm's reach.

'Sir! Just returned from the Front with the pigeons, sir! Yesterday, in fact.'

'Is that a fact! Well, today is another day, Private Lovelock. The Front needs you and, lucky day, for you, only a mile or two up the road. Get your gear and follow me.'

'Sir, but shouldn't I stay with Ted here? Gone for a piss, sir. In case we are called away, the pigeons…'

Lieutenant Whitehead's eyes were now only a foot or two away from Dickie's.

'Believe it or not, I am the one with the information as to when you leave or don't leave in the case of this bus. It stays here with Ted but, as you have nothing to do except read love letters, I have a job for you.'

'Say that about the British Army, you never have time to yourself if they can find you a job to do!'

'Spot on, Private! Hop to it. Big strapping lad like you, just the kind we need.'

Following the officer to the trenches, Dickie groaned. He put down his kit under a tree with the other soldiers' equipment and lit a cigarette, an expensive French one for export only. The tobacco wafted over the other recruits, a mix of British and French troops.

'No time for smokes, lads,' a sergeant called out. 'Get in and start clearing up, officer here shortly to inspect. Go to it.' He handed out bags.

Dickie stubbed out the cigarette, put it in his top pocket and hauled himself down in the squelching trench mud, his polished black boots yet again caked in clay. Picking up cartridges, identity discs and other metal, he fished out a watch half hidden in a duckboard and turned it over to see if it had any identifying marks. None. He pocketed it. Identity disks were lifted up over the trenches to patrolling sergeants as well as gas masks and helmets.

Searching for any lucrative merchandise, he found a cache of photographs, all damp and stained with God knows what. Before handing them over, he examined them. Proud, earnest faces stared up at him through the streaky brown stains, a child in a professional photographer's pose next to a smiling, yet anxious-looking, over-dressed mother. 'To my beloved Geoff, love always, Cecily.' He tossed it in the bag.

He continued to gather damaged useless items. Feeling the pull of his long overcoat trailing in the mud, he glanced at the French soldiers along the trench with their practical overcoats, corners pulled up and buttoned at the waist. Only trousers and boots were muddied and heavy. When the signal was given to leave the deep trench, his coat, thick with clay, pulled him down.

'Here, help you.' A big-bearded French soldier in front of him was at his side.

Scrambling out he offered a hand, Dickie mustering enough grace to look as if it was normal practice, no shame attached.

'*Merci, mon brave*! Ah, Dickie's the name. You?'

'Thomas. But don't pronounce the s like you do.'

'Ah, Toma, this right?' The soldier nodded.

'Don't s'pose you know any places around here for music, dance?'

'Here?' Thomas laughed as he spread out his arms in an expansive gesture.

'Well, close by, *mon ami.* You know, in the vicinity.'

'Yes, yes, I understand. Chez Victor, down a small street from the square, is very, very good. Rue Tisserant.' He winked. 'They like you English there. Drink a lot!'

As soon as he could brush the clay off and wash, Dickie would go there, see if Ted was up to it.

Back at the bus, he stripped, shivering in the damp, cold air, washed in cold water before rubbing himself down to warm himself. After dressing, he draped his coat over the front lamps for the mud to dry out. Then he would attack it with a wire brush, boots first.

He and Ted sat down for tea, crouching inside the bus for warmth.

'Found us a place to go tonight, just in the village, not far from here, reliable source,' he announced.

'Ah, Dickie,' Ted said. 'We're not stopping.'

It was not said with regret, the less time with Dickie the better, Ted unable to be himself around him after Dickie's callousness towards Dawkins and his own culpability. No army questioning had taken place nor had Ralph brought up the subject of the sergeant's visit just before he had been found dead. Maybe he hadn't heard anything, the pigeons occupying him. But he felt uneasy. Did Ralph know what he and Dickie had done? Or hadn't done? Had Ralph overheard Dawkins promise to court-martial them for stealing?

They took off shortly afterwards for bus depot repairs, Ted maintaining silence during the journey. As they entered the town, Dickie broke the quiet, 'What's old lover boy upstairs up to now he's not able to send his pigeons out?'

Ted sighed. 'Ralph? You know him, quiet as the grave, no doubt groomin' 'em.'

Dickie snorted. 'Best fucking groomed birds in the world. Should take more trouble over himself and take himself off for a night out with humans.'

213

'I don't think he likes our breed, Dickie, not an easy lot to handle, to get on with. Lay off him, he don't mean no harm.' Dickie shrugged.

Ted found the garage, swearing when he saw the queue of buses. A harassed manager came over. 'Be with you soon, mate, assessment first, then…' Look around you, priority first.'

They sat on board, listening to Ralph pacing up and down. Later a garage mechanic examined the bus. 'Piston's shot to pieces, so's the crosshead bearing, nothing too serious' in broad Yorkshire. 'The name's George.'

'Ted.' They shook hands. 'How long?' Ted asked. 'Got over sixty birds up there.'

Ralph ran down the stairs. 'They can't stay here, they think it's night time, too dark in here for them, time to fly.'

'Ah, Ralph, this here is George. He's from Yorkshire, but you'll get to understand him! He'll do his best, for sure. Get us on the road again'

'Can't stay here, all, they're all awake, getting ready to go. Got to move the loft. Now.' Ralph began to rock on his heels.

Dickie chipped in. 'Really, Ralph, can't you see what George here has to do to get this bus back on the road for your precious birds? It's not all about your fucking birds, you know. These buses,' he pointed to the line-up, 'they carry men. What's more important, eh? Them pigeons or men?'

Ralph punched him. Dickie fell backwards, tripped over a large metal wheel and landed hard on his backside.

Ted swore, went over and hauled him up. 'Go and sit over there, chum,' he instructed, pointing to a stack of wooden boxes.

Dickie glared at Ralph, brushed off his uniform and ran his fingers backwards through his hair.

Ted put his arm around Ralph. 'Follow me.'

Calling over his shoulder to George, he said, 'George, can you get a start? I know we's not first in line but you can see our little dilemma here.'

George nodded reluctantly.

Ted took Ralph outside into the square and found a small café, a table outside free.

'Sit down. Please.' Ralph stood immobile, looking over at the depot, his shoulders shaking.

A waiter approached.

'*Deux cafés, et cognacs, garçon, merci.*' Ted placed some coins on the table. 'Alright, Ralph, calm down, sit please.'

Ralph became voluble with an unaccustomed brandy inside him and blurted out his thoughts to Ted. No one had manners, no understanding of others, pigeons not asking him stupid things. They were just there, no words to get in the way. They responded to him in their own way. People didn't.

'All bastards, every one of them "cept you, Ted.' Ted ordered another round and gradually coaxed Ralph's previous life out of him.

Ted kept an eye on the depot while listening and watched for a waving mechanic beckoning them back. Ralph's voice came in waves then silence as he stared at his hands on the zinc table next to his third cognac.

Adopted by an uncle – his parents were financially and emotionally unstable – he worked with pigeons, training and racing them for him, a bit of a rogue by all accounts.

Ralph enlisted as soon as war broke out to escape a nasty situation, some mischief with illicit betting and birds being mishandled. Ted drank the dregs of his strong coffee, sat back and waited for Ralph to continue. The small voice emerged again.

'They know it's race day, the routine changing a bit. Some of 'em are quiet, and some of 'em are big mouths.'

He put on a crooning pigeon voice. 'I'm gonna win this, I'm gonna win that! All about winning, nothing else, the birds forced to fly even when poorly. Uncle Albert, well, he – and others, mind! – did some terrible things, cruel things to birds.'

Ted sat forward. 'I can't imagine what they would be doing but there's no need to say. Distressing you, so leave it alone.'

'Never talked to no one about it, Ted. He'd control the pigeons to think they have chicks about to hatch with false eggs under them, just to get them to come home after a race. Or he'd do cruel things like widowing, separating lifelong mates, so they fly back in a panic to the lofts to get to their mates. They mate for life, see? Live longer than some of these poor soldiers will,' he pointed to the square's milling troops, '30 years or more.'

'So, what did you do?' Ted gently pushed the brandy glass towards Ralph.

'Couldn't stop him doing it! Said I'd tell on him so he beat me up. So I signed up, got into a terrible jam at Wipers, treading on dead bodies in sodding trenches, howitzer blowing' em sky high in the air. Couldn't cope after that, so they sent me to train pigeons. Helps but don't rid me of it, no sir, it don't erase.'

He downed the cognac and stood up. 'But you, Ted, I..., you..., well, you treat me...I'll be OK but only when I'm with you.'

Ted reached over and left a light hand on Ralph's shoulder. They were silent for a while before Ralph became restless. 'Whatever's happening in that garage?' he said and stood up abruptly.

They returned to find their bus parts all over the oily rough cement floor. George emerged from underneath the bus, wiping grease and sweat from his brow.

'Not the right size of piston in the place, not ready until tomorrow. I sent for the right parts, so your bus should be up and running by midday. Find yourself a billet somewhere.'

George nodded curtly and walked towards the long line of other buses, a swarm of drivers following him. He gesticulated angrily, mopped his brow again and strode to the first bus in the queue.

Ralph rushed past Ted and ran up the stairs, Ted following him. They found Dickie by the cages, stroking their silver-streaked backs, a gentle cooing sound heard. For the first time, Ted saw faint, fleeting smile emerge on the pigeon handler's face towards Dickie.

~

That evening, Dickie persuaded Ted to go out on the town to look for entertainment and a drink or two. Ralph declined, preferring silence to loud voices and what he imagined would be raucous music. They had found billets in a house the café owner, near the garage, offered as refuge. But Ralph was adamant to sleep on board the bus.

Ted and Dickie walked around the town, its typical northern French architecture now familiar to them. Passing a fountain in a quiet square, they stopped to locate a café or bar down a side street.

'Listen!' Ted instructed. 'Sounds lively enough down there,' he said, pointing to a *ruelle* big enough only for bicycles or pedestrians. 'Come on, I'm starving.'

'I'm ready for some plonk and some good lookers to serve it,' Dickie grinned.

They hurried down the street and found themselves at a large hall. Lines of Belgian soldiers and cavalry lined the entrance, Belgian, French and British flags decorating the partly shelled, handsome square granite building.

They joined the throng and watched as a string of generals and other top brass arrived, ribbons, medals and polished buttons decorating their dress uniform. Soldiers in uniform from the three countries followed them inside. A brass band played.

Ted thought he saw Kitty in grubby boots, a muddy, battered leather coat and breeches with a woollen hat pulled down, partly obscuring her face but dismissed the thought. She would be better groomed for such an occasion and what would she be doing around here? He calculated they were a good fifty kilometres away from where she might be.

'What the brass here for? What's going on?' he asked another driver who ambled over when catching sight of Ted and Dickie.

'Something to do with Verdun, bit of morale boost, singing and speeches. Me, I'm not bothered. Going to find a drink. More cheering than all this hoopla.'

'*Venez, venez, entrez, oui, vous*!' a man at the door beckoned.

'You go if you want to,' Dickie pushed him. 'I'm off to find some entertainment, looks a bit stiff, a bit proper.' He disappeared back into the crowd.

Ted shrugged his shoulders, more intent now on Kitty than his stomach. Taking off his hat he entered the hall and found a seat on the side near the stage. Looking around the assembly he searched for her. The lights went down and he gazed at the stage.

A comedian took to the platform. A few risqué jokes later, he was quickly bundled off, a large woman following on to a fanfare of stirring music. Warm applause rippled around the hall. Ted recognised her: Lady Inglis. He had often seen her carrying a writing case and a campstool into canteens, sick bays, hospitals and soldiers' billets to take dictation from soldiers who were too ill or too illiterate to write their own letters home.

Her voice boomed. 'Men of England, who join arms with those of France and Belgium, we salute you and ask you to keep the faith in foreign lands but never forgetting who you fight for, for Verdun, now upon us. And who is it for? For the kings of Britain and Belgium, president of France and all countrymen and women, those back home who cherish you and urge you to fight the good fight. It's for you, for all of us present. And for our children and their children to come. Here's to Victory!'

Rousing cheers and stamping feet rose up, the hall quietening down again when a general came on stage. Joined by other high-ranking officers, they launched into *The Gondoliers* followed by *Von Tromp Was an Admiral.*

Come out like an honest foe.
For there is still a whip at the mast,
And it's strong and long and fast,
Though you ravage and slay and sneak away,
You'll have to fight at last!
There's still a whip at the mast,

And it's strong and long and fast,
And dogs that bite
And will not fight
Shall be whipped to death at last!

The general winked at the audience after the song. *'Admiral von Tirpitz has got the push!'* The applause was deafening.

'He got the push from the Kaiser! One more Hun down!' went up the chant.

Lady Inglis quietened the throng. 'We have a very special guest tonight. Come all the way from England to help you on your way with good cheer and a good heart. Please welcome Mr. Ivor Novello!'

The curtain at the back of the stage swung back to reveal a young man at a piano. The first note brought everyone to their feet, Belgians and French soldiers joining in, the words of *Keep the Home Fires Burning*, the meaning of the words evading local soldiers who emulated the English voices as best they could.

They were summoned from the hillside,
They were called in from the glen,
And the country found them ready
At the stirring call for men.
Let no tears add to their hardships
As the soldiers pass along,
And although your heart is breaking,
Make it sing this cheery song.

Keep the Home Fires Burning,
While your hearts are yearning.
Though your lads are far away
They dream of home.
There's a silver lining
Through the dark clouds shining,
Turn the dark cloud inside out
Till the boys come home.

Ted left the hall before the final verse, his eyes and cheeks moist. He leaned against a wall outside and reached for a kerchief in a trouser pocket.

'Will this one do, Ted?' He looked up, embarrassed. Kitty smiled at him. 'Come on. You look as if you could do with some cheering up.'

Ted wiped his face and blew his nose. 'Yes, I could. Sometimes it's all too much.'

She led him down a confusion of narrow streets to a bistro. Ted cheered when seeing only locals in the small restaurant.

'Soldiers haven't found this place, too far off the beaten track,' Kitty nudged him. One of my favourite around here, get some good *onglet*, the red's a bit rough but quite acceptable.'

Over their thin steaks, potatoes, green salad and local wine, Kitty made him laugh, made him feel good, wise, kind and caring again.

The reminder of past feelings welled up inside. Putting down his knife and fork, he covered his head with his hands, Kitty unravelled his knotted hands.

'Ted, Ted. You go right ahead. No shame for a man to cry, a good releasing crying.' Moving her chair next to Ted's she put both arms around him.

'Crying's not just for those at home, missing their men. I bet many men have cried around you but you've not seen them. They do it in the dark, when they're alone. On the battlefields, running toward the enemy, or away from them. We all cry for different reasons, don't we?'

He nodded. She went on. 'Fear for life, mourning the past. Even the injured try that stiff upper lip until they, well, Dora and I, we say, you don't need permission to blub, you know.'

Ted started to tell her about Dawkins but the fear of losing this wise, caring, loving woman, stopped him. She saved lives, he didn't. Hadn't. He grabbed her hands. 'I'm talking gibberish. Let's get out of here.' She nodded and led him to the small apartment she shared with Dora and to her bed.

Chapter 25: Western Front

September, 1917

Famous World War One Volunteers: *Gertrude Stein, poet, playwright, feminist, volunteer driver for French hospitals. Jean Cocteau, filmmaker, ambulance driver. W. Somerset Maugham, author, British Red Cross Ambulance Corps. Maurice Ravel, composer, volunteer truck and ambulance driver. Ernest Hemingway, author and journalist. American Red Cross, wounded. Ray Kroc, founder of McDonald's Corp, trained in Red Cross Ambulance Corps. E E. Cummings, poet and painter, ambulance driver, France, 1917. Imprisoned five months in France on suspicion of espionage. Walt Disney, cartoonist, filmmaker and businessman, enlisted in American Red Cross Ambulance Corps.*

Ted looked at the handwriting on the enveloped delivered to him. It was not Kitty's bold script but Norah's, her small, rolling handwriting, thickly clustered on the pages, felt like a denser read than usual. He'd set it aside for later.

Kitty came to his mind, replaying last night's lovemaking after the town hall event and dinner: how he had lifted himself carefully off the tiny bed, leaving her sleeping. After picking up his clothes and boots – his movements careful, over-exaggerated so as not to wake her – he let himself out of the bedroom and into the kitchen where he dressed. Rummaging around in the disorganised space he found paper and pen and sat down at the table to write a note to her.

Folding it in three with her name on the outside flap, he placed it against a jam pot on the linoleum table cloth.

In the first few sentences, he was formal, stilted, almost apologetic, the remaining three paragraphs warm and longing.

'What a rotter I am for leaving you, for not saying goodbye to you, wonderful woman that you are! You deserve only the best. Instead I got the best, bucked me up no end to share another night with you. Never could I ever dream of this happening to an old East End geezer like me, a good ten years older than my pretty, strong, fighting woman. A gentleman never asks a lady her age. You are funny. And wise. So wise and accepting 'bout the deaths you witness, people you care for at the end of their young lives. You'll make me think twice now before I gets so angry, so damned defeated sometimes, Dickie, well. What my schoolmaster said was true. Familiarity breeds contempt. I can picture him now writing it on the blackboard and we had to copy it down a hundred times. But not toward you! Never you! But what a reckless idea you had! Suggesting I get home, saying I got dysintry! What would our grans say about the modern girl! No romance left in the world, I bet! One way to get home but, like you, honourable nurse, I must resist them thoughts. Couldn't hold my head up. I know people do it but where's their morals? I want to see you and your trusty Triumph soon, and will, come hell or high water – and shells. You matter. A lot. I'm getting soppy but you bring the best out in me. Cheerio for now, my girl, my one and only. Ted.

He knocked against a teacup as he got up, cold tea spilling on a soft-covered journal. Swearing, he wiped the liquid off the front with his handkerchief, the name on the front now smudged. Kitty's Diary. Damn! He examined a few pages to check on any damage and came across an entry she had written last week.

September 4, 1917: *My poor little boy Rudd died yesterday. He had been with Dora and me for 15 days suffering from gas poison, pneumonia, bronchitis and has been extremely and dangerously ill all the time, but only the day before yesterday he realised that he was not going to get well. I am glad to say we never left him night or day and he was fond of us all. Yesterday was a difficult day to be 'Sister'. He kept whispering all sorts of messages for home and his fiancée. Then he would call 'Sister Kitty, I do love you. When I'm gone, will you kiss me?' I did kiss the boy before he died – first for his mother and then for myself – which pleased him. Ted came by later and helped me get him ready for his burial. He's a godsend, that man, such a help to the injured we care for, the house now in better repair than ever by my lovely man. Never want to be parted from him.*

Ted wiped his eyes, carefully closed the diary and left it next to his note. Before leaving, he went back to their bedroom to gaze at the sleeping figure before making his way to the bus depot. It was drizzling and there was no sign of Dickie. Taking quick steps up to the top deck, he swung open the door. Ralph was cleaning out the cages.

'Ralph, you seen Dickie?'

Ralph looked up. 'No, not a sign of him. Can we go now? This bus been rocked a lot when they lifted it up, everything topsy turvy now.'

'I'll check with George.'

He climbed off the bus to find the mechanic who gave him the all clear with 'Ready now, Ted. But go around them craters in the road, promise me? Don't want to see you anytime soon!'

'Do my best, George! Cheerio now.'

Ted waited for a while for Dickie to appear then briskly crossed over to the square to see if he was loitering in a café, his usual way of dealing with responsibilities. He caught sight of him coming out of a side street, the weight of a bulging rucksack slowing his gait.

'Come on, Dickie. We're ready to go! Get a move on! Sergeant's getting frisky.'

Dickie grinned. 'Sure, sure. Let's go. Heard last night, spot of good news, about…'

'Save it for later, chum, later.'

Dickie scowled and lagged behind Ted on their way back to the depot and lazily mounted the bus with his heavy load. Ted called out after him.

'For crying out loud, hurry! And you're driving, Dickie.'

'Fine, fine, whatever you say, boss.'

'No need for sarcasm, Dickie, no need at all. Let's all pull our weight, eh? Buying gifts, were you?'

Dickie turned around and gave a quick laugh. 'Friend of mine, trader, met last night. Gave me some stuff for safekeeping.'

'Mind you leave me some room in there,' Ted said sharply. 'We share that space, getting a bit crowded, bit of a magpie, you are.'

'Of course! In each other's pockets, you and me.'

A sergeant bustled up. 'Ready now? Finally? Move your bus out but careful backing out, it's a tight corner.'

Inside, Dickie sniffed the air and frowned. 'Oh, bugger!' He flung his bag on the bed and quickly unlocked his food cabinet. A brown liquid spread along the floorboards. He reached in and lifted up a smashed bottle.

'There goes the Reserve Royale,' he muttered angrily, watching the crested label floating on the bottom of the cabinet. 'Damned fools, mechanics!'

He left the broken glass and fumes, climbed up into the driver's seat and reversed the bus quickly out of the garage, the sergeant waving his arms in protest.

'Steady on there!' Ted remonstrated next to him.

Dickie settled down to a sedate pace once on the road. Ted breathed heavily to calm himself then relived his night with Kitty over and over in his mind as the bus gained speed, Dickie driving over potholes and dirt ridges, the bus lurching. Ted yelled at him to go around them to save returning to the depot. Dickie slowing when joining a convoy.

'Say, what did they do to the chassis?' Dickie hollered over the noise of nearby engines. 'You notice too we don't bounce on the bench any more, getting a sore backside!'

But Ted was asleep and only woke up when they reached Hollebeke, the hotly-contested ground of Hill 60 and onto Zwarteleen and St Eloi.

Dickie pointed out telephone wires strewn along the route, the tangled mass rendered useless by constant shelling. 'Ralphie's pigeons are needed, for sure. No other way now of getting in touch with the Front.'

Ted stared ahead, muttering. 'Glad you can finally see why they're useful.'

~

That September, battles raged around the Ypres-Comines canal, cutting through the front lines three miles from the town's medieval Cloth Hall for the second time during the war.

Transport and ambulances weaved between the base and the advance lines at a slow pace on the narrow country roads.

Ted heard the klaxon of emergency vehicles dashing in their direction. Dickie, behind the wheel, seemed paralysed or unaware of their rapid approach.

'Get over to the edge, Dickie!' he shouted. Dickie swung the large steering wheel to the left. Ted slid swiftly over on the bench and grabbed control. 'You're in France, not at home, you fool! On the right side!'

An ambulance passed them within inches followed by French cavalry, their whips cracking, the steel hooves of their horses striking fire from the flint *pavé* like Vesta matches on dry boxes.

The bus slowed and shuddered to a stop avoiding a ditch. It tilted to the right.

Dickie slumped over the wheel, breathing heavily.

Ralph ran to the front of the bus, narrowly avoiding being struck by a whip.

'Fuck, fuck, fuck!' he yelled.

225

Ted and Dickie followed him upstairs, the cages and the pigeons' paraphernalia in disarray, Ralph's flock in distress.

Ted said forcefully. 'Sorry, mate, let's get this righted. Dickie, get down and push to the left.'

Dickie disappeared downstairs. 'Coming! Just a tick!' followed by boxes opening and closing in the lower cabin followed by a curse.

'Another brandy gone, dammit!'

Ralph and Ted moved the cages and tethered them tightly, Dickie joining them.

'Oh, go away, Dickie, it's all done now,' Ted said in a resigned voice. 'Drive us out.'

The bus's wheels screeched as they searched for traction, a bus behind them letting them out into the traffic.

Several miles on Dickie swore, craning forward in the murky gloom. Processions of German prisoners slowly focused into view, escorted by French and British soldiers with fixed bayonets. 'Must be 'round two hundred!' he shouted above the noise.

The vehicle convoy came to a stop to let the slow march-past of prisoners.

'They been trying to get into Ypres for nearly two years, and they're almost there!' Dickie laughed. Ted sighed with exasperation.

Ralph ran down the stairs and knocked on the dividing window. Gesticulating, he mouthed his displeasure at the noise, Ted nodding.

'Turn off when you can, Dickie.'

Spotting a turning to the right up ahead, Dickie sounded his klaxon and held out his arm. 'Turning right, turning right!'

Soldiers scattered as he drove straight at them before turning down a small track. Soon the only sound was a chorus of cooing and Ralph's soothing voice.

'Really, Dickie, did you have to do that?'

Dickie shrugged. 'They're Germans, deserve all they get.'

'They're people, like you and me, Dickie,' Ted said quietly. 'While you was watching how fast they could move,

I looked at their faces. They don't want to be here anymore than you do.'

'Take all we can get out of this war, but 'specially showing them Hun we're superior to any of them. Me, only thing I could see was helmets on their fat heads. And their watches,' he muttered.

Ted shouted. 'You really take the biscuit, you do!' Dickie shrugged.

They drove in silence for the rest of the journey, Ted wordlessly pointing to a place down the track. Dickie parked abruptly on a strip of bare land, heavy rain smacking the ground and threatening to fill an adjacent crater, the bomb's jagged remnants littering the edges. Ted climbed down and ran up the stairs.

'Ralph, check outside, will you? You happy with the location?'

Ralph opened the canopy, peered out and nodded. 'When it clears, we'll see. Bit brighter eastwards, what we want.'

While Ralph readied his flock, attaching messages to their bodies, Dickie scrubbed the floorboards, drinking in the brandy fumes. He cussed at the grey-brown water, muddied by clay and cursed the lack of brandy.

Ted walked over to the ridge to view the surrounding land. He walked for a while along the track, thinking about Dickie. His attitude was beyond the pale. As he edged around a large crater, he vividly recalled visiting Hector, a bus driver taken to a field hospital after being injured when his bus, carrying soldiers, hit an unexploded bomb in a crater. The bus, once a number 24 taking passengers from Pimlico to Hampstead Heath, was demolished. Hector was lucky to be alive.

'Weren't supposed to drive the bus that day, anyways, mate, so here I am, lying here with a Blighty wound. Leastways, this will see me home, the only good thing coming out of it.' But his walking days were over. Sparing no detail, Hector stared up at the ceiling on his narrow hospital cot as he talked.

'The battle noise was echoing all round us, couldn't hear ourselves speak, horses panicking, men falling like billy-o. See, the Hun confused us with them SOS signals up all along the zone, like red stars. Better than the Battersea fireworks! Remember them electric thunder flashes there? Used to go as kiddies, we did. Only bigger and better.' Ted often thought about Hector and if he survived the shock of a double amputation.

Looking at the craters and their depth, the churned-up earth, rotting, fallen trees and absence of wildlife, Ted was surprised anyone had survived. Turning on his heel, he walked slowly back to the bus. There was no sign of Dickie.

Ralph stood smoking by the bus. Nodding at Ted, he murmured he'd wait for an hour or two before releasing his chosen birds. Ted took off his long coat, hung it up in the damp quarters and lay down. Drifting in and out of sleep, his thoughts turned to Kitty again to soothe his anger. This love and compassion couldn't be happening, not to him, an old man like him. Ruby had teased him when seeing him off that he was 'still quite handsome in a way.' Turning over on his narrow bunk, he was aware of Norah's letter rustling in his breast pocket.

Norah. Shivering, he got up, put on his boots and another layer of clothing over his vest and braces and looked outside. The sky looked clearer.

After making tea, he filled his flask and sat down to read the letter.

Ted,

September 4, 1917

We, Ruby and me, at work, the whole canteen, watch more men leaving for the Front, conscription really strong now, the canteen now filled with women. But, my dear, what does this mean? I can only think it means more men, more bus drivers, toddling off to war to relieve you so you can come home. The length of time since we heard your tread on the doorstep, all those months of heartache now turning into years. We will pass the third anniversary of you leaving us next week. Makes no sense to me. But every coward and slacker thinks fighting is wrong but you done it. Well, not fighting but taking all those men to war, hundreds and hundreds of them all cramming into our buses we used to take to the West End for a show. They rounded up 18 to over 40 year olds, they say, and even married men! You'd be too old now. Now, them that won't fight will be made to. Ruby was telling me of a man who said to her he couldn't harm anything so beautiful like us human beings but when the other side want to kill you, what else you going to do? He just hadn't thought it through proper. Ruby says there'll be rewards for us women when their jobs come up. Good news for women, she reckons, quite the little fighter these days, must be all that driving making her feel like a man. What do you think? Oh, my dear, you can make up your own mind when we see you. And you get to meet our little one, a roly poly chap who stands on his chubby legs and shouts. Happy boy, is our Will. He's only afraid of them Zeppelins, well the noises of the bombs falling, ducks under our skirts and howls. One of them airships loomed out of the night sky near work, some as big as battleships, a right sight. Search lights followed it. I'll close for now but just had to share the spark of hope with you. Feel I just talked to you.

Odd what writing can do! Your Norah.

Ted got up. He paced back and forth in the tiny space, five strides up, five strides back, holding the letter. Well, I never, I never! he muttered then stopped. Why had no one mentioned conscription? Examining the letter, he looked at its date: early September, 1917.

Away from the canteen for long periods with the bus, skirting along the Front's perimeters, the subject hadn't come up with anyone. Kitty wouldn't have known about the shift in policy when they last met, he guessed. But they had other things to talk about.

He didn't know whether to feel elated, hopeful or pessimistic about going home. Not for good, mind. Wouldn't get indefinite leave. Not in these times. Not with his experience. Unless, he thought as he unlaced his mud-caked boots and sat on his bed, unless a lot of men signed up for driving. Maybe they would. They'd see it as a safer bet, no fighting. But then the training would take too long. Dickie hadn't any training but he was a seasoned chauffeur, a driver used to the road, to mechanics. Billy, now, precious little experience driving but he cottoned on fast learning the ropes with him. Maybe that's what the army would choose to do in desperation. Send them out with a day's training and a uniform. Needs must.

He, other drivers and soldiers weren't sheltered from the news of casualties, the numbers of deaths. Hell's teeth, they could see for themselves the carnage happening before their eyes. They read copies of the Daily Mail, spoke among themselves, climbed down into trenches to retrieve the belongings of the dead. Over half a million killed so far, or wounded, or missing. Norah said 18 to 40-year olds. He was now 48, way past this age group.

He sat paralysed on his hard, cold bed. What could he do, who could he ask in this desolate, abandoned place? Not Dickie nor Ralph. They had their own motives for being here, in the thick of it. He thought of his own reasons, tracing back to that hot summer of decision three years ago when he had made up his mind. And the reason? To have the last adventure? Before he was put in a 'too old' category forever, on the scrapheap? He rationalised his thoughts then. As he'd not fought in any war to defend his country, driving a bus for troops was the nearest he could aspire to. What could go wrong?

When he had signed up, it looked like duty crossed with an exciting adventure, almost a jolly. He wouldn't be away from his family too long, wouldn't upset his life too much, a bit of a thrilling hiccup, a change, a minor key challenge. And he wouldn't have to fight, would he, nothing that brutal, that fatal, that final. No, he'd just be driving the same old bus but, in another country, just different passengers. Granted, all those boarding his bus would have a purpose. To fight the enemy. But so did those buying a bus ticket from Dalston, from Trafalgar Square or Shepherd's Bush. To get somewhere, to do something, achieve, have a goal in life, to work most likely, to a bank, a surgery, hospital, insurance company, to the law courts on the Strand to be a responsible juror, attend to a sick relative, go to a music hall, a concert, a film. He hadn't thought it through, he admitted, and now there was a chance, a slim one, he might be sent home, even for a brief period. Or for good. If younger drivers signed up, that is. But why would they?

Then he remembered Hector. He might not survive for much longer. After all, they were right at the Front, in buses, easy targets.

Reaching over for a pack of Woodbines, he sat back after lighting a cigarette. *'Norah, it's just not that straightforward, that spark of hope,'* he thought at the first draw. Then he thought of Kitty and smiled but felt a knot in his stomach and groaned loudly. He'd lose her. No, not her.

Chapter 26: Home Front

November, 1917

The "Wheel of Fortune" a positive Tarot card, suggests destiny, fortune, success, luck, and happiness. What goes up must come down, so the wheel keeps turning, turning, turning.

'Two zepps and a cloud, Geraldine.'

'Coming up, Ruby.'

The cook dished two sausages and a pile of mash onto Ruby's plate and handed it to her. 'Where's your ma, haven't seen her today.'

'Feeling a bit poorly, thanks for asking. Should be as right as rain by tomorrow though, she reckons.'

'Come on, Rubes, move up. We're hungry too!' a voice said behind her.

Ruby gave a crisp nod to the worker and joined Frances at a trestle table away from the draughts.

'Well?' Ruby asked. 'Well, how did you get on?' She picked up her knife and fork.

'Mr. Watson, well, doesn't want to go, he's fighting it. Can you believe the man?'

Ruby looked up from her plate. 'He can't not go, it's conscription, he's got to! He's young and fit!'

'Well, youngish, let's not go overboard, late 20's. Not married...'

'...and we know why not,' Ruby interrupted. 'Not with a nose like that.'

'Ruby! He's alright, quite fair to us, really, but he can be a bit impatient, demanding more and more work done, like lightening. Sometimes my hands are in a blur, they work so fast. Got mine up to ten fills a minute.'

Ruby bit into a sausage. 'Gristle, that's all we get.' Taking a lump out of her mouth she sliced off another piece in hope.

'But what's his excuse? He's not lame, no family. So, what?'

Frances picked up her fork and played with her food.

'He's going to the Military Service Tribunal with his excuse, work his excuse, says it's of national importance.'

'He's right there,' Ruby admitted. 'But he's not the only one, there are thousands of you in that department. I go in there and can't believe my eyes still, after all this time. It's bigger than Trafalgar Square!'

'I'd make a good supervisor of all of them, rows and rows and rows of 'em.' Frances said, her mouth full.

'Anyone can train for it, learn the ropes. He's not essential!' Ruby teased Frances.

Frances flicked a bit of mash at Ruby. 'Thanks, my friend!'

'No, no, Frances, sorry!' Ruby giggled. 'What I meant is that's how them at the top will see it, and on that panel too, I bet. You? You'd make a fine Super!'

'I'll fight for it, don't you worry!'

Frances pushed her plate away, picked up her pudding and spoon and put it down again with a sigh.

'Eat up, Frances, never know if it's going to be your last. Think of the starving.'

Frances gave her a wry look. 'It's very yellow! What they put in that custard? Like them women over there.'

'I know what you mean, a bit like my Mum in a way.' Ruby stopped eating.

~

Norah returned to the munitions factory floor the next day. She had gained a wintery pallor after a wet autumn, a pale-yellow tinge added to the already-sallow look. She glanced at the rows of women in explosives, many of them joining at the same time as her. Their stained hands wrestled under the domes of glass on the table as they filled up the cases with black rock powder. Norah's cap kept slipping back on her head, her fringe now a coppery colour thanks to the TNT. Ruby said it was quite fetching and hid her disquiet.

Norah and others in the shell-filling stations had new orders: to strip and change into a uniform and remove their corsets. No wire, no metals and fiddling with hooks and eyes before and after a shift made it more comfortable, at least for the less well endowed, like Norah. When she washed the yellow off her hair at home, it returned the next day after a day's work. The pallor returned with a permanent sickly hue, like a late winter's sky.

They had been issued with overalls, some older women complaining about wearing trousers. But Norah found them much easier to move in and gladly discarded the billowing itchy garments.

Ruby had petitioned the superintendent's office for overalls too to drive the cranes and was given them after badgering Mrs. Stockwin. She found them liberating and urged Frances to ask for permission too. Soon, most women, noticing increased mobility around the Arsenal, signed up for them, Ruby and Frances seen as leaders, girls to come to if problems arose.

Mrs. Stockwin had established monthly meetings with the pair. On the next agenda several items had been put on the list which Ruby and Frances had drawn up.

'Mrs. Super, ma'am, these boots. Still nothing happening 'bout them,' Ruby mumbled as she ran her finger down the points to be discussed.

Frances nudged her, digging her in the ribs. 'Speak up!' she mouthed.

Ruby continued in a forceful tone. 'Our shoes are not fit for working in twelve hours a day, all that standing. Like me, running around on that crane, getting on, getting off in all sorts of weather and on stones and rail tracks. It hurts my feet. I soak them for a good half hour when I get home. Look at the state of my boots.' She undid her laces and lifted one up. Mrs. Stockwin glanced at them. They were battered and rotting in places.

Frances added to the request before the superintendent could answer. 'My feet ache in bed. Just some sturdy boots, that's all we need, like the men have.'

Mrs. Stockwin looked at the pair, ignoring the boot Ruby continued to hold up. 'I have looked into this but the cost for booting thousands of women is very high. I do believe sharing the cost might get this request moving.'

'You mean, we pay for our boots?' Ruby said. She sat back, fixed Mrs. Stockwin with a frown and laced her boot up.

Frances kicked her under the table.

'Yes, that is a possible solution, one suggestion we can discuss.' Mrs. Stockwin looked at Ruby, challenging her.

Frances chipped in. 'This wage now. Some of us need all we can get for children's care, money can't stretch to this. And pay the rent and feed us, coal prices so high.'

'One thing at a time, ladies! Let's go back to the boots now.'

'How much, Mrs. Stockwin? For us, for the company?'

'Half and half, ladies. Half you pay, half we pay. A good deal, and a fair one, I believe.'

Ruby looked at Frances then stood up. 'This is a matter for the union, ma'am!'

'Please sit down, Ruby,' Mrs. Stockwin said quietly. 'No need to get on your high horse over this. War is expensive, we all need to compromise.'

'Do as you're told, Ruby, please, dear,' Frances urged. 'A word with Ruby in the hallway and then come back, please, Mrs. Stockwin?'

235

'Be as quick as you can, girls. You have work to do, and so do I.'

Frances pushed Ruby into the hall and closed the door.

'Don't be such a hothead, Ruby! The first thing unionists do is learn to negotiate, not rush in with both feet and demand things, not the way to do it!'

Ruby looked down at her shoes. She had seen to the soles several times now, adding a further expense to the family purse.

'Look at these, Frances! And yours are the same.'

'Yes, they are, and many of us are in the same boat, dear. But let's think now. If we ask too much now what about the crèche we want for the children? And the health care, now? All important. We come in too strong and we'll get a cartload of no's.'

Ruby was silent and shifted against the wall.

'Hmm, guess you're right there, bit too hasty, I was. Union idea got to me, fighting for rights and all.'

Frances folded her arms on her overall. 'But by compromising, isn't that a better way?'

Mrs. Stockwin peered out from the door. 'Are you coming back in or have we finished our discussions for this month?' She was not smiling.

Weeks later a notice went up in the changing rooms and in the canteen on the boot deal. Most women chose to pay half the sum after arguing with management. Ruby and Frances wore theirs in by walking most of the way to work, then took the bus back home after a long day. Weeks later, Ruby still felt a sense of shame, mixed with misplaced pride, for her outburst.

~

Norah sat down and eased her boots off after stepping inside the front door. Sighing, she picked them up and walked stiffly to the scullery and examined her footwear for a rogue nail.

Sitting down on a bench by the cold kitchener, unlit for the evening meal, she rubbed her feet and wished she hadn't

236

invited Ethel by for a game of tarot cards. Returning to the scullery, she bent down to wash the yellow off her skin and looked in the mirror. Without her cap on, the coppery fringe looked raffish against the rest of her brown hair.

After drying her face and hands, she headed back to the kitchen and lit the cooker after filling it with coal and riddling it. Blue flames flared up, lumps turning from black to the colour of rust, a match for her hair.

Ruby was upstairs with Will, putting him to bed. Norah decided she and Ruby would eat the remainder of the soup. Lifting the ham bone from the pot, she placed it on a plate and stored it in the cold scullery. The bone would make a second soup.

She hadn't heard from Ted since writing to him about conscription. Where was he? Did he not receive her letter? There was no comforting field card either, often his way to communicate via a quick note able to assure her. But there were fewer as the months and now years passed. The tarot cards needed consultation.

'Mum, those cards won't tell you anything!' Ruby retorted over supper when Norah mentioned the game ahead. 'I'm going out if you're playing again tonight, second time this week. You'll be reading the carrots in the soup next!'

'Fine, dear.' Norah said, putting down her spoon. 'It's just a bit of fun for us. Dad is fine, don't worry about him. He's, he's, well, busy...' she added lamely.

~

Norah lit a lamp over the table and got out the box of cards when Ethel arrived. 'Trying a different tack tonight. I'm transferring energy to the deck.'

Ethel watched as Norah shuffled them again and again then carefully put them in order from Fool through the World, followed by each of the suits, from Ace to Ten, then Page, Knight, Queen and King.

'Why you doing all this?' Ethel asked, impatiently stirring sugar into her tea. We never done this before, have we?'

'Handling cards helps them to be more like you,' Norah replied patiently, intent on getting them in order. 'Geraldine, next to me in line, she says it's good for hunches, creates new paths, spiritual forces.'

Ethel shrugged.

'Know what I do when I get up out of bed?' Norah asked as she spread them erratically face down on the table. 'Choose a card, spend some time looking at the figures, at the colours.'

'Why do you bother, Norah? It's just a card game. For fun,' Ethel said crossly as she bent over the table, helping to straighten the cards.

'No, it's not just a game, really. It brings out the emotions, what them figures are doing, who they remind you of, how you feel about them.'

Ethel sighed. 'Have it your way, dear. They can't guide us, see our situations, predict the future.'

Norah was silent then started playing them vigorously, slapping them down on the table. Dust fell from the cards.

'You storing them in a dirty cupboard or something?' Ethel teased.

'No, certainly not, Ethel! You know I keep a spotless home! I keep it tidy for baby, for Ted case he come through that door any day. It's earth. From the garden. I bury them in the garden to get rid of negative energy.'

Ethel bit her tongue and frowned.

Norah turned over a card. The magician. 'Good, good!' she exclaimed excitedly. 'Now you choose one, Ethel.'

The Sun showed its warm rays, another 'Good!' from Norah.

The Moon created a small clap of appreciation as did the Star. Norah's turn revealed the Fool. 'The best possible one! Perfect combination, Ethel. Just perfect.'

'We never played like this before, you sure it's telling you anything?' Ethel asked.

'They all mean happiness, good feelings, something good going to happen!' Norah assured her. Picking up the cards she shuffled them again.

'Now it's your turn, your luck changing tonight. Like mine.'

Ethel turned over the first card. The Devil. Disaster. Further cards made them both wince. Norah packed them away in her wooden Tarot card box soon afterwards and placed a few dried herb branches on the top of the pack.

'What they for?' Ethel said, picking up the tea pot.

'Oh, those. A bit of thyme, rosemary, good for better spirit understanding. Increases 'em. Ruby thinks it's all stuff and nonsense! No soul, that girl.'

She paused, picked up the box and held it to her thin body, more sprite-like than ever. 'But if you had a gemstone, that would be even better, like the ruby, now, the best, shows devotion, love, being generous. You can't ask for more.' Ethel turned away to the scullery with the tea pot in her hand.

~

Ruby heard the clatter of the metal letterbox from the kitchen. She put down Will's porridge and wiped her hands before going to the front door. Norah, scrubbing the baby's soiled clothing, heard it too and wiped her hands. Will sat banging his spoon in his high chair which Ted had made for Ruby from dark wood, the stained padded, patterned tea cosy on the headrest needed replacing.

Ruby picked up the envelope. 'From Dad, Mum. Letter from Dad!'

Norah walked swiftly into the kitchen. 'Give it here, dear!'

Sitting down next to Will in the kitchen, she looked at the envelope absentmindedly patting her grandson's arm. Ruby poured a cup of tea for Norah and reached for the porridge warming on the kitchener. Will knocked the tea cosy off the back of his high chair and Ruby put it back on. 'No more, little man, for the fifth time already this morning!' She laughed.

'Mum, some porridge?'

'What, dear? Oh, yes dear, thanks, a little.' Norah had discarded the envelope on the floor and was reading the letter. It was a short one. She gave a shriek. 'He's got leave, he's got leave! Coming home, at last!'

Ruby pulled Norah up from her seat and danced her around the table, only stopping when Will started screaming.

'Shush, little man! Quiet!' Ruby hugged him. 'Read on, mum! When's he coming home?'

Norah sat down again and continued to read.

'...but, my dear family, I don't know for how long or when they'll give me leave but it shouldn't be before too long. We need to get these new drivers up to scratch, all recruits, most of 'em wet, raw, untrained. Not London lads, they say, rough geezers from the North but at least they're on their way soon. My captain, mentioned him a few times to you, diamond officer, says so and says they can spare me for maybe a week.'

Norah put the letter on her lap. 'A week, only a week. And we don't know when, maybe two months away.'

She put her hand to her mouth. 'I shouldn't have picked up another card, that jack. Bad, too hasty. My fault.'

'Mum, what are you talking about? Nothing to do with the silly cards! Senseless! He's just being given leave, nothing more, nothing less.'

Norah ignored her and finished reading. *'I will write again, when I know. Had a difficult time with Dickie and wouldn't be surprised if he just disappeared. He's a funny bloke, charming when he wants to be but bit of a slacker, suits himself. He does get around though, I'll say that for him. Charms the legs off all them Frenchies.'*

'Can't say I'd want to meet him,' Ruby commented, picking up Will after wiping his mouth. 'But granddad will be pleased to meet you, my little man. You're charming too, aren't you?' She nuzzled her hair in his face and Will laughed.

Norah put the letter in a cake tin reserved for his letters and returned it to its pride of place on the dresser. She felt disquiet, Ted's words lacking in excitement, more duty-like. He seemed more wrapped up with Dickie than home. She'd consult the cards again tonight, hoping for a sight of the Man with Three Staves, the card symbolising strength, effort and the end of troubles.

Chapter 27: Western Front

January, 1918

'My platoon's terrier, one of the brave animals, a mascot and, part of the fighting machine against the Hun, set a record by killing over forty rats in our trench in a few minutes. One of our trench pets. Napper, a big mongrel, has a kitten he tucks in to his coat for warmth. They will have their own graves. Quite right. They bring solace and hope.' Lt. Clifford McCrae.

Ted and Dickie sat apart in winter sun outside an army field canteen with mugs of tea and cigarettes. They watched the new sergeant approaching.

'Here comes trouble,' Dickie muttered, more to himself than to Ted.

'You two, Lieutenant Buxton would like to have a word with you. In the office, now.'

'Sir, be right there.' They returned their mugs to the canteen and walked over to the office.

'Done anything I should know about before we go in?' Ted asked quietly.

'Now, what would make you say that, boss? Tucked up in bed just like you last night, nice and early. Good game of cards though, won fair and square!' Dickie pulled out a wad of francs.

Ted glanced at them. 'Fair and square, you say. No tampering with the cards like before, then?'

'Nothing to do with me!'

'Anything else?'

'I swear, nothing since that time in December, didn't know she had an old man. Didn't know he'd be so, well, possessive about his grog.'

'Alright then, Dickie, we'll just have to see what the brass wants with us.'

They entered the makeshift, long, low building. The lieutenant broke off a conversation with a corporal. 'Ah, here they are. Sit down, lads. I understand you two are at a loose end while your pigeon loft is stationed for two days near the Front and you're not needed. We're short of men, short of good, strong men like you who can do a weighty job and do it properly.'

'Yes, sir. We wasn't skiving, knew we had some free time but…'

The lieutenant interrupted Dickie. 'Now, drivers, this is what I want you to do. Go with the corporal here – Corporal Leonard Cleeve – and do a spot of apron wiring. He'll teach you the ropes.'

Dickie gave an involuntary laugh.

The lieutenant gave him a sharp look. 'Not in the line of fire, you're not proper soldiers, just part of the ghost army, so there's no real danger. You'll be gone for two days. Near Vimy Ridge. Get cracking.'

'Sir!' They clicked their heels.

Cleeve, the corporal, a short squat fellow with restless eyes and a brusque manner, waved them to position themselves behind him with a curt 'Follow me, drivers.'

Dickie ran up beside Cleeve. 'What about our kit, Corporal?'

'You'll just have to do without, rush job, no time to wander over at your leisurely pace. I've been watching you, Lovelock! So forget about your pomade and mirror.'

Dickie scowled and joined Ted.

'Boss, aren't you going to say anything? Surely our right? I was going to the barber's today, shave off this beard, getting a bit manky, the ladies not appreciating it.' He laughed.

Ted sighed. 'Just leave it, Dickie, no women where we're going, I bet you. Force yourself to eat the usual grub soldiers eat for once, not the fancy stuff you lay your hands on.'

Dickie grumbled under his breath as he followed Ted into a yard, Cleeve walked towards high coils of wire and barbed cable next to a pile of metal and angle irons and pickets. He pointed to an open truck. 'Fill that up with them rolls and the other stuff by it. I'm back at noon to see it done properly.'

Dickie drew out a smart pocket watch. 'Only nine now, corporal!'

'Private Lovelock, I would like to remind you that you are in the Army too, not just a bus driver. What does it say on your pass?' He didn't wait for an answer. 'I thought so. Army Service Corps. And what's the word to remember here?'

'Army, corp.'

'No, in this case it's service, you are doing a service to the Army, to the empire.'

He walked away then called over his shoulder. 'You'll find water and rations in the truck.'

Ted clapped Dickie on the back. 'Buck up, now, for God's sake, Dickie! Let's get going. I should be on leave so it's no picnic for me neither, mate.'

Walking over to the truck, he took off his outer wear and picked up a water flask.

The barbed wire started to cut through their hands as they manhandled it onto the truck, the small, tough jagged points digging into their flesh. 'Like Jesus on the cross,' Dickie said, 'only I'm no fucking Jesus!'

'Never was a truer word said,' Ted said under his breath. He searched for some material to bind around his bleeding palms. Finding some old jute cloths, he tore one up to wrap around his hands, tore off smaller strips to tie them securely and returned to work.

Dickie swore like a navvy as he lifted a bundle, his brow moist with perspiration. Spying the makeshift gloves, he shouted. 'Got some of that for me?'

Ted looked at him. 'Make your own! Stuff in the cabin.'

By noon, the truck overflowed with barbed wire and jute bags which Ted had commandeered for any loose items, the sacks now firmly positioned alongside the wire.

Cleeve strode into view, eyeing the work and the now empty yard.

'Good work, lads. Bit of initiative too, I see,' he said, fingering the jute bags. 'Fine, fine. Just one thing though.'

'Sir.'

'The yard's a mess, bits of broken wire all over the place. Were you really going to leave it like this?'

'No, sir, but no broom or rake,' Dickie muttered, resting against the truck, touching painful scratches on his head, his uniform torn by sharp barbs.

'Digby, you had the initiative to move the truck and find the jute, a hunch of mine. Now you do the same for the yard, Lovelock.'

'I'll go sir, Dickie's got a few bad cuts 'n all.'

'Kindness, a rare thing, Ted, but so is diligent work from some.'

Dickie nodded gracelessly. 'Sir.' He wandered off to the engineer's yard and returned with a stiff broom and a bag.

Dickie was silent as the corporal drove the lorry out of the army base and onto the road after a bite to eat. Ground-up turnips now replaced scarce flour for their bread. Looking inside the ration box, he snorted at the tins of Maconochie stew, his stomach heaving.

They drove north to the Vimy area through La Targette, the hamlet now largely deserted, then down an unmade road, arriving in a wooded area mid-afternoon which revealed open fields and churned earth in the distance. Rabbits bounded across the track.

Cleeve put the gear into neutral and turned off the engine. No guns in the distance fired, no artillery or other sounds peppering the landscape.

'Right lads, we'll reconnoitre the area and start apron wiring after dark.'

'In the dark?' The corporal ignored Dickie, addressing his remarks only to Ted.

'Sort out the pickets and angle irons into manageable chunks for carrying after we've done the scouting.'

Before dusk fell, they carried the wire and items to the chosen sites, Cleeve instructing them on the technique before starting on the wiring.

'First of all, you put a fence of pickets this far apart,' Cleeve said, demonstrating the distance. 'Then you put these little angle wires down and make a fence of four strands of barbed wire, usually four maybe one less, one more. Understood? Speak to me! Yes or no?'

'Yes, sir!' they shouted in unison.

'Not so loud. Jesus, don't have any sense, you buggers? Listen now. Next step. At about ten or twelve feet in front and behind you, zigzag the wire through those angle irons, at an angle. Understood? An angle!' he emphasised.

A whispered, belligerent yes was heard from Dickie.

'Now, I want you, Lovelock, to work on the area we identified before. The Regent Street trench. Just imagine yourself back on that fucking posh boulevard.' He laughed. Dickie flinched. He'd get him for that.

'Ted, you're on the Kiwi Tunnelers trench. Can you see it in your heads, your positions now?' He heard a muffled yes.

'Off you go. I'm on Tipple Trench. I'll give a whistle when to return, finished or not. Bring any unused wire and equipment back with you. Army's not made of money, you know. But if you see any searchlights or hear them Huns, scarper back. Got your mallets, cutters? Face blacked up?'

'Done,' Ted said. Dickie hastily reached in the bag for the boot polish, smearing his face.

'Leave gaps in the wires but not gaps to see from them German trenches,' Dickie muttered, as he made his way over the flat fields. 'Blimey! How am I s'posed to judge that, eh, Mr. smart Alec Corp? Lions led by donkeys, for sure.'

The pearlescent moon, a faint shadow emerging and vanishing behind clouds, afforded some light beyond the distant forest to his right, stiff pines filling the horizon. A frost lay heavy on the ground, churned-up trench mud ever-present despite the January temperature. Siting his wire at an angle as directed, Dickie swore as he rolled it out, cutting lengths as he measured it then picked up the mallet and hammered one of the metal pickets into the ground before cutting the length. The noise ricocheted across the land. He froze and looked across at German territory. No lights, no commotion, no sounds at all. Breathing shallowly, he moved on to the next picket, dug into his pocket and drew out part of a jute sack which he wrapped around the mallet and tapped it more lightly this time.

Hell's teeth, this was going to take an age and the patience of a saint, he thought as he uncoiled yet more wire and moved it along the area. Running out of range in one direction he glanced at the abundant leftover wire and cursed. The cutters were not up to the job to penetrate more swathes of the stuff as he rubbed his sore, red-marked hands. He'd just bundle it up and leave it there. Heaving some into a trench, he decided to call it a night and listened for the corp's whistle. There was no sound. 'Wind's in wrong direction,' he reasoned. Shoving leftover angle irons, pickets and the mallet in his sack, he started to walk back.

The moon disappeared behind thicker clouds, scudding traces of light now gone but he could still make out the outline of bare trees in the distance.

'That's where we parked. Better be,' he muttered. 'Reach those trees and I'm home and dry.' Heaving the sack over his shoulder he ducked down when seeing lights and hearing garbled speech followed by silence, the lights extinguished.

His breath was forced as he hurried toward the treeline and safety. Stumbling in the dark his foot caught a barrage shell hole. Tumbling into a trench he slithered down the muddy bank. The heavy bundle plummeted after him, catching him on his shins. Yelping with pain, he sat for a while, dazed and muddied.

Moving gingerly, he swore, sweat pouring down his back. How was he going to climb out of this watery, stinking hell hole? There must be fire steps around, or, failing that, a dug-out he could climb into until the light. An overwhelming stench filled his lungs and he retched.

Reaching in his pocket for his Gauloises and matches, he shook one out, struck a match and lit the ground around him. A German helmet glinted in the mud, the owner's body attached to it and sprawling in water between split sandbags. Dickie gave a muffled shout then shot up, moving as fast as he could along the trench, tripping over other corpses and bags, trying to ignore his shin pain.

Clinging on to the uneven side of the trench wall, he stumbled and fell. Gibberish preceded the Lord's Prayer, some of the words remembered from childhood.

'*Our Father which art in Heaven, hallowed be thy name, lead us, lead us not, down the road to temptation.*' No, that wasn't right. What was it now? *Lead us not into temptation but deliver us, yes deliver us, deliver me from this fucking nightmare! Where are my ciggies? Still got my matches, but what's the fucking use without ciggies?*

His voice rose in the night then lowered. *No, no, mustn't panic, them Hun will butcher me! Want my old life back! Out of the army, back in London, not in this shitty, shitty, shit...want my good times, oh why ruin it?* He hunched over, covering his head, his breathing shallow, his throat dry. Muttering to himself, his mind drifted back to his old life. *Good, easy job with Harmsworth, hah! snitching his mistress from under his nose, raiding his cellar. Escape, you daft bugger! Go to ground! The lord'll get another mistress, his wine cellar topped up. And me? Out in the cold but I got away with it, escaped, didn't I? Not Wormwood again, no thanks. Hellhole prison.* He raised his head. *No, this is the real hellhole!* He beat his head with his fists then forced himself into a less painful position *Join the fucking Army! Never find me here, old Harmsworth. Bit of a laugh to start, bit of a bore driving that damned bus with all those bleedin' birds, Ted a good bloke though. Give him that. He going to spill the beans 'bout Dawkins? Christian, Ted is, but he didn't save him either. No, no fucking Christian!*

Shifting uncomfortably, he stifled the urge to shout out his jumbled thoughts. *Some tasty women around too giving me tasty food, anything I want really. Here's a bottle to see you on your way, mon cher, make sure you come back for more, you big boy, they say. Come back for more. Come back for more. I will, once I'm out of this fucking misery of a place. Marry one of 'em, settle down, buy and sell my stash, buy and sell, make a killing, those fucking bodies with their watches, their gold, them abandoned houses stuffed with goodies. Not doin' no harm. They're dead anyways! Always lucky, me, lucky ol' Dickie they call me. Smart ol' Dickie, I say. Our Father which art in Heaven, hallowed be thy name, lead us,' lead me out of here! For Chrissake! Shit, shit, shit! Just do it, Lord! Think I can't mend my ways? You watch me, Lord!*

He lit another match and saw that he had reached the dug-out. Climbing in over rubble, discarded kit and empty shells after making sure there were no bodies, he found an empty place away from the stench, talking to himself until his voice was raw and hoarse. *Jesus. Mother. Fucking beating father. No chance, dad, no fucking chance of seeing me again, want to live, I'm lucky Lovelock, I'm always fucking lucky. Aren't I? Jesus. Mother!*

He felt movement then fur brushed across his face, his mind seeing giant rats bigger than dogs, their teeth digging into his skin. Flailing wildly, he jumped up, banging his head on duckboard and fell unconscious. He did not hear Cleeve's faint whistle.

~

An army team, headed by Cleeve, found him the following day. He and Ted heaved themselves down into the trench and pulled Dickie to his feet. They helped him to the shelter of the trees, a light, wet snow falling, the vista clear of all adversarial action in the desert of shelled trees, their mutilated, carbon-burnt branches haphazardly, unintentionally signposting misery.

'Looks like a clown, all that streaked polish on 'is face,' Cleeve muttered as he grabbed Dickie's legs, Ted his upper body.

The team carried him in the truck, one of them retching at the damage rats had done to Dickie's lolling head and drove him to the nearest casualty clearing station near Arras where a doctor diagnosed pneumonia and shock. Ted remained at Dickie's bedside to see him settled and to talk to the medical officer about his prognosis. The restless, bustling hospital smelled of carbolic and decay, sounds of the sick and dying filling the air, cheerful voices of the nursing staff and patients on the mend blending in.

Ted sat on a stool by Dickie's flimsy fold-up metal bed. He counted sixteen beds down each side of the rough, wooden structure and tried to imagine each patient's reasons for taking up a bed while waiting for Dickie to wake. White blankets with a large red cross on the front gave the ward a pristine look. Four nurses, their complex white headwear cascading down the back of their grey uniforms, weaved between beds and pushed trolleys containing bandages, basins, creams and other nursing paraphernalia.

Dickie had been given an end bed away from draughty windows. His head was swathed in bandages, doctors removing most of his hair to clean the rat bites and stitch them. He had been dressed in flannel pyjamas, layers of blankets laid on top of him, and talked in his sleep, Ted catching a few words. *Harmsworth, Dawkins, damned fucking birds, get off! Lord!* Ted got up and rubbed his face.

A nurse came over to see if Dickie was awake and turned to Ted.

'You look as if you could do with a scrub and a seeing to yourself, you know, those wounds on your face getting infected, for sure if we don't look after them.'

'Barbed wire work,' Ted explained unnecessarily.

'Of course, I know,' she replied. Of course she would have.

She led him to a makeshift shower room and handed him clean clothing. 'Take off your uniform and give it to me. I'll see it's brushed clean.'

'What, now?'

'Private Digby, yes. I seen more bodies alive and dead than you've had…'

'…hot dinners! Sorry, sister.'

He undressed swiftly and handed over his clothes after emptying his pockets and stood under the shower for as long as the water remained warm. He slicked back his thick greying hair, his face shiny and polished after scrubbing hard, deeper wounds causing him to flinch. They needed to be seen to. He dressed in unfamiliar clothing.

The nurse bustled over. 'Sit over here, I'll do your dressings. Then you can have a cup of tea.' Helen. She was from Norwich and had been at the hospital for a year.

'Haven't had any home leave yet but it's the same for most of us,' she said, dipping a swab in alcohol. 'This will sting a bit.'

Ted jumped in his seat. 'Well, if that's the worst damage I'll have, I count myself a lucky devil.'

'Doesn't really count as a Blighty wound, you know,' Helen laughed. 'Desperate, they are, difficult to understand how you can do a really bad injury on yourself. But maybe you just can't take any more.'

'Don't need no Blighty wound, thanks, to get me home, been promised some leave but only when backup drivers are trained. But it could be in a month of Sundays.'

'Never mind, eh? Just be glad you might be going home one day without one or all of those missing.' She nodded towards a limbless soldier, Ted glancing at him and at another soldier with bandaged eyes.

'What about Dickie?' Ted asked as Helen cleared away. 'Think he's in a bad way, bad enough to be shipped back home?'

'Wouldn't like to say, not up to me. Duty medical officer will make that judgement.'

Ted stayed the night in rudimentary quarters adjacent to the hospital. After a proper cooked breakfast, his first in many months, he paid a visit to Dickie.

He was lying on his side facing the door, his breathing laboured, a rough cough rattling his throat. He lifted a shaky hand when hearing Ted's voice. Ted bent over him.

'How you feeling, old man? Quite the turn you gave us, not turning up yesterday. What happened to you?'

'Can't really remember. Did I blubber 'bout Dawkins?' Ted moved abruptly away.

Dickie closed his eyes. His breathing became more rapid, his body shaking.

'Best you don't make him talk, dear,' a nurse said as she pressed a towel to Dickie's face. She wiped off the sweat, patting around wounds. Ted touched Dickie's visible shoulder lightly and wandered outside.

The camp bustled with wounded soldiers, transport, supplies and motorbikes. He walked down the road, feeling a bit unsteady on his feet. Leaning against a gate, he looked out over the countryside and the road leading out of the camp.

A trail of dirt followed a motorbike. It came closer. He willed it to be Kitty. Or Dora. She'd be able to give him news of Kitty, second best. The bike slowed down, a small, slim man in the saddle.

Ted turned away and wandered back to the ward. Sister Helen broke off from paperwork and came over to him. 'Doctor would like a word with you.'

She led him over to Dickie, his pain evident.

'Hi Ted.' The voice was barely audible. Ted bent over him. 'What you doing sitting up with that cheesy grin on you, you dunderhead!'

'I...I... just...' Dickie had a coughing fit, Helen helping him to water. A doctor came over, took Ted by the elbow and led him away.

'He says he wants to leave, go back to the bus, doesn't want to go to the bigger hospital for treatment for his pneumonia.' The doctor paused and looked over at Dickie's bed.

'He's fit enough but he's in a rotten way after nearly 20 hours in a waterlogged trench, and he's probably got an infection too from the stagnant water and those stinking bodies. He can't and won't want to' – he laughed abruptly – 'return to work. But he's quite agitated, seems to be champing at the bit to be on the move, back on his bus, very attached to it. Quite commendable!'

Ted looked over at Dickie. Stupid bugger. 'I am stumped too, doctor,' he lied. 'You'd think he would want a rest from all this, 'specially what happened to him, terrible for mind and body. I just…' He paused. 'I'll tell the corporal he might be re-joining the bus when he can but when he's well enough. That might help calm him.'

'You know him better than we do, I daresay. But we can't let him go until he's good and ready. As for you, there's no infection so back to work for you.' He gave a rueful smile.

Before making his way to find transport to take him back to the pigeon loft, Ted walked over to say goodbye to Dickie.

'Don't worry about you and the bus, old man. See you on board very soon.' He winked and Dickie gave a faint knowing smile. He touched the side of his nose twice and tried to wink before coughing.

~

Dickie re-joined the bus three weeks later laden with parcels. He had lost weight but not his swagger. 'Well, here I am, you lot. Good to see you. How are those birds of yours, Ralph? Champion, I bet.'

Ralph grinned faintly.

'And Ted, any news of that leave yet?'

'No, not yet, Dickie. Welcome back, I'm sure. You're looking rather thin, feeling up to working again? Don't strain yourself too much first few days, a week maybe.'

'Don't fuss so, my mate. I'm topping, and so is Helen. Fine gal if ever there was one. Fit as a fiddle. Know what I mean?' He gave an amused bark. 'Now, must go and put these away, been on a bit of a shopping trip.'

Picking up his packages, he walked to the bus and closed the partition. Ted heard him coughing then restless snoring came from the bottom deck. He wondered why Dickie had been released from hospital.

The following day a vehicle drove up, a sergeant alighting, followed by a sallow figure, a slight man no more than twenty. 'Show private Bracey the ropes, Ted. This is John Bracey. He's your replacement during your week's leave. Starting tomorrow.'

Looking Ted up and down, he added, 'That's a shocking old uniform, Ted, to travel in. Go to stores and get a less worn one. Yours is for the bonfire. Give a good example for the army at home, eh?'

Ted choked out a welcome to Bracey then turned to hide his tears.

Chapter 28: Home Front

February, 1918

'The sergeant sent for me. He says, 'Private,' he says, 'I've just received this morning intimation from the War Office that leave can be started now. I've chosen you to be one of our first to go home for four days to England, on leave.' I took off my hat – steel helmets weren't invented then – and I put my Army-issue hat on the bankside and put a bullet through it. So that when I went home back to England wearing a hat with a bullet hole through I could say, 'That was a near one.' And that's what I did.'

Ted caught the mail cart taking him as far as Chocques station. As he waited on the platform, he glanced at his reflexion in a window. Norah would have a go at him for losing bulk, a gaunt face staring back at him. An old photograph, the image of his father returning from Mafeking, came to mind.

'Come to this, Ted, lad, it's come to this, looking like your dad now,' he muttered under his breath. 'Whatever can Kitty see in me? Just an old turnip, me.'

Turning swiftly away, he looked down at his boots, mud clinging to the sides. A clean-up on the boat to try to rid them of the many layers of dried, dung-coloured heavy clay, was called for. Might as well play the soldier walking through his front door. Home. But first get rid of the lice.

Hunting for his house key before leaving the bus brought him out in a cold sweat. He removed belongings from the locked box under his bed and scattered them over the scruffy flooring. Finding the key, he whooped. Fingering it during the journey home reassured him he'd get in, just in case Norah and Ruby were both at work. There was no time to tell them when he'd arrive, not even the day or week, even month, the sergeant just springing it on him. He couldn't imagine how the sallow, new recruit would be able to stand up to the likes of Dickie but that was his problem. Now for Boulogne to catch the boat to Folkestone, then the first train to London, the journey eating away into his time.

On the way over to the war with Billy, the young chap had been seasick, the bus still painted red and with its Shepherd's Bush destination on the front. Charles Hawtrey's show was advertised on the side, Hayward's Military Pickle on the other side. Now Billy was dead, a father too, although he never knew it. The bus was now a grey, unwieldy pigeon loft with carbuncle structures on both sides of the top deck, pigeon shit covering the top flooring. Shrapnel had hit sides of the bus and the headlamps hadn't worked for over a year.

Boarding the train, he watched the French countryside go by, marvelling at the few signs of war as he neared the coast, villages seemingly untouched by disaster, people with baskets combing the markets for produce. But looking more closely at the stalls, he noticed few vegetables or meat. Although neat and tidy, people looked threadbare, thin.

As the French shoreline receded, Ted stayed on deck for most of the journey to Folkstone, buttoning his uniform up to the neck to ward off the chill February air, the jacket a size too large, allowing a freshening sea-wind to spiral down his back. It seemed so strange to be on moving transportation he wasn't in charge of, with no difficult passengers to control, no mud to trample through or brush off. Taking off his cap as gusts blew harder, his thick hair whipped around in whirling dervish fashion. A sudden drenching squall forced him into the fug of the buffet where he drank a lacklustre cup of tea and smoked a cigarette.

Arriving at Victoria Station late afternoon, he waited for a bus to the East End, feeling a lump in his throat seeing so many red buses charging in different directions: Lambeth, Battersea, Kensal Rise, Regent's Park, Oxford Street, Putney, Westminster. Joining the crowd of people queuing for buses, he curbed his natural instinct to head to the driver's seat when a bus came along. There was an angry rush to get on board before it halted at the stop, Ted drawing back, his kitbag squashed in the melée.

'Come on, my soldier, you've done your bit, you get on first.' Ted turned to his benefactor, an elderly woman who pushed forward with her basket, caught hold of the rail and cried, 'Let the soldier on first!' The crowds parted, some clapping him on the back.

Ted hid his tears and managed a faint 'Thank you, ta ever so, thank you very much!' Walking upstairs, he found a seat facing forward, his kitbag on his lap. He wanted to see London again, feel at home once more.

His pride turned to dismay as the bus passed Zeppelin damage done to the Lyceum Theatre and along the route in Holborn too. Rubble and twisted metal lay in swathes down residential streets, a school lying in ruins. London showed off its suffering from the top deck.

Getting off a fair distance from home to stretch his legs, he turned into Saxon Road, staring at it as if discovering it for the first time. He passed neighbour's homes, gas lamps, one or two with torn notices, battered bicycles leaning up against railings, a discarded child's hoop lying on the road. Their home appeared unchanged, the windows perhaps not as clean as usual and the flower box was missing from the front room's window sill.

Reaching for his key, he turned it in the lock. There was no need for it, the door was unlocked. All was quiet. No child charged from the kitchen, no smell of soup drifted from the kitchener. Norah usually had a ham bone stewing away for stock, or vegetable peelings when the end of the month was reached. Bending down to take off his dirty boots, he took them and his dirty kit bag to the scullery.

Removing his socks, he opened the garden door and stepped outside. The shed door looked in good nick but needed a coat of paint, a chore he would do during his leave. Maybe he'd turn over the remaining beds if they yielded to the shovel, help plant some early seeds with Norah. Maybe put the net up for the fruit and vegetable crops to keep the birds off. Or was it too early? Norah would know. He went back into the scullery to retrieve his dirty boots and kitbag to clean them later in the garden, sat down on the bench and yawned.

He awoke when he heard Norah's voice. 'It's freezing in here! Did you leave the garden door open, Ruby?'

He sprang up. 'No, it was me, dear.'

Norah cried out and ran to the garden, Ted taking in her rust coloured hair. It made her look odd, thin, tired. Old. He stretched out his arms, not sure what to do.

'Ted! Ruby, it's Dad, in the garden!' Putting her hands over her face, she burst into tears. Ruby joined them and threw her arms around him.

Will appeared at the doorway, tried to bounce down the small step and screamed. Ted released himself and looked at the child, wiping away tears. Ruby picked Will up and walked back to her parents.

'This is Will, dad. How long you got, Dad, how long?'

He didn't reply but took Will from her, lifted him in the air and laughed.

'Never long enough. Never,' he finally said, looking at his grandson.

~

Norah made a scratch dinner and set it before Ted and Ruby after Will was put to bed despite Ted's protests but the child had become cranky. Ruby whisked him off upstairs. 'You can make a fuss over him tomorrow, Dad, when Mum and I are out at work.'

'Ruby, really, you can't ask your Dad to look after him,' Norah said with alarm. 'He wouldn't know what to do! That's a woman's job and you know it! He'll go through to Ethel's as usual.'

258

'You have to work tomorrow, both of you?' Ted asked.

Norah ladled the vegetable and lentil soup into bowls. 'We didn't know you was coming back, dear, did we? Got to give them notice, but maybe in special times...' her voice trailed off.

Ruby re-joined them and sat next to Norah. She wanted to see her father opposite her, sitting down, at home, not out of the side of her eyes. 'Oh, tired little man. Went right to sleep.'

She helped herself to some bread. 'Work, it's not easy. We'll try, Dad, but with so many men going...'she paused. 'And now the married men too, them who's fit. They have to, we're seeing them go already.'

'What? But it was only singles having to sign up!' Ted said, tucking his napkin under his chin.

'Dad, you're in the thick of it! You should know! Last week, now all the marrieds too, and I can tell you, they're not happy about it, 'specially the older ones. Set in their ways. But if they got no problems, no two left feet, they go.'

Ruby nudged her mother sitting next to her. 'And we get their jobs!' She laughed.

'I'm not ambitious like you, dear, happy with my lot but could do with another day off, for sure, to catch up around here.' Norah replied.

'Why, dear?' Ted raised his head from the soup bowl. 'Doesn't Ruby pull her weight? Only teasing, mind, Ruby!'

'No, she does, of course. She's a good girl, our daughter. Goes out a lot, mind, always out with chums evenings. But then she always puts Will down first, good mother, she is.'

Tears sprang in Ted's eyes, a lump in his throat preventing him eating the chunky soup. He stared into his bowl. Norah had decanted the last of the preserved tomatoes into the soup to bulk up the meal she and Ruby would have been sharing that evening and had found the remains of a brisket bone in the cool box. The meat, still clinging to the bone, was added to the soup for a richer flavour.

Norah looked over at him. 'Don't you like it, love?'

Ted coughed. 'It's the best meal I've in a long time,' he whispered.

'So, what don't you eat these days, Dad? Bet you go to some of them fancy places the French like, eat food we never had. Hear they eat things like snails. Imagine!'

'Not fancy, really, called *estaminets*, simple food, eggs, omelettes with mushrooms and cheese my favourite, good bread, wine a bit rough.'

'Wine! You drink wine!' Norah looked over at him. Ted picked up his spoon and finished his soup.

'Sometimes,' he said between mouthfuls. 'We do get some time off, you know, that poor old bus been down so many roads, over and over again, zigzagging all over the shop. We get to know all the cafés, owners, good blokes, most of 'em. Now pigeons upstairs with Ralph, told you 'bout Ralph in my letters, he...'

'Yes, Dad, I read them too. Know all about him.' Ruby got up and cleared her bowl. She brought some cheese over with pickle.

'Ethel, now, she's a good sort. Looks after Will, and her own. Gets a good chunk of my wages though. But don't know what we'd do without her. Don't get no attention from Billy's family, only seen the kid once, when he was born.'

Norah finished her soup and picked up Ted's bowl. 'That's because Billy's house was damaged, they had to move away, to Essex or somewhere, isn't it, Ruby?'

'And half their street. That reminds me, Mum. Hannah, you know Hannah Collins?'

She looked at Ted. 'She works with me. Her middle sister Lillian managed to get a job as a clerk to a photographic slide manufacturer. Man's work! We're going places, women, for sure.'

Ted sat back in his chair and looked at her. How could someone change so much? In so little time? He glanced at Norah. Had she changed too, underneath her yellow pallor? Early days, Ted, take it easy, don't jump to wrong thoughts. You've just arrived home. What would Kitty think of him here? In the midst of his family? They had an understanding, a shorthand to communicate. Here, it was like walking in a mire, an ocean of incomprehension. He looked down at his empty plate.

Norah pushed the cheese over to Ted, got a spoon for the chutney from the drawer and passed it to him. He took a breath and glanced at Ruby.

'I'm impressed, dear. Don't know Lillian but she sounds just like you in a way.' Ruby grinned.

'Them French girls get jobs like this, Ted?' Norah said.

'I don't know, dear, never meet them, but do meet some nurses, British girls, one from Norwich not long ago, Helen, fine woman, looked after Dickie when he was carted off to hospital after he fell in....'

'Spare us the details, Dad, we got enough to be getting on with here. Mum and me been to see a few films to feel less, well, down with it all. We seen, oh, what's the last Chaplin one, *The Bank,* wasn't it?'

'Double bill one with *The Tramp,* do you mean?'

Ted fidgeted. 'No films where we are, like to see one maybe if there's time. We make our own entertainment mostly, my harp, sing-alongs, sometimes an army evening do with,' he paused. 'Oh, you never guess who came to one of them northern towns, near Belgium!'

'Who, dear?' Norah smiled.

'Ivor Novello, he played the piano. In a bombed hall, for the soldiers.'

He went into the scullery, picked up his harp from his satchel and launched in to *Keep the Home Fires Burning.*

Ruby joined Norah on the bench and moved from side to side and sang.

~

That night in bed, Ted didn't settle. He got up and moved to the floor to sleep. The bed was too soft and he found Norah's closeness claustrophobic. Wrapping a spare blanket from the foot of the bed around himself, he finally slept after mulling over the last few days' events. How could life have changed so much in just three years? Or was he being naïve? Kitty often teased him that he was an innocent abroad at times. Ruby seemed so old, so poised, in control. Norah, now, there was a difference with her too, the wind taken out of her sails, her skin ochre yellow against the brass tint of her hair. He'd have a word about dyeing her hair, didn't suit her one bit.

Norah woke him with a cup of tea. Putting it on the chest of drawers, she bent down.

'Dear, I must go to work. Will's next door with Ethel but you can take him out to the park, a lovely day for February. Ruby and I will try to get some leave. Don't know if we can but we'll give it a go.'

Ted sat up and scratched his two-day old beard. 'I'll come with you. Don't want to miss a minute with you and Ruby. Then I'll come back and Will and I can go to Victoria Park to see the ducks.'

He dressed hurriedly, rummaging around for clean civvies which Norah had packed carefully away in the wardrobe. Throwing on a heavy long jacket over a shirt and tie, he hastily tied his brogues after pulling on his trousers. Slicking his hair back in the scullery with water following a quick wash, he downed cold tea left over from their early start. The beard would have to wait until he found a barber on the way back from the Arsenal. Picking up his cap and a scarf from the peg, he put them jauntily on. Norah giving him a shy smile.

His confidence weakened as he walked alongside Norah and Ruby, not knowing what to say, how to act. Ruby put an arm around him. 'Come on, Mum, you do the same!'

Norah followed suit, Ted spread his arms around them, tightening his grip on both women, not wishing to let go. Ruby was as plump as Norah was thin, too thin.

Ruby said, 'Dad, you going to grow a beard? Might suit you, you know. What do you think, Mum?' Norah glanced up at him. 'Hmm, maybe.'

'Not likely, dear, not allowed for a start.' he gave Ruby a grin. 'I'll get a shave at Victor's before the park. It'll be gone when I see you next.'

Norah let go of Ted. 'Victor's not there, Ted, shop bombed, happened in the night, few weeks ago, the flat demolished. He and Elena, well…' her voice faltered.

Victor. The elderly Italian had been like an uncle to him. Ted had visited him just before he left for the Front to say goodbye, Victor giving him a good trim and a talking to.

'Mind you look after your mind, and your man's body!' when handing him some French letters by the passage leading to the door. Ted had laughed, shocked at this uncharacteristic gesture. He now felt sick. Yet more change.

Recalling the contraceptive's uses, he blushed, removing his grip around Ruby. 'That's too bad, too bad! Victor, never done nobody harm, ever.'

They arrived at the Arsenal, Ted promising to meet them when they had finished work. Ruby flung herself at him, hugging him, her jaunty step receding into the maze of roads within the armaments complex. Norah waved goodbye, walked away then turned back to see Ted.

'Until tonight!' she called, smiled shyly, waved again and entered the sturdy Arsenal Gatehouse with its hinting clock and zealous flagpole. He watched her thin figure until she disappeared.

Ted made his way to Victor's on Bow Road and examined the smoke and wood damage to the barbershop. Bending down, he read a notice on the door – CLOSED INDEFINITE – and stood looking at the shop recalling their many chats while the barber whittled down his dark hair. Victor was the first to notice grey hairs taking root, his English not improving over the decades he knew him. '*Ma lei è ancora giovane!* Too young, you are for this *capelli grigi*!' showing him a cluster of grey strands.

Walking away, he wandered down side streets, not really caring where he went before recalling his need to find another barber for a shave and haircut. Passing a row of shops, a flame-damaged pole caught his eye, the familiar red and white painted spiral shaft in need of painting or replacing. The name above the door was roughly abbreviated from Pohlman to Patch. Patch, Harry, prop.

He studied the worn exterior and peered in the window. Two barbers' chairs and a bench for waiting customers and two basins filled the small interior. Shelving housed jars, lathering, shaving bowls and brushes, razors, towels and an array of scissors. The new proprietor had not totally erased the previous owner's nationality, gold Gothic etched lettering still visible on one of the mirrors. The business looked clean enough, though.

Was this the German barbershop he and, oh, what was the soldier's name, the soldier he helped on board to join other prisoners, talked about? His cousin owned a business somewhere nearby. Ernest. No, Ernst! Ernst. He entered. A short, fat man around fifteen years his senior emerged from the back room, rubbing his hands on a towel.

'Wet shave, sir, and how's about a trim?'

Ted hesitated then sat down in the swivel chair the barber had whisked clean with his towel. Rubbing his rough chin, he replied, 'Thank you. Yes, two-day old stubble never looked good on anyone.'

'You're right there, sir.'

The barber threw a towel with practised ease around his client's neck and shoulders.

Ted sank back in the chair, enjoying the odd sensation of someone looking after him, just him, no rows of soldiers lining up to have shave and cut, and no salty language or sham jocularity.

He watched the barber preparing the lather, a thick pure white foam emerging from the shaving bowl. A stout, thick brush, heavy with foam, was applied to Ted's jaw and cheeks.

'Fine day, sir, for a February. Any plans?' Ted was silent, trying to formulate his thoughts. Well, no, he didn't have to drive a bus past convoys of soldiers going one way, prisoners-of-war trudging the other way, ambulances tooting to clear the way. Nor did he have to deal with Dickie and an increasingly silent Ralph, finding the next meal or locating a remote area for the best place to send and receive messages from the Front. No filthy latrines, either and no lice.

'Cat got your tongue, sir?' The barber's voice jolted him into the present.

'No, no, sorry, well, I'll take my grandson to the park, Victoria Park, the best in the area. Bit parky but I'm sure he'll love it.'

'Yes, sir, it is, your grandson a lucky chap indeed to have a grandfather like you.'

Ted gave a sharp laugh. 'He will be, got to get to know him. Never clapped my eyes on him 'til yesterday.'

'Oh, that right?' the barber looked at Ted in the mirror.

'Just back from the Front, away when he was born. Thinks I'm a battering ram already!'

'So, at the Front, eh? Terrible, terrible. Not what it was 'sposed to be, over in a jiffy.'

The barber reached for a cut-throat razor and began shaving Ted, his deft, slow movements soothing and comforting.

Ted was silent again, thinking of Ernest. Ernst. Was he still alive? Was this his cousin's business at one time? He pointed to the Gothic script carefully etched at the top of a mirror, the beautiful lettering at odds with the rest of the interior.

'Harry, you Harry, the owner?' The barber nodded.

Ted pointed to the script. 'Why is that there?'

'Used to be a German who worked here. Owned it. Now interned, like the rest of the Hun. Good riddance I say. Just like you must feel, soldier. You seen what they're like up close. We see them flying around in them Zeppelins in these parts, monsters, all of 'em.'

He flicked lather into the sink and began shaving Ted's right cheek. He stopped and pointed to the script. 'Know what that means, Sir?'

'Yes, I do. *Gott Mit Uns.* God is with us.'

'Think they own the world, they do. They don't. We're the superior ones. Right, sir?'

Ted remained silent, his eyes closed. He opened them when the remaining lather was removed.

'How's that, sir? Close enough for you?'

Ted rubbed his chin. Smooth as a baby. He looked in the mirror. Those barbed wire scratches still dominated part of his chin, but the skin had hardened, a second layer now beginning to form.

'Good,' he replied. 'Now just a trim, nothing too short, Harry, or my missus won't know me.'

The barber motioned him to the basin. Ted leaned over, his hair brusquely washed.

During a towel dry, he asked, 'What happened around here anyways?'

'Riots. Them Russians was punished, anyone with a foreign name, but really people looked for German shops to stone, to burn, to throw bricks at. Ol' Pohlman was dragged away, crowds shouting at him, pretty nasty it got. I hear he's not far away, not like most of them foreigners, shipped off to the Isle of Man. He got lucky, just in Islington, detention camp, not far enough away for my liking.'

Harry clipped Ted's fringe. 'Short enough for you, Sir?'

Ted nodded. 'What? Interned near here?'

'Yes sir. The funny thing is old Pohli, roly poly, as I like to call him, he's making limbs for our soldiers there,' he snorted. 'Serve 'em right, I say.'

'You buy the business from him, then?' Harry stopped cutting and held up his scissors.

'What do you think? Not bloody likely!'

Ted was silent for a while, watching the barber in the mirror as he bent over his customer.

'My wife, she worked at the German Hospital, in the laundry. Well treated, she was, German manager very kind to his staff.'

Harry's head came up, his look belligerent. 'She German, your wife, then?'

'No! English as you and me, just saying they're not all bad 'uns. Hard-working, clean, correct. Least, that's how she found 'em.'

'Now all them lot been rounded up too, from the hospital, I bet. Wonder how they like the bracing Isle of Man air!'

Ted's collar was swept of hair, the towel removed. The barber held out his hand, Ted reaching in his pocket for loose change. Opening the door to let Ted out, he said firmly, 'I sees it as poetic justice. Them Germans killed my father. Boer War. Tit for tat. They gets everywhere, not here though. English around here.'

'You got your work cut out for you,' Ted replied. 'Any thoughts about them Jews living round here?'

Harry turned his back on him, flicked Ted's hairs from the chair with the towel and started to clean the sink with its ends.

Ted walked briskly to the bus depot on Shrublands Drive, passing damaged shops, cursing the war and people like Harry, their kneejerk reaction towards foreigners. Hurt first, ask questions later. Or not at all.

Pausing at the entrance he looked around before entering the canteen, Mrs. Dillon, the cook and a girl, a server he didn't recognise were behind the counter. He took off his cap. Mrs. Dillon gave a shout. Frank Titcomb, his bus partner, looked up and grinned.

'Ted, Ted! Me old mate!' Frank stood up from his bench, upsetting it. Leaving it where it had fallen, he walked quickly over to Ted, took his hands and pumped them up and down.

'Here, steady on, Frank!' Ted laughed.

Mrs. Dillon left her kitchen and came over. 'Ted, me old darlin', how are you?'

'Mrs. Dillon, I...' Ted smiled broadly and shook her hand. 'Wonderful, wonderful to see you.'

'I'll get you a cup of tea and nice piece of fruit cake. No eggs, mind, can't get 'em for love or money. Tasty, though!'

Ted and Frank walked back to the bench, uprighted it and sat down.

'How'd you get out of the hellhole, Ted? Is it for good? You coming back to join us? We miss you something terrible.'

He added 'By the way, you don't look too bad, all considering, them marks on your face, though, nasty. How'd you get them? Had a bit of a trip to the barber's, I see, always were a handsome devil.'

'Maybe compared to you, my old friend!' Ted joked, punching him on the arm.

'Here, mind you don't spill my tea! Anyways, how long you got or, well, what's happenin', Ted?'

'Got 'til Saturday, then back I go, drivers needed, ones with experience, the geezer who's replaced me, well, he's something else. Don't know how they train 'em but them inspectors shouldn't have signed him off for another month or two. No experience and, really, don't want to be there in first place, conscription not always the way to go in my mind. Least we really wanted to go, beginning of the war.'

'And now?' Frank asked

'How can I put it, Frank? Something you wouldn't wish on your worst enemy. Not by a long chalk. No.'

Mrs. Dillon interrupted with Ted's tea and cake. 'How's your Norah then? Hear you're now grandparents, that Ruby, well, always was a good-looker. And smart.'

'Not smart enough, finding herself in the family way so young,' Ted said. 'But he's a beaut, a fine lad. Takes after his dad, my young driver, killed. Gassed.'

'We heard tell,' Frank said. 'Nice lad, I'm sure, Ted. What a way to go and all. We lost a few drivers from here, you remember Clifford, Arthur, oh, and the Kelly brothers, both of 'em? George and Howard are still out there.'

'Kind of out of step who's who now, Frank, you see my bus…'

'And then there's Den, Den Quinnell, Irish git, he's out there too and Joe's turned into a conchie. Him and a few others took it upon themselves to say they're more Christian than most! Can you believe it? Albert says he's short-sighted, be useless in battle anyways.' Frank laughed and punched the table. 'How the hell does he get away with driving a bus, for god's sakes?'

Ted listened to the gossip around the depot, the happenings in the area, the anger at the beer being lowered in strength, Percy's missus running off with a black man ('but I don't believe it. Who'd do a thing like that?'), the price of coal, sugar shortages. 'And to cap it all, Ted, we're asked to do more shifts and work with women conductors! I ask you!'

'Women are good workers, I met a...'Ted protested.

Frank got up and put his cap on. He offered a handshake. 'Ted, can't believe the time's gone by so swift, look at the ticker! Got a bus to drive. See you before you go, eh? Want to hear more about it. Don't be a stranger! Thanks for the tea, Mrs. D!'

Ted sighed and pushed his tea away. He felt like an outsider. Walking across the yard to the staircase inside the hangar, he climbed the stairs to the manager's door and knocked.

'Come!'

Ted took off his cap and opened the door. 'Mr. Craven, I...'

A young man looked up from the desk. 'Hullo? Mr. Craven, you're seeking? Gone, had a heart attack last year, retired now. Can I help?'

'I'm Ted. Ted Digby. I drive, drove buses for the depot. Out in the Front now and just hoping to see my old boss, a good mate.'

'Oh, hullo Mr. Digby. No, as I've said, no Mr. Craven here now. I've taken on his job, can't help you then. Look, sorry, mate, please shut the door behind you. And...and mind how you go!' he called after him.

Ted walked slowly down the stairs and out of the depot. Walking back home along city streets rather than the planned detour to Victoria Park, he opened the front door with a sigh and sat down in the kitchen. Making himself a cup of tea, he took it outside, finding the house warm, suffocating. He drank it without tasting the strong brew, then tossed the remainder into the winter beds.

Walking over to the shed, he lifted the latch and peered inside. Shutting it abruptly, he sat down on the garden bench he'd made. His, Norah's and Ruby's initials had been roughly carved into its back. He traced them with his fingers over and over again, then felt more initials when shifting to catch the moving sun. One was a deep, rough B, the other a W. He outlined the B, stroking it, removing tiny twigs and dirt. Good girl, Ruby. But where did he belong now? Kitty would know. Would Norah?

Stretching out on the bench he fell asleep, his dreams obscure, frightening, no comfort found in reveries, every twist and turn tinged with sadness, dismay and anger, distorted, ugly, raw faces from France appearing and disappearing. Gasping for air, he sat up, covered in sweat, lay down again, drew his jacket around him and curled into a ball.

He fell asleep again, the adjacent church bell waking him. Getting up, he had a wash and returned to the garden shed. It was in disarray, nothing put back on shelving he had put up and marked TOOLS, TWINE, NAILS, SEEDS, LABELS, LARGE CLAY POTS, BEDDING POTS, PAINTS, BRUSHES. His bike, hanging up in the corner, was covered in cobwebs, a few slugs attached to the wheels and handlebar.

Taking off his jacket, he rolled up his sleeves and set to work, emptying the shed, sweeping it clean, checking the door hinges for rust and treating them with oil. He hammered some more nails into the shelving to make them stronger. A pile of items to discard landed on the grass before he repaired roof panels. Replacing the remaining items, he surveyed the shelving. Scowling, he removed everything, checked them for cracks, for damage, each nail in the box scrutinised for any rust or imperfection. All the shelving was dismantled, the floor and walls swept again, the roof inspected for water damage. He stared at the stains formed on part of the roof and one side from the neighbour's overhanging mulberry bush.

Reaching for a stiff brush, he fetched a bucket of water, stood on an upturned box and scrubbed the roof until his hands and shoulders were sore. The marked side resembled ugly purple blemishes the colour of wounded flesh, rotting skin and bone. He got another bucket of water and scoured these until the wood had been returned to its natural pine.

The shelving, side by side, military fashion on the grass, was scrubbed of all marks. Rusted paint pot rings, flecks and daubs of paint, tool and clay pot markings all went, his shirt, his arms and upper torso wet with water and sweat.

He re-built the shelves, placing them in the exact position they had been for the past twenty years, filled them again and stood back to survey his work. The labels would have to be re-done. Picking up the labels, he placed them face down on empty shelving and dug into the thick paper with a broad black pencil, tracing the lettering over again until each word stood out boldly, assertively. It was now easy to find short nails in the sorted-out tins, each label tacked on their appointed place, the corners hammered in. After hanging his cleaned, oiled bike with its pumped-up tyres on a new, larger set of hooks, he returned to the doorway to look at his efforts. Satisfied, he picked out a wide paint brush, located the primer and painted the outside wood. Reaching down for the tin of green paint, he coated each side with diligence. He hadn't noticed that the sun had long set, moonlight illuminating the quiet garden. Nor did he hear Norah or Ruby returning home.

'Hello, dear.' Ted looked up, startled, when Norah appeared. 'What are you doing home so early? Coming to fetch you, I was! Are you feeling alright, my love?'

'It's past 8.30, Ted.'

He put down his paint brush. 'Oh. Caught up in what I was doing, love. Dear, can't be!'

Ruby joined them. 'Dad, we waited for you, waited an hour. We thought something had happened to you. Get back, all safe and as well as can be expected from the war, then you just disappear. Haven't seen you for over three years and look what happens!'

Ted moved over to the bench and sat down. He put his head in his hands.

'Everything's a bit, well…' Norah came over and sat with him.

'Doesn't matter dear, just as you're alright.'

'It's not alright, Mum. Dad promised to take Will to the park. He painted the shed instead. I don't know! And Will's still at Ethel's, poor dear!' She turned and went into the house, slamming the door behind her

Chapter 29: Home Front

February, 1918

Ighty iddley ighty/ Carry me back to Blighty/ Blighty is the place for me/ Put me on the train for London town/ Drop me anywhere/ I don't care! If it's Piccadilly, The Strand or Leicester Square. All I want to see is my best girl/ Cuddling up again we soon should be/ So it's ighty iddley ighty/ Take me back to Blighty/ Blighty is the place for me! Florrie Ford song.

Ted woke up early on the third day of his leave, recalling where he was. He turned over and remembered with a jolt that Norah and Ruby were able to spend the day with him.

'Dad, the Arsenal does have a heart,' Ruby declared at last night's supper after struggling to talk to him, 'but it doesn't show it often! Special time off, 'cause of you.'

The night before, Ted had joined Norah in bed, only her rust coloured hair visible above the sheets. She had gone to bed early, he had followed soon after. Was she awake or pretending to be asleep? He slid under the covers and lay there for a few minutes before turning over, nudging his body closer to hers.

She lay rigid before murmuring, 'Ted, oh, Ted, I don't know anything anymore, just hold me.'

He kissed her, the memory of his nights with Kitty taking over. Her willingness to have the kind of sex he had always craved filled him with sense of betrayal, of shame but also with satisfaction before the urge to enjoy the same kind of carnal pleasure with Norah took over.

'Norah,' he whispered, 'how's about we do it this way?' He pulled up her nightie, past her thighs to her breasts and kissed them softly before moving up to her neck and mouth, his urgent, hard grasp on her breasts making her cry out.

Tearing off her nightdress, he entered her, thrusting himself with a ferocity neither of them had experienced together, Norah fighting him off before giving in without pleasure.

Later, after a muttered 'sorry, dear, don't know myself these days,' he moved onto the floor with a pillow and spare blanket before falling asleep. She had kicked off the covers in the night which landed on him, awakening him from a troubled sleep.

In the dark, his mind raced: his meeting with Frank, the barber's hatred and distrust of anyone foreign, the conchies who wouldn't fight for King and Country, their weak reasons for not taking up arms against the enemy. And what of Ralph's experiences as a soldier? How it had affected him, now unable to communicate to anyone, just his pigeons. Who was right? Maybe everyone should become a conchie, live peacefully under the Boches. Norah had worked with them, found them an agreeable, kind type: efficient, clean, slightly rigid perhaps. These thoughts were crowded out by the sight of Dawkins, his hands moving, his eyes pleading, the smell of the sergeant's graveyard-to-be. Stifling a cry, he rubbed the sweat off from his chest and groin with his hands and blanket and lay face up in the dark listening to Norah's restless sleep.

Getting up, he folded his blanket and Norah's discarded nightie and dressed before tiptoeing downstairs past Ruby's and Will's door. Picking up his cigarettes and matches on the way to the garden, he lit a cigarette and pushed back his shirt sleeve to study the time. Ruby had adjusted his watch last night to British Time with relish. 'You're home now, Dad,' she had said softly. Almost dawn. He'd go for bike ride before they woke up. Maybe go up as far as the Grand Union Canal up northwest or to the Limehouse basin in the east and reach the Thames.

Reaching for his bike in the shed, he lifted it down from its hook and left by the side gate. He was unaware of Norah watching him from the window as he mounted and cycled away.

He returned two hours later, red-faced, shins aching, to find Norah and Ruby in the kitchen, Will making a happy sound as he greeted his grandfather.

Ruby helped Will with his porridge. 'Morning, dad.'

Ted bent down to kiss Will and gave Ruby a peck on the cheek. He went across to Norah muttering quietly, 'morning. What you making, dear?'

'Mutton stew, using some of the pearl barley, some carrots, for tea.'

Ruby looked up from wiping Will's mouth. 'Specially for you, dad.'

Ted smiled gratefully at her. He swiftly blurted out a few cheerful words, more than he felt.

'Dear, your mother and I are tackling the garden for an hour, after breakfast. Then we'll go to the park. And the day will be special for Will too. Have something to eat in the pavilion when we're peckish. What do you say?'

He and Norah got to work on the beds for spring planting, the conversation desultory, stilted. Each shovel, forced into the untended hard ground, sounded in Ted's head with a *Daw-kins! Daw-kins! Daw-kins!* until he could no longer bear it.

He threw down his shovel when he smelt the bright, sickly unnatural-looking marigolds which Norah had planted last year. Now a dark brown hue mottled with age, their pungent aroma reminded him of putrid wounds, making him retch, Norah not asking why. She picked up the dead flowers and threw them on the compost heap.

Ted opened the shed door and studied the seed packets of Brussels sprouts, onions, carrots, potatoes and peas for spring planting. They would stay there for Norah to plant in a more forgiving soil, their delicate tendrils growing up on the latticework against the wall separating home from church property, but he would not be here to see them.

274

He went inside after murmuring to Norah, 'Let's go, dear,' washed his hands, put on clean boots and a warm jacket and called out 'Ready, everyone, for the park?' He carried Will on his shoulders, Ruby pushing her son up on his padded backside when he slackened his grip on his grandfather. Norah beside her. The park was crowded, even for a weekday. Uniformed men and women walked or lounged in the park, collars up against a chill wind.

Ruby pointed at the soldiers, 'Dad, you should be in uniform too, so we can be proud!'

'Ruby, sometimes a change is as good as a rest,' he frowned at her.

The uniform had been folded away for Norah's sake. After last night, she might be glad to see the back of him. He stifled the thought of putting on the full kit the day after next, the jacket's rough material chafing him on the neck, leaving permanent marks. Norah wouldn't touch the blemished skin.

They joined nursing staff pushing elderly patients and children taking advantage of the bright winter's day. Ted recalled how French and Belgian children dressed, contrasting their cut of clothing and footwear. He was used to seeing neat *tabliers* over boys' and girls' garments, hearing their muddied boots or *sabots* clacking along cobblestones. These young ones at home lacked the pinched, sallow look, a tougher breed, but the boys' Norfolk jackets looked far too jaunty, out of keeping with war. The children's white socks tumbled towards ankles during their skipping or running down park paths. He clutched his grandson's chubby arms tightly. Feeling Will's weight, he winched him off then crouched down beside the teetering child, pointing out birds of many colours at the aviary, Will favouring any yellow ones.

Ruby raced ahead to claim one of pavilion's tables tea rooms. It was as if nothing had changed, Ted feeling alienated despite the familiar surroundings. They sat over their cakes and tea, conversation laboured despite attempts at normality. Ruby broke one of the many silences with an assured voice.

'Dad, I've joined a union, a women's federation one and been to meetings with my friend Frances. She's the one who talked me into it, remember? From my letters? They're good people and Arsenal's fine with it, helps, in fact, big changes now for working women.'

Ted nodded. 'Dear, most enterprising of you.' He turned to Norah for her comment. Wintery sunlight, shining through the bay window, caught her hair and skin, making her look more fragile than ever.

'Bless you for writing so often, Norah. Can't tell you how much we all love that time of day or week when the sergeant comes up with a bundle of 'em. We almost shove the others out of the way, trample over 'em to read news from home. I've kept the lot, I have, stashed in the bus. Will'll be able to read 'em when he's a granddad, show him how much he's welcome in the family.' But no feelings came to him when spouting these well-meaning words, all waffle.

Ruby stiffened. 'Yes, I'm sure he'll be interested. What his nan and grandad wrote, but in what his mother did too, doing now, right now, dad. Support for women, now we're taking over some of the jobs too. Men are leaving, they have no choice, but what's not right is we only gets paid a little, doing men's work.'

Ted was silent as Will held his thumb in his grasp, gazing at the child who grabbed at a piece of cake Norah offered him and sucked on it, kicking his legs in contentment. Ted was conscious of Norah laughing for the first time that day and offered him the rest of his cake.

Trying to catch Norah's eye and failing, he looked out of the window and stared at the passing visitors, seeing nothing but hearing pigeons cooing, their sound rarely out of his head.

Turning to Ruby, he said firmly, 'But dear, them's are men's jobs, need stamina, strength, something women don't have. Besides, they have work at home. How can they do both? And both well? Specially they got dependents, babies, children like Will? Not natural. Not 'less you give everything up, just work. Still don't have the power. So pay can't be the same. Takes twice as long for a woman to do a man's job.

Man's work, you're doing. In men's clothing, your mother writes. That's not very womanly, is it?'

He thought of Kitty and others like her, women who reached out for others' sakes, a feeling of betrayal, of duplicity overcoming him. He blushed, wiping his brow, the thought coming to him that it was acceptable for women other than his own family to do men's work, not his girls. Fine, if they wanted to nurse or do the laundry. Women's work.

Ruby looked angrily at him before adopting a neutral tone. 'Dad, women together give us more power as a group. We put safety into work where it didn't exist before.' Her voice rose. 'And we show men we can do the work, 'specially where we work, in munitions, and we're learning new skills. Men are now having to go to war, them at the right ages, them that can pass the medical. Stands to reason we get paid same wages as them men.'

'Ruby,' Ted said, sitting more upright in his seat. 'Ruby, do you think the war will last forever?'

She shrugged. 'No, 'course not. No war does.'

Ted looked at her. 'So, what do these men do when they get back? Sell matches, flowers on the streets? Go begging? Not enough jobs to go around. The country's broke, surely, after a long war, all that money spent on the things you and Norah make, them shells, those cartridges.'

'But we're good at what we do! Other countries will need what we make, won't they?' Ruby argued.

'The world will be sick of war, sick of people being killed, sick of them bombs in cities. And so close to home! Why, from the canal today, when I was cycling, some of those houses look just like matchsticks, people queuing at soup kitchens, not a life anyone wants.'

He put his shaking hands under the table and grasped them tightly together in an attempt to still them.

Norah moved in her chair. 'Dear, don't get so het up. We're trying to enjoy your time with us, so short, must make the most of what we got. Not much to ask, eh?'

Ted unclasped his hands and put one on Norah's arms resting on the table. He brushed past her tea cup, moved a hand up to her face then touched her hair.

'And this – *this* – Norah? Temporary, or will you always have this colour of hair from now on? Not natural, this dye, just like women doing men's work.'

Norah flinched. 'Dear, all the women fillers' hair goes this colour, it's part of the job. The managers wouldn't want to harm us. They need us and treat us well, good cheap meals, new uniforms, far more practical to work in. Besides, it's nice to be with other women, just like at the laundry. And the pay's good. 'Course it's long days but we're used to it now, aren't we, Ruby?'

Ruby didn't reply. For the rest of Ted's stay, she kept her distance.

The days passed slowly, Ted unable to feel how he fitted into family life. He persevered the first few days, taking Ruby and Will out for a treat to buy new clothes for them and buying Ruby tickets to see a show with Frances. When he broached the subject of her union work, it was met with a look of defiance, the subject not discussed again. He told her about Billy's last days but she ordered him to stop. Nor did she show any curiosity about Billy's or Ted's life in France, Ted's relationships with Dickie and Ralph, his fears, anxieties about the future, the end of the war. It was the present – her present – that mattered, and that of her boy but also of her future role in the unions, women's needs and wants over men's.

Ted decided to concentrate on Norah who tried to break the silence between Ted and Ruby.

'Please, Ruby, do try to see your father's point of view,' she ventured. 'And Ted, Ruby has her views too, life here's changing.'

Ted put an arm around his wife but she shrugged it away, got up and cleared the dishes off the table. She remained mostly silent during these encounters, not taking sides, her eyes pleading for them to stop bickering. They would shine with tears too, her worn hands with their enlarged knuckles and yellowing nails a new source of anguish, of guilt, for Ted, for not being able to provide a less hard life for her. He stopped voicing his unhappiness to her about their daughter and the manly work path she had chosen. Batting away thoughts that he might be ignorant, out of touch after over three years at war, his natural stubbornness got in the way of acknowledging these profound changes. Will was the only one he felt truly comfortable with, Ted's feelings towards the little boy was also out of love for Billy, the son he might have had and had lost so cruelly. But who had also betrayed him. He found it odd that Ruby was not interested in the father of her child and his last months of life.

He took Norah out to the pictures one evening, away from home tensions. She had reluctantly agreed, telling him about a film the girls were talking about over shell-filling. *East is East,* a drama centered around East End people, a story of a young woman in a poor neighbourhood inheriting a fortune and joining high society.

They walked to Lyons Corner House on the Strand after the film. It had been their favourite rare treat. As they walked, Ted declared that he wished Ruby could inherit some money to live without working, Norah disagreeing.

'That heiress was never happy, that's why she came back to Poplar and work and family.'

'Know your place, you're saying,' Ted agreed, reluctantly. Money would make a difference to Ruby and to Norah, put a stop all this difficult, dangerous man's work and live a more leisurely life, a middle class one, like Kitty had before deciding to help others in France. She'd go back to her nice life after the excitement of war, of riding motorbikes and nursing at the Front. What else could she do? Besides, Kitty had a son who needed her. He'd lose her.

Over ham, bread and butter, cakes and tea, Ted urged Norah to give up work.

'It's too dangerous, my love, your hair, well, what else is it doing to you? All them girls going the work there, I seen 'em. So many of them have the oddest skins I ever seen. Not healthy.'

'Ted, you know you don't get paid enough for our wants, 'specially now with Will part of the family. I get paid much more than at the hospital and, anyways, no one's been sick, off work. We're proud to be called canaries! You always said I was like a bird and now I look like one!' She poured some more tea, Ted watching her bony wrists struggling under the weight of the large tea pot.

Blowing on her tea, she put her cup down after a scalding sip. 'A few explosions, you're right, dangerous working with that powder but all them shells, they're needed. I'm quick and good at it too. You felt my arm muscles in bed,' she said in a low, accusing voice. 'All that pounding is good for them.'

Ted reddened, squirmed in his seat and glanced at the tightly packed tables. He admitted to himself that the night he had sex with her wasn't half as pleasurable as with Kitty. No give or take. Norah might have been a rag doll for all the energy she put into their love-making. Love? No, far from it. Servitude, more like.

'Grant you that!' he mumbled. He looked around the beautiful art deco room. 'Look at them Nippies, good job, why don't you go for that? Lot safer, cleaner.'

Norah glanced admiringly at the distinctive maid-like uniform with a matching hat.

'They all smile a lot, nice job, granted. But they don't take on married women, Ted. Didn't you know that? Besides which, I'm content, got used to it now. But it would be better if you came home for good, be the way we used to be. My cards sometimes aren't too cheery.'

'Your cards! What cards are these?'

'Tarot. I play with Ethel.' She looked at Ted. 'But most-like alone. The joker has to be turned up with the good omen cards like the stars, the sun, the magician, definitely! And if they're not, I do them 'til I get there. Can't go to bed at night, 'til I see them turned up, all in a row, telling me all is alright.'

'Why is the magician there, why does it have to be there, Norah?'

'That's me, 'course. I magic people, well, in cards anyways.'

Ted looked at her with dismay. 'What's the joker, dear?'

'It's you, Ted. You're my joker.'

~

Ted woke the following morning with a plan. While getting dressed, he told Norah that he had received a message to return urgently to France as his replacement driver had disappeared. Making the bed, Norah looked up and nodded. 'So be it, Ted. Today?' He hated himself for lying to her. Hurrying to the post office to send a telegraph to Kitty after saying goodbye to Norah and Ruby before they set off for the Arsenal, he took Will next door to Ethel, hugging him for a long time before handing him over.

His message read 'Meet me Boulogne tonight? Stay Hotel du Globe again? Able to?' He waited for a reply, drumming his fingers on the telegraph clerk's counter.

The reply came quickly. 'In Boulogne with patients boarding hospital ship. At Globe after seven.'

~

That evening they found a table in a café, the town lively with soldiers, many of them Australian and Canadian enroute to war or invalided out. After a meal of stew and cheese, Ted relaxed and broached the subject of his home leave.

'Actually, Kitty, mine wasn't…wasn't quite…well…' He stopped and looked embarrassed.

'Not quite the homecoming you expected, dear Ted, was it? It never is. Great expectations, you're a hero, people are excited, then they don't know what to do with you. You realise you're talking to people who don't know what you do over here. And they don't want to know.'

'Exactly it! They don't!' He stared at the table and at the empty *pichet* of wine. Signalling to a waiter for another carafe, he put a hand on her arm, grasping it tightly.

281

'Impossible to tell them really just how it is, Kitty. You want to tell them the story of how men are alive one moment, and the next, they're dead. People don't seem to realise, you know, what a terrible thing war is over here. You can't explain the awful state of things, of how you live like animals and behave like them. They just don't ask or don't want to understand it…'

Kitty interrupted and looked directly at him. 'Ted, they can't bear any more misery than they can cope with, plenty of that at home too without adding more about this place. As you say, they wouldn't understand anyway, Ted,' she added in a low voice. 'You know that, I know that, always an anticlimax.'

'What's it going to be like when we go home for good, Kitty? Will we have anything in common with anyone anymore?'

'Not sure if I want to resume my past life, dear. And you?'   Ted was silent, his hands on hers. His bleak look was all the information she needed. Kitty leaned over and kissed him on the mouth.

Chapter 30: Western Front

July, 1918

Offences in Respect of Military Service:
Section 4: The most serious military crimes, including deserting one's post, convincing a superior officer to surrender, throwing away one's arms in the presence of the enemy, assisting the enemy, corresponding with the enemy, or showing cowardice in the face of the enemy.
Section 6: A wide range of crimes including plundering, leaving one's post without orders, physically attacking another soldier, stealing from civilians; revealing secret passwords, being drunk at one's posts and making false alarms about attacks.

Dickie, whose only reminder of his trench fiasco was a constant cough left over from pneumonia, changed gear, the bus struggling up an incline. The heavy vehicle, with its lopsided pigeon loft load, wasn't used to hills with its unwieldy structure. He had taken over all the driving from John, Ted's replacement, the lad an incompetent fool in his opinion. But John shared the same itchy fingers as Dickie, both of them thieving more openly while Ted was absent, Dickie showing him more subtle ways of obtaining and selling items on to troops and locals.

They didn't restrict their tastes to the more luxury end of the market – watches, clocks, pendants, small art objects easily transportable in their kitbags and on board – but they also developed a good line in plucked geese, eggs, vegetables, fruit and any kind of sweet they could lay their hands on. The food and drink items were only for sale to soldiers, not to locals, John thriving under Dickie's cunning tutelage.

'Here, watch me,' he said as they approached trenches after a battle. John followed him over mounds of earth to bodies further away from other soldiers clearing up, crossing the line to fallen German soldiers.

'Rich pickings, my son. Just watch out you don't get nicked, steady does it.'

He lowered himself carefully down into the German trench, John acting as lookout. Watches, the more up-to-date type, always sold on quickly, Dickie teaching him how to search bodies on the battlefields, targeting German officers, their expensive tastes worn on their wrists, even in battle, or in their pockets, a nice line in Deutschmarks also gathering momentum.

Dickie also became known to a select group as purveyor of fine wines and brandies. What they couldn't sell was taken to dealers he had struck a bargain with in Belgian and French towns. He didn't ask for home leave which puzzled sergeants and officers, dismissing this as an unusual but commendable conscientious streak, serving King and Country. Other officers and batmen – their cleaners, valets, cooks and general factotums – turned a blind eye, enjoying liquid luxuries thanks to his skills.

John knew of rumours that Dickie had a woman in every town, the stories growing about his burgeoning fatherhood which he denied with a chortle. 'Me, a dad, can't even look after myself, let alone any kid, 'specially a Frenchie. Couldn't speak to the lad, could I?'

When Ted re-joined the bus after his leave, John was moved to a bus driving soldiers which he didn't like. Constantly on the road, it was not like driving the more congenial pigeon loft, staying for days in one place. After a few months relentlessly driving or as a bored second driver, he disappeared one March day.

Letters to Ted from home over the months since his return were few and far between, his bus off the radar due to relentless, erratic movement along the Front. When they were distributed, Ted store them away for a while before opening them. Norah blanked any personal comments, reporting mostly on Will's progress and how the seeds she had planted in late May had now developed into a cornucopia of fruit and vegetables for summer eating, storing or preserving for winter.

You'd be ever so pleased to know we keep your shed nice and tidy and swept inside too. I replaced one of the labels, the one with Tools as it fell off and slugs left a mess on it. The slug's gone to another world too, horrid things. Ruby's right proud she managed to get the Arsenal to have some cress going in the building so Will comes with us every day we work there, happy as a sand boy to be with so many other kids. Well, she didn't do it all on her own, but the way she talks you would think so! But you know our Ruby, not a shy wallflower.

Norah didn't write anything about herself. She knew that Ted was displeased with her job, best to avoid mentioning her work and her increasing ill-health. Sometimes she wished she was a Nippie. She'd wear the hat to cover the rust coloured hair and run from table to table in smart, sophisticated surroundings, a band playing, receiving smiles and tips from appreciative toffs. Fair's fair. But she was married but didn't feel married. The joker and the magician, those elusive cards which she secretly played on her own, were hidden away in her bedroom, away from a mocking Ruby, leading her increasingly to despair.

~

Months passed, the bus constantly on the road as it zigzagged along the Front. Ted and Dickie manoeuvred clogged roads passing or being passed by swelling numbers of soldiers on foot – Scottish, English, Irish lads alongside Indian, Portuguese and others – as well as many horse-drawn wagons. Mounted horse numbers grew too as well as a multitude of trucks, motor ambulances and artillery guns. Another ninety – they were told – London buses joined the nearly 1,000 double deckers already at war and packed with soldiers, the wounded or prisoners-of-war.

But the Somme was not evacuated of civilians. Despite nearly four years of war, a few locals continued to live near the firing lines, their bus passing homes with laundry fluttering in the air, chimney smoke spiralling into a mottled war-grey sky.

When they weren't travelling to various strategic points for Ralph to unleash his birds, the bus was seconded to the Royal Engineers for Dickie and Ted to sink bore-holes for water and lay pipelines, Ralph looking after his birds on board. Other than the Somme, the Ancre, and a stream between Vadencourt and Contay, there was no other water to be had and horses and men needed it.

'Dickie, there's a good chap, get on the end of the tank with Robert here,' Ted shouted to Dickie who lounged on the drivers' seat by a swollen river. A small team of soldiers, hoisting the water tanks onto wagons, shifted the heavy loads with shouts and curses.

Dickie ambled over, reluctant to move from the vehicle after a wet outing, the July weather unseasonably rainy. They had just come off duty after eight days of laying pipelines, the sergeant giving them time off, Ted too exhausted to do anything except sit and stare until called to help.

Hours later, Ted watched nearby trucks revving their engines in the sticky clay with their load of two-gallon petrol cans. Bound for troops in the trenches, the cans were used to transport hot tea, kept warm wrapped in hay. Other trucks followed, carrying rations and ammunition for those in shell-holes.

He idly speculated if some of the equipment had been made by Norah or transported by Ruby from the depot to the vast arsenal's rail lines.

'Ted, Ted, start the motor,' a commanding voice shouted.

'Ah, sergeant, you promised Dickie and me a whole day to rest up at least. What's the big rush?'

'What's the big rush? You ask in time of war what the rush is, Private Digby?' The sergeant banged on the side of the bus with an angry fist.

'You've caught the Dickie bug, you have. Doesn't suit you, being offhand. Take the bus and pick up some soldiers. Been poisoned. Take 'em to the clearing station, you know where the nearest one is.'

'Poisoned!' Ted sat up. 'What, gas again, you mean, they been gassed?'

'No, they didn't clean out the fucking tea tins from oil properly, whole load of sappers out there laying pipes shittin' themselves something terrible. They're writhing all over the place.'

Ted shook his head. 'Hang on, we pick them up in this bus, our home, Dickie's and my quarters, filled with pigeons and all? Pigeons who don't like to be wakened, Ralph says, until they're good and ready! Them soldiers shittin' and vomitin' all over the place, on our beds?'

The sergeant reconsidered. 'Then take Harry's bus over there. He's on sick parade. Yes, that's the ticket, smartish, now.'

'I'll do a deal with you, sergeant. You get Dickie up. He'll bitch like hell – and you give us a double tot of rum tonight. How's that?'

Ted slid into Harry's bus, a groggy, complaining Dickie beside him. The double decker, used for transporting soldiers rather than a pigeon loft with its double carbuncles on either side, felt lighter, like a gazelle compared to their lumbering elephantine one.

'Happy days,' Dickie grumbled as they helped the sappers on board the bus once at the destination. Some had taken off their soiled uniform trousers and had thrown them in ditches, exposing bare stained brown legs, others retching and gasping for air.

The clearing station had been alerted, soldiers shown the way to their quarters after arriving. After a shower, nurses guided them to makeshift tent with rows of beds and a dressing station. Ted got back on the bus with scrubbing material, he and Dickie reluctantly dealing with the reeking, choking interior, swearing and holding their breath.

'I'm stripping, washing outside,' Ted grumbled after surveying the cleaned space and jumped down from the bus. He took off his clothes, spread them on the engine and washed, stretching his arms while he scrubbed.

He looked up at a passing motorbike. Kitty.

'I'd know that body anywhere! Hello, Ted.' She revved the bike then turned it off. 'Don't get too close,' he muttered, 'stinking job, just finished, clothes smell somethin' terrible.'

'Look, what you think I've been used to out here? Come on, get dressed and we'll have a brew.'

He blew her a kiss, followed by a sheepish grin as he struggled into underwear.

She whistled then looked around her. 'Is that Dickie lurking behind the bus? Hey, you!'

Dickie sauntered up. He looked immaculate in a clean uniform. 'Ah, Kitty, a pleasure.' He bowed in an exaggerated fashion then turned to Ted. 'Here.' He threw him a uniform. Ted picked it up and pressed the stiff khaki cloth to his nose. Pristine. He grinned.

'Where'd you get it, Dickie?'

'Money and fair words, money and fair words, chum.'

Ted didn't care, it smelled sweet. 'Just a mo, Kitty.' He started dressing and looked up when he heard Kitty swear, her voice strong. 'Got a bone to pick with you, you bugger!'

Dickie's reply was nonchalant. 'Why's that, sweetheart?'

'Wipe that innocent look off your face!' Kitty held up a fist at Dickie.

Ted called out. 'Hey, what's this all about?'

'Stay out of this, Ted, none of your business,' Dickie muttered.

Pulling on his braces over a clean shirt with a snap against his chest and hastily fastening his fly buttons, Ted stepped into his boots before striding swiftly towards Kitty and put a protective arm around her shoulders.

'What's going on, Kitty?'

'He did me out of a whole wad of money, sold the jewellery I gave him to buy medicines then had the utter,' she repeated angrily '– *utter audacity* – to tell me they only fetched a few francs. They were real diamonds in the brooch and bracelet, not cheap paste.'

'Hold on to your hat, dear!' Dickie said in a soothing voice. 'I'm glad I caught up with you. The dealer made a mistake, owned up, he did, just saw him the other day.'

Drawing out a substantial wad of notes, he peeled off a generous number and handed them to Kitty, winked at Ted who glowered at him, then disappeared into the packed camp.

'He is a one,' Kitty said. 'He's going to get into trouble one day, if I have anything to do with it.'

Ted nodded. 'I know and I agree, one day for sure. You alright?'

'Of course. You and I have had worse things to deal with. Must get on, dearest, now I have some money from the rascal to ferret around for some food for my newcomers. Dora's coping with them best she can. Better run, tea at another time, eh? Cheerio!'

Ted had held her hands, not letting go. He started to call her 'darling', picked up from officers' who cavorted stylishly with nurses, his confidence growing over time with Kitty and who reciprocated with darling, dearest, lamb or love.

He pulled her to him. 'Let's meet up, darling, miss you something terrible, I do.'

She laughed and whispered in his ear. Turning, she waved a cheerful goodbye.

~

They met up randomly, unexpectedly, and without ownership of one another, during the months beyond the battles of the Somme and those of the Ancre, Serre, Miramont and Le Loupart Line. The warmth of her body, her eagerness to give in to him created an increasing longing for her, their meetings not always by chance. He learnt where she often drove her

289

motorbike and would head on down roads in case she was there, his pulse quickening when hearing the familiar roar of her bike. Ted increasingly spent his spare time at the farmhouse if in the neighbourhood where Kitty and Dora looked after the injured, lending a hand with the repairs and helping incapacitated soldiers write home. When at work during a prolonged period of exceptional frost, they continued to dance around northern France's roads in hope of meeting up.

~

Soldiers jostled around a series of flyers pinned to the walls at a camp's canteen. Dickie barged his way through the crowd, calling out to Ted to join him. He started reading the text.

Hah! The General! Haig's written to us!

Certain outstanding features of the past five months' fighting call for brief comment from me. In spite of a season of unusual severity - a chorus of agreement went up *- a winter campaign has been conducted to a successful issue under most trying and arduous conditions. Activity on our battle-front has been maintained almost without a break from the conclusion of last year's offensive to the commencement of the present operations. The successful accomplishment of this part of our general plan has already enabled us to realise no inconsiderable instalment of the fruits of the Somme Battle, and has gone far to open the road to their full achievement.* 'Says you!' Dickie interjected.' What we achieved, eh, boys?' Jeers went up. *The courage and endurance of our troops has carried them triumphantly through a period of fighting of a particularly trying nature –* British understatement, boys, fucking more than that! *– in which they have been subjected to the maximum of personal hardship –* a mix of cheers and groans rang around the soldiers *– and physical strain. I cannot speak too highly of the qualities displayed by all ranks of the Army.*

Dickie sat morosely over a plate of canteen food later, not touching the grey-brown mass after sniffing it.

'They'll just start all over again, more fodder from Blighty bussed around this fucking continent, more bodies, then they'll ask again, more bodies. But we defeat them and they defeat us and the generals write reports to cover their own asses. Not triumphant, in no way, shape or form.'

'What's Churchill playing at?' Ted said, getting up from the canteen table. 'Leaders, eh? What next? Just sending us more troops, Americans now. Can't move for 'em.'

'Rumour has it we paid for their uniforms and all,' Dickie said. 'Where's the money coming from?' But he also thought of good American watches to flog, a nice little earner to serve him well when the fiasco ended. If.

Chapter 31: Western Front

August, 1918

Marching – left, left!
Along the road in the evening the brown
battalions wind,
With the trenches' threat of death before, the
peaceful homes behind;
And luck is with you or luck is not as the ticket
of fate is drawn,
The boys go up to the trench at dusk, but who
will come back at dawn?

All too soon, it was late summer. The soldiers from the second battle of the Marne were laid to rest, air battles adding to the bombardments and death tolls. Drainage systems collapsed, the sun never peering through the clouds long enough to dry the ground, Armies on both sides squelched through clinging, pudding-like mud.

Ted lost all sense of time, of ever feeling clean and well-fed again. Dickie's extra, exotic supplies had all but dried up, apart from the occasional caught rabbit or filched chicken. It didn't pay to dwell on his own creature comforts, best to cease imagining going back home. From the reception he'd get he wouldn't fit in anyway. He despised himself for longing to see Will more than Norah and Ruby. Those who shared his life now understood him, Norah's letters reminding him of his alienation. Life had changed out of all proportion.

Talk around the camps was over decreasing supplies of Army food too. Ralph, rarely one to voice an opinion, was moved to make observations.

'Down from six ounces of meat a day to once every nine days.'

'Very precise of you, chum, 'Dickie commented. 'You sure?'

Ralph spurned any attempts by Dickie to supplement his diet with the latest game in season. 'I don't eat birds,' was his terse reply when handed a leg, French grouse Dickie's choice of meat, if he could snare it, rather than one bite of Maconochie's tinned stew. He sometimes found a local woman who would cook it for him, repaying her by lying next to her then stealing from her vegetable patch, the garden shed looted too for sales. But mostly, the men's diet deteriorated. Thanks to the bus's erratic zigzag across the Front, Dickie escaped scrutiny by the local population, never in one area for long

Dickie laughed. 'Well, you know the solution, it's in your hands, Ralph. My, them birds, mighty tasty!'

'*Don't,* don't say it, Dickie. You're an unfeeling man,' Ted joked, making a face at the turnip bread but eating it after dipping it in his nettle soup. He reckoned there were more weeds now than ever in the grey-green broth, some leaves too.

'Ah, Ralphie, me ol' mate, wring a neck and let's have a feast!' Dickie said, laughing. 'You only tease the ones you love!' he called after the swiftly departing Ralph taking two steps at a time up to his flock.

Talk in canteens included heated discussions about women. Sex, of course. This itch was never far away from their minds, the *filles de joie* kept busy when they found the time and the energy, visits to French brothels by British soldiers officially sanctioned.

But it was more than just sex. Women, they reckoned, were taking over the world, on the buses as conductors, as street cleaners, football teams of women now playing in clubs, in leagues, a man's world being usurped. Norah had written of lady typists being engaged to work at New Scotland Yard and had described her first sighting of a woman police force volunteer in long skirt, military-style jacket and large felt hat.

In a letter, she wrote: *That hat! looks like an upside soup plate! I hid my laughter from them when passing a pair of them! Someone's named them copperettes, too, just silly.*

But more disturbingly came the disapproving information, mostly from the Daily Mail, Dickie's old boss's paper, that women were found flat out in the gutter drunk, fights in brothels by soldiers a common occurrence, petty crime committed by women. Rowdy hoydens, without a moral compass! They have too much money for their own good, thundered the paper. And they want the vote! What next, a woman prime minister? Ted and the other men laughed when they read the paper's article. It was all too farcical. But women like Ruby now, nothing seemed too far-fetched, Ted grudgingly concluded when alone with his thoughts. But Kitty, she formed one of the new ranks and was wonderful. Maybe it wasn't too fanciful after all. Ruby contested that young, modern women knew no boundaries, they would not be fenced in, corralled like some dangerous beasts by their masters. She wouldn't give up wanting justice for all munitions workers, egged on by Suffragettes' battles.

The drivers argued over their soup and stew about women's roles. One said they were unstoppable, the old order teetering.

Dickie voiced his thoughts. 'Look at Kitty on her motorbike, free as a bird! But still attached to a man, eh, Ted?'

'But with a sense of duty to others!' he retorted. My daughter, Ruby...' his voice trailed off, the complete sentence remaining a duplicitous thought.

~

One late August morning, back on old stomping ground near St. Quentin, Sergeant Todd, a friendly West Country man, approached the bus, Ted under the bonnet. He poked his head around, clutching an oily rag.

'Want me, Sarge?' The sergeant handed him a letter, apology written on his face.

'Sorry Ted, been round the houses looking for you when it came in, then forgot. Just found it. Buy you a drink later.'

Ted scowled, then wiped his hands on his dirty cloth and took the letter. Not recognising the writer's identity, he opened it and read the signature. *Your loving daughter Ruby,* a rare letter from since he had set out in September, 1914. Not that he expected one. On the top right-hand corner, Ruby had marked July 16. He'd have the sergeant's guts for garters.

Dad,

Will is loving his nursery. I teach him to say grandpa when we look at your photograph we took when you was last here, near six months ago. He's a big boy for three, well, soon, and happy too. He's in the nursery school I helped to open for the Arsenal! It's got a link with you. Met this soldier's mother, a lady, Lady Julia, put up the money. So it's named after her son. Very down to earth, just like anyone, really, not snobbish but looks it! MP's wife. He died at somewhere calls Loose, only 21, only child. It's a lovely wooden building just for the kids of munitions workers. I feel right proud! Frances just had a baby, in March, Alfred's his name and he's here too. Soldier father. Sound familiar? He had another family so guess she won't see much of him after she found out too late but Alfred's a nice baby. Will don't know what to make of him yet. Puts his hands to his ears! But I had to move closer to the Arsenal, single mother, like me, or you don't get a place in the nursery. Even though I helped make it happen. I moved home nearby with Frances and Alfred in May with Will, the new house just a treat after our old one and ever so close to work, couldn't be better and right opposite a big green. It's called Well Hall Garden City. Don't need to do that long walk to Victoria Park anymore but no ice cream here or boating lake, just the dirty old river… Mum thought it made sense. Saves us money too, all that travelling. Mum staying at home, thinking you'll be back one day. But will you? Work too with union makes more sense to live here, very busy working getting equal pay, not something we're going to get overnight but we do the same work so what's the problem? Men! But reason for writing really is to let you know Mum is far from well. Ethel's been a good neighbour, looking after her. She went to the doctor and he said that she was a drinker 'cause she was falling about and she couldn't hold herself up, like she's drunk! Mum, I ask you! She don't drink! I have a tipple Sundays sometimes but she has one once in blue moon, even less now you're not here to take her out. So the doctor told her to come back again when she was sober. I told him she don't drink but he says she was tipsy so I took her back home and put her to bed. Nasty colour, that yellow making you feel sicker than you are, guess that could be part of it. Trouble is that awful Leaving Certificate them politicians say munition workers have to accept. No one, not even Mum, sick as she is, can leave their job. You have to go to a tribunal and you're punished if you don't have that cert. I'm going to change this. Watch me! My new address is below, 'case you get the time to drop me a line. Good move for Mum too, no small child charging about, no extra money needed for the two of us. Real shortage of food these days, rabbit instead of mutton, can't get any for love or money, forget salt beef, your favourite. But we get sausages. Think they're made of sawdust. And I swear them loaves are shrinking. Must get out my old school ruler.

PS. My team won against Beckton. The Final! There's a grand picture of us in the Arsenal hall of us. We look ever so jaunty in our striped shirts! 6-3.

PS: I hope you're doing fine, not too tired and having some rest along the way. Those pigeons coo you to sleep?

296

Ted reached under the drivers' seat for his box and put the letter away. He'd reply to it later and write to Norah too. Letters to her had dropped off quite considerably, neither of them finding the words. Kitty's letters, short and endearing, came thick and fast, Ted replying with alacrity. He'd written to Frank at the depot months ago, but he'd not heard back.

Photographs too bulked up the box's contents, ones of Kitty and him favoured over family ones, he admitted to himself. Dickie, with his stolen camera, a Verascope which neatly fitted into a small knapsack, had suggested a keepsake photo one day when they were together.

'Hop on Kitty's bike behind her,' he instructed, angling the camera at them.

Ted knew the picture intimately and gravitated towards it whenever he stored a letter away. They were both leaning forward, pretending to be going like the wind, their smiling faces looking at the photographer, not the road.

Placing the box under the seat, he hopped down from the cabin then glanced up at the pigeon loft's windows on the upper deck. Ralph had opened them wide for extra air to waft through, the smell still overwhelming. Ted wondered how he managed to sleep with the odour of pigeon shit invading his nostrils. The lad remained a mystery to him but he had a firm understanding of Dickie, his pattern of life's needs and wants very clear. Their shared knowledge of Dawkins' death was rarely mentioned or alluded to, both wary of one another. They kept out of each other's way, a knowing sideways glance all it took.

The bus was solidly stacked with Dickie's takings, his gains, to sell on at everyone else's expense. He had run out of officer buyers recently, too many deaths amongst the commanding ranks to make a fast buck. But he still had the French dealers, mostly further away from scenes of battle, a lucrative market as local buyers needed to replace items after their properties had suffered war damage. Dickie was always amongst the first scavengers after bombings, with rich pickings from houses, farms, cottages and even hotels, Ted marvelling at his daring.

Ted grimaced at the state of the protruding, bruised, streaked wood on the bus's side, damaged by striking overhanging branches and low roofing. Whatever would the depot say about the state of his bus these days?

Wandering down into a nearby wood, he sat down in a glade in the sun. It was peaceful and he lifted his face to the heat, too little of it this disastrous summer. His mind reluctantly turned to Norah and her illness. How serious was it? Every sense told him it was but Ruby's letter down-played it, as did letters from Norah, never mentioning how she felt. And she hadn't written about Ruby's leaving. Recently, it was all about the tarot cards, how they weren't playing fair with her, always the joker turning up at the wrong place at the wrong time.

Chapter 32: Home Front

November, 1918

We've answered Lloyd George's call to arms,
Keeping things going to at home.
We're really helping our country, us girls.
But my skin's turned to yellow
And my hair's tied up all the time.
I swallow dust when I breathe in,
And should be in my prime.
For the first time us women
Are as important as men.
Nine and half hours of shifts we do,
But we get paid less than them.

Norah stood in line for her meal. Holding onto a counter, her sallow complexion mirrored the day's pallid wintery sky outside. Picking up her tray, she found a nearby seat and looked at her food, her one meal of the day. She had given up cooking at home, her energies non-existent.

She looked up when a superintendent entered the canteen. Holding up a clipboard, he bellowed for quiet. Women put down their cutlery and stopped their chat, others rubbing their sore feet and hands, ignoring him. Some swivelled around on canteen benches, trying to see the speaker. 'Get out the way, you fat cow!'

'Didn't I call for silence?' the speaker bristled.

'Yes, Mr. Carey,' a few teased.

'Good! When I call your names out, stand up and shout out your presence.'

'Mrs. Mary Dunlop.' 'Here.' 'Louder! Mrs. Geraldine Clayton.'

'Here.' 'Miss Bernice Tully.' 'Here, sir.'

Norah sat quietly, surveying her uneaten meal. She had struggled to get to work, half-heartedly filling the shells that morning, She glanced at Ruby at another table looking mischievous, grinning about something Frances was whispering in her ear.

The names droned on, the supervisor's voice hoarse. 'Mrs. Norah Digby. Mrs. Norah Digby.'

Mary Dunlop, standing next to her, bent down and shook her shoulder. 'You, Norah, you're called. Stand up.'

'Here, here!'

Mr. Carey turned to the last page on his clipboard, read out another dozen names then looked at the women standing. He always had a hangdog look, as if the end of the world was nigh. Women joked he probably looked like that on his wedding night, the look permanent either before drawing back the sheets, but definitely after.

He cleared his throat and parted his legs, as if ballast was needed to get him through whatever he was about to say.

'Ladies, we heard yesterday the Russian Front collapsed.'

Cheers went up and were quickly quelled by those who knew better. 'They're on our side, you silly nincompoops!' came a strident voice. 'Our allies, ninnies!'

Mr. Carey parted his legs even wider. 'The Imperial Russian Army has virtually disintegrated, a civil war now sweeping across Russia.'

'Why's he tellin' us this? Didn't know we was in for a politics lesson!' Mary hissed to Norah who ignored her.

'This means...' he hesitated '...means, ah, now.' He rushed his words. 'There will be fewer armaments made at the Woolwich! Those standing are to be laid off, starting today. Finish your day's work, collect your pay and return home.'

There was uproar in the canteen, bread pellets and rice pudding thrown at the hapless Carey who batted missiles off with his clipboard before turning and walking swiftly away.

Norah's first thought was one of relief. She sat down and wept, covering her face with her yellow hands, but cried with gratitude. She would no longer have to trudge the miles to work, stand for twelve hours a day and fill shells. She despised her yellow colour, her coppery hair, her weak body. The cards had never predicted her failures. But then, she had not tried to find out about herself, Ted the joker uppermost on her mind when the cards came out late at night.

Ruby fought her way through disgruntled women to her mother. 'Mum, I'll fight this, fight for you to keep your job. They can't do this, after all the work you and them's done for the war effort, just... just chucking you out when they feel like it.' She put her arm around Norah.

'And look who they got rid of,' Ruby carried on. 'Oh, not them classier women, just the lower ranks. We'll see about that!'

'Dear, don't make a fuss just for me. I'll find something else when I feel a bit more like working. Just not now, eh?'

Ruby left her sitting in the canteen, her shift about to start. Norah left to change and go home, not able to face finishing her shift or to say goodbye to her workmates. Clutching her stomach, she stepped out into the icy November air and vomited, her innards gnawing and cold.

Home no longer felt like home. Ted had deserted her first, now Ruby and Will. They had moved out leaving her alone for the first time in her life. She hated having no one to cook for, no reason for getting up in the morning apart from making munitions.

Ruby called around on her next day off. Letting herself in, she pushed Will in front of her and closed the door, the cold air inside hitting her.

'Will, wait here, sweet boy.' She settled him down in the kitchen with a biscuit and a toy and walked slowly, quietly upstairs.

She smelt the stench before she reached Norah's bedroom door, the odour churning her stomach. Opening the door, she retched.

Norah was lying on the bed, still in the clothes she wore on the day of the layoff. Her hair, clothing and bedclothes were matted with sick.

Ruby went over to her, covering her nose with her scarf. Kneeling down towards Norah's chest, she listened but couldn't make out any breathing, no rise or fall of her tangled clothing. She put her hands over her eyes, her hand darting over her mouth after a sharp, shrill noise. Ethel. She'd go to Ethel. She'd know what to do.

Running downstairs, she slipped on the mat, knocking her arm against the front door. Pulling it open, she ran next door and banged on it.

'Ruby, whatever's the matter dear?'

'I...I can't...'

Ethel grasped her arm. 'What can't you? Slow down, there's a good girl.'

Ethel smelled the vomit as soon as she took the first step on the narrow stairs. Clutching her thick winter skirts, she ran up to Norah's room and opened the door.

'Oh, my, oh, dear. Ruby, you go downstairs and heat up some water. Clean your poor mother up.'

Ruby shook. 'But she's dead, she's dead! Hot water's not going to bring her back to life!'

Norah shifted in the bed, turning toward the noise, a rasping sound coming from her body. Her yellow face and hair looked deathly against the stained, stenching bedclothes.

'See! She's alive, Ruby, go get some water then call on the doctor. Run!' Ethel opened the window, covering Norah with a clean blanket after stripping her clothing and bedding.

Norah woke up in the East London Hospital a day later and remained there for a week before being discharged. Ruby was told she would need constant nursing and, under no account must she be allowed to get up, prolonged bed rest the way forward. Anaemia, liver and blood problems were great obstacles, the harassed doctor in charge of the large ward informed Ruby, advising her 'that with nourishing soups, our patient may overcome this foul poison in her lungs and organs.' He was brisk. 'Who will look after her as I understand she lives alone?'

Ruby paid Ethel to deal with her mother. Now she would deal with the Arsenal.

~

Ruby and Frances knocked on the Chief Superintendent's door. Mrs. Stockwin rose from her chair and put her arm around Ruby. 'My poor child, how is your mother after her terrible ordeal?'

'I don't understand why you shove my mum's illness in the past, Mrs. Stockwin. She is and will remain far from well, likely, for the rest of her life.'

'Now, dear, she is getting the best treatment at the East London, I am told.'

'No, she's at home, her home now, can't afford the luxury of hospital. My mum's savings from working here is paying for the doctor and paid for the hospital. She most probably will never work again so how's she 'spected to get along, live?'

'Come and sit down and let's talk about this sensibly. You know, girls, I am on your side. Always have been, always will.'

She sat down and pointed to the chairs opposite the desk. Ruby looked at her and remained standing, her face set. Frances put her arms around her and pushed her to a seat.

'My mum,' Ruby began, her voice wavering, 'my mum's been a loyal worker here, over two years, never had a day off sick, never skived, never thieved nothing, took nothing for granted. That's how she is, we are.'

'Dear, Norah has been a fine example to all. Not of word of complaint about her. Or from her, for that matter. But what can we do?'

'She needs compensation, Mrs. Stockwin! And…and any woman who works here who gets sick, or injured, or laid off.

Not in three or ten years' time, but now! When she needs the money to pay for the doctor, medicine, her care. Household expenses like the coal, the oil, the...'

Frances interrupted. 'Yes, Ruby, I think Mrs. Stockwin gets the picture. Let's not use up too much of her time but see what can be done. Something practical.'

'Good advice, Frances.' Mrs. Stockwin smiled at Ruby then smoothed down her dress as if it were the oracle, the font of knowledge to guide her through this challenging meeting.

Looking up she put her hands together on her desk as if locked in prayer.

'Now, as you know compensation is only forthcoming if,' she stressed the word, '*if* you are injured in some way *if* you know the Workman's Compensation Act as well as I do. Money is only given for accidents caused by serious and wilful misconduct due to the negligence of the company you work for.'

Ruby rolled her eyes. She had still not learnt the art of diplomacy in her negotiations.

'All well and good, ma'm, but don't using dangerous chemicals over a long time like lyddite, TNT and the like, mean it's a problem with the work? People like my mum need help too when it's the Arsenal's fault and...'

Frances interrupted her again. 'And neglect by them factory doctors too who *never* but *never* came by, seen on the workshop floor like we was told, checking our health!'

'Doctor said she was drunk! Drunk! I ask you!' Ruby looked at Mrs. Stockwin defiantly, her voice strained.

The superintendent pressed her hands together then touched a cluster of pens in a holder as if they held the key to strengthen her under pressure.

'Look, girls. Girls! I am on your side and all that you say should be put into practice but, as yet, it seems to be patchy. Only those injured in the infrequent,' she looked at Ruby and saw an indignant eyebrow raised, 'yes, infrequent explosions we've had here. Unlike Silvertown's this year, now that was a real catastrophe not yet visited here.'

'But could happen, Mrs. Stockwin, or them Zeppelins coming over us again like they did and drop another bomb. You're forgetting a man was killed, lots injured.'

'No, I'm not forgetting at all, Ruby. That's a case in point, only one killed and that was due to the Zeppelins, not caused by our work here.'

'Alright, so it hasn't happened here but what about them girls in other armaments around the country? One girl was blown up three times! She didn't lose her sight, or an arm, like the girl working next to her – blown off in bits all over the shop, or a leg or die but plenty of 'em did and will do. My mum, she's one of them canaries, loads of canaries working with this poison!'

Steadying her shaking hands, she stood up. 'Granted, the pay is better than sweeping the streets but they're sick, sick too!'

'Management says, and I'm reluctant to relay this on, quite honestly, but you may already know,' Mrs. Stockwin paused and played with the corner of a file, 'Management says that some women have a propensity, a... '

'A what, what's that mean?' Ruby interrupted.

'Ssh! Don't be so rude, Ruby!' Frances said impatiently. 'It's...'

Mrs. Stockwin interrupted, her words tumbling out in impatient staccato starbursts. 'A tendency, a leaning toward absorbing toxic substances and therefore should be removed from that work when it begins to be noticed.'

'But if the doctors aren't there noticing, then they won't be moved to other work,' Ruby said, warming to the argument. 'Clear and simple!'

Mrs. Stockwin sighed and stood up. Clearing her throat, she clutched at her brooch.

'Today we established that compensation is out of the question. Have you contacted the relief funds? Maybe you should try that.'

'And who runs this, and why should I have to rely on a charity to get some benefit for mum when it should be the Arsenal? Answer me that!'

Mrs. Stockwin led them to the door and opened it. 'It's the Ministry of Munitions. Try them. And good luck!'

Ruby and Frances stepped into the corridor. Mrs. Stockwin called after them.

'Perhaps she could consider outdoor work in future, the Women's Land Army now recruiting those laid off. Please pass on my best wishes to dear Norah.'

~

That evening Ruby wrote to Ted.

Dad,

You must be wondering why you received two letters from me in a short time and none from Mum recent times. Well, sorry to say she was laid off, some excuse about the Russian Front and no need for so many shells and all. Over 200 women got rid of. I ask you! But she was taken ill and after a spell in hospital, back home, that powder affecting her bad. She won't work for a time, her savings used up for nursing her. Ethel's looking after her, born nurse she is, deliverin' babies – first to see Will's blond mop! – and now seeing to mum. As I do the accounting for mum and have done for long time now, I'll make sure some of your wages pays for Ethel. But it means only one breadwinner now, you, so you keep well, do you hear? I can look after myself and Will, my wages enough to be getting on with, and sharing costs with Frances in our new home I wrote you about. Had a right ding-dong with the Arsenal about getting some compensation but no. Won't hear of it. Says I should try charity. Since when have our family done that! Never. Christmas round the corner, never felt less like it but my boy will want it so he shall have it. Hear from you, dad. We'll cope an' all.
Your Ruby.

PS. Mum says to say hello, love.

Chapter 33: Western Front

November 1918

German counter-attack has been repulsed by the Companies occupying the Hauteville Trench. During the day the bombardment of the position continues. No infantry attack in Sector 1. A deserter gave himself up at Bois Carré. Name of Pvte Alexander Smithson.

Ted received Ruby's letter a week after she had put it in the red post box on Roman Road, a short distance from their home on Saxon Road. He imagined little Will being lifted up by his mother to put the letter in. He was shaken by Norah's illness but was not been given permission to have any compassionate leave due to 'lack of drivers like you, Ted. And that's final.' Kitty was his solace.

The bus criss-crossed from Rheims to Arras with pigeon messages from General Haig to frontline staff. The relentlessness of posts to and from the pigeon loft pointed to an escalation along the front, rumours and propaganda confusing those who listened to talk and read notices. Ralph was exhausted but exhilarated by his birds' prowess and their staying power, few only shot down by German marksmen. The Canadian Army had recruited Cree and other Indian Natives as snipers for the allies' side, their impressive natural huntsman tally making marks in despatches and in messages, their downing of many German pigeons a formidable feat which Ralph wrote up diligently in his records. His feelings for birds, even those flying for the enemy nevertheless caused him sorrow, his birds, their birds, all prized, all valiant, trustworthy, worthy, courageous.

He studied incoming messages, figuring out the coding early on, strictly against regulations. Drawing out a battered, small notebook hidden behind a favoured pigeon's box, he wrote, 'Very violent bombardment of our lines, send relief to Souville urgently.' The message joined the hundreds of carefully, meticulously written entries; Ralph's writing was tiny, as if an ant had mistakenly picked up a pen and was trying to find its way back to its nest through dense grass.

According to Captain Greenwell of 17th Battalion, King's Liverpool Regiment, the Germans have withdrawn troops to take them to the right bank. On the Somme Front alone, over 400 hundred operation messages came back from the attacking forces.

He studied the messages for movement, for logistics, for defining moments in the war and felt proud he had a part in it. Ted became gradually aware of more of a cocky step in Ralph but couldn't fathom this out. Why was the man so much surer of himself as the war deepened?

Ralph wanted to treasure this record forever, his eyes gliding over the entries with elation. When he deciphered the message of smashing the Hindenburg Line by new-fangled tanks tossing up enemy machine guns as if they were toys, driving German infantry to ground, he whooped with joy, initially suppressing the desire to run down the steps to Ted and tell him the good news after decoding the message. He gave the message to the despatch rider and slid onto the drivers' seat next to Ted who was napping. Glancing around for Dickie, he caught sight of him on his uncomfortable bunk, writing a list.

'Ted, interesting.' He leaned forward and whispered, 'Hindenburg Lines been tumbled, broken, smashed up, biggest tank battle ever!' Ted sat up from his hunched position and stared at him.

'Say that again, Ralph.'

'No, Can't. You heard.'

'Hindenburg's been what?' But Ralph had already started climbing the steps back to the loft.

Hindenburg! How had Haig done it? Surely not! Surely this had to be the turning point. Ted jumped down from the cab and turned up his collar against the driving rain. His mind started racing. Maybe in a few months' time he'd be back nursing Norah. And Kitty? How would he see Kitty? There had to be a way of never losing her, thoughts of betrayal fluctuating like a shifting tide, sweat forming on his brow.

The pigeon handler kept the next battle news to himself.

Northern end of the Bonavis Ridge and Gonnelieu sector: swift advance of enemy's infantry followed by bombardment has overwhelmed our troops, both in line and in immediate support, with sudden attack. Send reinforcements with utmost urgency.

Soldier talk raged over the scant meals and tainted gas canister tea on General Haig's novel tactics. British pride was puffed up by the number of tanks daringly put into operation, their use dispelling the notion that the Hindenburg line was impregnable, but optimism was again dashed with the news of a shortfall of nearly half a million soldiers to end the war. The war would continue, propaganda escalating. In one attack, troops captured the entrance to the St Quentin canal tunnel. Inside, a kitchen where German bodies lay, an Allied soldier's remains were found in a cooking cauldron, wild claims that the enemy was boiling down the dead passing from soldier to soldier.

~

Dickie was getting anxious about his cache. He didn't have enough space left in the cabin and would have to either sell larger items or discard them to fit smaller objects in, the acquisition of yet more jewellery the best possible option. He had joined forces with Albert, an American soldier, a renegade who saw the opportunity for riches other than his lousy pay, as he put it, by entering into the antiques trade with Dickie. With his useful French – his mother was Belgian-born – Albert took the larger items off Dickie, exchanging them for coveted American dollars. Under cover of darkness in the Soissons area after German bombardment of Paris, he loaded them onto a cart and took off during a rest and recreation leave for the capital, successfully selling them to Paris antique dealers, eager for a good price from an American, apparently residing in the south of France. He returned, having also sold the cart, to re-join his platoon, he and Dickie continuing their methods under the distracted radar of their armies.

To keep Ted sweet, Dickie tucked wads of dollars under his rough pillow, Ted never acknowledging the sudden windfalls over the months. Placing them in the box containing the letters and photos, the money would come in handy for Norah's care when he returned home. Or would he find his way to Kitty's home in the Midlands and start a new life with her with the proceeds? Thoughts of Will managed to stem the deceitful tide most days.

~

Ted arranged for the bus to go to the garage for repairs to its rear axle one raw early November morning, volunteering Dickie to remain on board with Ralph and help him muck out the pigeon shit. A meeting with Kitty was upmost on his mind, time for Dickie to pull his weight who, to his surprise, readily agreed.

'Why you doing this, Dickie?' Ralph had asked, in an unusual display of fluency. 'You always like to get out, enjoy them dames a bit when in town.'

'Sometimes, a bit of brotherly solidarity is called for,' came the unconvincing reply. Ralph had shrugged and handed him the shovel. They had got to work, Dickie sweating profusely and retching. When they had finished cleaning out the top deck, Dickie patted him on the back, pushed him towards town to have a hot meal.

'I'll join you later,' he gasped, 'just need a lie-down and a brush up.' Ralph looked at him, shrugged, fed his pigeons and left.

Dickie hurriedly washed then climbed back up the stairs to the loft with goods to stash behind the cages during Ralph's absence before sauntering into town.

~

Ted continued to receive updates from Ruby on Norah's condition and her battle with workers' rights.

Sometimes, Dad, I wonder why I do it, some people not bothered about joining forces, joining the union. They think we'll do it all for them. And I guess we will 'cos we want justice for the munitonettes. More lay-offs and there's nothing we can do about it. Leastways, we got one success. They can't dismiss a girl in the family way now if the man isn't also discharged. You won't be surprised to know them dads are more likely to be soldiers. A victory for sure. And girls are allowed back to work too when babies are born. The crèche is stuffed with kids. Will is a little helper, likes to be with the tiny ones and make them laugh. Tickles their feet, under their chins. He is a one! Mum got up today when went over but looks terrible thin. Least colour's better.

~

Ted ran up the steps of the bus to talk to Ralph. November rain lashed down on the two worn carbuncles forming the loft, grey paint now virtually non-existent on the upper deck due to more branch damage and exposure to the elements. Ted was not advised to repaint it, 'better things to do with your energies at this stage of the game, Ted,' the sergeant advised.

Ralph crouched down, talking to cooing pigeons and feeding them water. He looked up. 'Ted, you want something?'

'Ralph, you got an hour or so to spare? You'll like what I'm going to show you, chum.' Ralph got up wordlessly and followed Ted to a nearby field. Excited pigeon handlers surrounded a grey structure, armed patrols standing guard.

'German pigeon loft, captured yesterday,' Ted said excitedly, leading him closer.

Ralph climbed into the loft after exchanging a nod or two with other handlers and examined the equipment. Ted followed him. Ralph counted thirty pigeons and picked one up to examine it for messages.

'Too late, mate, for any info, already taken by officers,' a handler informed him.

'Not a patch on our birds, smaller, not fed on a good diet,' Ralph sneered. He turned to Ted, pointing to a small piece of metal. 'A camera, a tiny camera. Them officers wouldn't know what to look for,' he said with quiet satisfaction.

Ted gave an admiring whistle. 'So well hidden and secured. Typical Huns! Got to give it to them. Attention to detail, eh, Ralph? Show it to the officer in charge. Maybe they missed it.'

Later that day, Ted got news that the film had yielded some interest. Ralph and the other trainers were offered the pigeons. They burst out laughing and shook their heads.

'Howay, man. You must be joking!' one said in a broad Geordie accent. 'Them birds aren't called homing birds for nought! Straight back home with the lot of them! Only fit for roasting!'

'Oh, no you don't!' Ralph was indignant. 'Give 'em to me. They need looking after!'

'What? All thirty of em, in our bus, mate?' Ted shook his head. 'No space, no extra food for 'em.'

The crowd faded back to their buses, Ralph only remaining. He carefully removed three birds, smuggling them back to the bus at dusk.

~

'What does 'toute le mond ala bataiy' mean, Ted? You been messing 'round with more Frenchies than I have had hot dinners!' Their dining fortunes had suddenly picked up when Dickie had uncovered a stash of tins and bottles in an abandoned disused cellar while looting a remote house, his first find for months. He and Ted were sharing a bottle of champagne and *foie gras* with a side helping of tinned *gésiers* which were frying. They enjoyed a lull in the rain and sat on logs in a forest scattered with pine needles, Ted picking handfuls up and throwing them into a nearby stream to make a flat space for the bottle and cut glasses which Dickie had nicked from the scullery.

Ted blew on the fried chicken gizzard before answering then ate the meat, a contented sigh following.

'Dickie, That's not true, you have more contact with the locals, but I guess you don't talk much to the women, why are you still so bad at French! You mean *tout le monde à la bataille!*' He exaggerated the final word with a French flourish to show Dickie he knew a thing or two after four years and as many months in France. The pine wood was near the Front but there were no sounds of action, of battle, of troop movement. The smell of the food wafted up to Ralph who took no notice.

Ted raised his glass and stared into the crystals, nearby pine trees distorted by their uneven pattern. 'That geezer Foch says to battle, all to battle, I bet you. That's what it means.'

Dickie flung a handful of pine needles at him. 'Alright, Mister Know All, who the devil is Foshe and what's he got to do with anything?'

'Foch leads the Frenchies, like Haig our lot. Who'da thought them Frenchies could pull it out the bag? Paper says we advanced two miles but you know what them Foch soldiers did?'

'No, no idea, go on, tell me, you old bugger!' Dickie leaned over and filled Ted's glass. 'More of this where it came from,' he said, lifting up the bottle and viewing the dregs.

'Go on, guess what them Frenchies did!' Ted raised the glass to his lips. 'Give up? Five. No, no, not five of them kilometres they're so fond of, but five of our miles, that's what! Some going, eh?'

Dickie replied indignantly. 'But Churchill – he was there, over here then, said it was a British victory, the best one we ever had in the war!'

'Ah, you don't want to believe all that mumbo jumbo British propaganda all the time, mate. Your old boss Harmsworth's now in charge of propaganda, didn't you know? Must be good at it, dropped thousands of leaflets all over the shop here. It was Foch. Let's drink to Fochie boy.'

'Only if you drink to Haig and that little squirt Churchill!' They clicked glasses and started on the *foie gras*.

'Pass over the bread, there's a nice chap,' Dickie urged, eyeing the fattened smooth duck liver and took the remains of a round brown loaf handed to him.

~

Shortly after the drivers' lunch in the woods, Foch delivered his ringing cry to the Allies to attack. He had pinched out a salient line in Lorraine before French and British forces had again assaulted the Hindenburg Line, firing a barrage of nearly a million shells in twenty-four hours. Ted liked to imagine it as a parting shot by all the women laid off from the Arsenal. In his mind's eye, every shell had a name, the name of the woman etched on each one who had filled it with lyddite, burn-in-hell TNT.

They heard rumours too that Ludendorff's spirit had been broken. 'Who?' asked Dickie. 'Or is that what, or where?'

'Ludendorff, you blockhead, keep up!' said Ted as they drove the bus to Lorraine. 'He's the Hun's general, same type as Foch.'

According to their sergeant and others, there might be hope now of winning after wholesale surrender by so many German troops. If complete catastrophe was to be averted, an Armistice could be the only outcome.

Ted wondered if Norah, on her invalid's bed, surrounded by tea and crocheted blankets, had turned over the Tarot card predicting the Armistice. It was definitely on the cards. But the cards could never have foretold the death toll and destruction – nor its hiccupping repercussions.

Chapter 34: Home Front

November, 1918

We don't half get tired these days,
But there's money jingling in our pockets, we says.
But here we are again,
Be fine after a cuppa, after the strain.
What will this day bring?
Does it matter anyway?
We're only women, they say!
Am I glad I'm a munitionette?
Well, it's the war -- not peace -- way.
Yes – and no –but I'll stay!

After the women's layoffs from the Arsenal, Ruby fretted about her employment, a sense of despair escalating when news of a conceivable peace floated in the air. At the prospect of losing income and independence, she had enquired about training as a bus conductorette but was informed this job would go to men after the war. As an Arsenal driver her skills might be snapped up by transport companies but' *Men only back from the Front, love'* was the default message, Armistice said to be close. She argued the toss with Arsenal depot managers; not all men had survived, jobs needing to be filled. But the answer was always the same. *'Men first, love. Then we'll see.'*

'It's not right we should give up our work for the men coming back,' she debated with small gathering of munitions workers who had met in a storeroom to discuss union membership.

'What can we do, Ruby?' asked one, a young girl with pinched features, a look of distrust on her face. 'They need to support their families when the army's finished with 'em.'

'And don't we, Margaret, don't we too? Look around at all the women, no men at all. Some abandoned by their men, others never having one at all, just pregnant by a soldier. Like me. Like Frances here. Not 'specially proud of it but life wouldn't be the same without my little chap.'

'Me and all too,' said another. 'And we got used to having good money, don't want to go back to basics now, being a housewife, just a skivvy again.' All were crushed by approaching loss of independence.

'So, what's the answer then?' Ruby asked. 'We fight for our jobs here or fight for equal pay in other jobs with not so much hard physical work?'

Margaret leaned against one of the storeroom's assembly surfaces. 'After the war what's left for the likes of us is laundry, sewing and domestic service all over again. And married women, like me, can't get jobs, employers saying all we want to do is take time off for our kiddies when they're sick.'

Ruby put a reassuring arm around her and nodded.

'Join the union and let's fight for equality,' Frances urged, 'as Ruby's said over and over again at this meeting. If not this union, then another one. Plenty of them getting on the bandwagon for women, not just men, so support them. Don't just sit there and whinge, ladies. Jolly well fight for what you believe is our right.'

Ruby returned to work after the meeting. She had promised to get support from the major organisers of the Women's Federation and report back.

She got into her crane and started with a load to the railway lines, working steadily until tea time. The foreman came up to her as she got down from the cab. 'Just one more load before you take that break, Ruby.'

'OK, Jim, just one the one mind, you can hear my tummy rumbling all the way to Westminster!'

She climbed back on the cab, frowned at the load then lifted the stack. The unevenly stacked shells tumbled like lumberjack logs jostling for space on pulsating rapids. She hit the brake, the force of the sudden stop causing them to cascade from a height onto a jutting railway track. The explosion was heard miles away. Ruby was just twenty. Armistice was days away.

~

Ted heard the news of the Armistice as he drove to Mons. He pulled up in the bus park on derelict land next to traces of a church and graveyard, parking near the road to get an early start for the following day. Climbing down from the bus, he walked with Dickie and Ralph to find the nearest *estaminet*. They entered the town square and were met with a blaze of music, excited voices, horns sounding.

Dickie surged on ahead. 'Party time!' He spied a group of women offering drinks to the crowd.

Ted went over to a driver. 'What's up Harry?' A leaflet was shoved in his face. 'Read this, my old man, read this and, and…' His arm was taken by a woman. '*Danse avec moi, cher monsieur!*'

Ted read the paper under a street light. Ralph huddling by his side.

Official Radio from Paris - 6:01 A.M., Nov. 11, 1918.
Maréchal Foch to the Commanders-in-Chief.
*1. Hostilities will be stopped on the entire front beginning at
11 o'clock, November 11th (French hour).*
*2. The Allied troops will not go beyond the line reached at
that hour on that date until further orders.*
MARECHAL FOCH
5:45 A.M.

A woman approached with a tray of wine glasses. *'C'est vrai, c'est tout à fait vrai! Regarde, signé par notre cher, brave maréchal Foch!'*

Dickie joined them. 'Bottoms up, mates! Isn't this the most, most...' Ted grinned and grinned and let out an uncharacteristic whoop. Dickie whooped too, Ralph shyly trying one small sound and gave up with an embarrassed look.

Dickie leaned towards Ted. 'Arranged with those gals over there, well, two of 'em, to meet up at their best estaminet for a spot of celebration. Let's go!'

Ted put his arm around Ralph. 'You too, oh no, you're coming too, got to be with us on a night like this. We're going home!'

Ted burst into tears several times during the evening, thinking of Kitty. Norah and Ruby would be so excited. And Will too.

'Sorry, sorry!' he muttered. *'Non, non, c'est naturel, Ted, le bonheur commence avec un peu de tristresse, ces jours-ci,'* whispered one of the women clasping his arm.

'Guess it's natural, cry with happiness, cry with sorrow, cry, cry, cry!' Dickie mocked and ordered more champagne. Ralph found drinking quite pleasurable, after all. He had never tried it much before but this was a special occasion and let himself enjoy a glass. Surely Mother would understand.

'What you going to do now, Ralphie?' Dickie put his arm around him. Ralph stiffened then relaxed.

'Start up my own business, pigeon training, I 'spect, not really much time to think about it, you know, 'bout three hours, if you must know.' Dickie bellowed with laughter.

'Good plan. And I want to help you with it. Here.' He handed Ralph a wad of notes under the table. 'You been a good mate to me, Ralph, just want to see you set it up with a bit of cash I've been lucky enough to make recently.'

Ralph looked down at the cash and shook his head. Dickie leant over and whispered. 'Put it in your pocket, don't flash it about. It's yours and I want you to keep it.'

'Thanks, thank you, you're...'

'I like to surprise people, gives me a funny feeling, doing something good for once, eh?'

'Hey, what you two doin' over there?' Ted slurred, his arms over women's shoulders. Releasing them, he picked up his glass.

'Dickie, me old mate, tell me, what you goin' to do when you get back home? Back to your flashy cars with that Harmsworth? Or back to running them milk floats 'round Hackney? Ha, ha, ha!' He laughed until tears ran down his face.

'Truth be told, Ted, what I'd really like to do is get on one of those little horse-drawn canal boats in the south of France and lie in the sun for the rest of my life. That sounds like a good plan. And plenty of champagne-sipping with the prettiest woman in town wearing some of the *bijoux* I shall buy her.'

'Steal it more like, you old bugger.' Ted drained his glass, poured himself another one and lifted it high. 'Here's to you two old buggers and to you two darling demoiselles. Let's toast Foch, not the Boche!'

Dickie picked up the bottle, filled Ralph's glass up and topped Ted's and the girls' glasses. 'Let's drink to Foch. Down in one! Here's to Haig!'

Ted leaned over to Dickie. 'You've not got a drink, dear friend, my old pal. Pour yourself a glass now. Keep up, keep up with us!'

Dickie lifted the bottle to the light. It was empty. '*Garçon, garçon!*' He looked around. 'All drunk, them waiters too, I bet. I'll go get another. Back in a tick. Toodaloo!'

~

The next day, Ted and Ralph woke with thick heads in beds they didn't recognise and no recollection of how they got there. Ted looked around for Dickie and smiled.

'Gone off with them women again! Good 'ol' Dickie!' He fell back on the bed and into a deep, untroubled sleep. After a late breakfast, they lit cigarettes, had another coffee and asked around for Dickie. No one recalled seeing him.

Ted fastened the last button on his overcoat. 'Come on, Ralph. Let's go back and start the bus. He'll not be far along the road. Not like Dickie to want to walk.'

They rounded the corner where Ted had parked the bus, a few vehicles now on the move but all were passenger buses, no grey-carbuncle pigeon lofts in the square. Ted scratched his head. 'Where the heck is it? This *is* where we parked it yesterday, isn't it, Ralph?'

Ralph nodded unconvincingly. He'd never felt so rough. Ted walked over to a corporal in charge of the traffic chaos who was surrounded by drivers and soldiers, all clamouring to find out where they should go next. Ted finally made his way to the front of the queue. 'Seen our bus, corp? Pigeon loft? Seems to have disappeared. Ralph here, he's worried 'bout his pigeons. Need a feed and water.'

'No, not seen it. Sure you parked it here last night? Look a bit the worse for wear, you do. Had a good night, did you?'

Another soldier stepped over to them. 'The pigeon loft? Saw it go off last night.'

'What?' Ted lit another cigarette. His hands trembled. 'Who was driving, for crissakes?'

'Just the one in the cab, looked like quite a tall chap.' He reflected. 'Yes, he was in uniform. Like you. Cranked the bus up frenzy-like. Keen to leave the war behind!'

~

Dickie drove through the night to Calais, stopping in St. Omer to pick up a large consignment of artefacts and jewellery from a dealer in the early hours, his insistent hammering on the door waking the trader and his wife. Twelve hours to the coast after placing his goods in the bus, he reckoned; it struggled to keep up with his urgent demands. At the port he talked his way onto the ship sailing for Folkstone with a wink and a nod and slipped a generous fifty-dollar tip to the seaman handling paperwork.

'Can't wait to get to my girl, know what I mean?' The seaman laughed and waved him on. 'Hope she's still there for you, mate! But you won't win her over with that vehicle!'

Before dawn broke on deck he opened the pigeon flaps and shooed the birds out over the sea. 'There you go, my lovelies, find a new home, like us lot.' Closing the flaps, he lit a cigarette and laughed uncontrollably.

The unwieldy bus clattered down the ramp at Folkstone, Dickie taking the Sussex road. England had never seemed so peaceful, so proper, but yet somehow foreign. He had been away for over three years.

Before Uckfield, he made an abrupt turn along the River Usk then down a track which led to a barn hidden by a wood, invisible from the road. He stopped and grinned. The future had arrived. Opening the large barn doors he drove the bus inside then closed them. Walking over to a rusted old trunk, he checked the contents before lying down on a bed of hay and falling asleep. When he awoke, he washed in a bucket of rainwater he collected outside by a side door, changed into civvies from the trunk before bundling up his uniform and all other army items. Lighting a fire behind the barn, he threw his army belongings into the flames and stared into blaze, watching his past life as a soldier vanishing into the Sussex cold air.

Satisfied that no traces remained of his army life after raking over the ashes and removing any metal, he let himself back inside the barn. Picking up a suitcase next to the trunk with the initials of his past employer in embossed gold lettering on leather, he climbed inside the bus, opened the storage under the bench which had doubled as his bed and removed a strong case with jewellery, watches, signet rings and other small items. Filling the suitcase, he tried it for weight, then squeezed in smaller items. He climbed the narrow staircase to the pigeon loft and rummaged around the back of the cages for further stashed goods. God, the stench, even without the birds! Carrying the trinkets down to the trunk, he placed them inside alongside other saleable goods. Another day. Rummaging around the bus, he pulled out

Ted's belongings and scattered them on the floor. Poor Ted wouldn't see his photos, his precious letters or Billy's violin again, he laughed. Finding the wad of dollars he had given Ted, he pocketed them. Poor old Ted, missed the bus, didn't he? Time for change, all change.

After bolting the barn doors with a thick lock and chain, he stood for a moment to check on the vigorous ivy which had grown profusely over the barn, nodding with satisfaction. He set off down the country road, hiking a mile to catch a bus to Uckfield, the weight of the suitcase stretching his arm and leg muscles. He would return over the months to empty the bus of its valuables, never to return after plundering it.

The bus drew into a stop at the train station, Dickie caught the first train to London and chose a quiet compartment. Lifting the heavy suitcase with difficulty onto the rack, he soon fell into a deep sleep. He was jostled awake by a heavy hand when the train came to London Bridge, its final destination.

'Ere, mate, you gettin' off the train before we makes the return journey?' Dickie shot to his feet and stared upwards to the luggage rack. His case was still there. A smile spread over his face. 'Yes, yes, must be going, thank you, thanks, mate!'

He joined the throng with its many sellers of Union Jacks, out in force to continue the Armistice celebrations. Musicians and dancers had taken over the roads near the station, the noise of the crowds deafening. A young woman playfully pulled on his arm, dragging him into a circle to dance with her. He shook her arm off, declined with a bow but with a fleeting glance of irritation, not in the spirit of the day. Buses, with cheering masses on top decks, sounded their horns.

He ducked down a side street heading towards the river and disappeared into the throng. Less than 24 hours ago, he had been sitting on a bus near Amiens with Ted and Ralph.

~

Ted and Ralph made their way to the officer in charge to report the missing bus, both agitated, hungover and confused.

They entered the makeshift HQ, the officers laughing when hearing about the bus and its cargo of birds. Ted gave their names.

'Any reason why this would have happened?' said one. 'High jinks after the Armistice announcement, most likely. A bit of a joke. Probably around the corner, that's all. Mind you, it's been over thirty or so hours now, a lot of confusion going on today, but, nevertheless…'

The officer paused, motioned for them to sit then lifted his cap to rub his hair, and picked up a list. 'Ah, here we are. Which one of you is private Digby?' Ted nodded with relief and smiled at Ralph.

'Seen your name in another file, somewhere, just a moment.' The officer left the room and returned with a paper. 'Private Gant?' Ralph nodded. 'Would you mind waiting in the outer room?'

Ralph stumbled to his feet. The officer turned to Ted. 'Private Digby. I have some rather bad news.'

'Norah, it is Norah, my wife? She's been ill, munitions work, see, in hospital a while back. Relapse? You can tell me, have to know.'

The officer came and sat down next to Ted. 'No, nothing about your wife here. Unless her name is Ruby?'

He paused before adding, 'You see, there's been a very bad explosion at the Arsenal…'

'How bad?' Ted rose swiftly from his chair, his voice faltering.

'Bad. The worst. I am sorry. So very sorry. War's a risky thing.'

Ted fell to the floor, curled into a ball, his arms covering his head. Surrendering to despair, his tortured sounds of rage filled the room, '*Why? Why? Why?*' His reckless gamble for adventure four years ago had turned into a suffering beyond his wildest imagination. He had not been at home to protect her, to guide her. Instead, he'd all but abandoned Ruby and Norah at the worst time, at the outbreak of war.

Chapter 35: Home Front

July, 1919

Daily Mirror, July 19, 1919: *London became the focus of nationwide Peace Day celebrations. A huge military camp sprang up in Kensington Gardens and thousands of people descended on the capital. Hundreds spent Friday night in parks and streets to secure a good position along the parade route. By eight o'clock on Saturday morning it was almost impossible to cross Trafalgar Square. Nearly 15,000 servicemen took part in the Victory parade, led by the Allied commanders. In Whitehall the parade saluted a temporary wood and plaster monument, the Cenotaph, dedicated to 'The Glorious Dead'.*

Ted pushed Norah in her wheelchair to the Albert Hall's main entrance, positioning her so that she could watch the procession. Bus depot work colleagues thought he had adjusted to life surprisingly well since returning six months ago for duties behind the wheel but his silence and expression told another story at home with Norah. Will, an excitable four-year-old, and Frances, with Alfred, her son, followed them. The vast throng parted to give way to wheelchairs, the injured, the war invalids. A large banner – wrapped around the entrance to the red brick and terracotta circular hall with its glazed wrought iron dome – declared a warm welcome to ex-servicemen and their types of transport which had all played a vital part in the war's victory.

Buses, lorries, motorbikes, ambulances, heavy guns and howitzers from numerous brigades followed petrol and steam vehicles, staff cars joining them, all transport manned by servicemen and women, Ted scrutinising each one for a glance of Kitty. His bus, his home for four years, and Billy's and Dickie's, should have paraded in front of the building too but Dickie had seen to that. Ted never ceased to wonder where the bus had been taken.

It lay hidden in a Sussex barn, the pigeons long gone too.

Ted had yearned to see it restored to its iconic red London double decker status with its advertising and destination signage covering his well-worn route from Shepherd's Bush to Clapham, Wembley, Epping and all points between. Ding, ding, Westminster, ding ding, Piccadilly, ding ding, Fleet Street. All change. But if it couldn't be his own gritty vehicle, he refused to drive one of the buses that had returned from the Front to London. He marvelled that a quarter of the 1,000 buses requisitioned by the army had survived the journey across France and Belgium, returning for passenger duty. But passengers avoided this reminder of the war, only choosing to board newer buses. No longer useful, on the scrapheap.

Dickie. What had he done with the bus? Ted knew why it had been taken, the vehicle listing to one side thanks to Dickie's shameless pilfering. Ted had benefitted from it too. He had a true understanding of why the French loved their food and drink, not like at home where a sausage roll or a jellied eel was about as good as it got. And don't forget a pint of brown ale to wash it down. Does the job. That was enough for many but not for Ted now. And the bribery money? He pictured the scene: Dickie, finding the roll of dollars, stuffed it in his pocket. Norah had not benefitted. There was no money to spend on her for extra medical help.

He glanced at other buses of similar vintage as they processed around the building's distinctive archways. Throngs of supporters, families, servicemen and women lined the route to cheer them on. Did they know how many challenges their bus had been put to use for, the major changes to its structure to fulfil its mission for over four interminable years? Did they pause to think of those who worked on them, the passengers they carried, the sights they had endured on the Western Front, and of the French, the Belgians who died in their many small ruined villages and towns? As Kitty had said to him when he returned to duty after his bitter home leave, maybe they had enough of their own troubles to think deeply of others elsewhere.

Choking, he tried to control his tears when spotting his fellow drivers. Picking up an impatient Will, and to distract them both, he pointed to a few of them and waved, the child joining in.

'See, my boy, that's George, and, oh, look, there's Jack, such a nice lad.' Will squirmed. Ted loosened his grip on his grandson and passed him to Frances.

He glanced at the invitation Norah held in her hands and looked up at the entrance number. 'This is our entrance, dear. I'm going to take you inside now. Quite a ceremony! Our seats are quite close to the stage. Maybe the Royal Box too!'

Norah looked up at him and smiled faintly to please him but had little interest in the event. She was not used to crowds, to noises, to excitement, or to life. She had inwardly died, her former life no longer existing after Ruby's death, her mind and ill body fenced in by inconsolable loss. The munitions canary look had not deserted her.

Ted wore a black coat over black trousers despite the hot June day – 'pay respects, respects, king and all,' without much faith – his greying hair now longer than it had been at the Front and accepted by the Dalston Bus Depot where he took on part-time work on the same pre-war route. It suited him, gave him time to look after Norah and help with raising Will.

But Ted had felt increasing remorse since setting foot back in London, his lack of fatherly love and support towards his daughter during the last years of war, a source of guilt and a daily reminder when he looked at Will. Norah had nothing to be ashamed of, always there for Ruby, for Will. Selfless. No one, not even Kitty, his wise, loving Kitten, could have convinced him otherwise. His grief was like a frontline bereavement, a portable tomb gnawing at his guts. Nor did he feel that he had a country. It had been lost in 1914 but he hadn't understood its cost until returning home. Except that it wasn't home anymore. Only Will made him feel alive.

Once he had travelled down countless French and Belgian roads, many of them leading to Kitty. Now there were just innumerable dead ends: the Norah he no longer knew, sorrow and anger for the loss of Kitty.

He was fearful of losing the memory of Ruby too. Was she really edging towards oblivion in his mind? To help regain a sense of his daughter, he ran his fingers softly down her pencilled growing stages etched on the kitchen door panel on her birthdays, studied photographs of her as a child, a young adult, a mother, an Arsenal footballer with her team. The last photo, sitting on her crane, winching munitions on to a railroad wagon, made him weep uncontrollably. He had put it away and didn't look at it for years until Will found it one day in a shoebox on top of his grandfather's wardrobe, appealing to him to confirm that this was his mother.

Inside the Albert Hall, Ted pushed Norah's wheelchair next to his aisle seat, Frances sitting next to him with Albert on her lap. The stage had yet to fill up with the speakers, their guests and the master of ceremonies.

Ted excused himself. 'Back in a mo.'

Norah gave him a quizzical look. 'It's about to start, dear. Hurry.'

He moved quickly, apologetically, through the crowds, his eyes seeking out his chums. Ralph: would he see him? And Kitty? She must be here. But how would he feel seeing her? Would he scoop her up in his arms, forgetting himself and not caring who saw him, or would he react nervously, with just a nod? No, that would be too heartless. He had sent her telegrams via a poste restante address and had one loving reply to his Bow post office. Pressing against the throng, he made his way around the curved hallway but saw no familiar faces, the commencement bell urgently ringing for stragglers.

Hurrying back to his seat before the royal party took theirs in the Royal Box, he glanced back to the entrance for one last look. In the mounting hush, he saw a familiar broad back standing on stall steps, the man turning around when a thunder of clapping erupted for the king.

Dickie's sleek dark hair, one of his many striking attributes, stood out as did an expensive frock coat showing a fine pocket watch chain, a top hat clasped under one arm. He appeared to be alone. His slim, upright, patrician figure stood aloof from the audience as if he couldn't bear to be associated with them, his superiority breath-taking. Dickie seemed to have taken on the persona of Harmsworth, his old boss.

Ted, sweating, wiped his hands on his coat and excused himself again. Norah threw him an exasperated look. Walking towards the stall steps, he crossed over aisles to reach Dickie.

An usher put his hand up. 'Really, sir, do have the courtesy to sit down, the King is…, find your seat, sir, this is not…'

He stopped, blocking views for seated guests and scanned the area where he had last seen Dickie. Spotting him again, he moved quickly despite further protests.

Dickie caught sight of Ted and started to walk quickly towards the exit, putting on his top hat. Ted swiftly followed up the steps trying to catch up with him.

'Sir, please find your seat, the King…, you won't be…'

He ignored the ushers and pressed on outside.

Dickie stood on Kensington Road hailing a hansom cab, several parked by the Albert Memorial. Ted quickened his pace to a run.

'Dickie! Dickie!'

Dickie stopped, looked around and stared at him before getting into the cab. Ted gasped for breath as he ran. Reaching the cab, he called out. 'Dickie, for pity's sake, stop! Give me my letters, my daughter's letters! I want them back! Kitty's too, and the photos! Under the driver's seat. Please...you've got them, you bastard, you…!' Dickie gave a short laugh and grabbed the door handle, shutting it forcefully.

'Drive on!' he urged the driver who shrugged and put his foot on the pedal. Ted fell onto his shoulder, struggled to his knees and watched the cab disappear down the road towards Knightsbridge. Inside the Albert Hall he heard loud cheers interrupting the final chords of the National Anthem and wept.

Chapter 36: Sussex

May, 2000

Stricter enforcement of parking regulations gets the go-ahead
*Much has been done to ease the path of buses through the main part
of Brighton and Hove, so that they provide an attractive regular
and reliable service. Money, raised by fines for drivers who park on
double yellow lines and at a bus stops, will be ploughed back into
better traffic management, benefiting all road users including
motorists and bus passengers.*
The Argus, 30 May

Jason, 11, and Danny, a year younger, had recently moved
into a Sussex village with their parents. They explored their
new surroundings one afternoon, their mother shooing them
out of the house while she finished unpacking boxes of china
in the garage.

'It's not spitting now, out with you! Don't be late for tea,
mind, your dad's picking up your granddad, tea'll be at the
usual time.'

The boys crossed the quiet country road to see what the
woods had in store. A broken fence, partly covered in
brambles, promised adventure. Jason wedged himself into an
overgrown, dense hedge, scratched an arm and snagged his
Bob the Builder T-shirt before reaching the other side.

Danny jumped up trying to see over the hedging. 'Hang
on, Jason, wait for me! Found anything?'

Jason shouted at him. 'There's a bumpy old road, must
go somewhere. You coming or what?'

Danny put his Westlife cap on backwards, crawled
through the hedge and joined Jason. Unkempt long grass,
once kept down by tractors or cart use, lay bleached by
decades of sun and neglect. Danny picked up a stick and
aimed it Jason with a firing sound, the boys chasing one

another down the road. They stopped when they saw an old barn.

'Been abandoned,' Jason said unnecessarily, approaching it.

'Fucking perfect den!' Danny breathed, looking at the rust on the large door's lock, the missing tiles and faded chipped, rain-damaged wood. Ivy stretched partly over the dented roof like a warm, mottled green hat.

Jason hit his younger brother on the arm. 'Where'd you learn to swear, Danny? Mum'll be cross! Dad'll be…watch yourself!'

'From you, 'course!'

Jason grinned. They rattled the heavy padlock; the silent barn resisted their entry. A cat emerged then ran into bushes. Rooks called out their wretched cackle in nearby trees.

Circling the barn, the boys searched for another entrance but failed. Gathering a pile of discarded bricks, they made a series of uneven steps and climbed onto the roof, Jason pushing Danny up. Once on top Danny lent a hand to haul his brother up. Clinging onto their vantage point, they could see adjoining fields and the road to the village. A bus went by then a Ford Fiesta trying to pass it. An airplane dozed in the sky.

Danny squinted in the sun, moving gingerly on all fours along the roof and pointed. 'That our house?'

Jason nodded. 'Just to the right.' He shuffled along towards Danny and inhaled a musty smell. Brushing aside dead vines and twigs, he uncovered a hole in the tiles and looked down. Broken side slats allowed light into the barn.

'Look! There's a beam we can hang from! A ledge too with some hay, looks like. Come on, let's get inside!'

Removing tiles to make a larger hole, they winched themselves down. When their eyes adjusted to the gloom, they found an upright ladder and climbed down to the dirt floor strewn with hay.

'Think we'll ever get out?' Danny asked as he missed a rung.

'Same way we came in, I guess,' Jason, down first, replied unconvincingly.

'Hey, look at this, Danny, an old...don't know. Somethin' to do with a farm?' He pointed to a vehicle. He answered his own question. 'Too high, it's an old, well, sort of like a bus, I guess, seen this funny jutty-out engine in one of granddad's mags but those flappy things on the side, a bit weird.'

'This old thing? Couldn't get from A to B!' Danny mocked.

They peered in the bottom deck with its debris, old clothes, bottles and broken wooden seating then climbed the stairs to the top deck.

Danny held his nose, his voice taking on a nasal tang. 'Ah, gross! Birds, I guess, been nesting here! Look at all this shit!'

He moved forward to some cage-like structures. 'Must be somethin' here, good way to hide things in smelly places, puts people off,' he mumbled.

Jason pushed past him and rummaged around in the mutilated cages, one loosening before it crashed by his feet. An old notebook tumbled out. Jason picked it up. Inside the front cover were faded words: *Property of Ralph Gant, pigeon handler. Top Secret.*

'Look, look at this. Spy stuff!' They peered at the writing in the gloom.

Hindenburg Line smashed through with numerous tanks, crushing down enemy wire for infantry to pass, smashing up enemy machine guns, driving German infantry to ground. Taking enemy by complete surprise six miles east of Gonnelieu to Canal du Nord. Our own infantry followed and, while the tanks patrolled the line of hostile trenches, cleared the German infantry from their dug-outs and shelters.

Danny grabbed at it. Pushing him away, Jason shouted, 'Wow! I'm keeping this one. Find your own!'

Danny grumbled then ran downstairs to search the lower deck after poking a piece of wood through the debris in remaining cages with their crusted shit. He kicked away dusty empty bottles of champagne, picked up a rusted, dented tin and read the faded label.

Maconochie World Famous Rations
A sustainable and economical meal for the family.
1/6 d. per tin

Jason joined him and peered at the tin. 'Weird! Tramps camped out here, maybe? Must be really old, funny old money or what!' Danny tossed it aside.

They moved on to the drivers' open cabin, tested the steering and played with the gears then the corroded headlamps, one coming off in Danny's hands. He chucked it on the hay.

Pulling a loose board up under the drivers' seat, Jason threw it next to the headlamp after he had read a faded, water-stained advertisement. *Charles Hawtrey, your favourite comedian, at the Apollo, limited season only!* He hauled up a wooden box from under the board.

'Gold! Must be!' he breathed and prised the lid off. 'Letters, it's only letters. Look, pictures too. What a looker!' He stopped at a picture of a young girl from another era, her hair piled high with a ribbon. 'Wonder how old she is.'

They examined the letters more carefully and found a legible address on the back of some of the envelopes. It was a London one, not too far from their old East End home and grandad's flat and where they had walked his terrier.

Jason put the lid back on. 'Going to take these to granddad, he loves all this kind of old stuff. Here, take the box,' he ordered Danny, tucking the thick notebook he had taken from the pigeon loft in his jacket pocket.

He struggled with the large box as they rooted around for other items and found a mildewed oblong case stashed away under one of the long benches, the catch sticking. Jason prised it open with a metal bar from the drivers' cabin and lifted out a violin. The strings dangled from the fingerboard, its tuning pegs no longer turning. The bridge at the instrument's pinched waist showed signs of wear and the wood beneath it was scratched and worn.

'Someone played this to death or the rats got at it,' he remarked. 'Wonder if grandad can do something with it?' He turned the old instrument over. 'Look, Danny, some scratched stuff on the back!' They took turns to make out the roughly etched lettering stretching down the violin's body.

William Boyden Cotgrave. Billy Boy!
Left Hackney! – 15.9.14

Danny gripped on tightly after reading the final entry, Jason letting go. 'All yours! What you going to do with it? And how are you going to take the box too?'

Danny shrugged and made a face. 'I'll manage, don't you worry!' He paused. 'Might flog the violin and some of the stuff in the box, make some money.'

'C'mon, let's go, Danny. Can't wait to show granddad.'

Finding a loose board on a barn wall, they knocked an adjacent one out with an old pitchfork before squeezing out into the sun with their findings.

~

Will Digby was an old man. His once-fair thick hair had turned streaky ash grey, similar to French clay clods his father, Billy, had lain under for the past eighty-four years. His son's age now. He had inherited his mother's small nose and unswerving brown eyes but not her temperament. Her sense of duty, yes, but not her zest to push boundaries. He was a homebody, living in his mother's and grandparents house all his life. He was more like his granddad whose love of gardening and any type of motor had been part of his life since Ted had assumed the mantle of fatherly care and love.

As a young man, Will, preferring to call himself Will Digby, not Cotgrave as no relationship had been formed with his father's family, felt no need to move home when taking up an apprenticeship at Ford Motor Cars in Dagenham along the Thames. Ted had looked after him ever since his mother's death when he was three and regarded Ted as his father and mother, with no remaining recollection of Ruby, Norah too ill to take part in his rearing. They rarely mentioned Ruby, his grandparents' eyes filling with pain whenever her name was brought up. But they kept a photo of her on the kitchen dresser and touched it before climbing the stairs to bed. Will picked up their habit from an early age, his first attempts causing the frame to fall and break on the stone floor. Ted carefully shook the glass off the photo in the bin and took it to the shed to repair it. Will watched the attention he had taken over the picture frame, his grandfather's practical hands working skilfully to recreate the talisman.

Norah, housebound then bedbound, had little awareness, only sparking to life when Will turned over a few Tarot cards in front of her on the bedspread, her yellowed, blotched hands only reacting eagerly when the joker came up. She died when he was seven. She had known about Kitty, finding a letter from her to *Dearest darling Ted* and a photo of the nurse hidden in a hat box from Dunn and Co in the shed but didn't have the strength to challenge him. Or wished to know the truth. The letter and photo had taken on the creased, bent look of being kept in a pocket and Norah imagined that Ted had kept it in his uniform, possibly a breast pocket. They were hidden under a smart brown fedora she had never seen Ted wear. Will had discovered the box on the top of his grandparents' bedroom wardrobe which Ted had transferred from the shed after her death. He asked Ted about his findings, Ted placing a knowing finger on the side of his nose and smiling.

After Norah died, Ted relied on Ethel Flynn from next door for housekeeping and laundry, Auntie Eth a strong presence with a no-nonsense sense of order.

Ted sometimes disappeared for days or longer when Will was older, returning with a jaunty step and a hum. He'd get out his mouth organ after these absences and play popular tunes. Soon Will knew the words to It Had to be You and Five Foot Two, Eyes of Blue which Ethel scolded Ted for teaching the boy.

Ted stopped playing for some weeks after an Army Corps reunion, the names of the dead who he and his colleagues had served with, read out, Ralph Gant's name among them. 'Shot hisself, couldn't cope with civvy life,' Ted was informed. 'Only 36,' another one said.

Will watched from his bedroom window when Ted, returning home after the meeting, dug up two of the beds he had recently carefully planted and tore at the vegetation and heavy earth with a savagery that frightened the thirteen-year-old. A few days later, Ted bought new plants, poppies and sunflowers, gently easing them into the soil.

He retired from the bus depot at sixty-five and took Will to transport museums around the country or to motor racing meetings.

Kitty and Doris nursed patients on the front line until Armistice. Kitty, on returning home, had come back to another type of conflict. Her husband deserted the family when Lesley, their only child, had developed polio. Her letter to Ted outlined her new life, that of nursing her son, but promised some time away when respite care could be organised. *My dearest man, you and Lesley are my life, make no mistake. The sadness I feel is being separated from you as well as the suffering my poor boy is going through but, knowing that we'll meet monthly is a great solace. And no uncomfortable beds either! But isn't the food grimmer here than in France! Now, that we'll miss! Shall we plan our next time away soon? Doris is able to step in to suit us. How's the second weekend in May for you?* They met for decades until Kitty's sudden death in 1957.

Ted, at 87, remained strong in body but was increasingly melancholic, the past mentioned with increasing clarity. Will and a frail Ethel looked after him until his death in 1958.

Will cleared out his grandfather's bedroom and found more photographs carefully wrapped in tissue paper in the hat box. They all featured the same woman, the hairstyles making him smile. In one faded photo, she was laughing, seated on the front seat of a motorcycle with Ted behind, his grandfather, handsome in his uniform, she in equally manly service clothing. Another photo featured her in more rounded middle age with a backdrop of a lake and mountains. A pencilled note on the back gave its destination and date as Lake Windermere, 1946.

He looked through the neat stack, the woman now older and seated at a table holding up a glass, her eyes crinkling with love at the photographer. Despite her advancing years, she flirted with the camera with a knowing smile of trust. He felt a pang of jealousy, mixed with remorse that Ted had not shared her existence with him. Sighing, he placed the box on Ted's bed, sat down, and examined the photographs more closely. Turning them over, he saw his grandfather's fine hand, *Kitty dearest,* and the date. Some featured them both, Ted sporting a natty trimmed beard in later ones. Many had the location: Broadstairs, Eastbourne, the Isle of Skye and one located in France, *Armentières, June, 1956.*

Will, like his grandfather, had also been involved with a married woman, a colleague's wife. He hadn't paid too much attention to Ted's sudden, unexplained absences, suspecting he wouldn't have been told the truth, and he didn't want to be questioned about his own deceitful relationship. He married Jean after Ted died but it was an uncomfortable five years, Will finally alone in the house after Jean's departure. Modernised over the decades, and conveniently near Bow tube station, there was no question of a move. It looked smarter than when his grandparents had bought it decades ago. The conservatory was the first alteration Jean had added, the scullery now a downstairs toilet and laundry room. The panel with Ruby's height measurements, marked by Ted since her fourth birthday, remained intact, Will occasionally tracing his hand over the wood.

There was little else of Ted's past apart from the photos, his Army bus badge and other war paraphernalia, which surfaced when Will cleared out his room before Jean moved in. He examined a book of Shakespeare's sayings, dedicated to Ted from Kitty. Leafing through the slim volume, he came across starred quotations, others underlined with an exclamation mark.

Love is a smoke and is made with the fume of sighs. Romeo and Juliet

Love sought is good but given unsought is better. Twelfth Night

Who ever loved that loved not at first sight? As You Like It

One half of me is yours, the other half yours, Mine own, I would say; but if mine, then yours, And so all yours. The Merchant of Venice.

Will suddenly envied his grandfather.

A neighbour bought the wardrobe later on that year after Ted's death, returning with a parcel. 'Seems this fell down the back panel, fished it out,' he said, handing over a notebook. Soiled green and eaten around the edges, the cover's title bore Ted's name, the notebook chronically capturing the crucial years from landing at Rouen's port in September 1914, the diary ending in 1919. Will examined its bow shape and reckoned it had been in Ted's back pocket.

Flicking through it at first before reading it from cover to cover, he glimpsed Ted's neat, even handwriting, some entries in faded ink, others in lead pencil. The left-hand column bore a date, a central one the destination, and, on the right, the purpose of the visit or comments about the place, war, people and even food. French and Belgian names peppered the diary – Amiens, Rouen, Fremont, Arras, Neuve Eglise, Ypres, Merville, Chateau Belge. Kitty's name came up often alongside what looked like a code, a single letter sprinkled like confetti over the years throughout the diary. Will laughed. Dirty old bugger!

He carried the book to the conservatory to read with a cup of tea. The afternoon light faded into darkness before he turned on the lamp, his tea left as he digested the diary, his attention growing as he approached his grandfather's many entries in the first two years of war. *Billy don't know what's hit him, sick on boat crossing! Billy home for his dad, not well. The lads joining in Billy's fiddle playing, fine player – and music hall mimic! Billy died today. Fine funeral, my son. So sorely missed. And him a father to Will and don't know, ever. Ruby will cope, we'll all cope. And well. We must for his sake, Ruby's and the little boy's. Hope little 'un grows up with the same sweetness as his dad. But Billy did betray me, just the once. But glad he did, or no Will.*

Will wiped his eyes and put the book down then picked it up later, re-reading the same entries before moving on. One later entry caught his eye, stopping him in his tracks. Moving the diary closer under the lamp, he slowly read the faded lettering.

Dickie and me, we let the poor bugger die. We could have saved Dawkins, drag him out of the trench. Now we'll be court-martialled and executed. Unless they don't find out. Oh, God, what we done? Dickie says Dawkins deserved it, sergeant had it in for us from beginning. Right royal bully, for sure. Cruel. Only he and I knows what we done. Haven't done and should have. Maybe Ralph sees more than we think, he'll tell on us. We're finished.

Will put down the notebook and gazed into the dark garden, only the outline of the church spire over the fence coming into sharp focus. What had Ted done? Upright, honourable, his granddad. Without him, he would have been without a home, a family, always looked after him, he had. Mother and father to him. Wouldn't he have done the same for others in trouble? What had the sergeant done to the drivers?

Getting up, he took his cup to the kitchen and put the kettle on. Briskly cleaning the cup of its stains, he re-used the tea bag, pouring water into the cup, the bag floating to the top. Just like Ted had always done. Returning to his chair, he re-read the entry several times before putting the notebook down.

It lay in the conservatory, gathering dust for months. Picking it up one autumn day, he stared at it before burying it in a neglected corner of the garden before the soil became brittle and hard. Unearthing a package where he dug, he examined the colourful characters forming a pack of cards, one catching his eye. The joker. He shrugged then recalled Norah's obsession with the card then carried the package to the bin.

~

Will Digby, in old age, was about to relive a past life he had all but buried with one sharp ring of his doorbell. Lifting his eyes from the BBC's Grand Prix race between Hill and Schumacher at the Nürburgring Ring, he ignored the bell's intrusion and settled back into his armchair, his arthritic fists tightening during a critical lap.

'Come on, Damon!' he called out irritably as the driver slowed in the drenching, skidding rain, swearing when the buzzer went again. Glancing at his half-eaten crumpet and warm tea on the table, he rose uneasily, steadying himself on the table's edge, the brew slopping over onto the saucer. 'Bloody 'ell, what next!' Turning the TV down he walked to the front door.

Two men stood on his doorstep, the younger carrying a box, the older one a long flaking black case. Will looked them up and down with a frown, impatient to be rid of them.

'You selling religion? Always two of you – dead giveaway. Before you say anything, no, a devout atheist me.' Will turned to shut the door.

The older man spoke quickly. 'Are you Will Digby? Was your granddad Ted, Edward Digby? Bus driver in the war? First war, that is! In France?'

Will stopped and turned back. 'Yes. Matter of fact I am. He was.'

The younger man came forward with the box. 'Look, my kids found this on an old bus, it's full of family letters belonging to the Digbys. Long story how they found them but we – my dad here – lives not too far away, around the corner in Hackney Wick.'

'You sure you're not trying to sell anything?' Will frowned dubiously.

The younger man grew impatient. 'No, nothing. We just want to give you some family mementoes! Think this could be one of your mother?' Removing the lid, he took a black and white photograph and handed it to the old man.

Will examined the picture. It was Ruby, mum, without a doubt. She wore a white dress, a bow in her piled-up dark hair, and fingered a necklace. She stood between Ted and Norah, Will's grandparents. He turned it over and read, *Ruby's 16th Birthday, June 21, 1914. Bow, London.* When he was growing up, a shelf on the kitchen dresser had the same photo in a plain wood frame which Ted had made in the shed. He smiled broadly, brushed the crumbs off his sweater and opened the door wide.

Will showed them into the conservatory through the kitchen, glancing at the flickering cars on the television as they passed the front room. Neither Ted nor Norah would have recognised their home, apart from Ted's shed which Will had carefully repaired over the years and which could be seen from the conservatory by well-tended colourful shrubs.

The older man placed the long case gently down on a table, his son laying the box next to it. Will motioned them to sit down.

The younger man removed the lid from the box and tipped it up to show Will its contents. Will leaned over and ruffled through its contents. Letters over the four-year period from Norah, Ruby and Kitty joined sepia photos, many of Kitty, others chronicling the bus, still in its original shape with soldiers mounting the outer back stairs, another with Ralph and his pigeons on the top deck with its unwieldy carbuncles, now a pigeon loft. Other photos highlighted food, cheery bar staff and scenes of deprivation and devastation, but mostly ones demonstrating a community of men. No officers, though.

'All too much to take in,' Will said after some minutes. He sat back in his chair and closed his eyes.

'Can I get you anything?' the older man asked.

Will shook his head and opened his eyes.

'What else you got there? 'he asked, pointing to the case. 'You musicians or something?'

'No, but we think this belonged to your dad. We read some of the letters, hope you don't mind, Mr. Digby.'

Opening the battered case, the visitor lifted out a violin. Strings hung from the fingerboard, the woodwork and scroll were scratched and marked with stains. 'We dusted it down a bit, dirt and cobwebs gone but... see here?' Turning the violin over, he pointed to the back. 'See this?'

He passed the instrument to Will. Etched on the reverse side were a series of place names and dates. Will read the engravings his father had made in France before he was born.

William Boyden Cotgrave. Billy Boy!
Left Hackney! – 15.9.14
On Ol' Bill with Ted Digby.
Seine – France! – 23.9.14
Bassee Canal – 10.10.14
Messine battle – 12.10.14
Festubert – 23.11.14
Wytschaete – Belgium! 14.12.14
Xmas Day – St.Yvon – 3:2 Fritz won footie
Neuve Chapelle – 10.3.15
Gas! – St. Julien – Apr.15
Ted lookin' after me like a real dad. What a man.

The older man asked after a long pause: 'Would you like to see where your dad lived, on the bus? We'll take you there.'

Will looked up, suppressing his tears, and nodded. 'Both dads.'

End

Acknowledgements

My love and thanks to my insightful early readers Jo Gibson, Jane Weeks, Sue Gilson, Jos Sampson and Kate Preston and to my family in the UK and Canada for their support. I am equally indebted to Hugh Ribbans, artist extraordinaire, for his cover and chapter linocuts to enhance the story. http://hughribbans.com

Extensive research at Imperial War Museum, London Transport Museum, Dalston Museum, BBC, Bishopsgate Institute, The Long, Long Trail, Army Service Corps, Base Depot, Royal Logistics Corps Museum, Chichester Library and many research books including *Zeppelin Nights, Fighting on the Home Front, My War Diary, Tommy's War, Forgotten Voices, Dictionary of Tommies' Slang and Songs, Trench Talk, Trench Orders, Love Letters of the Great War, My War Diary, Elsie and Mairi go to War, Woodbine Willie, The Beauty and the Sorrow, Thirty-Odd Feet below Belgium, Destination Western Front, Women in Britain 1900 – 2000, Women on the Warpath, London, The Story of a Great City amongst other research.*

Carol Godsmark is a UK-based Canadian writer, journalist, chef and PR professional and grew up in a diplomatic family in Canada, Czechoslovakia, Switzerland, Denmark and England. She is the author of six non-fiction books and a novel, **Stalin's Czech Guests**, based on her childhood growing up behind the Iron Curtain. **Number 60 to the Somme**, a performed play co-written with Greg Mosse, is grounded in research for **All Change.** She has an MA in Creative Writing from the University of Sussex.

In memory of my grandfather, Joshua Edward Reynolds, WW1 Canadian engineer, whose life was shortened by his duties at Vimy.